Praise for Stan Washburn's

INTENT TO HARM

"There are some things most people take for granted. Small towns are safe. Police officers can handle anything that comes their way. Rape happens to somebody else. In this frighteningly suspenseful crime novel, these assumptions and others are swept away.... *INTENT TO HARM* is a . . . fast-moving police procedural whose nonstop plot twists keep you reading.... Washburn forces his characters to face the darkest sort of evil, and to consider how best to overcome it. That he does so in a no-nonsense, conversational style only makes the experience more intense and the novel more powerful."
—Christine Watson, *West Coast Review of Books*

"A chilling but very human portrayal.... This police procedural . . . is no ordinary blend of research and office tedium. As the suspense builds and investigators grow increasingly frustrated with their lack of success, so grows the humanity of their concerns, both personal and civic.... Washburn holds [the] suspense to [the] end."
—Florence Gilkeson, *The Pilot* (Southern Pines, NC)

"Washburn does the best job since Thomas Harris' *Red Dragon* in setting the reader inside a victim's home.... Then Washburn takes it further ... from her mind into her heart after the crime."
—Paul Foreman, *Birmingham News* (AL)

INTENT TO
HARM

STAN WASHBURN

POCKET BOOKS

New York   London   Toronto   Sydney   Tokyo   Singapore

This book is a work of fiction. Names, characters, places and incidents are products of the author's imagination or are used fictitiously. Any resemblance to actual events or locales or persons, living or dead, is entirely coincidental.

POCKET BOOKS, a division of Simon & Schuster Inc.
1230 Avenue of the Americas, New York, NY 10020

ISBN: 0-671-88458-1

First Pocket Books paperback printing April 1995

10 9 8 7 6 5 4 3 2 1

POCKET and colophon are registered trademarks of Simon & Schuster Inc.

Cover art by Gerber Studio

Printed in the U.S.A.

This book is dedicated to
Berkeley Police Inspectors
Al Bierce and Larry Lindenau
with great respect.

Acknowledgments

In reading pages of acknowledgments I used to think that *my* book, if ever I wrote a book, would be the pure product of my lonely genius. Now I've written one, and I know better. So let me join the parade of honest authors in acknowledging the following:

This book first found its voice in Jane Vandenburgh's writing class. It has passed through several drafts, and several friends read one or more of them and gave me thoughtful comments. They are Sandra Bails, Al Bierce, Anne Civitano, Gretchen Grant, Andrew Hoyem, Diana Ketchum, Larry Lindenau, Adria Petty, Dan Quinn, and Jack Stub.

My wife, Andy, and my children, Anne and John, read *all* the drafts, made crucial suggestions, and delicately talked me out of many grievous errors.

Thanks to my super agent, Fred Hill; publisher Bill Grose; and my editor, Jane Chelius, who knows when to touch the tiller and when to leave it alone.

—Stan Washburn

1

She lay tense and perfectly still, listening.

She thought that there was someone in the hallway just outside the room. She thought that she could hear him breathing. She thought that she could hear the slight brush of fabric, of a shoe across the carpet, the giving of the floor-boards as he moved his weight.

She had been dreaming about an intruder who stood in the doorway watching her sleep, watching while she shifted and turned in nightmare. She was sure that she was awake now, but she thought that he was still close.

She could make out the shape of the half-open door in the faint light from the curtained window. From her pillow she could not see anything, but someone standing in the darkness of the hall could see her. She did not know whether someone could see that her eyes were open, but she did not dare to close them.

She was too frightened to do or say anything.

After a time she felt, rather than heard, that he was moving away, down the stairs. Still she waited. She could not hear anything.

With great care, so as to make no noise, she reached for the phone on her bedside table. It was not there. The phone was on a long cord. She could see from where she lay that the cord ran the other way, across the hall and into the study, where she had left it the night before.

She did not dare get out of bed to get to it.

The house creaked from time to time, as houses do. The refrigerator cycled on with a busy hum, ran for a while, and then cycled off with a dying murmur followed by a shudder. Occasionally there would be a bit of wind, which dragged the branches of nearby trees across the roof and siding, gently rattled the windows, and, tormentingly, overlay in its fitfulness potentially more important noises.

She thought that he was still in the house. He was somewhere downstairs.

Several times she was on the point of deciding that she was surely alone again. She would begin to relax her attention and gather her courage to cross the hall to the phone. But each time she would hear some creak, some click, some brushing sibilance which might not be clearly suspicious but which was also not clearly innocent. And each time this happened her heart leapt, and she stiffened again into the most rigid concentration, lifting her head and turning it slightly this way and that, pressing first one ear forward and then the other, straining for advantage.

It was a long time before she decided that, yes, she was alone. Even then she waited cautiously a little longer, to be sure.

It was still dark when she pulled back the covers and gently, carefully, put her feet on the floor.

She wanted the phone. Outside her bedroom door was a very short hall leading to the stairs in one direction, the bathroom in the other, and the study opposite. There was a hall light, but the switch was at the top of the stairs. She was not a fearful person, and she had no reason to suppose that the man was there, but nevertheless she was reluctant to go out into the dark hallway. She thought he had gone downstairs—she thought he had gone altogether—but she could not be sure.

The cord lay across the hall and disappeared into the study. The telephone was at the other end of it. There was no getting to it without crossing the hall. Her instinct was to dart across the hall and into the study, but she hesitated; she could see from the bedroom doorway that he was not in the hall, but she did not know that he was not in the study.

What she dreaded was the moment of encounter.

She crossed the hall firmly, turned on the light, and glanced quickly around. There was no one.

A sudden, violent gust lashed a bough across the window behind her and almost stopped her heart. She snatched up the receiver, dropped it to the end of its bouncing cord and fell to her knees to recapture it, lashing with her hand at the live-seeming object in its crazy bounces. She caught it in her fingertips, almost dropped it again, grasped it firmly. Instantly she realized that she had turned her back to the dark doorway. She spun around.

The doorway was empty.

She punched in 911, and a moment later heard the professional, slightly bored voice of the police dispatcher.

There is not much crime in the predawn hours, and within minutes the house was surrounded by several rookie officers in high hopes of a little action at the end of a quiet night. When the handling officer had ascertained that the intruder was probably gone—indeed, that the whole thing might have had more to do with sleeplessness and a lively imagination than with criminals—there was widespread disappointment. The rookies searched the house and grounds thoroughly, if noisily, and then were shooed away by their training sergeants back to their own beats.

The handling officer took her carefully over the house. There was nothing missing or out of place. The computer, the stereo, a camera, a TV—untouched. They went around all the windows and doors. Everything was locked, as it should be. There was no sign of entry. There was no sign, he told her frankly, that anyone had been in the house at all. And with the whole place freshly searched, and an officer beside her, she began to wonder whether she hadn't let the shadow of a bad dream run away with her.

The following evening she met her boyfriend at a restaurant. He was a fireman, not given to pushing the panic button. After hearing her tell about her night he was inclined to agree with the police that there had been nothing to it.

Finally, he decided definitely that the intruder was imaginary. Usually she resisted his tendency to tell her what she thought, but this time she was glad to listen.

They decided to skip coffee, dropped cash on their bill, drove pretty quickly to her house, and went straight to bed.

Afterward, he fell asleep. She was hungry again, and went down to find a snack. Going up, she had been preoccupied; but as she came down she had a sensation of things being unfamiliar. She paused at the foot of the stairs. The little living room was lit only by the light from the kitchen passage, but it seemed to her in looking around as if things were not exactly as she remembered them, as if everything had been picked up and then put back in a slightly different place, skewed just a little. Couch cushions, magazines on the coffee table, the fireplace tools, the knicknacks on the mantle; it was as if the whole place had been jiggled. Even the books in the shelves seemed in places to be more tidy, and in others less, than she remembered them.

God, she thought. This is creepy. But she smiled at the same time, partly because she thought that she really must be imagining it—what could have done it?—and partly because tonight she was not alone in the house.

"It's like a movie," she said aloud, and the echo of fiction reassured her. But she checked the lock on the front door, just to be safe, and then went to check the kitchen door, too. It did not occur to her to pull aside the curtains in the breakfast nook and check the latch on the window there.

She got her snack and found her book—pretty much where I left it, she thought, but yet, perhaps not *exactly* where she had left it—turned on the reading lamp and settled into her big chair.

At some point she dozed off. She dreamed that she was sleeping in her big chair and that the man who had been in the house the previous night had come into the room and sat down in the chair just opposite her own, five feet away. He was there now, if she opened her eyes he would be right in front of her, his eyes fixed on her face. She knew that he was waiting for her to wake up. She also knew that if she was aware of this, she must, in fact, be about to wake up, and that he would know. This consciousness snapped her awake so fast that without meaning to, knowing it would give her away completely, she jerked upright and shot her eyes wide open.

The chair opposite was empty.

Her chest was heaving, her heart thumping with a slow, heavy violence that she had never experienced before. She had never experienced a cold sweat either, but her forehead was icy, and a little trickle of perspiration ran from her scalp down the sides of her face. The palms of her hands were clammy. Her arms and legs felt rubbery. She could barely hold herself up in the chair.

It was only after several minutes in which there was no sign or sound of another's presence that she could bring herself to turn her head to look behind her.

The room was empty.

There was only her boyfriend upstairs. There could be no one else.

She sat limply in the chair for several minutes. Her heart slowly regained something like its normal rhythm.

She got up as soon as she felt that her legs would support her. The little bungalow, usually so cozy, now seemed immense, full of dark corners. The foot of the stairs was only ten feet away, but it looked like a long distance, and to reach it she would have to pass the door to the hall closet, which was uncharacteristically ajar.

"It was just a *dream*, goddam it," she said aloud.

She stepped quickly to the stairs, closing the closet door firmly as she passed. Then, still hurrying, and with her back turned partly to the wall so that she could keep an eye on the hall below her, she slipped upstairs.

It was not until she was at the bedroom door that it occurred to her that she had not switched off any of the lights downstairs. Reflexively she turned to go back down, but then she thought of passing the closet door again.

No, she thought. To hell with 'em. And for good measure, she left the light burning at the top of the stairs as well.

Her boyfriend was on the side of the bed nearest the door, where she usually slept. Carefully, she climbed over him and snuggled deep into the bedclothes, next to the wall. He was a solid young man, competent and composed even

5

in sleep, immensely reassuring. A gentle shaft of light from the hall fell across the bureau at the foot of the bed and illumined the room softly. God, she thought, I'm like a kid, with night-lights to keep away the spooks. But it reassured her, childish or not. For a few minutes she watched contentedly over his shoulder. There was nothing to see or hear throughout the silent house.

Soon they both slept.

At some point in the night she opened her eyes.

It was several seconds before she remembered that when she had gone to sleep the room had been lit from the hall. Now it was dark, with only the faintest light coming from the window.

She was wide awake. The man was in the bedroom doorway, less than five feet away, a silhouette only slightly lighter than the blackness of the hall beyond. He was leaning back against the door frame, his weight settled on one leg as if he had been there for some time.

Involuntarily she cried out and jerked to her knees, pressing back against the wall. Reflexively, her boyfriend lurched up against the headboard. In the moment of waking he saw the man. A moment later the doorway was empty, the footfalls on the staircase muffled and rapid.

"My *god!*" she whispered. "It was *him!* It was *him!* It was *him!*"

Still half asleep, her boyfriend clambered out of bed and stepped to the doorway. There was no one there.

The phone was beside the bed. They called the police, and then they went downstairs. All the lights were out. The hall closet and the kitchen door both stood open. The cord of the downstairs phone had been pulled out of the wall. One of the benches from the backyard picnic table stood below the window of the breakfast nook, and the row of lively little blown-glass animals which had lined the sill lay in a disconsolate tumble on the ground outside.

The call was broadcast as a burglary just prior, meaning that the responsible was at that moment in flight. The location of occurrence was in the beat adjacent to my own, and I was in good position to respond.

You estimate two minutes for a relatively calm and collected reporting party to make the call, explain what has happened, give the dispatcher enough information to begin broadcasting, and for the dispatcher to put the information out. A person can cover a long block in a minute, or more if he's in a hurry, which fleeing burglars usually are. But say he's not an athlete. We'll say that at the moment a hot call is broadcast, the responsible can be anywhere in a circle of two blocks' radius, or roughly twenty square blocks. If it takes you two minutes to respond, the radius is, say, three or four blocks, and the area is fifty or sixty square blocks. So theoretically, after four minutes you have him somewhere on ten or twelve miles of city streets.

In this case, the description given by the dispatcher was "Male, unknown age, unknown race, average height and build, dark clothing." That eliminates women, which is something, but since women don't do a lot of burglaries it doesn't help a great deal. It also eliminates males who are obviously young enough to be identified as juveniles, and elderly men, and anyone wearing such bright clothes that you would notice him even in darkness, and midgets, and basketball players. Anyone else fits. So somewhere on these ten or twelve miles of city streets you're looking for a man of any race between, say, fifteen and fifty-five, anywhere from five feet six inches and 120 pounds to six feet and 200 pounds, wearing almost anything not notably conspicuous.

You might get lucky and see someone running, for example, or out of breath, or sweating as if he had been running recently, or who might see your patrol car and look nervous, or try to duck out of sight, or even turn and run away. Burglars have been known to struggle along the street with stereo components stuffed under their coats and the wires, with cut ends, dangling around their knees—that happened once to me. You hear of criminals who are so frightened by the pursuit that they flag down the first squad car they see and surrender, just to get it over with. That hasn't happened to me.

And all this assumes that the burglar didn't have his car parked around the corner, in which case he's probably already home watching TV with his mother.

But there are ways to cut the odds. Often there's a direction of flight. That reduces the search area by about half. And some escape routes are more dangerous for a fugitive than others: a quiet residential street has little traffic, pedestrian or vehicular, so what little there is gets attention. That means that the sooner he can get to a big street with lots of traffic, the less he'll stand out. But if it's late enough so that there's no traffic on the big streets, he'll use side streets because they're harder to watch. He'll probably avoid large open areas such as parks and schoolyards because he can be seen from a distance.

Bad guys tend not to hide near the scene and wait until the coast is clear. It's human nature to get as far away as possible. Besides, it's hard to judge a hiding place in the dark: a shadowy corner looks great until a headlight passes across it, and then it's nothing.

In responding to the fireman's call I thought, He won't have gone across the park to the south, and he probably won't have gone into the neighborhood to the north. He's probably driving by now, so if he's heading west he'll be long gone by the time I get around. Eastbound, there are two large streets coming out of that area; one of those leads to another residential district, and the other heads downtown. I'll sit on the downtown route.

So within two minutes of the initial broadcast I had my black-and-white parked in shadow under a tree on a secondary cross street about two spaces back from the downtown arterial. Facing west, I could also see for about three blocks down the secondary street. In my rearview mirror I could see two blocks up, so that if he were to use one of those side streets I might see him going across. Of course, there was no vehicle description, but people in a hurry very often drive differently than people who are just going home: they speed, they roll through stop signs, they tailgate and jink back and forth, left and right, as if trying to get around the car ahead. From the radio I knew that four other squad cars to the west and south had taken spots based on a similar process of probability and opportunity. Two cars went straight to the scene, the one place in town where we knew for a fact that this citizen was *not*, but it makes the victim feel better when you show up right away.

We had as fair a chance at this fellow as you usually get. But we didn't get him. Maybe he crossed the playing field. Or maybe he sauntered through the neighborhood to the north without anyone taking notice. Or maybe he picked a good hiding place and waited out the search. Or maybe he was in one of those cars that went quietly past one of the spots, driving cool and not standing out. Or maybe he was just fast, and was outside the perimeter before it was set up. Maybe he was really cagey and outsmarted us, or maybe he was just lucky. Anyhow, he got away.

The intended victim was uncertain what to say when the handling officer arrived to take the report. It's hard to sort out exactly what happens between sleep and waking. When the moment came for her to describe what had happened, she felt ridiculous talking about frights and apparitions. She said simply that she had been asleep, that she was awakened by a man in the room. The boyfriend told the same story. The officer, who had also taken her report the previous night, reported the incident as a probable robbery attempt, with the responsible losing his nerve and fleeing. There was no useful description of the responsible, and a quick dusting by an overworked technician revealed no fingerprints or other evidence. Without further leads, the officer requested that the case be suspended. A copy of the report was forwarded to the Robbery detail, and there the matter rested. An odd case, but lots of cases are odd.

The whole point of the cover around a crime is that you're waiting for the bad guy to run into your arms, and you get hyped up in expectation. Then when you come up dry you want to unwind a little before going on to the next thing. When I left my spot I drifted over to the supermarket that lies on the border between Walt Kramer's beat and mine, and where it was our custom at about that hour to meet for a few minutes to see a friendly face. Walt was already there, at the underlit extremity of the parking lot. Even in uniform, Walt has a massive, rumpled silhouette that you can spot from some distance. A ripple of dismay follows immediately behind him in movie theaters if he walks down the aisle, everyone afraid that he will settle in front of them and they will have to move; this makes him anxious, and if he can't get a seat in the back row he'll usually leave.

I pulled in next to him, facing the opposite way so that we could talk without leaving our cars, and so that nobody could approach us unseen. Walt and I had been friends in college and roommates in Basic School. Our preference in these little intermissions in the battle against crime was to talk about something else.

"Ah, Toby," he said when I pulled alongside. "What news?"

"Sara says to come to dinner tomorrow," I said. "She made a double recipe of a casserole that sounded very promising, but the kids won't eat it. Naturally, she thought of you."

Our house was in Walt's beat, a rather scruffy neighborhood of older houses largely inhabited by the less well-to-do university population. He and I worked the 3:00 to 11:00 P.M. shift. Dinner break came irregularly, any time between 4:00 and 9:00. I usually went home to eat, perching in the dining room with gun belt creaking and radio squawking quietly. If Walt got off at the same time, he would often come eat with me. If we happened to get off around 7:00, which is when Sara and the kids ate, we would all eat together. Occasionally, Walt would feed me at his apartment. He never planned for this, so his cooking consisted of bold, often alarming, improvisations.

"I dunno," he said. "Your kids will eat pretty much anything. Is Sara sure she wants to—"

The radio interrupted us.

"For 104 and 22, a family fight, violent." It was a midtown address. We waited to hear 104 and 22 acknowledge the call, because if they didn't Walt and I were the next closest beats.

"104 copy."

"22 copy."

If a call doesn't involve you, you just make a mental note. Walt picked up where he had left off.

"Is she sure she wants to palm off this casserole on an old friend? Who's going to look after you if I'm—"

The radio again.

"104 and 22, we've just had a second call. The reporting party's the grandmother at that location. It's developing into a brandishing via knife. 93, why don't you cover in there, too."

"To arms," I said to Walt as I picked up my mike. "93 copy." I flipped on the roof lights and started toward the downtown at a pretty good clip.

"Cars responding." It was the dispatcher who was taking the phone calls, bypassing the radio control supervisor to get information out more quickly. "It's now an assault via knife. Ambulance responding."

"Cars responding, make it Code 3, light and siren. 17, S-5, can you cover in?"

There were three cars there before me, standing empty in the street with their roof lights flashing away blue and red over the gathering neighbors. The first two officers had already gone in. The third, Sergeant D'Honnencourt, was just crossing the sidewalk, slipping his long baton into the ring on his belt, glancing up toward the open window of the apartment in question, and coming as close to breaking into a run as I had ever see him do.

2

It had never crossed my mind to be a cop. Sara and I weren't antipolice as such, but we were good liberals, and we entered on adult life suspicious of any activity that requires a uniform. After college, I joined a tiny publishing house which specialized in handsome editions of obscure texts. Sara began law school. We lived thin, much as we had done as students.

When Sara graduated and joined a small firm specializing in family law, we bought a fixer-upper and stocked its two sunny rear bedrooms with one child of each sex.

This state continued for several years. Then, rather suddenly, the publishing house was acquired by a larger, coarser company seeking to refine its image. They wanted the name but not the staff. I was offered two or three promising jobs by friends with other publishers, but we were reluctant to relocate, and I hesitated. Sara's firm was very flexible about her hours, but they didn't pay her much money. We needed my income.

Walt and I had been great friends since college. He had realized a small inheritance from an aunt, and with a little capital in his pocket he fell into the same genial error as many another bookish person with a degree and no specific

12

ambitions, and opened a bookstore. Sara and I were just married at this point, and many of the discussions which led to this doomed venture occurred in our kitchen.

Walt lived in bachelor digs and went out with a sequence of rather attractive, bookish women. His business neither succeeded nor quite failed. I often went by the store to visit. He would loom like a great corduroy bear behind the desk near the front window, glaring up the quiet side street to the main drag, where the students streamed past on their way to classes and to other, more craftily located bookstores. We drank many espressos and discussed how business was sure to pick up.

At about the same time that I found myself on the bricks, Walt found that he had run out of money. He had only had the one aunt. A police officer customer who attended his going-out-of-business-sale mentioned that the police department was hiring. This cop was working the 3:00 to 11:00 P.M. shift and going to graduate school during the day. He said there were a number of bright people in his platoon, and he said several sincere things about making the world a better place.

Walt came over that evening. He told Sara and me what the cop had said. We all laughed uproariously. Then Sara said that she believed in making the world a better place, and of course Walt and I agreed. I asserted the dignity of all necessary work, and Sara and Walt agreed. Walt said he thought parasitic intellectuals were pitiful, and Sara and I agreed. Then Sara, who had been paying the bills when I got home, asked what entry-level cops got paid, and Walt happened to know.

The next day Walt and I went down to the Personnel office together. We figured it would give us time to regroup. And a couple of good liberals would be a wholesome influence, we thought.

When we got out of Basic School and were assigned to the night shift (11:00 P.M. to 7:00 A.M.) training platoon, our training sergeant was Barry Dillon. Walt and I tended to get more theoretical instruction from Barry because we were older than our fellow probationary officers. Barry liked to perform for an audience who could appreciate the subtleties

13

of his work. Walt was thirty-two when he was sworn, and I was thirty-one. Most cops start several years younger than that, and between the fact that they are, as a group, without much life experience, flexibility, or sense of humor, they can be a very unresponsive audience for an instructor. You can mold them when they are like that, and make very good stuff out of them in two or three years, if they survive, but it's hard to like them very much in the meantime. They're too dumb even to recognize that they're being molded, let alone notice how well it's being done or feel thankful about the care that's being taken over them. Walt and I, on the other hand, were more educated and more skeptical and thus more conscious of what was happening to us. Barry loved that. He'd been a cop for twenty years, and in that time he had formed a style based on the contrast between his looming, intimidating appearance and his almost child-like ebullience of spirits. He was good at what he did, and proud of his skill. He loved the night training shift, because that is where you find the most ignorance.

Barry was full of little lectures. Sometimes these popped out at roll call, when the whole watch sat around the big squad room table and listened to the reading of the log highlights for the previous sixteen hours and other housekeeping matters.

"You always gotta remember who you are and what you want," he told us once. "You're a cop, and you're dealing with people for a reason. Don't be distracted. Last night there was a little incident in the squad room. I name no names, Dwornenscheck . . ." Everyone looked at Patty, who laid her head on the table and covered it with her arms. Some woman officers adopted the unflappable affect which their male colleagues have traditionally regarded as professional, but Patty was not among them.

"Go ahead, Barry," she said. "Humiliate me." The previous night Patty had arrested a pimp who told her while she was bringing him in about how his girls were high class and that he wouldn't employ a dog like Patty to pass out towels in his massage parlor, let alone service his customers, who trusted his taste. He made the point at some length. It made her so mad that when they got to the Hall of Justice she shoved him into a holding cell without checking it out for cleanliness first, which you're supposed to do, and went away to recover her breath. When she came back there was a fat packet of heroin on the floor. She couldn't charge him with it because she couldn't swear that the room was clean when he went into it. He laughed in her face.

"Well, if you don't get embarrassed in this business it means you're not trying," said Barry. "And if you're not trying, you're not doing your job. So it's Patty tonight and someone else tomorrow. Look, people. If somebody calls you names, don't get mad. If somebody tries to butter you up, smile, but don't be fooled. If they think they're smart and you're dumb, they'll get cocky. They'll get careless, and you'll be waiting. If they think you're dumb and they've put one over on you, don't straighten 'em out. Let 'em think it. It's no part of your job to educate jerks."

Sergeant D'Honnencourt, who was sitting beside Barry, added, "The gentleman was paying our colleague and our department a high professional compliment by his behavior. He knew that he could be rude to one of our officers and still keep his teeth. That's something we can all be proud of. Right, Dwornenscheck?"

She pulled herself up and said, "Right, Sergeant," which was what you said to D'Honnencourt.

Sometimes Barry would give his little chats individually. Once over coffee he told me, "This is a small town, Parkman, and that makes a difference to a cop. Out of a hundred thousand citizens there are only so many criminals, and after a couple of years you oughta know a lot of 'em, what they do, what they're like. And you oughta know all the little populations, too. The university people, what they're like. The professional people. The blacks. The whites. The Latinos. The Asians—all the *different* Asians. And professional blacks are different than poor blacks, just like professional whites are different from blue-collar whites and hippie whites. They're all different; they all have something different in mind when they call you, or when you arrive without being called. You treat 'em all fair, you'll be effective, but

15

they all think 'fair' is something different. You gotta know what they want."

He told us these things proudly, like a master carpenter exhibiting the contents of his tool chest, bringing out each object and expatiating on its right use. He would loom over you with his pale blue eyes floating in his great pale face, his curly flaxen hair gleaming like a halo, and emphasize his points by a sudden volley of jabs with an enormous fingertip against your chest, or a flurry of whacks on the back with a great, horny hand.

"And son of a bitch, *you can do something about it*," he would whoop, jabbing. "You know your job, you know who you're dealing with, you can get things done. You can give people what they deserve, good or bad. That's the great thing about being a cop: you have discretion. Defense attorneys, they're stuck with whatever jerk comes along and they have to make the best of it. The D.A.'s got some flexibility, he can adjust the charges or dismiss, but what he's got to work with is what we give him. But all the attorneys, all the judges, they're dealing in paper. They're dealing in stories. They're dealing in excuses and recollections and lies. Us— we can do *justice*"—several hard pokes—"right on the spot. The players are still breathing hard when we get there, they're still in the heat of it, they haven't made up a fable yet—hell, they don't know they need one yet. They're glad to tell their side straight, they still believe in it. You can take care of some honest bozo who's just unlucky, and Mr. Slick goes off to jail.

"That's power. That's the power to do good. You got it. Use it. Protect the weak. Nail jerks. That's what it's all about."

It was a heady anthem for a good liberal: Protect the weak. Nail jerks. Don't hesitate.

With Walt and me, at any rate, who were nearer his own age, Barry discussed his private life with equal pride and candor. We came to reckon time by the eras of Barry's entanglements. When we were sworn, it was Bette. Our two years of probation endured through the tenures of Pauletta and Elaine. We had completed our third year and decided that we liked being cops before June had been supplanted by Maya.

Barry always knew his girlfriends' measurements and cup sizes, and it was never long before we knew them, too. Maya's were 36C-29-38.

He was a graduate student writing his thesis in a little apartment that had once been a hayloft at the very rear of the homeowner's property. During the most recent election campaign he had hung the poster of a radical candidate in the window above his desk. This window was invisible from the street; indeed, the only person who could see it was his immediate neighbor, a conservative woman of middle age. She had been greatly offended by it. They had had one or two stormy conversations, and then stopped speaking. It annoyed her greatly that his desk overlooked her garden. It pleased him to think that it annoyed her.

He had discovered that it relaxed him, at the end of a long evening of writing, to turn off the lamp and simply sit for a while in the darkness, looking out of the window. One night, he had been sitting this way for a few minutes when he saw a man slip into the woman's yard and stand close to a large shrub. It was fascinating: in the darkness he seemed to disappear once he stopped moving. He seemed to melt into the shrub, to disappear.

Perhaps, the student thought, this was a Peeping Tom; the woman's bedroom window overlooked the garden, and there was a small gap in the curtains. He snickered. Even if the peeper was lucky there wouldn't be much to see. He thought of her indignation if she found out, and snickered again.

When he looked back from the woman's window to the garden he couldn't see the prowler at all. He thought he could distinguish a figure near the place where he had first seen him, but now he had to admit that there was no way to be sure. He watched for a while longer, looking for movement, but there was nothing.

No doubt whoever it was had given up and gone home.

He was very tired. He moved slowly around the room preparing for bed. He thought about his work as he was

17

drifting off to sleep. He didn't give the prowler another thought.

"Why doesn't Barry just hang a memo on the bulletin board? To save time," mused Walt one evening on our back steps.

"A memo?" I prodded the charcoal. "Are we still discussing Maya's dimensions?"

"Right. To: All Personnel. From: Patrol Sergeant Dillon. Re: Mon Chérie Amor. Cute nose, nice hair, a little short in the leg, but she's got knockers from *here* to *there.*"

"Mom, what are knockers?" asked Jocelyn, our daughter, who was nine, and had a pattern of appearing unexpectedly in doorways.

"Walt will tell you," said Sara, who knows how to run a taut ship.

"Walt, what are knockers?"

"It's how you know somebody's at the front door," said Walt after a moment's hesitation.

"But why from here to there?" persisted Joss.

"Oh, that's just an expression," said Walt. "Oh, look, a squirrel. I hope the cats don't get it."

"No fear," said Joss. "John Marshall is getting fat and Robert Peel is shy."

Our first cat, despite being a female, was named John Marshall, after the first Chief Justice of the Supreme Court, and always given the whole handle, never merely "John." The second was named Robert Peel, after the father of the modern police force, as a compliment to me.

"Anyway," persisted Joss, "if it's just an expression, what does it express?"

"Are you going to be a lawyer, like your mom?" said Walt.

"I don't know. What does it express?"

"It expresses that her knockers are big enough so that they can be heard all the way out in the backyard," said Walt, who had at least gained a little time.

"We just have one knocker, and it's pretty small, but you can hear it fine."

"Well, maybe his girlfriend doesn't hear as well as you

18

do, young lady," said Walt severely. "Really, Joss, it's very egotistical to think that everybody else is just like you."

"I guess you'd rather not tell me," said Joss tactfully.

Perhaps moved by pity, Sara said, "Toby, why don't you and Walt start the hamburgers. Joss, please set the picnic table. Adam, please help your sister."

Adam rolled slowly over on the grass.

"But first wash your hands," added Sara.

"Oh, okay," said Adam. He clumped up the steps, chanting to himself, "She's got *knockers* from *here* to *there*. She's got *knockers* from *here* to *there*," and disappeared into the house.

"How nice it is," I said, spreading the coals, "to have intellectual friends to uphold the tone of discourse around here."

"*God*, Toby," said Walt. "What species of child are you raising? Where's that little minx going to find a man tough enough?"

"Oh, you never know," said Sara, who was arriving with the condiments. "I found her father."

"You mean she'll have to settle for someone unworthy," said Walt gallantly.

"I never thought of that," she said. "Or at any rate, I don't dwell on it. Dear, the kids'll want theirs well done. The fries'll be another minute. Walt, another beer while I'm in the kitchen?"

Walt was active in the Explorer troop attached to the department. While we ate he told us about the encounters of hormone-drenched adolescents with the modern world.

"Walt, what are hormones?" asked Joss. But Sara, sensing danger, explained for him.

"She's got *hormones* from *here* to *there!*" Adam began.

"Bedtime," Sara and I said simultaneously.

Over coffee Walt said, "Toby, what did you make of that burglary-in-progress or whatever it was in the north end the other night?"

"I didn't make anything of it." There was a little pile of salt spilled on the picnic table, and I was drawing spirals in it with my finger. "The guy got away. They usually do."

"It was Jackson's case. He said the victim woke up to find the responsible in the bedroom, just standing there."

"Very odd behavior for a robber."

"Yes. It's . . ."

"Just a sec," I said. "Adam's in bed, but where's Joss?" We looked around. Through the window we could see the top of Joss's head as she followed Sara around the kitchen.

"What did Jackson make of it?" I asked.

"He said it looked like a peeper or an incipient rape, but he made it a burglary because he didn't think anyone would try to rape a fireman."

"Jackson is becoming quite a snob."

"Yes," said Walt. "But if it were a robbery, the guy wouldn't have been just standing there. And if it was a burg, he would have burgled, but he didn't. And there was that intruder call the night before. Pretty odd."

"D'you think it's some kind of stalk?" I said.

"Could be. It's odd."

"In any case," I said, "we're not likely to know. So I won't worry about it."

Sara's voice had been heard giving Joss bedtime injunctions. Now she appeared in the doorway. She said, "I've come out to join you and enjoy the evening, if you think you can keep it comparatively clean. What aren't you likely to know?"

Walt recapitulated.

"I don't like the sound of that," said Sara. "And why, my dear, are you not going to worry about it? That was only ten blocks from here. *I'll* worry about it."

"Well, I meant professionally," I said. "If we don't catch him at the time, and he doesn't leave any evidence behind that would suggest who he is, and he doesn't turn himself in, and his girlfriend doesn't rat on him, then he's home free."

"I don't like that," said Sara.

"I wish not liking it changed anything," I said.

"Well, I know it's a workaday calculation to you heroes," she said. "But it's a big deal to us peaceful lawyers and mothers."

"Ah," said Walt, stretching with theatrical luxuriance. "Home life. Nothing like it. Kids and a mortgage, and on top of it all the question of whether your sunny, honey-suckle-draped cottage is going to be invaded by psychopathic disembowelers. There's something to be said for the bachelor's existence, after all." But to my domesticated ear there was a note of discontent in his voice, and as it happened Sara's arm was at that moment resting on my shoulder with the careless intimacy of old acquaintance. So perhaps I sounded a little patronizing when I agreed with him. And Sara, who would usually have replied to such a speech with something tart, said nothing at all.

Shortly afterward we folded up the tablecloth, carried the glasses into the house, and Walt wandered off home.

"Walt's lonely," Sara said.

"Well, of course he's lonely," I said. "He's alone." It's always possible to fit one more glass into a dishwasher if you do it right, and this was the problem which was principally engaging my mind at that moment.

"Melanie's really lonely, too."

"Yes."

Sara had played the viola since childhood, and she managed to keep it up even during law school. After we were married she found her way into a chamber music group, and there she met a flutist named Melanie. They became great chums, and made a point of getting together to play duets two or three times a month. Our two families were often together. It was very convenient for us, because Melanie's children, Mike and Heather, were baby-sitters of genius.

"She doesn't talk about it, but of course she is. Mike's going off to college soon, and Heather's a dear, but she's not company. She's fifteen, and her mind's elsewhere."

"Yes. And . . ."

"Yes. And then there's Walt. He's . . ."

"Honey, wait a moment. A moment, if you please." I had got the glass in. I straightened up. Sara is usually so sensible. I said, "You're not thinking of trying to mate Melanie and Walt."

"I am."

"Oh, *really*, Sara."

"Toby, why not?"

"We tried before. It was a flop. Melanie thinks cops are

21

tacky—she makes an exception of me because she knew me when I was in something genteel and she thinks I'll get over it. And Walt doesn't like commanding women. That pretty well licks the platter clean. Remember New Year's Eve? They both got tiddly and seemed so chummy, but then they started talking seriously, and that was the end of it."

"That was ages ago."

"It was the wee hours of January first. This is the fourth of April."

"Well, they're both still lonely."

"It's a mad scheme."

"We'll think about it," she said, which is her way of saying that the subject is not closed.

Right after she was divorced, Melanie had gotten a dog, a large black dog with long hair. He was rather an old dog at the time I'm thinking of, very placid and friendly, not pushy, not destructive, very easy to get along with. A dull animal, really, full of unassuming dog virtues. The only odd thing about this dog was that he had such a very active dream life. Of course, animals dream. But this dog dreamed a lot, and got very involved. Melanie liked to speculate about what the dog was dreaming. She loved to spin out a fantasy about it, preferably something philosophically or culturally obscure.

If the weather were cold or dreary Melanie would have a fire, and the dog loved to sleep close to it. On this one occasion the dog was asleep on the hearth rug, right in front. You could tell that he was dreaming: his eyes were moving under the lids, his nose wrinkled as he smelled, he stirred and kept changing position. He was growling in a very confident way, and holding his tail back. It looked like a very satisfactory dream: whatever it was he was doing, he seemed to be winning.

The only problem was that he was awfully close to the fire, and Melanie began to worry that he was going to roll right in. She got down and pulled rug and dog together a little farther away.

The dog was making little kissing sorts of noises, twitching his ears, very engaging, I guess. Melanie was so engaged that on an impulse she bent down and kissed him on the nose. Instantly he twisted half over on his side and snapped at her face, the upper canines catching her cheek just below the eye, and the lower beside the nose on the other side so that he really had a grip on her; he gave several very hard shakes, jumping to his feet and straining backward as she screamed and tugged back on her hands and knees, trying to pull away. For a moment Sara and I were frozen, as one is at such moments, but of course we jumped up and got him off. He backed into a corner, snarling, while we pulled Melanie to her feet and got her into the kitchen, where there was water and we could clean her up and see what to do.

She had several deep punctures and gashes in her face. She was pouring blood, and still only barely comprehending what had happened to her. We were trying to grab towels or whatever could be of use to stop the bleeding, running around giving each other contradictory advice and telling her in loud, worried voices that it was okay and everything was going to be fine.

Then the dog appeared at the kitchen door, all sociable, tail wagging, ready to be friends. He came straight to Melanie. I started to push him away, thinking that she would be scared to death of him. She saw what I was doing and stopped me. She threw her arms around the dog's neck and told him that it was all right, and that everything was going to be fine, how Mummy loved him and it didn't hurt a bit, all the time bleeding copiously into his fur.

3

Up the street from our house, at the corner of the main drag, there is a bus stop used by schoolchildren from across town. A man struck up a conversation with two young girls there after school. They described him later as being old, thin, earnest, and pleasant. He told them that he was a magician; more, that he was a Hollywood talent scout. He asked them about themselves. He flattered them on their intelligence and appearance. He told them some quite probable-sounding tales about utterly unknown ten-year-olds who had turned Tinseltown on its ear.

When the bus came he got on with them and continued their conversation. The briefcase he carried contained the properties he used in his magic, he told them, which he would show them another time. But he made quarters appear behind their ears and made the girls a present of them. He got them to write down their names and addresses, and put the slips of paper into the briefcase. He told them he would be calling them about screen tests.

Then he made a mistake. Grown-ups, he said, often got very jealous of their children's success. Many a promising career had been ruined because of this, and so they must not tell their parents that they had talked to him. At the

24

next stop he got off the bus and started walking in the opposite direction.

Along with the classic injunctions against going into strange houses and getting into cars, the girls had been told always to tell if someone says not to tell. They told, and their mothers called the police. All this happened on a Friday.

On Saturday morning the report of the investigating officer, headed "Suspicious Circumstance re Possible Attempt Child Molest" ("Possible" because there had been no overt act, and the motive was thus conjectural) was placed in the Sex Crimes detail's "in" tray, among others.

The commander of Sex Crimes was Sergeant Leo Gadek. There were several other cases in a pile on the corner of his desk, all reported during the past few days, which seemed to involve the same man. Some of these were suspicious circumstance reports, but most were sexual molestations. The man was variously described in these reports, and details were few and unreliable. Not all of the reports mentioned magic tricks. To a police officer who thrives on hard information all this was very unsatisfactory.

Several of the reports had not been made until days after the incidents described, and even establishing a chronology involved a lot of guesswork, but it was becoming clear to Gadek that a substantial series had been in progress for three or four weeks. He gave it to Blondie Moore, the junior of his two officers. She was known as Blondie, despite her trim black Afro, because when she was interviewing for the department the Personnel officer was pompous and patronizing and when he asked her if she had a nickname she said "Blondie," just to be difficult. But that's how he addressed her for the rest of the interview, and he passed the word on. Everyone in the Personnel office called her Blondie. The name preceded her to Basic School and followed her back to her training platoon. By that time it *was* her nickname.

Blondie spent most of the day organizing what facts were known, doing file checks, and phoning neighboring jurisdictions to see whether they had anything similar.

The occupants of offices near Sex Crimes had learned not to step through their doors without looking out for Gadek. He barreled up and down the narrow Hall of Justice corridors absorbed in bad photocopies and illegible reports. A picture was forming in his mind of the man he was looking for. He was coming to think of him, quite personally, as "the Magician."

On that same Saturday afternoon the Magician got into conversation with an eight-year-old boy playing by himself at the edge of a neighborhood park. He did not mention the movies. He made a quarter appear from behind the boy's ear and made him a present of it. He showed him a trick with a handkerchief. Then, indicating his briefcase, he described some of the tricks he could do if there were any place nearby where his rivals couldn't spy out his secrets; those bushes over there looked thick enough. In the bushes he made the boy promise not to reveal the magic secrets. Opening the briefcase, he did several tricks. Would the boy like to learn how to be his assistant, and do magic too? He blindfolded him.

There was a patter of mumbo jumbo. In the midst of this he told him to "kiss the angel's tongue."

Almost immediately, the boy began to retch. He tried to pull away, but the Magician clamped both hands over his face, digging a finger behind the angle of the jaw just below each ear to hold him. He proceeded while the boy struggled to breathe, astonished by the pain.

When he was finished, he ordered the boy never to tell anyone, because if he did, the Magician would know. Then he hurried off.

The boy did not really understand what had happened, and he told his mother about it. Her first reaction was to make him promise never to tell anyone, ever, and then to confine him to his room. But the following day, heavy with misgivings, she called the police to make a report.

On Sunday there were reports of two incidents in addition to the one from Saturday afternoon: one child had refused to leave the house and began bursting suddenly into tears, a pattern which lasted for several days until the truth came out; the other was taken to the emergency room when her mother, doing the laundry, found a pair of her underpants black with blood. Parents often did not find out for days that anything had happened, and when they did they would often react so violently that by the time the victims were interviewed their stories were an impenetrable miasma of denial, apology, and exculpation. Inexpert beat officers often had great trouble making out just what it was that had occurred. Child victims are frequently poor sources of facts, and these victims were frightened, confused, deeply conscious of their parents' shame and outrage, and heartbreakingly unsure as to its object. Questioned by an imposing uniformed stranger while their parents paced and fumed, they fidgeted, mumbled, wept, omitted, forgot, embroidered, contradicted, invented, denied. They did the best they could.

All this, combined with sometimes dilatory completion of paperwork, meant that by the time a case reached Sex Crimes the trail was cold, the evidence muddled, and the victim uncooperative. But there was usually something new to be learned, even so.

Together with the reports in hand, the three new incidents established the rate of reported molestations at three a week over a period of three weeks.

On Monday morning Gadek went to the captain of Detective Division and proposed a special detail. The core would be the two Sex Crimes detectives, Blondie Moore and Eddie Agnelli, supplemented by Patrol officers on overtime, and supervised by himself. The captain approved, and by the afternoon a slip of goldenrod paper was thrust into the Third Platoon sergeant's "in" tray.

Roll call for the Third Platoon began at 3:00 P.M. with a reading of highlights from the Daily Bulletin, the record of all calls for service received since the platoon went off duty at eleven the previous night. Dillon and D'Honnencourt sat at the end of the table, each with large mugs of Patrol coffee, and Barry with the Bulletin in front of him. The platoon sat around the squad room table, changing flashlight batteries, tinkering with equipment, and taking a note from time to time.

"At 0033, Low Class Liquors—excuse *me*, Low *Cost* Liquors—reports an attempt robbery via gun. The responsible, our old friend Donnie Wonner, was unfortunately too drunk to stay awake long enough to complete the crime, and was apprehended by our own Henry Lomus in an unconscious condition on the floor of that establishment, clutching in his alabaster arms the weapon and the boodle. Congratulations, Henry."

A ripple of derisory applause. Lomus bowed from his chair.

"At 0135, we have a report of a stolen car." Everyone picked up their pens and scribbled down the description and license.

"At 0928, Bilbo's Head Shop reports the Mystery Flasher urinating on the fireplug in front of that establishment. Guys," said Barry wearily, "the lieutenant wants the Mystery Flasher busted. Patrol Division takes too long to get to fireplug pissings. The brass are beginning to get the idea that you are not taking this as seriously as they are. So let's do it."

He thrust his hand down the back of his shirt and scratched vigorously.

"At 0955, in front of Ocean Canned Goods, an injury truck-to-car. Beats 1, 2, and 7 share that intersection. Please spend some time bringing law and order to that shopping district generally, and to that intersection in particular, traffic-wise."

D'Honnencourt ran his eye around the table at the officers assigned to those beats, all of whom immediately looked firm and decisive.

"At 0957, Memorial Med Center Emergency reports a walk-in rape victim, a woman living alone, age fifty-three. Victim was attacked at around midnight while asleep in her house. Responsible described as adult male, nothing further. Entry probably via door cheat from the garden in the rear, but the initial investigation was unable to pinpoint that with certainty. Neighborhood check turned up a resident in the adjacent property which overlooks the garden and who saw an unidentified man lurking on the victim's property just prior to that time, but like a good citizen did nothing, zero, zip, at all about it and now feels like a complete jerk. I bet we all figure he's got it right this time, one time too late." Applause.

"At 1227, Hortensia Plata reports being the victim of a

purse snatch via rat pack in front of Big Bill's Bowls. At least six juveniles, approximately junior high age, including at least two females, knocked her down, grabbed her purse, kicked and punched her several times, and fled westward from there. Guys, we've got nothing on this, no description, no nothing. But you beat people in that area can always step out of your cars and chat with any groups of kids you see hanging around in a pugnacious way, explain that we've been having this problem, and ask if they have any suggestions to make. They won't, but if you're lucky you'll get some guilty reactions that you can work with. If you're really lucky somebody might run. If we can come up with a face, Plata might be able to ID."

He pushed the Bulletin away.

"Ladies and gentlemen," said D'Honnencourt. "We have one or two little housekeeping matters.

"I have noticed that the standard of neatness and polish in your uniforms and equipment has declined recently. The purpose of your uniform is to promote recognition and inspire respect. If you don't maintain it, or if you don't wear it neatly, you create confusion in minds which may be confused enough already. I don't want to waste our time here by beginning every roll call with a formal inspection"—his eye lingered briefly on Walt, who stirred uneasily in his chair—"but I will, unless you young people can manage this by yourselves."

"On another matter, Sergeant Gadek in Sex Crimes has a recent series of child molestations, all presumably by the same responsible. He is forming a special detail to work this case during the after-school hours. Normally, we wouldn't be looking at you people to work this one because it means taking you off part of your regular shift, but for various reasons we're in a bind, and so we'd like to get two volunteers. If you're interested, see me after roll call."

There were training schedules and vacation schedules, and one or two admonitions from the higher echelon. Then we were dismissed. We lined up at the equipment room window for radios and cars. Then I circled around to D'Honnencourt.

"Sergeant, I'd be interested in Gadek's detail."

"Ah, good, Parkman. You're certainly ready for that. You haven't done any of these Detective Division specials, have you?"

"No." I'd admired DD from afar—plainclothes, big cases. Romance.

Walt appeared, looking comparatively neat at the beginning of the shift.

"Kramer, does this interest you, too?"

"Yeah," said Walt. "Yeah."

You could almost see D'Honnencourt's eyebrow go up inside his head, but he'd largely given up trying to imbue Walt with any active sense of punctilio. He suppressed the snub he would have given a younger officer.

"Very well," he said, "you've got it. You'll work tomorrow starting at two o'clock P.M. and going till seven. Casual plainclothes. Then you suit up and finish up your shift here." There was a moment's hesitation, and then he said, "I should explain, Kramer, that 'casual plainclothes' means clean, although perhaps not ironed, slacks, an equally clean shirt, perhaps with a collar. Appropriate shoes. A coat or windbreaker suitable to the time and season. Are you clear on that?"

Walt glanced at me with his hunted look.

"I'll check him out, Sergeant," I said. "He'll be okay."

"Thank you, Parkman." We talked past Walt as if he were some monstrously overgrown idiot child. The irony was that he must have been high in D'Honnencourt's good books to be worth all this extra fuss.

"Report to Sergeant Gadek in the Sex Crimes office," he said. "He's an interesting officer. You'll learn from him if you listen carefully." He passed into the sergeants' office.

"We've *made* it," said Walt, "*Detectives*. Inspector Javert. Sherlock Holmes. Hercule Poirot. Sam Spade."

"Dogberry," I said. "Chief Inspector Lestrade. Inspector Clouseau. J. Edgar Hoover. Now come, and let us discuss your *ensemble*."

On Monday evening the neighborhood check following the Saturday incident came up with a woman who had seen the Magician. She was a single mother, a neighbor of one

30

of the victims, and she had had a very clear look at him hanging around near where the children were playing. She had not alerted any of their parents or called the police. She wasn't on the lookout for crime; she was lonely. She was hoping that if she could attract his eye she might be able to strike up an acquaintance. She had studied him with longing. A police artist interviewed her the next day and produced what she declared to be a good likeness.

Mindful of my promise to D'Honnencourt, I went by Walt's apartment on Tuesday afternoon to inspect his outfit, which, as it turned out, was deficient only in the article of socks. We were out the door in good time, breezed through the squad room, past Service Division, down the narrow corridor into DD, and arrived at the Sex Crimes office promptly at 2:00. The door said SEX CRIMES in gold letters on the glass. Very often when you passed by this door you would see a motel sign hanging on the doorknob, with a picture of a sleeping woman, glamorous and underdressed, and the text "Please Do Not Disturb." Someone had lined out the "Please" so that the sign said "~~Please~~ Do Not Disturb." This meant that someone in the office had an interview or a "cool call," a call which mustn't sound as if it were being made from the Hall of Justice. Anyone wishing to communicate with the office when that sign was out could only leave a message with the DD secretary at the end of the hall.

Sex Crimes consisted of one small room, almost completely filled by three desks, two filing cabinets, a small bookcase and four chairs. Besides Gadek, Blondie, and Eddie Agnelli, there were four other overtime Patrol officers already there, sitting on the desks. Walt and I pressed through to the far end and sat on the windowsill. In this office, apparently, "two o'clock" meant "one fifty-nine."

Gadek closed the door and said, "Okay, guys. What we've got here is a serial child molester. We started getting reports last week, and to date we've got nine reported hits occurring over the last three weeks."

Blondie had compared the series to prior cases of known sex offenders, but nothing matched, nothing came close. She had queried every nearby jurisdiction, without result. There were no perpetrators of similar crimes to seek out in a succession of fleabag hotels, no apartments to watch, no lineups to organize. The Magician appeared to have sprung pastless out of the primordial muck. The only course open to us was to consider the pattern of his activities so far, try to predict where he would go next, and be there when he appeared.

Gadek had read the reports and reread them, pictured the partial bits of information they contained, assembled them in his mind. He distributed copies of the drawing that the artist had made with the help of the lonely woman. Then he described the Magician for the detail.

He would be a man who looked old to children, but probably wasn't actually very old—about forty—worn-looking, thin, and haggard rather than aged.

His clothes would be decent, clean, and all respectable: slacks, polo shirt or dress shirt, windbreaker, baseball hat. Everything all right in itself, but nothing quite going with anything else. A wardrobe out of St. Vincent de Paul's, a bit of this and a bit of that purchased as funds permitted.

He would be where children are found in numbers. He always hit after school. He was careful to find the right victim in the right circumstances. He had never taken his victims far from the place where he first encountered them, so he would be looking for children close to some hiding place.

He seemed to prefer boys as victims, but there were girls as well. He was known to have approached two girls on a bus and got their addresses and telephone numbers; there might be others he had scouted in this way; he was not known to have made any attempt to follow up. He would probably avoid the schools and playgrounds he had hit already, so the detail could concentrate on whatever other places we could think of where conditions might be attractive to him. We could cruise or pick a spot and sit on it, our call.

"We've leafleted the schools on this," said Gadek, "and one thing you might notice is whether there's any reaction, any more adult presence than usual. If there is, be careful they don't rise up to you. We don't want to spend all afternoon being chased down by Patrol."

He divided us into teams of two, pairing Walt and me. He assigned each team a quadrant of the city, and sent us off.

Walt drove. Even in plainclothes and his own car, a light gray two-door, he drove like a patrolman, easing along with his eyes on the block ahead, pausing at each intersection to look long and carefully up and down the cross streets, hanging sudden U-turns and doubling back to look again, shifting over to a parallel street for a block or two, maximizing the street and sidewalk scanned as we moved slowly through our quadrant.

"Maybe we'll just keep moving," he said. "It shouldn't make any difference which way we do it. We don't know where to expect him, and it keeps me awake."

"That's fine with me."

We circumnavigated a park. "I think we can forget about this one," I said. "There's no place for him to take a kid. Not enough cover."

Two blocks away, an elementary school. There were children in the yard, and several adults. They looked carefully at us as we drove past, obviously alert. One of them held Gadek's leaflet in her hand. "We can forget about this one, too," said Walt. "He isn't going to get anywhere near this place."

Walt and I had worked together many times, but this was the first time we had actually shared a car. Every Patrol officer has his own style, and Walt's was restless and questing. We never quite stopped, never went fast, never followed the same street for more than a couple of blocks. We moved from school to school, from playground to park, the nose of the car constantly twitching like a nervous compass needle. We saw people we knew. We chatted about the bad actors we noticed on the street, their histories, their addresses, their hangouts.

"That's Paulus Downey," said Walt, indicating a large young man walking past us in the opposite direction. "You know Paulus?" I didn't. "He's a burglar. A dumb burglar. The last time he was caught he stole a key from a friend of his, and then one night when he knew the friend's family were out he went into their apartment and stole their TV. He'd given this caper a lot of thought, and he knew he

didn't want to carry the TV through the hall and down three
flights of stairs. So he brought a rope with him. He tied the
TV to the end of the rope, took it out on the balcony, and
lowered it down to the garbage area. What he didn't think
of was that the people on the first and second floors might
notice this TV going past their windows on a rope. Sure
enough, they did notice, and being decent working people
who earn their money and don't like burglars, they both
called the police. Two neighbors out of two called the cops.
So when Paulus came down to the garbage to pick up the
TV he was arrested. Of course, he was out in a couple of
hours. Paulus loves the juvenile justice system, and the juvenile justice system loves him. He provides employment for
an officeful of county bureaucrats and psychiatrists. They're
determined to fix his soul. But Paulus hasn't got a soul.
Paulus looks at the beautiful world and all he sees is the
opportunity to take things away from the people who've
worked for 'em. He'll be eighteen next month, and shortly
after that, no doubt, he'll become a guest of the state for a
considerable period. But there'll always be another Paulus."

I laughed. "I guess it's been eating at you," I said.

Walt stopped at the end of the block, eased into the intersection, and looked carefully in each direction. "I'm sorry
we can't stop Paulus," he said. "I bet he's dirty."

But he didn't repine. Even while he talked he was driving
and scanning, searching the streets for whatever else might
be of interest.

There were places that were more promising than others.
We looked for a combination of children in quantity, and
bushes or fenced-off yards where they could be taken without attracting notice. And since the Magician didn't seem
from the description to be prosperous, and might therefore
not have a car, we also favored places that were close to
bus lines. As the afternoon wore on, we fell into a regular
little circuit around the dozen or so most promising sites,
except that Walt never went from A to B via the same route
twice, seldom approached a site from the same direction
twice in a row, and snaked back and forth among them in an
almost random order. You want to avoid being predictable.

"The last victim, that boy," said Walt at one point when we'd been silent for a while.

"Yes?"

"It just occurred to me. He's just Adam's age."

"Yes."

"Comes close to home."

"Yes."

"You thought of it before."

"Oh yes," I said. "It kind of jumped out at me."

Each of the other teams worked their quadrants in their own ways. The team in the northeast cruised until they had picked what seemed to them the single most likely spot, then spent the rest of the afternoon watching it. The third team, in the northwest, picked the principal intersection bordering their quadrant and watched every car, bus, and pedestrian that passed through in either direction. Several times they had spotted look-alikes, and followed until they could get a better look, but nothing turned out to be promising on closer inspection. The fourth team, in the southeast, cruised and sat alternately. We all worked diligently. While we were doing so, we later learned, the Magician molested a girl of eight near New Middle School, a place he had not previously visited in the northeast quadrant. The place had been given a low priority because although there was plenty of cover there had been a major adult presence, and the team had seen several copies of Gadek's leaflet. But it appeared that the adults stayed only until the last classes had been dismissed, and the victim, a neighborhood child, had been entirely alone in the schoolyard when the Magician approached.

Also that day, a woman came home to find an unlocked window in what had once been the maid's bedroom by the kitchen. She lived alone in a large, old house with big windows close to the ground.

She rarely entered the maid's room. She spent some time trying to remember when that window had last been opened. She couldn't remember. She decided that it must have been unlocked like that for months, although she could have sworn that she would have noticed it if it had been. It was a little unsettling, because the window was both low and shielded from the neighbors by bushes.

It was some time after dark when she went to put out the garbage. She flicked on the outside light (the stairs were a little tricky) and saw a man standing against the fence at the end of the yard. He was in shadow and perhaps thirty feet away. She couldn't see him clearly, but his face was toward her, his eyes were fixed on her. He had been watching her.

She backed quickly through the door, slammed it, and snapped the wire hook-and-eye that secured it. If he came after her he had only to put his weight against the door to burst in, and for the first time she felt the full dimension of her vulnerability. The bag of garbage slipped from her hands, and she ran into the living room and called the police. The man did not try to come in.

It was in every way a routine prowler call. The officer who looked around the yard told her that the ground was too hard to find footprints, and there was no other sign that anyone had been there. Doubtless she had, in fact, seen someone; perhaps a burglar, perhaps a Peeping Tom. Several squad cars had cruised the neighborhood and found nothing. He told her that she was inviting trouble by not having proper locks, and she agreed. He said that he would come by frequently for the rest of the night.

In fact, he did come by several times that night. Everything looked fine: the porch light burned, the light on the rear stairs burned. The first time he came by there was a light in a window upstairs; after that, all the windows were dark.

The next several nights he made a point of noting the house when he passed by it on his way to other business. It always looked the same. He had no way of telling, really, if anything was going on inside.

4

On Wednesday we repeated Tuesday's cover.

On Thursday, our briefing included a summary of Tuesday's molestation, which had been reported Thursday morning. There was nothing to add to the physical description, and no other new information. When we hit the street we repeated the cover without result.

On Friday, the same.

Saturday was my day off. Sara cleaned and I shopped. I drove to the market. Just east of the market is a school, and by the crosswalk a stop sign. I stopped. I looked right, I looked left, and there was the Magician.

He was half a block away, walking stiffly toward me at a brisk pace, his gaze fixed on some children playing in the schoolyard on the southwest corner. He was older than Gadek had said he would be, but in every other particular—clothes, figure, manner—he was unmistakable, and his resemblance to the drawing was almost uncanny. He carried a briefcase.

There was a car behind me; I couldn't sit at the stop sign. I pulled half a block east, out of his sight, hung a U, and parked midblock, facing back the way I had come. I was driving the family station wagon and wearing nondescript weekend sorts of clothing, so I didn't think he would make me for a cop. I also had no radio, badge, or gun, which complicated my next step. One possibility would be attempting a bust then and there, and getting some neighbor to call the police. I rejected the idea. It was always a possibility that he might be tougher or faster than he looked, so that I might not be able to make an arrest effective single-handed. One of the worst possible outcomes would be to let him know that the police were onto him, but without holding him. He could then destroy whatever evidence he might have among his possessions and disappear. Even if he couldn't get clean away, if he were able to get home, or even simply ditch the briefcase, we might lose any chance of prosecution. It seemed best to follow him, then, until I could find an opportunity to call in for reinforcements.

All this thinking didn't take long. He had turned the corner and was coming toward me at a good clip, eyes fixed on the children. It was clear that if I intended to follow the man I didn't want to begin the process by giving him a good look at me, so I fished a map out of the door pocket, spread it as wide as I could, and buried my face in it. Out of the corner of my eye I saw him pass close by the car, and after a few seconds I took a glimpse in the rearview mirror. He didn't seem to have noticed me; he was still heading east. He was also walking surprisingly fast. I got out hurriedly and started after him.

My whole experience up to this time had been in Patrol, of course, and in Patrol you do chasing and intercepting and pouncing, but you don't do following. I *had* actually followed people on one or two occasions, but only at night, never for more than a few blocks, never someone who was alert to the possibility, and never anyone who mattered very much. It turned out to be a subtle craft, and the lessons came quickly.

I was wearing a leather car coat with a fleece collar, a large and unfortunately noticeable garment. By the time I was on the sidewalk in pursuit he had reached the corner; he turned north, and as he did so he glanced quickly and carefully around. I blanched. When, in kindergarten, the teacher looked sternly around the room, each tiny heart knew, *knew*, that its secrets were an open book—guilt is convinced of its own plain face. He was perhaps a hundred feet away; he must have seen me plainly. Now an innocent man might argue that I should not fear, I was only walking up the street, nothing suspicious in that; and if I turned north too, well, why not? But I wasn't, in this sense, innocent, nor was he. If he were to look back and find me coming around the corner still behind him he probably wouldn't assume that I was a cop, but he would notice; and after he had turned a time or two more, and I was still there, there would be no doubt in his mind. So clearly it was essential that if he looked back he would see either nobody or somebody different. On the inspiration of the moment I whipped off my coat and put it over my arm. This would change my silhouette and color considerably.

He stopped and stared again toward the children in the playground. Perhaps he rejected them as being too numerous, or too far from any secluded spot. Then he looked right at me without any noticeable reaction, turned, and walked briskly away to the north.

So far so good. I put my coat back on and hunched my head down as deep into the collar as I could, bowed my legs, and lost a good six inches in stature. It was difficult to walk quickly in this ridiculous position, but I was satisfied that I would look quite different to a casual glance. But before he had looked back again I came to a recessed doorway close to the sidewalk. We were falling into a rhythm; if there had been time to count, perhaps, I would have found that he glanced around every certain number of steps; whatever that number might be, I felt that it was coming up, and rather than burn my shrunken silhouette unnecessarily I ducked into the doorway and watched him through the wisteria that grew around it. A moment later he looked back, and of course there was nobody there. I popped out, still shrunken, and followed once again.

The trouble with doorways, driveways, and suchlike private places is that the tenant, or a neighbor, will sometimes notice and take exception; if loudly, it's a great problem. Or sometimes they call the police. If I had had a radio, of course, I could have advised the dispatcher of my description and whereabouts. Without a radio I wouldn't know until it was too late, and the last thing I wanted was to have a couple of black-and-whites come screeching up and lay a stop on me. Some of the daywatch officers wouldn't know me, and by the time it got straightened out the Magician would be long gone. So it seemed best for me, as well as for him, to assume that I was looked for and to avoid the notice of the authorities. I adopted his habit of periodic examination of the street in all directions, and so we slunk along.

At the next corner we turned east, toward the junior high, a large campus with semideserted areas of shrubbery, uninhabited stretches of outbuildings, and a children's playground close to the street. But before that there was a small shopping area, and in that shopping area, I happened to know, on the other side of the street, a streetside pay phone. Half a block before we reached it he looked back and paid my shrunken silhouette the compliment of inattention. He pressed on. I straightened up, skipped across the street and up the opposite side to the phone. I was almost opposite him now; I could see his face, concentrated, tight, eyes scanning as he strode along.

I had change for the phone. Sometimes you don't.

I identified myself to the dispatcher and asked for Control. Control was a patrolman from my shift, lucky again. The Magician was at the corner ahead of me, and if I had to do a lot of explaining I might lose him yet.

"Turner, Parkman. Y'know Gadek's molester?"

"Yeah?"

"I'm looking at him." And I gave him the location.

A long truck pulled up to the corner and stopped for a woman with a stroller and a small ambulatory child. I couldn't see him.

"Outstanding, Parkman. Ya wanna do a stop? I've got three cars in the north end."

The lady seemed to be having trouble with the child, and the truck was still blocking the view. I could see eastward, however, and he should have been in view by now, but he wasn't.

"No, no; no uniforms. Has Sex Crimes got anyone on the street yet? The detail is supposed to be out at two-thirty."

"It's only one o'clock now. I'll call down—hold on."

"Make it snappy, Turner," I said. "Hell, I can't see him anymore."

The truck was pulling away now. I could see the whole block up to the next street in both directions. He wasn't there.

"Parkman, Eddie and Blondie are in the office. They'll be on the street ASAP."

"Hit 'em on the air. Gadek's description is good, tan over brown, baseball cap, carrying a briefcase. I've lost him; he must have gone east or south from here. I'm starting south."

South was the shorter block, and he could have covered it more quickly. He might have continued east and gone into one of the shops along the street, but I doubted it. I ran.

At the corner, nothing.

A short block in either direction, but ahead led back to the school where I had first seen him, and left circled toward the junior high. I turned left and ran again.

The next corner, nothing again.

I ran south and at the next corner, cursing, breathless, and wondering what I would say to myself if he got away, I found Blondie in the vice squad's old blue Mustang, borrowed for the day.

"Eddie's got him," she said. "We figured he must be heading for the south side of the junior high, and that's where he was. Gadek's not in the office, so we've made our own decision. We're gonna follow him and see if we can on-view an approach so we can tie him in by MO even if the kids can't identify him. Get in." She laughed. "You've been running."

Her radio was lying in the passenger's seat. I held it while we circled after Eddie. The Magician cruised through the junior high and came out the other side. This was empty schoolyards and courtyards with lots of corners where it's hard to follow close and impossible to follow at any distance.

We circled past them on a parallel and parked on a side street. Blondie got out and sauntered up to the corner, sticking her face into some rosebushes when the Magician stalked

41

past quite close to her, glaring down our street and pressing on, returning westward toward the spot where I'd first seen him. Blondie stepped out after him, I slipped behind the wheel and pulled up to the corner. Eddie appeared and jumped in.

"Outstanding, Parkman." While I set out in cautious pursuit of Blondie and the Magician, Eddie called Dispatch to get us another radio and to clear Channel 2 for us. Channel 2 is used for lower priority messages than Channel 1, or, as in this case, for special details.

As it happened there was a patrol unit only a couple of blocks away; he had been following the chase on the air and hanging back just out of sight, hoping to be right on the spot when and if we called for backup. This enthusiasm now cost him his radio. We swooped past his location, seized it, and pressed on after Blondie.

We followed the Magician for the next half hour or so. We wound back and forth through the streets. We traded clothes with each other, put them on, left them off, following for two or three blocks while the other two hovered in the Mustang, then trading off. Blondie was the shadow when he arrived back at the neighborhood park where he had made the attempt on Thursday.

Suddenly he stopped. Blondie couldn't see what he was seeing, but she could tell that something had occurred; this was the first time he had come to a stop in all the time we'd been behind him.

We saw her slip into a carport. A moment later she came on the air.

"This may be good," she said. "He's near some kids."

Eddie moved quickly to within half a block, parked at a fireplug where nobody would hem us in, and dropped the keys on the floor where any of us could get them. Then we sat, waiting. We could see Blondie; we couldn't see the Magician. She was moving again, slipping out onto the sidewalk and quickly away, stopping at the fence that separated the park from the neighboring houses.

"He's got close to the kids," she whispered into the radio. It sounded very close in the Mustang. "Two kids. They're near some bushes, out away from the apartments. I can't hear him, but I can see. He's put ... he's put his briefcase down." Blondie was excited. "He's talking to 'em."

Eddie said, "Y'know, I'm feeling good about this one."

"He's opening the briefcase."

We couldn't see Blondie; she had slipped along the fence into someone's backyard. Christ, I thought, I hope the owner doesn't jump her.

There was a sudden hiss of static on the radio. "Bingo! He's doing the trick with rings that other kid described! Bingo!"

There was a judgment call here. The longer we let him go on before stopping him, the more evidence we would have. But if he actually got into the bushes with one of those kids, even briefly, the consequences could be grim.

More static. "Somebody's coming. I think it's their mom. She's calling 'em. He's shutting up shop. He's heading west into the apartments. Keep him in sight till I can talk to those kids!"

Eddie started up and we roared west, across the railroad tracks and up to the apartments, a series of long two-story units with courtyards between them and bisecting them, and communicating balconies: a complicated sort of place. The Magician was not in sight.

"You drive around to the other side in case he goes straight through," said Eddie. "I'm walking in this side and see if he's gonna cut back out this way."

But it was Eddie, and not the Magician, who appeared a few minutes later on the other side.

"How could I have missed him? This is crazy. Look, you go in the east courtyard and cut back through; I'll take the west courtyard and do the same thing. We'll have him ... oh shit, here he is!" He was perhaps a hundred feet away, coming out of the east courtyard, coming right to us.

"The hood," muttered Eddie. "Pop the hood!" I reached in and pulled the lever. Eddie threw up the hood and we draped ourselves over the fenders. How could he miss us? We had been behind him for an hour; he had seen us many times. He approached the car. It occurred to me that my radio was lying in plain view on the driver's seat. He went past us without a glance, paused to peer around the street, and stepped out briskly again to the west.

"He's looking for uniforms," I said. "He's looking for kids and uniforms. He's been looking right through us."

He might well suppose that he was looked for, but it had probably never crossed his mind that there would be detectives shadowing him about the streets. His mind was on cars with roof lights and shotguns, and, of course, on children. He wasn't thinking about us.

And so we began to follow him more boldly, closing the distance to reduce the chance of losing him again.

And we began to wonder what could be keeping Blondie. As soon as she had established the connecting MO, we could make the bust. This was certainly great fun, but I wanted to wrap it up. I had now been a party to losing him twice; my stomach was sore from the tension. I wanted this over. But she didn't call us, and it was pointless calling her. There was nothing to do but keep on with what we were doing. Eddie took the opportunity of his next turn in the car to call for a perimeter cover, four patrol units, one in each quadrant, whose job it was to monitor our channel and hover not less than three blocks from the Magician's position. If we should lose him again they would be available to close in without delay; and when the moment came to make the stop they would make it overwhelming. So we continued.

And Blondie persevered. The mother was a good left-wing lady who viewed the authorities with profound mistrust. It took a while to work through this before Blondie was allowed to speak to the children.

There is a sense of high drama about these things. Every unit on the street, every monitor in the station, would have been following the chase from the time Eddie had begun to use his radio back at the junior high. Units in the eastern beats would be shading into the downtown; midtown beats would be as far into the west as they thought they could get away with; the western beats were now involved in our perimeter. The sergeants would be on the prowl around the edges, as was right and proper, to monitor the arrest and ensure that everything went by the book. Everyone wanted to be in on this, or at least to see it done. You spend so much time writing parking tickets, booking drunks, picking up dead rats from people's driveways, enlivened by the frequent dashes to respond to silent alarms which, like as not, turn out to be false, that you feel almost a Christmas joy at having something important. You become a cop thinking about bank robbers and women screaming for help.

Everyone was waiting for Blondie.

We were striding along the fenced grounds of yet another elementary school, the Magician forty yards ahead of me, when her voice, strong with satisfaction, crackled into my earpiece, and Eddie's, and every car, and every monitor.

"66, 122. We got it. We got a go."

It was the perfect spot: there was no escape for him.

Eddie came on the air: "Cars on the cover from 66, we have a go. Perimeter, move in. All units move in."

It went down quickly after that. I broke into a run. All around, a block off in each direction, there was a sudden roar of engines and squealing of tires as each patrol unit, hanging out of sight around the nearest corner, accelerated madly inward to the focus. The Mustang flew past me along the street, nearly colliding with the first of the patrol units coming from the opposite direction. The Magician had frozen at the initial explosion of sound. Then he turned and started to run back the way he had come, saw me, and turned again. Eddie jumped the Mustang very romantically across the sidewalk and right into the chain-link fence, blocking him. Eddie leapt out as I dashed up. We grabbed the little man between us, spun him around, and slapped him flat over the hood of the car. The hurtling patrol units, sirens howling, roof lights blazing and blinking, filled the street almost completely, and a wave of uniforms poured over us.

"That was pretty good, Toby," said Gadek. He was chuckling. "You had good breaks, of course. But you saw them, and did something with them. Let's see, this was your day off, wasn't it? Well, there are compensations."

5

She was very fond of the garden behind her ground-floor apartment. The tiny patch of ground with its enclosed patio had been her chief inducement for moving into the building, and although the upper floors had pleasant vistas over the rooftops of the neighborhood—and were, besides, more secure in a part of town where burglaries are frequent—other considerations could not outweigh the pleasure of spending an hour or two each weekend tending the beds of annuals and perennials, or the solace of that quiet and ordered place at the end of the day. Only her upstairs neighbors overlooked it. Sliding glass patio doors opened to it from living room and bedroom, and there was scarcely a place in the apartment where she could not see it.

Lack of security did bother her, but she was confident that she had taken sufficient precautions. A friend had shown her a simple measure to deal with the sliding doors: you just lay a broomstick in the track, and then even if the lock is jimmied the door can't move. She had done this with both the living room and bedroom doors, and on the same principle had laid small slats in the tracks of the sliding windows in the bedroom, bathroom, and kitchen. The front door had a strong dead bolt, and a second, keyless, dead bolt to close from the inside. She checked them each night before she went to bed, as regularly as she did everything else.

She was not without other safety concerns. One of the neighbors had her purse snatched by a group of kids in the parking area in front of the building. They grabbed it right off the trunk of her car while she was getting her groceries out of the front seat. And a few weeks before, someone had come over the back fence and through her garden, and climbed up to the balcony of the apartment above hers to burgle the place. The burglar had forced the lock of the sliding door with a screwdriver. The neighbors had not used broomsticks. They had them now.

And just three days before, she had found a fresh footprint in the flower bed. Someone had come over the fence, she supposed, and jumped from rock to rock and then to the patio. In one place he had slipped and stepped in the dirt. Probably just a kid going through the middle of the block, but still, you can't help worrying. It was a big footprint.

She was thinking about all of these things at the end of a long day. It was still daylight at 6:30 when she ate outside on the patio, an early-spring treat which usually gave her great satisfaction. But tonight she wasn't soothed by it.

She had noticed some small dents along the bottom edge of the aluminum frame of the living room door, as if someone had been prying at it. The broomstick had been in place, so the door couldn't have been opened, but someone must have been trying. She hadn't gone outside the previous evening, but she was sure she would have noticed the marks if they had been there the day before that; that meant that someone had tried to get in either that day or the day before.

And ridiculous as it seemed, she had a disquieting sense that someone *had* been inside the apartment. She knew this could not be so, because burglars don't come in to look at your family photos, they clean the place out. And nothing was missing, but everything seemed—well, she couldn't even say what it was. So it didn't make sense, but still she was uneasy.

And there was that footprint.

In a city where there was a real crime problem it didn't occur to her to waste the time of the police over such matters.

Sergeant D'Honnencourt paused slightly in his reading of the Bulletin, and frowned.

"At 0055 hours the Parkside Theater reports the Mystery Flasher urinating on the fireplug in front of the main entrance. The first unit to arrive, an overtime fill-in from amongst ourselves, reports responsible 'Gone on Arrival.' GOA." He glowered at Dennis Page, who sighed.

"At 0420, numerous reports of gunshots in the street result in the discovery of the body, or at any rate the principal body parts, of Paulus Downey, age seventeen, and the apprehension a block away of Donald Wilson, known to us all, and one Denise Richardson, age fifteen. Wilson was found to be carrying a sawed-off twelve-gauge shotgun, still warm, under his coat. At issue seem to have been the proceeds from the sale of Miss Richardson's person. All three of these bright ornaments of the criminal justice system are now departed from our midst, one way or another."

Walt was polishing the switch contact on his flashlight with a little piece of emery cloth. McFadden had corralled all the ballpoint pens in his briefcase and was testing them to see which ones worked. Dwornenscheck was tidying her folder of report forms. Becker leaned back in his chair, head against one hand, the other poised over his notepad, a spare pen in front of him in case of need. The squad room coffee machine emitted its typical periodic gurgle-followed-by-a-hiss. D'Honnencourt's firm voice overlaid it all, warm, commanding, reassuring. It was like prayers at a big Thanksgiving dinner, except that it happened every day.

"At 0745, Bargain Gas reports a no-pay, described as a small, dark-colored foreign sedan with a bright red-primer right front fender, driven by a young woman with short black hair.

"At 0755, Delta Convenience Store reports the same vehicle, driven by a middle-aged male wearing a long forked beard and overalls, responsible for the theft of miscellaneous groceries.

"At 0910, Althea Norman reports being ratpacked and robbed of her purse at the same bus stop where we had the same crime last week. South end, look alive. This is probably along some neighborhood-to-junior-high route, and they'll come back along it after school. Hang around and see what you can see.

"Now, one or two housekeeping matters. First, we welcome the victorious return of our heroes from Sex Crimes' special detail. Well done, gentlemen." There was a rustle of comparatively sincere applause. Walt and I bowed from our chairs.

There were some training matters, and a vacation schedule, and then we were dismissed.

"Parkman," said D'Honnencourt as I headed for the equipment room, "Sergeant Gadek would like a word with you. Why don't you cut along to DD right now."

I was almost to the Sex Crimes office when Gadek came rocketing out the door into the narrow passage.

"Ah, Parkman," he said. "Busy day. Look, I wanted to talk you into a temporary assignment to Sex Crimes to do some interesting stuff, but I don't have the time now. Can you come around tomorrow?"

"Sure," I said.

"Time is gold," he said. "What if I start the paper now?"

"Okay," I said, and he was gone.

Wednesday, after roll call, I went down to DD again. This time I made it as far as the office door, but Gadek was reaching for the phone. He said, "Look, Parkman, it's gonna be a busy night. Why don't we bend an elbow at the end of the shift?" He had three report forms in his hand, and on the desk in front of him was a pile of eight-by-ten color photos of Paulus Downey in death.

"I don't get off till eleven," I said, surprised.

"I'll be here," he said. He hadn't taken his hand off the phone.

"Right," I said, and briskly as I said it he was already dialing.

I went to the typing room to call Sara, told her not to wait up for me, and I would see her in the morning.

"I'm bending an elbow with Gadek," I said.

"You're what?"

"Bending an elbow. It's something we veteran cops do."

"Oh, dear," she said. "Do they? Should you? Is there some occasion?"

"I don't know. I'll find out and tell you all about it."

"I was hoping for a little S-E-X," she said.

"So was I." You don't like to say, at such moments, that you'd rather go drinking with the boys. You say, Maybe I won't be too late.

"Maybe I won't be too late," I said.

"You'd rather go drinking with the boys," she said. Then she added, "I love you, Toby."

Becker was at the next phone, so I said, "See you later, old girl."

Most of the platoon was on the street by the time I got back to the squad room. Dispatch came on the intercom speaker and told me to call up to the Communications Center. I checked out my radio and car and then called Dispatch on the squad room phone. Dispatch said that a woman had called from out of state to say that she had just spoken to her father, a widower and retired admiral. He was deeply despondent, and she was afraid he might be suicidal. It was my case, with Walt to cover.

The admiral lived in a quaint little faux-medieval apartment complex with leaded windows. Walt met me outside. I repeated what Dispatch had said.

"I can understand it," Walt said. "Admiral Nelson got depressed. Seasick, too."

"He may find that very comforting and inspiring information," I said. "Hold it in reserve."

We went in. We would talk to him; if he was in reasonable command of himself we'd just encourage him to call his daughter back and reassure her. If he was depressed enough to be a danger to himself or to others, I could commit him to a county medical facility for a seventy-two-hour observation. I'd done that many times and never thought twice about it.

We knocked and the admiral opened, sixtyish, smallish,

thinnish, balding, mousy, alert about the head and eyes in a manner reminiscent of squirrels; not your idea of an admiral.

Our uniforms introduced us. I told him my name and Walt's. I explained that his daughter had called the police because she had been concerned about his welfare. When I was a sentence or two into this the admiral began to edge the door closed, but Walt put a large foot against it in a friendly way and held it open. In their telephone conversation earlier in the evening, I understood, she was alarmed by some of the things he'd said. Could we come in to discuss it?

The admiral sidestepped behind the door and tried to slam it shut, but Walt pressed door and admiral firmly back, and we came inside.

The door opened directly into the living room: couch and chairs by the window, tables, lots of bookshelves, lots of papers. I closed the door behind us.

There was a long silence. Walt and I stood with our backs to the door, and the admiral stood within arm's length, facing us. He didn't say anything. He glared at us in turn, a look which perhaps he had used in former times to wither negligent midshipmen. But we weren't shrinking subordinates; we were police who had the authority to ship him off to the funny farm, and his silence wasn't reassuring us.

Walt tried again. He tried several approaches. While he was trying them, I was running my eye around the room. The daughter had said that her father kept a pistol in the apartment. If it was there it wasn't visible. Of course, a gun could have been under any of the papers littered around, in any drawer, under any pillow. A person contemplating suicide might get it from its usual hiding place to hold, to look at. Hearing a knock at the door he might slip it anywhere out of sight. He might have it on his person, but I didn't think so. The daughter had described it as "big."

Meanwhile, the admiral hadn't spoken. Finally Walt said, "Admiral, your daughter told us that you have a gun here. Is that right?"

A trace of a smile.

Cops are hierarchical beings, and an admiral impressed us, even if he was an unimpressive admiral. But a standoff seemed to be developing, time was precious, and we needed to move ahead. Walt said affably, man-to-man, "Will you please tell us where you keep the gun?"

Sometimes if an object is mentioned a person will look toward it involuntarily. The admiral half turned, and his eyes flickered around the room as if, in fact, the gun might be there. I took half a step forward so that I could see where he was looking. He didn't seem to be looking at any particular place, but it was clear that there was a weapon somewhere nearby and that the thought of it was immediate and pleasant to him. Then, with the idea still playing on his face, he turned to us again, not quite directly, but quartered off. He was still looking back and forth between us as if he thought that he had only to wait and something specific and favorable to him would happen. As if he didn't need to deal with us because the whole thing was in process of resolution.

After a considerable pause I said, "Perhaps the admiral would show us where the gun is." This seemed such a childish ploy that I half expected him to laugh in my face, but immediately and quite matter-of-factly he turned and started for the hall.

Instantly we were beside him, one at each elbow. He stopped, seeming not to have anticipated that we would follow him. He looked back and forth between us. Again, the withering look. Amiably overlooking it, Walt said, "Show us."

The admiral started off again, more slowly, looking crafty. The hallway was narrow, and we had to fall in behind. We followed very closely.

A spare bedroom had been furnished as an office with desk and filing cabinets. As soon as we were through the door we stepped quickly to resume our places at the admiral's elbows. He stopped in front of one of the cabinets. We waited, watching his face, but careful not to lose sight of his hands. He stood for some moments as if to let us pass on, but we waited firmly.

He pulled himself up a little. He glanced furtively at each of us, as if invisible in the most secret recesses of his mind. Then stealthily, as if we might overlook it, he raised his hand to the third drawer and slowly drew it open. His eyes flickered again from side to side. He ran his forefinger negligently along the label tabs, and then in the middle of the drawer suddenly thrust his hand between the files. We were both ahead of him. Walt had his hand from the right, and I snatched the barrel of the pistol and yanked it out of his grip, pivoting away from him. He reached after it with his free hand, but Walt pulled him around the other way, gripping him by both wrists. He tugged frantically backward, trying to turn around, but could not. They struggled face-to-face, Walt pinning his wrists between them, the admiral straining to turn, suffused with a frantic energy, yanking and twisting against Walt's weight, stepping, writhing, and all the time his eyes rolled around over his shoulder, fixed on the pistol. I had backed off to the doorway, unloaded the pistol, and stuck it into my gun belt. I pulled my jacket closed over it so that there was nothing more to be seen.

The admiral stopped struggling. For a moment his gaze remained fastened on the front of my jacket, and then it drifted off into space.

Walt released his wrists. His hands dropped to his sides, and apart from that he made no further move. His shoulders slumped forward and his weight settled. He wasn't thinking about moving.

In all this time he hadn't uttered a word. He stood beside the looted filing cabinet as he had stood by the front door, except that now the cagey watchfulness was gone from him. His eyes rested vacantly on the wall. He merely waited, as if he had nothing more to look for, as if the event he had been expecting was no longer to be expected. The sense of possibility, which had been so arresting in the apartment when we arrived, was gone. It had boiled down merely to the pistol.

This sudden and terrible deflation troubled me. Better to have killed himself than fiddle around until his power to choose was stripped away from him. His life was his own business, but his weakness was an upending of the proper order of things, and I felt that it struck at me. It was as if, in overcoming him, we had played a terrible trick on ourselves.

We locked the apartment and bore him away, unprotesting, between us. It was what we were required to do, and after all, what else was there?

* * *

After dinner it was dark enough outside that the garden was barely visible, and the uncovered expanse of windows made her feel exposed in a way that it usually didn't. She closed the curtains and did the dishes. She watched the evening news and a comedy program she enjoyed.

She called her sister to chat about family matters. She didn't mention her sense of unease, although it hadn't left her; in fact, the longer she was in the apartment the odder she felt about it, but still she couldn't put her finger on the source.

She read a book until bedtime. Several times she felt uneasy, and looked carefully at the curtains, but they were fully closed; no one could be watching her.

Before she went to bed she pulled the curtains aside and checked the broomsticks in the doors and the slats in the windows. She read for a little while longer before turning out the light. She was longer than usual falling asleep.

There was no warning.

Her first awareness of his presence in the apartment was when she felt his weight on her back and his hand pressed over her mouth. He was strong and heavy, she was powerless. His mouth was close to her ear.

"One sound," he hissed very softly, "one sound and you're dead." The hand over her mouth suddenly shifted to pinch off her nose as well, stopping her breathing altogether. The other hand on the back of her head pressed her face into the pillow.

"Get it?" he whispered harshly, right into her ear. She struggled briefly against suffocation, but she could not even get her arms up from beside her. "Get it? One sound."

Desperately, she made a "mmmmmmm" sound, and he released her nose, but not her mouth. Nostrils flaring, she inhaled frantically, repeatedly, but otherwise lay entirely passive for fear that he would shift his hand again and smother her. He remained heavy and rigid above her, waiting.

When her breathing had almost recovered he said, "I'm going to take my hand off your mouth now. When I do, you're not going to move or make a sound. Understand?"

She hummed again.

54

But instead of releasing her he suddenly clamped her nose and leaned hard against her back. "Don't forget," he hissed, and then withdrew his hand.

He did not shift his weight. She still could not move, and it was hard to expand her chest enough to breath. She felt him straighten up for a moment, and then she felt a piece of broad tape passing in front of her face and around her head. He pressed it tight over her eyes and pulled the ends firmly so that they overlapped behind. Her hair caught in the tape and strained painfully.

He moved off her, but he kept one gummy hand hard on her shoulder. She heard the click of the bedside lamp. She had a slight sense of light through her closed eyelids and the tape, but she was quite blind.

He was tearing her nightgown down the back. She thought she knew what was about to happen. It would be much, much worse than that.

Several times in the next hours she began to scream, and instantly he stopped her breathing. If she was slow or inept he struck her across the face or boxed her ears, the blows bursting without warning into her blindness, irregularly but frequently, so that she reeled with the sense that there was no right answer, no possibility of grace.

She had no sense of time, only that it had gone on for a long while. She had learned quickly not to hesitate when he pulled her this way and that. Her few involuntary spasms of disgust and resistance had cost her heavily: her nose bled intermittently, and he had twisted her left arm until it had made a cracking noise to enforce a command. The pain was immediate and astonishing, and it was getting worse each time she had to move it. The sweat stood on her forehead from the pain. Insofar as she could she had withdrawn into some far, internal place, hoping only to endure.

There was a pause.

She was slumped on the floor, propped against the bed. Her ears were ringing. She could not tell where he was or what he was doing. Then her head was jerked sideways by the hair.

"I'm done with you."

He had not spoken to her since the beginning, and so the sound of his voice now was a surprise.

She did not move or change her expression, and he continued, "Pretty soon I'm going to leave. But don't forget that I know you. I know all about you. I know where you work, at the title company. I know what car you drive. You can't hide from me. You can't hide your family. I know where Mary lives, and Louise, and little Sophie." He made that little hiss he had. "Louise and little Sophie," he repeated, almost inaudibly. "So don't even think about telling anyone about this. You won't, if you're smart. Get it?" And his other hand clapped painfully over her mouth and nose. Instantly she hummed. Fairly quickly, he withdrew his hand.

But he did not release her hair, and he jerked it again so that her neck was twisted even more awkwardly.

"When I leave, you sit right where you are for an hour. Get it?" Her mouth was uncovered, but again she hummed. "Don't move a muscle. Maybe I won't leave right away. Maybe I'll just stand right over there by the door for a while and make sure. Get it?" She hummed.

He released her, almost gently, and then suddenly slapped her hard across the face. Her nose began pouring blood again; it ran back into her nose and mouth so that she thought she would choke on it. Humming in little bursts, she dropped her head forward to let the blood flow out.

She thought she heard him stand up. He took his time. Then she could not hear him, only the ringing in her ears. For a little while she could feel his presence: he was still there, watching her. She remained frozen, blood dripping down her chest. Then she thought that he was gone.

She continued to sit, absolutely still. The bleeding from her nose slowed and then stopped.

The time passed so slowly.

At first her whole attention was turned inward to her ears, searching for any sign of his presence. After a while, when minute succeeded minute without any sign of him, her tension began to slip away, and fatigue mounted.

She began to regain a sense of the room as her mind found it possible to register incidentals. The light was still on. The air was close and foul with the smell of vomit and feces. The carpet was damp and sticky. Her rectum burned. Her mouth was foul. Her arm hurt her terribly.

At last she made a small, exploratory movement of her good arm. Instantly she withdrew it, certain that the hand would clamp down over her mouth. When the wave of terror had passed over her and she realized that it had not, she made another small movement. And then another.

By degrees she eased and straightened her arms and legs, still leaning against the bed. Less cramped, she sat still for several minutes, trying to listen.

Then she began to pick at the tape. It stuck to her hair, her eyebrows and eyelashes. It took a long time to get it off.

When she could open and focus her eyes again she found that it was still dark outside. The bedside clock showed 4:15. She did not know when he had come, but it was probably before midnight. He had been there at least three hours.

The bed and surrounding carpet were smeared and stained. The dampness in the carpet beside her was blood. Her body was streaked and smeared with it, and with vomit and excrement. Her legs seemed apart from her, her arms, her belly, her breasts. She—the part that she now thought of as herself—had withdrawn to a point behind her eyes. From this viewpoint she examined her body with something like detachment, and with deep disgust. How could he *bear* to? She began to repeat it to herself, but the thought stuck on, how *could* he? Then she had a sudden, sharp image of something he had done to her, which she had seen only in her mind's eye, but in the room, in the light, she could see what it must have looked like, and at the thought her whole body jerked in a way that sent a sharp spasm of pain down her arm and distracted her. She was grateful: she much preferred the pain to the recollection.

Then she thought, I must call the police. She remembered his threats, but she hurt so much that she could not concentrate on them enough to be frightened by them; her life's training moved her. A good citizen calls the police to report a crime. She had to get help for her arm.

She found the phone. He had pulled the cord from the wall, but she knew where the wires should go. It occurred to her that if he came back now he would know what she was trying to do, and the thought almost panicked her, but she overcame it and fumbled purposefully with the wires until they seemed fixed. Glancing around her she lifted the receiver and heard the dial tone. Her hand trembled so that it was hard for her to push the right buttons—twice she misdialed and had to hang up and start again.

"Police Emergency."

It was not until the dispatcher answered that she realized that she still did not dare to speak.

"Police Emergency. Do you need help?"

She listened helplessly to the dispatcher's voice at the other end, asking, "Can you tell me the address? Do you need an ambulance?"

Her mouth opened and closed. Her voice simply wasn't working.

"Can you tell me your name?"

The voice, brisk at first, had grown gentle and concerned. Help was right there. It was agonizing not to be able to answer it.

"Is your mommy there?"

In concentrating on the repair of the phone she had at least partially displaced her pain and disgust. Now, with this connection to the world, they returned to her. She framed in her mind the words that she would have to speak, and began to realize what it would be like to pronounce them to another person. She felt the first livid flush of shame. The first of many.

The phone was useless if she could not speak, and she replaced the receiver.

She knew that physical evidence was of the utmost importance in rape cases, and that this included such things as semen and pubic hair, which are lost if the victim bathes before hospital examination. If she had been able to speak to the dispatcher while she was still in the immediate shock of the event, she might have permitted herself to be whisked away foul and stinking to whatever process of combing and scraping the apparatus of justice had devised as most productive in such cases. But she could not speak.

The pain in her arm was almost more than she could bear,

and she knew she must get to the hospital. Walking out of her apartment without washing was not possible. She felt guilty about it, but it simply was not possible.

In the living room with the phone she had noticed, without registering, how he had entered: one of the sliding aluminum window frames in the kitchen had been lifted right out of the track; and doubtless the marks on the living room sliding door had been made when he had lifted that out of its tracks and gone through her apartment to prepare his attack. The living room door was open now; presumably, he had left that way. She closed it again and locked it, futile as it was. It cost her a terrible effort to go near it, where he had last been, but it would be worse to be moving about the apartment completely unprotected. She went into the bathroom, clicked the tinny lock on the hollow door, and turned on the shower. She took a washcloth and a bath brush and shampoo, and cleaned herself meticulously. She stayed in the shower, washing, scrubbing, and rinsing, washing, scrubbing, and rinsing, long after she was perfectly clean.

When she was done she realized that she had not brought clothes into the bathroom with her. Next, she must unlock the door and go into the bedroom to get them. She knew that of course clothes would not protect her, but it was daunting to think of opening the door and walking naked into that room.

The thought that he might have returned, might be waiting for her just outside the door, passed over her like a wave. She could almost feel his hand on her face again. Her legs turned watery, her empty stomach heaved suddenly, and she sank down on her hands and knees until the spasm had passed.

There remained the opening of the door.

She thought that he was *not* there. Reason suggested that he was not, that he would be well away before dawn. The bathroom window was gray: dawn was coming. He would be gone, he would be crazy—but that was the wrong argument to use. She threw the door open. He was not there.

At least, not so far as she could see.

Her clothes were in the closet beyond the bed. The closet

door was ajar. The thought that he might—he could have been there, watching her, the whole time—if she went to it and opened the door and he was there, right in front of her, *within arm's reach*—she thought she was dissolving. She could neither retreat into the bathroom with its matchbook door and its useless lock nor come forward into the room, more revolting than ever with the dawn light adding its gray cast to the gentle golden glow of the bedside lamp. And to approach the closet was unthinkable.

She was still holding her towel, and she wrapped it about herself, tying the corners as tightly as she could with her injured arm, straining on the knot. Her hands were shaking. She sank down in the doorway, leaning against the frame.

She fixed her eyes steadily on the closet door: she felt that her gaze was all that held him inside. If she looked away, he would come out.

There seemed to be nothing else to do.

Softly, then louder, in rapid little bursts of monotone, she began to hum.

Time passed. She became conscious that it was full day. The room was unchanged. He was not in the closet. She was not immediately threatened.

She dressed methodically, as for a visit to the doctor: sensible underclothes, jeans and top. She noticed the stink in the room, but ignored it; she approached the bed as little as possible, moving around the apartment preparing to go out. She did not look at the kitchen window or the living room sliding door.

She unbolted the front door and stepped out into the hall without looking first to see if it was safe: she knew he was not there. The parking area was not frightening. She concentrated on unlocking the car, starting it and backing out. Her car was an automatic, so she could drive pretty well with one arm. She backed too wide and brushed the trash cans lined up against the fence, but she did not hear the scraping. The streets along her route were familiar, but she did not notice them. Her arm throbbed as if her heartbeat were shaking her apart. She stopped mechanically at stop signs and then pressed on regardless of the other traffic, nearly causing an accident. She did not hear the horns sounded in protest.

She had often driven past the hospital, but had never been inside. She turned into the emergency room driveway, past the doctors' cars, to the ambulance bay. Leaving the motor running and the door open, she walked quickly up the gurney ramp, failed to notice that the doors had opened for her automatically, hastened into the waiting room and stopped abruptly in front of the admitting nurse's station. The nurse took one look and jumped up to help her into a chair.

6

The admiral and his perturbation was only the beginning of a long evening fighting crime. My platoon was kept on the street even after the night shift came on, and what with one thing and another I didn't get off until almost midnight. I had phoned Gadek from a callbox to tell him that I was going to be tied up and wouldn't be able to meet him, but he said not to worry because he'd be working late. He was in the Sex Crimes office when I came in. The photos of Paulus were gone, but the rest of the mess appeared unchanged.

"Ah, Parkman," he said when I appeared in the doorway. "Let's get out of here." He murmured his address and bounded off down the stairs. I hastened to the locker room, changed, and followed.

Gadek was said to work harder than anybody else, get into more trouble, make more busts, close more cases. He was celebrated for a shootout as a young patrolman: on his lunch hour he had walked unknowing into the middle of an armed robbery at a hamburger joint. He walked in just as the robber, cash box in one hand and gun in the other, was running out. Without hesitation the robber jerked up his pistol, a small-caliber automatic, and fired at a distance of about two feet. He hit Gadek right in the middle of the forehead. By a freak of ballistics the bullet didn't penetrate the skull, but went between skull and scalp all the way around to the back of his head, where it exited feebly and fell down the back of his neck, inside his shirt. The robber saw the bullet hole appear right in the middle of his forehead, followed by a shower of blood, and naturally expected him to fall down dead. Gadek felt the smack of the bullet and thought his last moment had come, but he drew and tried to return fire. He was stunned; he was moving very slowly, and all the time the blood was pouring from the bullet hole and running in sheets down his face so that he was almost blinded, dribbling off his chin and soaking the front of his uniform. Everybody in the place was frozen in amazement, watching this zombie cop slowly raising his gun. The robber watched it too, unnerved. When it reached level, he threw down his own pistol and surrendered.

This feat was much admired, and the little round scar that Gadek carried in the middle of his forehead was considered a very notable badge of distinction.

Gadek was a Patrol sergeant when I was sworn. Mostly we worked different shifts, but sometimes we coincided. I found him precise, reasonable, hard to please. My reports would come back with firm little checkmarks in red pencil and the notation "See me S-19."

"Look, Parkman," he said to me once, "there are only thirty-two boxes on this form. I've given myself the trouble of learning what goes in them, and there's no reason why you shouldn't do the same. Now please just get it right, and then we can do some real police work."

"Right, Sergeant," was what one said at such moments, but in his case it was because he was, in fact, right. He didn't bluff, and he always did everything first. He was great to work for and I tried to live up to him.

In the fullness of time he moved on from Patrol to Detective Division. He was assisted by the fact that nobody senior to him was interested in assignment to Sex Crimes. And now here we were.

He had an apartment quite near the Hall of Justice.

There were family photos, mostly appearing to be nieces and nephews. There was a stereo and a lot of jazz records. There were CDs, but not many. The bookcase was jammed with the classics required in college literature courses, more jazz records, and stacks of sports magazines. There were several unframed posters for symphony and opera stuck to the wall, and a massive antique brass barometer, clearly an heirloom. The needle pointed to SETTLED FROST.

But the principal impression at the moment was paper: the carpet was covered with offense reports, some in stacks, some by themselves. There were little paths to allow movement around the place. The hall to the bedroom and bathroom was itself lined on both sides with reports. We threaded our way through to the kitchen, which, perhaps more for fear of dirtying his reports than any other consideration, he had left relatively unencumbered. He brought out a bottle of Pernod, of all things, ice, a small pitcher of water, and two glasses, and nodded to the kitchen table. This was covered with large graphs informally scrawled on sheets of butcher paper. Along the top were dates, each with a case number in parenthesis. Down the side was a long row of features:

> —knowledge of victims
> —evidence of pre-entry & prowl
> —objects rearranged
> —window pry
> —door cheat
> —disables phone
> —jumps victim asleep

and so on. There were twenty-five of these basic features: customary phrases (virtually all threats); sexual practices; modes of coercion; with checkmarks where applicable to each case. There were asterisks and footnotes indicating unusual features not included on the basic list.

"Jesus," I said.

"Help yourself," he said, indicating the bottle.

I'd never met anyone who drank Pernod at home. It seemed delightfully exotic. While I poured for both of us he smoothed out the topmost sheet on his pile.

"Did D'Honnencourt mention what I have in mind?"

"No."

"Ah, well. You did good work on the Magician detail, and I wanted to see if I could interest you in a little work for Sex Crimes. I've been to the lieutenant, and he says there's no way I can have another body permanently, but I can borrow someone from Patrol for a while. What we normally do is rapes, molestations, indecent exposures, registered sex offenders—all that sort of thing. It keeps us pretty busy. Just rapes alone, we get two a week on the average, and of course things get bunched up. Now we've got something new that looks like it's going to be very time-consuming, and we just don't have much time to consume.

"Over the past few months we've had an unusual cluster of rapes in the south-central part of town. I think most of them are by the same guy. They haven't been identified as a series because ... well, because of a lot of reasons, but I'm convinced there's a pattern. And I think it goes back a lot farther than the last few months. I took nine years of rape reports up to my cabin in the mountains and spent four days reading 'em. Four hundred and thirty-seven of 'em, to be exact. Reading that many cases quickly you can see patterns. Each rapist has his own pattern, and the similar ones kinda jump out at you. There's a whole bunch that fall into this one guy's MO, and then there are some that might or might not. One of the problems is that the investigating officers didn't ask all the right questions. There's a lot of reasons for that, too, but anyway, they didn't.

"It's gonna take a lot of reorganizing, a lot of reinterviewing victims to decide finally which cases are in this series and which aren't. It won't be pleasant. A lot of 'em ... well, it won't be pleasant. But I think we've got someone who's done maybe forty hits over four years, and he's gonna go right on doing 'em till he gets caught. If it interests you at

all, you'd be doing important work—a lot of it—and you'd
be learning fast."

His hand was resting on the paper.

> —tapes eyes
> —prevents breathing
> —kidney punch
> —boxes ears

Women in distress. Cries in the night.

"Yes," I said. "Yes, I'd like to work on it."

"Good," he said, and ran his hand eagerly across the
sheet. "You can see how this works. I've got the cases
here in this column, and MO factors here. The MO factors
are common in a lot of rapes, obviously, but the reason I
know we've got a series going here is that some of these
cases have twenty or more of these factors in common.
That's how come I raised up to this in the first place. I
kept reading these reports and these same factors keep
bunching up. Look at this," he added, and drew another
sheet out of the pile and held it next to the first for
comparison.

You could see at a glance that the checks for MO factors
present were much fewer and spottier in all but two of the
cases.

"This is twenty rape cases, consecutive by date. So I guess
it's a random sample. These two each have at least twelve
of the factors. None of the others has more than three. And
there's nothing in either of the two that indicates that they
were *not* done by the same guy. After I read all these"—he
waved toward the sea of paper in the living room and returned the comparison chart to the bottom of the pile—"I
went to the Department of Justice and read a bundle of
cases from statewide—about nine hundred of 'em—just so
I could be sure that there wasn't something odd about the
way our department writes these things up. I didn't find any
case—not one—that had more than four of these factors.
Other factors, yes, but not these.

"So I'm pretty damn sure that what we've got here is
one guy. Here, look at this"—another chart—"this is the

first one, four years ago. There may be others, but you can't tell from what we've got. There are four that first year. Next year two right off, January and February—then six months with nothing. Maybe he went fishing, maybe he moves around. Most likely the victims weren't reporting. Then two more. The next year, we get more: two in January, one in February, then nothing until July, then one each month except for October. Next year, fourteen altogether, pretty evenly spaced out. This year, eight so far, no pattern—again, they're probably not all being reported. That's thirty-eight reported offenses, twenty-eight I'm sure of and ten likely."

"And you can see that the first ones aren't so distinctive. That's one reason the series didn't get recognized before. The pattern was much less obvious at first. And during the last four years there've been three different guys in charge of Sex Crimes, and none of 'em was around long enough to get a handle on it.

"He's a burglar, probably, and most likely he started out raping women he happened to find at home alone. Just opportunistic. But he liked it, and it got to be the focus. See here: two years ago the numbers begin to pick up. Also, it gets worse for the victims. All along he's liked oral and anal sex, but here he starts doing the anal first.

"And at the same time that grinding the victims becomes more important to him, he also begins to get more violent. The first real injury was eighteen months ago, a sprained wrist. This year, a broken arm, done the same way but with more force. It goes along with the degrading sex: the victims resist, and he hurts them. Probably he sets it up so that they can't help resisting, and that gives him an excuse to hurt them. Here, another arm. Here. Here, broken eardrum. He likes to box their ears, which also makes it hard for them to hear what's happening when he leaves. If the pattern holds, it's going to get worse."

I was beginning to wonder if I was ready to be responsible for this.

"Look at the map." He produced a city map from the floor and spread it over the charts. It was sprinkled with colored dots each with a case number. "The black dots are the first year. Green the second. Blue, Brown. Red's this year. See, he started in the south end—in fact, outside our city limits; eight of these early cases aren't ours at all. Each year he's moved north, but it's not consistent, it goes back and forth."

He pushed the map away and splashed us each another finger.

"I can't do this series full-time—we've got too much other stuff going—but I'll do what I can. The lieutenant said I can borrow you for a week. You'll work out of Sex Crimes and at the end of the week we'll see where we're at. That okay with you?"

"Yes." Things suddenly seemed to be moving pretty fast.

"There's a lot we don't know. A lot of these reports have holes. Whoever did each investigation wouldn't always ask enough of the right questions. We need a lot more information.

"And we need something that takes us somewhere. We've got a pretty good picture of how our guy works, what he does, the whole thing; only there's nothing to tell us who he is. He's real slick. He only hits houses or apartments that are accessible from the ground, so he doesn't spend time in elevators or staircases, where he might run into someone. Nobody's seen him coming or going. He always hits women living alone or with small children. He must spend a lot of time identifying potential victims. He probably watches them somehow to make sure there's no man there, no boyfriend visiting. He always jumps his victims while they're asleep, and tapes their eyes first thing. He doesn't talk much, and when he does he disguises his voice, kind of whispers, hisses, so the victims don't even know what his voice sounds like. He always tells them details about themselves so that they'll know he knows about 'em, and he tells 'em that he'll know if they make a police report. But he never goes back, so far as we know.

"There's very little useful physical description. He's probably kind of old for a rapist—victims guess he's in his fifties. He's average height, a bit on the heavy side, very strong. His hands are soft. He's got a missing upper tooth—he makes some of his victims French-kiss him, and they can feel it.

"We've got some fingerprints that don't belong to any known victim or anyone that they can think of, but they don't lead us anywhere—they don't match local rapists or sex offenders. If we had a suspect, we'd try to match the prints with his.

"We've got semen and hair samples. If we had a suspect to match the samples we couldn't establish that it's definitely our guy, but with DNA testing we could eliminate him as a possibility or put him in a small category of the male population.

"But anyway, first we have to get a suspect.

"I'm hoping that if we go back over some of these cases, reinterview the victims now that we know what we're looking for, we'll get some useful stuff. Maybe when he started out he wasn't so careful. Maybe he said some things that didn't seem important to the beat man taking a case in isolation but fit with other things and give us something to work with.

"Here's some reading for you." He pulled a fat sheaf of report forms and narratives off the chair that had formerly produced the map. "That's the essential material in the twenty-eight cases I'm pretty sure of. Those are good investigations by reliable people. I've discussed the cases with them and I'm pretty sure we're not missing anything important.

"And these"—another sheaf—"are the most promising of the ones I'm not sure of. Some of these just have holes—they don't say what the victim was doing when the responsible came in, for example, or they don't say how he got in, or just when. Or they're not specific about what happened. A lot of cops just hear enough to know that something completes the Penal Code definition of rape and they stop there; they don't want to hear any more. Which is natural, except that different rapists have different procedures, and preferences, and problems, and if you want to connect a particular rape with a particular rapist you have to know everything that happened.

"What I want you to do is read the first pile pretty carefully. 'Pretty carefully' means *very* carefully—you really have to know what's what or you'll miss things later on." He paused and glanced at me.

"Right," I said.

"Right. Then I want you to start at the top of the next stack, contact the victims, make appointments, and reinterview them. I'll be doing it too, when I've got time from other cases—if I've got time I'll come along on interviews you set up. And the first couple we'll do together, in any case.

"Anyway, you'll be looking for MO stuff that got missed the first time and, of course, anything else good. Maybe the guy said something or let a name slip. You never know. And a lot of times victims are so messed up right after the event that they forget stuff, and then later when they remember it they don't think it's important and they don't call us back. So chances are you'll come up with some new things, and they may or may not be useful.

"If you're sure that a case *doesn't* belong, do me a very short memo saying why and go on the next one."

He paused again, but this time it was not so that I could say "Right."

"Parkman, have you done any rape interviews?"

"No," I said. "Just one initial contact and short report. Then Detective Division took it."

"How'd you do?"

"It was pretty grim. The guy was rough with her."

"Did it throw you? It's no disgrace if it did. I just need to know where you are."

I thought about it for a moment.

"I wasn't sorry to let DD have it, if that's what you mean. I sure as hell didn't enjoy hearing about it."

"D'you think you've got the stomach for a lot of that? Because DD won't be behind you on these; you'll be DD. This is a rough thing for these women. It's going to be hard for them to go through it again. It's a lot to ask of someone. What they say has to be received with sympathy. If you're shocked by it, or offended, or critical, then obviously whatever door they've started to open you've just pushed shut again. If you blow one, it's probably blown for good. Once a victim gets messed around and stops trusting us, then it's three times as hard to get anything going again. I know you can't tell me what's going to happen, but do you feel pretty secure about getting started on this?"

I wondered. I said, "Yes, I feel fine about it. You've sold me. I want to get this guy. That's why I wanted to be a cop, to rescue beautiful gals in distress and arrest bad guys. This covers both bases. It's what Dillon says: Protect the weak and nail jerks. If that means all this"—I patted the piles of paper—"then that's what I'll do. I feel strongly about this sort of thing."

"Good," said Gadek. "But be careful. I mean, about the strong feelings. I remember my first rape case. I'd been with the department a year or so, still on the night shift. I'd gone through the first stage, when it's all strange and new; and the second stage, when you think you get it but you worry about making mistakes; and I was just getting to the cocky stage, when you've seen it all and you can handle anything and there aren't any more surprises. Right.

"And I went to take a rape report. In those days we didn't have support services or women's advocates or anything like that. They told us to be nice, and that was it.

"The victim's a student. She's nineteen, intelligent, seems reasonable.

"So I'm in the victim's living room. It's incredibly neat. There are some books and papers on the coffee table, and they're all lined up at right angles and stacked up according to size, biggest on the bottom. There are some pencils and pens right beside them, all exactly the same distance apart. The whole place is like this. She sees me looking at this and she tells me she's been cleaning the apartment for the past two days. She says she wants it to be clean, and while she's saying this her eyes begin to fill with tears and she starts crying, just standing there in the middle of the room. I don't know what the hell's going on.

"Well, after a while she stops crying, and we sit down. I've got my clipboard and the offense report, and we start filling in the boxes—name, DOB, all that. Then we get to

71

the rape. When did it happen? Three days ago. So of course there's no physical evidence. She tells me that afterwards she stood in the shower for two hours and scrubbed herself all over with her bath brush. She used two bars of soap. She douched five times. She washed her hair five times. She washed the clothes she was wearing five times. Then she washed *all* her clothes. Then she began to clean the apartment. She hasn't been out once; she's been scrubbing the whole time. She takes three showers a day.

"Well, I'm a rookie but I'm beginning to see a pattern."

"There's no mystery about it at all. The responsible is her ex-boyfriend. About a month before this, they got drunk and went to bed—she says she was a virgin up till then—and the next morning she's filled with remorse and she tells him she isn't going to do it again. It's against her principles. He tells her after she's done it once it doesn't make any difference, blah blah blah. Anyway, for days he keeps trying to get her back in the sack. He brings booze but she won't touch the stuff. Finally he sees that being nice isn't getting him anywhere, and he gets demanding and they have a big fight about it. She breaks up with him. A few days later he calls, they make up, but pretty soon he's onto her again, they fight again, they break up again.

"Then three days ago she's getting ready for bed and he shows up at the door. He smells of beer but she lets him in anyway. He says he's been thinking about it a lot, and he's decided that she hasn't been fair to him. She's been leading him on and then she won't deliver. He tells her he wants it and right now. She tells him to get out. She's frightened. And the more frightened she gets the more insistent he gets. And I'm thinking, Yeah, this guy's like a dog, never run from a dog, never show fear, because if you do he'll attack you, he'll bite you.

"She gets up to open the door, and when she does he jumps her, throws her down on the floor, and gets on top of her.

"She's been pretty calm up till now, telling me about all this, but now she starts to break up.

"*She couldn't do anything because he was too heavy.*

INTENT TO HARM

She just wasn't strong enough to get him off her. She can hardly say it, she keeps collapsing into sobs, but she keeps repeating it: he was too heavy. It's the hardest thing about it for her, not that he raped her, which he proceeded to do, but that she was so helpless. She was just utterly helpless. And as she's telling me this she's curling up on the couch, it's like she's getting smaller and smaller. And I can see it, yeah, she's very slender, she can't weigh a hundred pounds. Her arms are really thin, her neck; so I'm looking at her while she's talking, and noticing all this. And then I notice that the smaller she gets, the bigger I'm getting: I'm sitting up straighter, I'm pulling my shoulders back; when I sat down I'd crossed my legs, but now I'm sitting with my feet flat on the floor and my knees apart. I'm just as big and imposing as I can be. Even my voice, I'm pushing it deeper. It's humiliating for her to talk about this and she keeps stopping, and I keep asking the obvious next question. My voice is getting very masterful, very commanding.

"She'd scarcely looked at me this whole time she'd been talking. Most of the time she looked at the floor, and sometimes around the room. But when she got to the moment when he raped her, when she feels him coming in and she knows this is really happening and there is nothing that will stop him, no word, no miracle, that she's weak, she's nothing; just when she gets to this she looks up at me, looks me square in the face as if to say, Tell me it wasn't what it seemed, that I've got it wrong, that there's some other way to look at it.

"But there is no other way to look at it, and I feel this jolt of contempt for her vulnerability. It must have been written all over my face. That's her answer.

"The hope in her face died instantly, and what followed was recognition, fright, a flicker of hatred. And then she's curled up again, looking at her feet. For a moment she doesn't say anything, and I'm suddenly realizing that she wasn't thinking about her boyfriend, she was thinking about me.

"Well, you can make too much of these things. She wasn't blaming me. But what she saw—what we both

73

saw—was that she was weak and I was strong, and that it is for me to choose whether she is to be protected or raped. She has no influence in the matter; all she can do is wait and see. And that I, who had devoted my life to protecting the weak, thought her weakness contemptible and her hope pitiful.

"This is a lot to learn from one exchange of glances. After that I had trouble following what she was saying, I was so distracted. But I finished my report, which took long enough to make it clear that I had slipped in her estimation from being a police officer, a disinterested guardian of order, to a man with motives. And that she was right, in large part.

"So, everyone has motives. No one is disinterested. I've thought about it a lot since then, and so long as your motives run in the right direction all is well. But at the time it seemed an awful bump down."

Gadek took a sip and chuckled. He said, "Once some coeds called the police to report a suspicious circumstance: a closet door wouldn't open and they thought an ax murderer might be inside. They were huddled in the living room when I got there, four gorgeous girls in shorty nighties and cutoff pj's. I opened the closet door, which had got wedged on a sandal. But they were all hyped up, so I took five minutes and I searched the whole apartment, all the closets, under the beds, everywhere. No ax murderers at all. They were so grateful, they all jiggled around the door to thank me when I left. A lot of long hair, boobs, and bare legs. Man, what a hero."

He took another sip.

"My rape victim never met my eyes after that once. When I left she just stood by the door looking at the floor while I told her what would happen next and when she would hear from me again. She closed the door right behind me when I stepped into the hall. The dead bolt clicked, and I heard this long gasp from the other side.

"I was in a real state when I went to deal with the boy-friend. Talk about having motives.

"I called for a backup unit on my way over to his address, and Barry Dillon was waiting for me when I got there. I filled him in, said I thought we'd be busting this guy tonight. That was fine with Dillon; any criminal—rapist? jay-walker?—go get 'em, that was his view.

"So in we go and knock on the door. The boyfriend's roommate opens and says the boyfriend is in the common room down the hall. So we go down the hall to this little lobby sort of place with a couple of couches and chairs. The boyfriend's the only one there. He takes one look at our uniforms and turns gray, I mean the color leaves him completely. I tell him in my most authoritarian voice that we would like to talk to him. I tell him why we're there, that his former girlfriend claims, and so forth. Does he want to give us his side of the story? He's sitting in a chair, and Dillon and I are looming over him. Well, what about it? And he begins to cry, and he says, yeah, he did it but he didn't mean to, he was drunk, he didn't know what he was doing, blah blah blah. And we ask him some more questions about the circumstances, and he tells us all about it, about what a tease she was, blah blah, just confirming her story with each and every word. And all the time he's shrinking into that chair, just shriveling, get-ting smaller and smaller just the way she did. But at the same time it's just pouring out of him, you can see how relieved he is to talk about it.

"He keeps looking up at us, like, tell me it was under-standable, tell me she was asking for it, anyone would've done it. And Dillon and I are towering over him, only this time I feel great about it. I remember her face, how thin her wrists were, her weakness. I'm looking at him, he's a jock, athletic, strong, bigger than I am. But he's pitiful now. I'm thinking, you son of a bitch, *she* couldn't stop you but *I* can sure as hell stop you. My thumb is hooked over my baton in its belt ring, and I'm very conscious of the weight of my pistol. You could do what you liked with her but I can sure as hell do what I like with you—I'm so immersed in this I'm almost not listening.

"Finally, he stops. He's said it all. I look at Dillon and he jerks his head at the door. There's a long pause—I'm still remembering the girlfriend, how she was curled up on the couch. Finally I tell him to get up, he's under arrest. He looks stunned for a moment, as if this were a complete non sequitur. Then he half gets up, but slipping backwards out of the chair, away from us.

"I have no idea what he intended; there was no way to escape there, only the corner of the room, but I'm on him like a ton of bricks, just leaping, catching him off balance and bringing him down hard on his side. I'm right on top of him with one knee on his legs and the other in the small of his back. One of his arms is pinned under him, but I clap a wristlock on the free hand and twist it around behind him, hard. I whack the handcuff on the wrist I have and shout at him to put his other arm behind him, all the time leaning harder on his back so he can't get it out from under him. He's just rolling his head and gasping with the surprise and the pain and he tries to say something but I whack him on the back of the head and bounce his face off the floor, ease off on his back, yank his other arm free and around, cuff it, grab him by the hair and spin him into a sitting position. His eyes are wild, blood is starting to pour out of his nose, his eyes are rolling between Dillon and me.

"This has all taken maybe fifteen seconds. Dillon steps behind him, bends down and takes the guy's wrist, the one I have in the wristlock. He looks hard at me and says, 'I've got 'im.' And he stands him up. I'm still kneeling on the floor. It's all running out of me, like the blood out of his nose. I don't feel strong enough to get up.

"It was a scary moment. I'd just completely lost it. I wasn't in trouble—nobody was going to question the way I'd handled any of this—but I'd always thought of myself as a good person who would do good things. I'm telling you this because you have the right instincts, and that's good. But instincts aren't enough. Even if you do this job just right you'll cause pain, and people won't thank you for it. When you make mistakes, which you will, they'll be mistakes you'll regret for a long time.

"I still think about those coeds and their legs and their ax murderer. I wish it was really like that, being a hero and protecting people who're grateful. But the people we deal with here have been victimized already. It's too late to protect them."

His glass was empty, except for ice. He crunched an ice cube in his teeth.

"Welcome to Sex Crimes." He laughed. The light fell across his face from the side and a little behind. It gave the scar on his forehead the appearance of a neat, black hole, like a new-made wound in that moment before it fills with blood.

7

I had all the equipment I needed to work plainclothes. I had a snub-nose .38 revolver and holster, and a belt clip for my badge; I tucked my handcuffs into the back of my waistband, one cuff in and one out, and there we were: Detective Parkman. Sara and the children were appropriately impressed. Dad was coming up in the world.

Detective Division functions diurnally, for the most part, so I was at the station by 7:30 Thursday morning, feeling very grand strolling through the squad room in jacket and tie, carrying my packet of reports. Detective Parkman. Nobody noticed.

There was nobody in the Sex Crimes office, but Gadek's desk was along the wall to the right, and on it was a note:

> Parkman
>   Our guy did another last night. We're at the hospital. Use Blondie's desk. Coffee is outside the lieutenant's office.
>
> Gadek

Eddie had the desk opposite Gadek's, by the door, and Blondie had the one by the window. There were telephone books, penal code, general orders, and mug books on shelves above the desks. There was a typewriter, the metal shiny on the convexities where use had polished away the paint. An off-brand computer terminal and keyboard. Snapshots of Blondie's nieces and nephews. A stapler. Three telephones, looking worn. Gadek's phone had taped to it a torn corner of paper with the injunction BE PATIENT printed in block letters. Taped to the wall above Gadek's desk were three or four snapshots of young women. It was unclear whether they were friends, or relatives, or perhaps the victims of crime.

The morning sun filled the office and drifted through the frosted glass of the door into the hall (fresh ocher walls, varnished oak trim, still-new ocher linoleum). There was a profound laconic dignity to the whole place.

I took my cup down the hall to the alcove by the lieutenant's office, where the coffeemaker was, and carried it carefully back. I laid the stacks of reports on the desk, found a yellow legal pad for notes, tasted the coffee, and began to read.

In the small parking lot below the windows of the Detective Division the secretaries from the mayor's office next door began to arrive, parking their cars in spaces prominently marked RESERVED PARKING SPECIAL INVESTIGATIONS BUREAU. Because of these signs, those parts of the criminal element who were interested in the matter made a practice of noticing what cars were parked there so as to be able to spot them when they appeared in the neighborhoods. For this reason SIB detectives were careful to park their undercover cars elsewhere. Undeterred by the troglodytic individuals in dark glasses and gold-chunk jewelry who could occasionally be observed writing down their license numbers, the secretaries parked there freely when they arrived each morning, half an hour or so late, and maneuvered slowly, stately, favoring their overloaded ankles, in the direction of the employee lounge.

I skimmed the first several cases to get a sense of their nature and the amount of detail and repetition. Then I started at the top again and read carefully.

The first case was just shy of five years old. The victim

was a meter reader for the electric company, fifty-five years of age. She had suffered only minor physical injury. I began to make notes. Soon I had a chart sketched out, much like Gadek's, but smaller and neater.

Eddie hurried into the office, dropped into his chair, and picked up the phone.

"Gadek's gone to meet the ID tech at the scene," he said while he thumbed his address book. "He wants you to come take a look." He murmured the address. "Enjoy."

I made a note and started for the door. Eddie caught my sleeve and pointed to the reports. "Just a sec," he said into the phone, and then, to me, "Don't leave 'em out," and returned to his call. The drawers of Blondie's desk seemed mostly to be full of sports equipment, but I found a place and managed to get the drawer closed again. I headed for my car.

There were two patrol cars double-parked across the street from the victim's apartment building, and the two uniforms could be seen on nearby front steps doing the neighborhood check: "There was a problem across the street last night, probably around midnight. Did you hear anything? Car doors slamming, breaking glass, raised voices? See anything? Anything unusual the last couple of days? Anyone hanging around? Strange cars? Would you ask the kids when they get home, kids pick up on all sorts of stuff. Yeah? Mine too, but what can you do? Look, here's my card. If you think of anything—anything at all—please call this number. Thanks a lot."

The ID van was in the parking area. Gadek's unmarked car (a beige American-built fleet vehicle with radio antenna prominent on the middle of the roof) was parked in the driveway behind it. A small group of neighbors stood around, waiting for whatever spectacle the occasion might provide. For a moment as I pulled up this was me, and they watched me out of my car and into the building without evident disappointment.

The ID tech was dusting for fingerprints when I came in. He had soiled large expanses of the more commonly handled parts of the furniture and walls with graphite powder and had progressed to the aluminum sliding doors in the living room, working alertly and systematically but with a discouraged expression.

Gadek was in the bedroom.

"I had the tech dust the windows first so we could open 'em and let the place air out," he said. "It was pretty bad before." It was still pretty bad.

"The victim's not speaking yet. He broke a bone in her lower arm, along with doing some other stuff. And then there's the usual." He was in the middle of the room next to a puddle which the shag carpeting had largely but not entirely absorbed, turning slowly, sometimes standing, sometimes kneeling down to get a different angle. Still concentrating, but in a slightly different tone of voice, he added, "He really put her through it."

I was surprised to find that it didn't touch me greatly. Little as I knew so far about this hit, I knew enough about our guy that standing in that stinking room I was able to picture the whole thing pretty well. But it was so far beyond my own emotional experience that I didn't take it in yet, and I was still pretty cool. It's a reflection on me, but there it is.

Rule one when entering a crime scene is that you don't disturb anything.

The carpet made small objects hard to spot. We also wanted samples of any and all spills and stains before they'd been walked on and tracked around. I waited in the doorway while Gadek spent some time pioneering little evidence-free paths between key points and marking them by laying down golf clubs which he found in the hall closet. Then I followed him around while he dictated detailed instructions for the gathering of samples, vacuuming the rug, bagging the linens, more dusting, and how it was all to be cataloged. There weren't any surprises about it; you just had to be systematic.

"As soon as you've got each sample bagged and labeled and entered in the catalog, put it in the hall by the front door. We've already gone over that. When you think you're done, call me and I'll come down for a last look. In the meantime, I'll be sending Blondie down to take a look if she can get away. Eddie's got something of his own, so try

to do without him. Nobody else is to come past the door."
And he stepped briskly out through the garden.

It went slowly and painstakingly. The ID tech took the
samples. Dry things were gathered into little plastic bags.
Since fluids may react chemically with plastic, he scraped
fluids onto pieces of paper and put them into paper bags.
All bedsheets and towels, whether obviously stained or not,
he bagged for later examination. I wrote out the labels for
each sample as he gathered it. Each label had to have the
case number, date, probable nature of the evidence, and
where it was found. All this had to be repeated in the catalog, with any additional details which either the tech or I
thought might be helpful later on. We went carefully
through the rug, combing the pile aside with our fingers.
The tech found a plain silver earring small enough to have
been worn by a man (and therefore perhaps not hers), and
I found a tooth fragment. Of course, you don't know what
significance, if any, these may have, but you collect first and
review later. Then we mopped up the messes we weren't
going to collect as evidence so that we could comb through
the carpet under them; this yielded nothing new. Finally we
vacuumed the whole apartment, putting in a clean filter bag
for each room. From the bedroom we got a good deal of
hair (some of it probably pubic and conceivably his), nail
clippings, crumbs of several sorts, a couple of glass beads,
some sort of fluff, carpet fibers, a good deal of lint, a sequin
(red), a tiny piece of wire, two very small white pills, small
fragments of apparent vegetable matter, some thread ends
(assorted colors), several small lumps of what seemed to be
tar, dirt, and a certain quantity of residual matter which
looked like sand but which might be anything. After each
room we turned the bag inside out onto a large sheet of
clean plastic, and then carefully transferred the takings to a
small evidence bag. I cataloged while the tech vacuumed the
next room.

Gadek arrived with Blondie in tow. He gave her a brief
tour, and then the two of them crawled slowly along the
hall, intently examining each of the bags we had laid out
there. The tech and I hovered like anxious hosts.

Gadek stood up.

"Prints?"

"Usables, but I don't know how much good they'll do," said the tech. "Nothing good from the doors or windows. The prints from the bedroom aren't much to speak of. Most of 'em from the kitchen, living room, and bathroom."

"Hers and her friends', most likely. Blondie, put that on your list. Who's been here in the last week so we can do eliminations. Also, there's an underwear drawer that's sitting open and all jumbled. The rest of the place isn't like that. I'd like her to go through her underwear and see if she can tell if anything's missing. If he's taking home souvenirs, we want to know."

Blondie returned to the hospital. Gadek went slowly through the whole place again, standing in one spot and scanning slowly, then moving, standing, and scanning again. Finally he said, "Looks pretty thorough, guys. Get that kitchen window back on its tracks and secure the place before you leave." To the tech he said, "Outstanding, as always, Jim."

Then he pulled me aside and said, "The neighborhood check was zip, zero. Doesn't something seem wrong about that? That kitchen window is directly opposite another apartment building fifteen feet away—a whole wall of windows. He stands between these two buildings and takes that window out? Now I can believe that you could do that in the middle of the night, and three times out of four nobody'd rise up to it. But I don't believe our guy would run that risk. He's done forty-odd offenses. If he took a one-in-four chance each time, he'd have been seen ten times. But nobody's ever seen him. He's not a risk-taker. We could be missing something."

"What do you think we're missing?"

"I don't know. I haven't thought about it yet, but I'm going to. You think about it, too."

He hurried off.

It was past three o'clock, and I felt the need of lunch. We remounted the window, locked up, and left. I picked up a hamburger and went back to the office, where I pictured the three of them with their chairs in a little circle, heads together, pondering the evidence and earnestly propounding theories. But of course it wasn't that way. There was a rapist out there; if we could find a trail of evidence that would lead us to him, that would take care of it. If we couldn't find a trail of evidence, and if he didn't turn himself in, and if nobody betrayed him, then we would have to intercept him on the street. It wasn't a theoretical case.

Long before I came to Sex Crimes, Gadek and his people had been spending what time they could devote to the series on basic elimination work. Information bulletins were prepared and sent out statewide in the hope that somebody in some other department might make some connection—perhaps to a bad guy who had a juvenile record, now sealed, but which somebody might remember. They had combed sex criminal registers. Somebody had spent a good deal of time with postal delivery routes, seeing whether any significant number of hits lay along any one route, especially when substitute carriers were working them. They had got the names of drivers for major stores, for parcel delivery companies, for taxi companies, meter readers, telephone repairmen, newspaper deliverymen—anyone who would be out and about, able to nose around without arousing suspicion. They had talked to the managers of apartments where victims had lived: What plumbers did they use? Electricians? Roofers? What building inspectors had been there?

With each name, we asked, Can he be eliminated? Physical description? How long has he worked this area? Any background of interest? And so forth.

Most names were eliminated quickly for obvious reasons. Some took a little longer. Usually one could find that they had definitely not been in the area—not a resident, different job, in prison—during one or more of our guy's hits.

There isn't a manual for this sort of thing; you think about it, and when you get some inspiration you go check it out. If you have a lot of inspiration, it takes a lot of time.

Gadek was alone in the office when I got back. Propped against the wall in front of him was an artist's composite drawing of a female hippie type. Next to that were four or five mug shots of women who resembled the drawing more or less. There were three offense reports spread out in front of him, which he was comparing and abstracting on a pad he held in his lap. His concentration was complete. He had other cases going beside our guy's rape series. This one involved a married couple who gained the confidence of teenage girls, usually runaways in bus stations. They would take them to wooded areas where he raped them while she waited in the car. I slipped in, got my reports out of Blondie's drawer, went out for a cup of the lieutenant's coffee, and settled back where I had been that morning to eat and read.

Eddie slipped in, moving fast. He closed the door behind him. Gadek looked up.

"I think this is going to be it," he told Gadek. "I'm going to call him now, and if he's got the stuff on hand we've got a go. The warrant's all made out, and there'll be a judge in chambers for another hour. Can we have bodies in twenty minutes?"

"I'll check," said Gadek, and picked up his phone. He dialed the Patrol sergeant's office. "Alphonzo, Leo. We may have a kiddie porn distributor ripe for squeezing in about twenty minutes. Can you loan me two uniforms? Great. I'll be right back to you." He nodded at Eddie.

Eddie dropped a comic book–size magazine in front of me. Crudely produced, the photo on the front showed a large, hairy man of about fifty naked on a bed. A black line was drawn across his eyes. Between his splayed legs lay an earnest-looking child of about six, also naked, with her arm inserted to the elbow in his rectum.

I turned the page.

"Cute, eh?" said Gadek. "He produces 'em himself. See the cable release in his hand? It's a self-portrait."

Eddie reached around the door and hung the Please Do Not Disturb sign on the outside. Then he closed the door, glanced over at me, murmured "Cool call," and turned to his phone. I knew that this meant that I wasn't to make any noise that could be heard by the other party, but then I saw Leo turning a switch on the side of his phone, and Eddie glancing at me again and hesitating in his dialing; sure enough, there was a switch on mine as well, to prevent it from ringing. I turned it down. Eddie punched the last number and pressed the Record button on the tape machine next to the phone.

"William?"

His voice was guarded, with a tight precision. It was a very distinctive sound, very recognizable over the phone.

"William, this is Harold. . . . Yes, that is correct. I am Walter's friend, as you know. . . . Of course you remember, but I think these little things are no more than good manners. I hope you agree. . . . Yes." He laughed a tight little laugh. "Yes, I am still interested. I found it as satisfactory as you described it. It was very . . . Yes, exactly. And in fact, several friends to whom I have mentioned it are also interested. Can you send me fifty more? Have you so many at hand? . . . Ah, Walter thought that you might. I am very pleased to hear it."

He did not change his expression of precise attention, but he gave a steely thumbs-up to Gadek.

"And you could send them to the same address? . . . Excellent. Then if I send you a package of cash this afternoon you should have it tomorrow. Will your package be ready to go out? . . . Excellent. And the amount? . . . Very well. And by the way, you mentioned a sampler of . . . Yes, exactly. How much should I add? . . . That is satisfactory, although if I may say so, William, I hope that before we have done much more business together you will find that a discount is appropriate, especially in the matter of my own . . . No, my friend, the fact is that your prices are on the high end. As I am sure you know. . . . Of course, you deliver value. Of course. But the customs of the marketplace suggest . . . Well. Well, we will discuss it further another time. And for now, you may expect a package tomorrow. . . . Yes. . . . Excellent. Good-bye, William." Gently, so as not to spoil the effect of mannered punctilio, Eddie replaced the receiver, but when it was fully down the mask dropped from his face and he almost shouted, "It's a go, a goddam go! He has the stuff on hand—probably a lot of it. We're going to have his ass in jail by dinnertime!" He hurried off to the judge's chambers with his search warrant.

Gadek snapped up his phone and dialed the sergeant's office.

"Alphonzo, Leo. We got it. Have 'em meet us in the north yard in ten minutes? Yeah, glad to have you—quiet afternoon? Good."

Gadek looked at me and at his watch. It was four. "Maybe you'd better do a bit more reading before you call it a day. There've been distractions. I'd rather you put in extra time now and then take an extra day off later. That okay?"

"Yes."

"Good. If Blondie comes in before you leave, tell her what's up. If not, leave her a note. This should take maybe three hours, depending." He hastened off.

I turned a page of William's pamphlet.

I thought, I'll never have another erection as long as I live.

I went through it. It was all pretty much the same. I stuck it back under the papers on Eddie's desk and turned again to my rapes. They seemed almost reassuring.

Some people register upset by refusing food, but I'm not one of them. I munched on my hamburger, now chilly-cold from sitting by the open window, and sipped the coffee.

Reading through reports one right after another gives a very strong sense of pattern: how he approaches, what he says, what he does.

I called Sara and told her I would be late.

"It's been a day," I said, "a real day. I'll tell you later. Be really nice to the kids."

Blondie tripped in, full of spunk. She'd been called out at five in the morning and going strong ever since. I told her about the raid on William. She told me that the rape victim had begun to talk. So far, they hadn't spoken about the case much; they'd talked about golf. Tomorrow they'd get down to brass tacks.

She got on the phone and called the apartment manager about getting a cleaning service for the apartment. The victim wouldn't be going back except to move out, but she couldn't face the mess, even for an hour.

"Can you get it done tomorrow morning?" she asked.

"She'll be coming out tomorrow or the day after, and she'll need her things.

"Man, it's been a busy day," she said as she hung up.

"You guys seem to be up to the eyeballs."

"Well, it's hopping, I won't say it isn't." She laughed. "It's this one last night that's really put us over, 'cause we had all this other stuff going already. Eddie's been working on William for weeks. He must be having fun right now."

8

Someone had been in her bedroom while she slept, and she knew it in the moment of waking. The bedroom door, which she always closed, was standing open. Her robe, which she invariably draped over the chair, was on the floor near the bathroom door. The dresser drawers were not all neatly closed. The little tray with three bottles and the glass of water was gone from the nightstand beside her bed. Someone had been right here, moving around her room, right beside her bed.

She retrieved her robe and put it on hastily, overlapping it as much as possible and belting it tightly around her. From where she picked it up she could see the medicine bottles on the vanity by the bathroom sink, where, presumably, they had been examined by the light from the window. Without waiting to see more she called the police.

Someone had been through the house from end to end.

Drawers had been opened, the contents lifted or shifted around and then restored, not precisely, to their previous places.

The patrolman who arrived had never seen anything like it in his eighteen months of service. He was tired, having been held over at the turn of shift to cover two open beats.

Still, he bent his mind to the problem. He was inclined to suspect a practical joke, and he questioned her at some length about friends and lovers past and present who might have a key and who might be puckishly inclined. She pointed out that she had found both front and back doors chained on the inside, as she had left them when she went to bed. There were lots of windows in the big old house, but they were all closed and locked. He went all around the house both inside and outside. There was plenty of concealment for an intruder, with the house on the end of a cul-de-sac and lots of shrubbery, but he was unable to detect any signs of tampering or to locate the point of entry.

It was a poser. He began to suspect some profound Freudian perturbation—"Freudian" constituting in his mind a vague and spacious category which included anything inexplicable concerning mental process—and he asked her if she had any history of sleepwalking. The question amazed her, but after an initial surge of incredulity she began to wonder. She had, in fact, been the family sleepwalker until well into adolescence. But she remembered the physical surge of fear she had felt at the moment of waking as her eye fell on the first signs that all was not as it should be. She had gone through the house, opening cupboards and drawers, and finding familiar-forgotten arrangements disarranged she had said to herself, he lifted this, he went through these, he spread these out.

It was hard to put into words. The patrolman still inclined to the sleepwalking theory. He wrote it up as a "suspicious circumstance: possible prowl." He offered to summon the fingerprint technician to dust the place, but he was not encouraging about results, and she would have to stay home from work until the technician came, which might be several hours. She declined, with a feeling of dissatisfaction. There was not much advice he could give her about future security because the house was already pretty secure, as houses go. Did she like dogs? Small, yappy dogs are the best protectors. And so he left.

Eddie was alone in the office when I arrived on Friday. He had had his fun raiding William, and he gave me the

highlights. They had gone to William's warehouse. The front
door to the office area was locked. They rang, and William
queried them via the doorbell-intercom. They told him they
were AirfreightCo, but unluckily AirfreightCo had been
there earlier in the day. The intercom fell silent. They
wanted to get in fast to prevent any destruction of evidence,
so they yelled *"Police! Open Up!"* When there was no response they took down the door with a battering ram they
had brought with them and stormed in, the uniforms first.
The inner door past the reception room was also locked and
they took that down, too. William was in the main warehouse room, frozen with fright, holding a large carton containing all sorts of great stuff. There was an incinerator with
more material stored immediately adjacent to it, but it
wasn't lit. He hadn't had time to destroy anything.

"We laid the warrant on him," whooped Eddie, "cuffed
him and put him in a chair by the door. Let him watch us
tear that place apart. We got all sorts of stuff. I took out a
selection." He held out a pile of pamphlets. The top one
had a photo on the cover.

"That's okay," I said.

"The arraignment'll be today. I'll give these to the deputy
D.A. to drop under the judge's nose. And the judge will be
Her Honor Nora Clements, number-one feminist. She'll take
one look at that pamphlet on fist-fucking and set his bail at
twenty-two-point-seven *million* dollars. He's begun his long
jail career. Parkman, I'm dancin'. I'm just dancin'."

And indeed he was, and he'd earned it. It was a pleasure
to watch him do it.

Blondie hurried in. She'd been to the hospital.

"They want to cut her loose this morning." I was in her
chair, and she dropped into Gadek's and grabbed the phone.

"They say her arm's as fixed as it's gonna get, and they
don't want to keep her. She's still barely talking. Hello, Mr.
Peterhof, this is Officer Moore. We talked yesterday about
getting the apartment cleaned? ... Right. So what's the
story? ... Oh, *no. Monday?* Oh, come on, you can do better
than that. ... Well, there must be another service. ... Look,
Mr. Peterhof, she's had a real hard time. A real hard time.
And there's no way she can go back into that apartment the

way it is, dig? You've been in there.... Right, well, she's coming out of the hospital today, and she's gonna need her things ..."

Gadek was beckoning me out into the hall.

"Look, Parkman, we seem to be crowded here. Why don't you take the reports down to Service Division. Speak to Sergeant Vanderloon. He's got an empty desk. When you're ready to start making appointments, come see me." He stepped into the office, hung out the Please Do Not Disturb sign and closed the door. I was reaching for the knob when the door opened and Gadek's hand appeared holding out my pile of reports. I took them, and the door closed firmly.

Sergeant Vanderloon led me to a vacant desk hidden behind filing cabinets near the booking desk.

"No one will disturb you here," he said. "No one can see you. Remember, young man, that if you want to get work done in this world you must be inconspicuous." And so saying, he left me. A moment later he was back.

"The coffee is just fresh, if you'd like some now."

"I would," I said, getting back up. He seemed pleased. We stood back to let a tired-looking rookie, Phyllis Canty, shepherd her prisoner to the booking desk, and then I followed Vanderloon to the coffeepot.

The prisoner didn't want to be there. Canty had placed him on a bench that had several large ringbolts fixed to the seat while she and an aide, a small woman, prepared the booking forms.

"Fuckin' broad," he said. "What'm I here for anyway?"

"Being drunk in public and disturbing the peace," said Canty wearily, not looking up from her writing.

"Fuckin' broad," he said again.

Barry Dillon appeared in the doorway, deep in colloquy with an earnest young patrolman.

"... so the judge threw it out," the earnest patrolman was telling Dillon. "Does that make sense? The guy is fleeing, he throws down the bag—God and all the world know it's full of dope—so the officer opens it up, finds the dope, busts him, and the judge won't admit it because the officer opens it without getting a search warrant. Does that make sense?"

"Sure it does," said Dillon amiably. "You can't just go around searching things. You know that."

"Well, it's just unimaginative report writing then," said the patrolman. "The cop should have said, 'The bag fell open when the suspect dropped it on the sidewalk, and contraband was observed.'"

"Fuckin' broad," said the prisoner again, louder. "What'm I here for? Can you tell me that?"

"*Think* about that," said Dillon. "*Think* about that. So he nails a jerk. The world is *full* of jerks. What about *him*? What about his *integrity*? If a cop isn't honest"—with an arm on each shoulder he was rocking the young man back and forth—"if he isn't *clean*, then what *is* he? How is he different from the jerks he nails? Cops got rules, jerks don't. That's it," he said, prodding the young man heavily and repeatedly on the chest with his forefinger. "Ask Van if I'm right." He turned to Vanderloon, who was carefully stirring imitation creamer into his coffee. "Van, am I right?"

"Quite right, Barry," replied that gentle man. "It sounds very square to say so, but it's just as your sergeant says—your honor is too high a price to pay for spoiling a lowlife's day."

"Of *course* I'm right," said Dillon, now giving the patrolman several avuncular thumps on the shoulders. "It's just what Van says: the world's *full* of jerks."

"Fuckin' broad," said Canty's prisoner, not for the first time. Canty was uncuffing him while the aide rolled out ink on a brass plate. "Why'ncha leave me alone?" He thrust both hands in his pockets and glowered at them. The group by the coffeepot stiffened up, but it isn't etiquette to interfere in these matters. Dillon and his patrolman returned to the squad room.

Canty was tired and cross. Her platoon had gone home three-quarters of an hour before, and she had already spent considerable time with this citizen.

"C'mon, Joey," she said. "Just put 'em up here and let's get this over with."

"What'm I here for? Will you at least tell me that? What'm I here for?"

"Joey, I've told you three times. Here's number four:

you're here for being drunk in public and disturbing the peace. Now let's do it."

"Right here," said the aide, indicating the inked plate.

"Fuck you," he said, and then, eyeing her up and down, he added, "Not that I'd care to. Fuckin' dyke."

"I'm getting sick of this," said Canty.

"Anyway, what'm I here for? You won't even tell me what I'm here for."

"Joey, what did I say a minute ago?"

"I got my rights. How come you ain't given me my rights? How come you ain't told me, fuckin' dyke?"

"Joey," said Canty. "I've been real nice to you. I've been real gentle, real nice. I'm about to stop being nice. The law requires you to cooperate in this booking process and that's what you're going to do, get the picture? Now just—"

"Fuckin' dyke," said Joey.

"Joey . . ."

"Fuckin' dyke."

"Last chance."

"Fuckin' dyke."

Canty took him firmly by the collar and the elbow closest to her, wheeled him around, and placed him up against the booking desk. Joey yanked his hands out of his pockets, pushed off from the desk, spinning, and made a snatch for the butt of Canty's long baton, which was right between them. She grabbed his hands and held the baton in its ring, but Joey was heavier than she was and he had her moving backward.

"Service Division!" bellowed Vanderloon toward the corridor, and we both jumped across the room. Joey had pushed Canty heavily backward against a desk and pressed her feet right back off the floor. She aimed a knee at his crotch but he twisted in time to avoid it. He withdrew a hand from the baton, snatched up a telephone from the desk, and cocked it back over his head, where I grabbed it, coming up from behind. Somebody slipped, and locked together we all went onto the floor in a pile. I must have hit my head.

There were shadows flitting over us from the direction of the squad room, and the room was thick with voices.

Things seemed to be moving slowly.
Canty?
Canty was gone.
Vanderloon?
Someone was congratulating Vanderloon.
I wondered what had happened to Joey.
I found I had a most unpleasant pain.

"Why don't you just stay right where you are, Parkman," someone was saying. "You had quite a knock."

"No, no, I'm okay," I said, but it was like being drunk: the more I tried to be okay, the tipsier I felt. In uniform it mightn't have been so bad, but it seemed wrong to lie on the floor in a necktie.

"D'ja see that?" someone was saying. "Vanderloon popped his collarbone just as sweet as you please."

". . . tougher than he looks."

"Just stay right there," said whoever-it-was. "The ambulance will be here in a minute."

Gadek went to the hospital as soon as he heard what had happened, but I was in and out so quickly that he missed me. He called me at home, but I was still en route. He called later and told me to take it easy.

Canty came by on her way home. She brought one of those awful florist's baskets. "I lost control of that one," she said. "I'm really sorry."

"Don't worry about it," I said. "The flowers are very pretty."

Eddie and Blondie came by at the end of the day. They brought chocolate-covered orange peel and a bouquet of marguerites. "Calla lilies are prettier," said Blondie. "The florist said these would be more appropriate, but from the look of you I don't know."

"We could bring lilies another time," said Eddie.

Walt heard about my mishap when he arrived for his shift at 3:00. On his dinner break he went by his apartment, picked out *The Mystery of Udolpho*, and brought it by the house.

"It's a key work in the history of early-nineteenth-century Romanticism," he murmured in a voice modulated to the sensibilities of a terminal invalid. "It's tedious and improbable in the last degree. It's just your sort of thing. You'll like it."

She got to work late, and stayed late to make up the time. It was almost dark when she got home. All about her was the evidence of the prowl. She could not shake the sense that she was not alone there.

It was too much. She would spend the night with her best friend, maybe a couple of nights, until this haunted feeling subsided.

She snatched up her purse and jacket and slipped out the door. Cursing the shrubbery, which seemed to be made of shadows, she hurried to her car, hastily opened the door, and locked herself in.

It wasn't until she had started the engine that she remembered that she had not looked in the back seat before getting in. In the shock of that realization she jerked her foot off the clutch. The car lurched and stalled. Wildly, her hand on the handle of the door, she craned over the seat and looked.

The back seat was empty.

Hastily, she started the car again and drove off.

The next day Gadek was at our front door at breakfast time.

"You have to stay put today, at least, I understand," he said. He placed a large manila envelope on the dining room table. "Your reports and notes. I thought you might be bored. Anyway, it'll be quieter here." And then he added, "I hope," with a droll smile at Sara.

Adam and Joss laughed.

"You're funny," said Adam.

"Yes," said Gadek as he hurried for the door. "Yes, I am."

We took the kids for a picnic. I spent a good deal of time lying on a blanket in the sun with my head on Sara's lap, an activity I've always found healing, especially when she runs her fingers through my hair and mutters endearments.

Sara has always ridiculed the traditional pomposities of my profession. She thinks that the worst dangers of police work are moral rather than physical. She thinks that cops who talk about "putting our lives on the line" are simply whining about a situation they have chosen for themselves. In the same vein, she doesn't like to hear disparaging remarks about the Supreme Court. She thinks the Constitution is a trim piece of work. But since I agree with her on all these points, she can afford to be amused by clichés.

"A husband lightly wounded in the line of duty needs plenty of looking after," she declared on this occasion. After the picnic she baked chocolate chip cookies and sent the children upstairs with them, still warm.

"Mom said to bring you these on your bed of pain," said Joss, standing at the bedroom door, "but you don't appear to be suffering very much."

"Maybe we'd better eat them," said Adam, "if you're not really suffering."

On Monday I went in for a checkup and was declared fit. I was in the office by late morning.

"I'm glad to see you," said Gadek brightly, "because I've just got approval to borrow you for several more weeks, till we get a little out from under. That okay with you?"

"Yes."

"Good. Here's a copy of your revised assignment schedule. Initial there."

I initialed.

"Blondie is going to reinterview our latest victim this morning. She's talking pretty well now, and we want to get a full narrative out of her before she forgets it or represses it. You go along and observe. Blondie's pretty good. Watch how she does it." He scratched his head. "After that, we've got some miscellaneous stuff that I want to clean up."

I went with Blondie to interview the victim. Then Eddie needed some spadework done on William, and, while I was at it, on one or two other cases where the D.A.'s office wanted more information than he had given them initially.

And we had an ordinary, garden-variety rape, a high school girl who was dragged into a car by two guys who took her into the hills above the university, pushed her into a grove of trees and both raped her. They were going to drive off with her clothes and leave her there, but then one of them came back and told her she was kinda pretty and how would she like to take in a movie? With truly admirable presence of mind she said sure, she'd go out with him if he'd give her back her clothes. He gave her the clothes, and while she was putting them on she said, how can I get in touch with you? And he said, look, only sluts call guys. *I'll* call *you*. But she said, no, her mother always answered the phone. So he said, oh, okay, and wrote down his number. Then she said, y'know, what's your name, since we're going out? And he told her, it's Tom. Well, Tom, she said, y'know I've got a real cute friend who might like to meet your friend. What's his name? His name's Bruce. And while they were standing there she was also memorizing the license number of the car.

As soon as she got back into town she called the police.

Tom and Bruce were in the lockup by dinnertime, but collecting all the evidence from the hospital, the car, and the crime scene itself took longer. And taking a narrative from the victim took time, especially since she began to come down from the adrenaline once she was in safety and it all began to catch up with her. She was scared and hurt in ways that "scared" and "hurt" don't describe, and during the hours I was with her that evening she was beginning to realize the dimensions of it.

All of this, and some odds and ends, kept me pretty busy. But Gadek said, "I think we might get going on the interviews by the end of the week unless we have some new cases come in."

"Great," I said. "I'm beginning to get frustrated. I want to nail this jerk."

"It's too bad he's not the only jerk in the world," said Gadek. "It'd all be much more orderly."

9

A few days after my injury we were all invited for dinner at Melanie's. Heather had admired a recipe of Sara's, and the two of them were going to cook it for everyone.

The houses on Melanie's street were all fairly old and large, mostly on deep double lots. In the middle of the block was what seemed like a forest, and in the middle of the forest was her carriage house. The driveway was hacked out of the shrubbery, which got thicker as you went farther from the street. The place itself was completely surrounded and overhung with enormous trees and lots of brush. Direct sunlight almost never reached the place. Away from the windows, the shadows quickly soaked away the light, and under tables or behind chairs it was dark and mysterious.

It had been a good-sized stable, with the lofts converted to two small bedrooms and a sleeping porch above. The stable itself was now the living room, and in simpler times someone had fitted large, low, wooden casement windows. There were several of these, each secured by a small metal latch and hinged with exterior pins. Standing outside with a small screwdriver, anyone could slip out the pins, pull the window out, and step right in over the low sill. It was your burglar's dream, the answer to our guy's prayers. Melanie liked to leave them hooked open when the weather was not absolutely cold. The neighbors liked to hear her music.

After her divorce Melanie had raised her two children by herself. In that spring, Heather was finishing her sophomore year in high school, and Mike was about to graduate and go off to college. Heather had the smaller of the two bedrooms, and Mike the sleeping porch. The sleeping porch was unheated, and during the winter quite cold. In Melanie's romantic mind this austerity was appropriate to the young male destined in future years to a life of affluence and power. It was her image of the sexes: herself and her daughter in their small, snug, virginal bedrooms of knotty pine, and her son (who was always given the best piece of meat at dinner in the absence of an adult guest) toughing it out a few feet away.

Melanie loved her carriage house, and the longer she lived there the more she loved it. And it was a magic place, if you left life's realities out of the picture. I made several little remarks and gave her the card of the police aide who did home security checks. I think my concern pleased her because it was mother-henish, and everyone likes to be fussed over a little. But she never did anything about it; she just said, "Goodness, Toby, you should relax your jungle instincts and enjoy the day."

I came to Melanie's straight from work, a long day helping Eddie do cleanup on his kiddie porn case against William— or, more precisely, against the father of the earnest little girl in his magazine, who had rented her to William by the week, knowing how she would be used, having used her in the same way himself. Adam and Joss saw me negotiating the path from the street and opened the door crying, "Yea for Dad!" They ran out a few steps, and I dropped down on one knee where we met, to be hugged. Of course, William's little girl loved her dad, too, most earnestly, and did what she could to please him; with that thought fresh in my mind, my children's embraces were too complex a phenomenon to receive in a simple spirit of enjoyment.

Melanie wasn't far behind to bestow her slightly remote kiss. If her dog had still been alive, he would have padded along right behind her.

Sara waved distractedly from the kitchen, where she and Heather were doing something intricate.

Mike, as head of the household, was tending bar. "I think you've got time for something before dinner," he said in his preppy respectful-familiar way as soon as I was in the door.

"I'd love a scotch, if you can manage one," I said.

"You shall have it," he said with assurance, as if I had made some humorously obscure request which he was, nevertheless, competent to fulfill. He disappeared into the kitchen in a manner reminiscent of comic English butlers. I could almost picture Melanie pressing old P. G. Wodehouse novels on him, trying to shape his taste in light literature.

Adam stood quietly, close beside me, as he sometimes does, a finger hooked through one of my belt loops.

Mike reappeared with my drink correctly presented in the customary short glass. Mike was interested in police work. He had wanted to join the department's Explorer troop, but Melanie had forbidden it. In the novels he had read the detectives drank whiskey, and he found my adherence to this pattern sophisticated and attractive. Now he lingered, hoping to chat, but Heather appeared immediately offering crackers and cheese, saying, "Officer Toby, sir." Then she said to Adam, "You don't get any," putting one in his free hand and another in his mouth. By the time she was finished charming Adam, Melanie had advanced to lift her very light gin and tonic and say, "It's so nice to have you here, Toby," and Mike, outnumbered, retreated to the kitchen.

Melanie is a good three inches shorter than I am, but when I think of her I'm always looking up at her. Her smile and the way her eyes meet yours is genuine, but there's a grip about it. I always have the impression that rather than feeling happiness she is choosing firmly to be happy. It's as if you could see the sweat on her brow sometimes. But she isn't ashamed of it. She expects equal effort from everyone around her. Mike and Heather sometimes showed the strain. Melanie had worked and gone to school and put her husband through his own training. She shed him when he proved unworthy, and without him she made a career of her own and raised two promising children. In season she attended the symphony and the opera, poured lemonade at

101

her children's school events, and donated regularly to conventional charities. She practiced her instrument every day. She kept her figure. She mentioned once to Sara that she had never come to the breakfast table less than fully dressed and made up. If everyone did as much, she felt, according to their conditions, the world would be a better place.

There was an edge to all this; I never approached Melanie without worrying whether my collar was clean, or if I had washed behind the ears. She had much the same effect on Sara. But you choose your friends selfishly, for what you need. Melanie's attraction was not so much her assurance as her discrimination. The products of her life—her children, her graceful surroundings, her music—were immensely attractive, and she had earned them by care, taste, and hard work. Sara and I could hope that in a few years the same well-directed effort would bring us to a similar place.

We sat down in big chairs in front of the fireplace. Adam squeezed into my chair beside me. I put my arm around him. He felt so solid there beside me, so safe. William had little boys as well as little girls. Joss had gone to help Sara and Heather in the kitchen, Mike was passing in and out carrying plates and silver to the round table on the other side of the room. The room was all wood, the lamps soft and golden. It was profoundly civilized, ordered and contented. But I was much absorbed by the thought that things go wrong, sometimes. Melanie's dog bit her by this very hearth.

Outside in the street the sun was still above the horizon and the treetops were golden, but in the carriage house it was twilight. The windows were big and pale.

"You don't have curtains, Melanie," I said, before I could stop myself.

"No, Toby." She smiled, half challenging, half overlooking. "I don't like the feeling of being shut in."

"Sorry. I didn't come to lecture you."

"You've had a long day, I take it." It was a riposte, but it was gently done.

"Yes. Pretty long." Melanie had some happier topic to chat about. Sara loves me and has always looked after me, but she has never cultivated, as Melanie had, the art of making gentle conversation calculated not to overtax at the end of a long day. By the time dinner appeared she had gotten two drinks into me—small ones, so that I felt cosseted by the repeated attention without getting anything like drunk—and done most of the talking herself, to spare me the effort, with periodic appeals to my superior information and judgment. I came to the table relaxed and sociable, happily appreciative of Sara's and Heather's labors, not realizing, until later, how neatly she'd done it.

Without any signal that I could detect, Mike and Heather jumped up at the end of dinner to attend to the dishes, assisted with much happy clamor by Adam and Joss.

We sat in comfortable chairs by the fire. Sara made one or two artfully ambient references to Walt. Melanie clearly pricked up her ears.

Heather's laugh came back to us from the kitchen.

Maybe I was a little drunker than I'd realized. I gestured at the windows and said, "Perhaps you should worry about her, if you don't about yourself."

Melanie turned square to me. She still smiled, but her lips were tight.

"Please don't be misled by your idée fixe," she said, "into thinking that it's fair to try to frighten me. You have no right to suggest that I'm not concerned about Heather. I'm plenty concerned. I think I'm making a reasonable choice. I'm not going to raise her to be fearful. I'm not going to cramp her."

"She's raised already. Reality she can handle very well. She—"

"Toby." She laid a hand on my arm. A firm hand. "Toby, I'm sure you mean it for the best. You've made your protest. You've made it several times, in fact. You've acted like a friend. Now please let it rest." And smiling still, she said, "Sara, let's try that Bach duet. Our Toby is tired and crabby. We'll edify him." And Sara, who agreed with me on the matter of Melanie's tin locks and exterior hinge pins, and who wished that Melanie would not refer to me as "our Toby," smiled a separate smile at each of us and reached for her viola.

* * *

When we left, Melanie said, referring to their chamber music group, "We should have a good turnout on Sunday. Plenty of Bach, and some Fauré, Toby," she added, turning rather unexpectedly to me. "You should enjoy it. I hope you can come. And bring Walt, too, if he feels like it."

Sara caught my eye and nodded discreetly.

"Ah, uh, yes, of course," I said. "I can't promise, but . . ."

"No, of course not," she said. "But come if you can. We'd be so glad to see you."

10

We were pretty well caught up on the odds and ends as we got to the end of the week. I'd read all the reports, summarized them, and finished making notes days before. I didn't think I'd miss the significance of new information.

"Okay," Gadek said on Friday. "Let's get going."

He hung out the ~~Please~~ Do Not Disturb sign and dialed the first number. I put my phone on the same line. Two rings.

"Hello?" A distracted-sounding voice.

"Could I speak to Jean Hayes, please?" he asked. In the background, a television and children. A pot on the stove.

The distraction was replaced by caution. "Who is calling?"

"This is Sergeant Gadek with the Police Department." You could almost hear her flinch. There was a pause, and then, bravely: "This is Jean Hayes."

"Mrs. Hayes, I hope this isn't a bad moment to call. It sounds as if you're getting dinner ready." His voice was sympathetic and alert.

"No, no, that's ..." Delay would not relieve her. "What ..."

"Mrs. Hayes, we're investigating a series of recent attacks on women. We have reason to believe that these may have been committed by the same man who attacked you. We're also concerned that things may have been missed in the investigation of your case which would help us now. I—"

"Just a minute." Her voice was tight. The television was off, and the children's voices were louder. "Kids." The receiver was some distance from her mouth. "Kids, I'm on the phone. Why don't you watch the next cartoon." There was some parley back and forth. The receiver came nearer her mouth. "Well, this time you can. Yes, take the chips out there. I know. Special treat." The television was audible again. "I'm sorry."

"I'll try to be quick. I know it's an awful big thing to ask, but I'd like to meet with you and go over this with you again."

"I told the other officer everything. I don't see . . ." Her voice was almost pleading.

"Some new information has surfaced in the time since your case was investigated," said Gadek. His voice was steady and reasonable. "The officer you spoke to didn't ask all the questions we wish he'd asked. As I said, this could be a great help in cases we're working on now, and it might help us arrest the man who is responsible for attacking you."

There was a pause. Finally she said, "Okay."

"I wouldn't ask it if it weren't important. I know it's a big thing. I'd like to make this as convenient as possible for you. Where could I meet you? You could come in to my office, or I could meet you somewhere else."

"Somewhere else. Not here. I . . . I can get a sitter and meet you at my friend's. I . . ."

There was still something unresolved. "How do I . . . I don't know . . ."

"Mrs. Hayes, I'm calling from the Sex Crimes office at the Police Department. It's in the phone book. Would you like to look the number up, and I'll hang up and you can call me back?"

Another pause. "Yes."

"Okay, I'll hang up. Look up the Police Department, then Detective Division."

"I've found it."

He hung up. "Well," he said, looking at me for the first

time. "That was easier than it might have been." The phone rang. "Sex Crimes. Sergeant Gadek."

"This is Jean."

"Good, Jean. Now, do you want to check with your friend?"

"No, I'm pretty sure it'll be okay." She gave the address. They agreed on the following evening, Saturday. Then he said, "Jean, I'll be bringing another officer with me. His name is Toby Parkman. He's also working on these cases. It's important for him to be knowledgeable about this."

She hesitated before saying, "Okay."

He hung up. "Well," he said, scribbling the appointment on his calendar. "That's one." He glanced at the next number on the list and began to dial again.

Saturday was Sara's birthday. We had arranged for Heather to baby-sit, a dinner reservation and theater tickets. Sara said we'd exchange the tickets and change the reservation, and she'd go to the movies. She was being a good sport, but she was thoroughly irritated, and feeling guilty for feeling irritated, and therefore more irritated than before.

The apartment door was on the chain when Jean's friend opened it. We had our badges already out. We made no movement toward the door until she had unchained it, opened it, and asked us to come in.

"I'm Sergeant Gadek. This is Officer Parkman."

"I'm Lois." She waved to a couch and chairs around a coffee table. "This is real hard on her," she said.

"All I can say is, we have to know what she can tell us. If there were any other way to do it, then that's what we'd do. I know how brave she's being."

"I'll get her." She went off down the hallway. Gadek stood by the couch, holding his folder. He didn't look around the apartment, or at me.

After two or three minutes Lois reappeared with Jean. Jean was thirty-three, I knew from reading the earlier report. She might have lost a little weight since then. Gadek introduced us again and thanked her for agreeing to meet with us. He repeated what he had told her on the phone: that we hoped that her case would shed new light on the current series. While he was talking she was advancing slowly into the room, eyes averted. There were several places she might choose to sit. He spoke quietly and matter-of-factly. After a hesitation she came to the chair next to him. We all sat down, the two of them next to each other, Lois in another chair. I sat farther along the couch.

It was beautifully done.

"Jean, as I explained on the phone, the officer who investigated your case originally was viewing it as a single occurrence. We now think that the man who attacked you has attacked a number of other women. It's important that we know exactly what happened to you. What I would like to do is have you tell us about it again, as if this were the first time you were describing it. You were there, we weren't. We have to see clearly how it went. If something comes up that we need to go into more fully, I'll ask you."

She nodded.

He said, "Jean, I know this is going to be difficult. If we come to anything that's just too hard, we can skip over it and then decide later if you want to talk about it. We can stop, too. We don't have to go straight through. If you need to take a break, that's what we'll do. I can't make this easy for you, but I want you to make it as easy on yourself as you can."

She nodded again.

"Okay." His voice was firm and level. "Thinking back to the day or two before the attack. Was there anything that you noticed that didn't seem right, didn't seem usual? Maybe something you didn't attach any importance to at the time?"

She said, "You mean, around the apartment?"

"Yes, or anywhere else. Anything that struck you."

"Yes, I guess I did. At the time I wasn't sure, but I've thought about it a lot. It was as if things had been moved around a tiny bit."

"What things?"

"Lots of things. Everything. It was like when you have a houseguest and they don't quite know where things go."

"You didn't mention that to the officer who took the original report?"

"No. I wasn't sure. I mean, it seemed so strange. And what are you going to say, I mean, with three kids and I'm noticing that things aren't where they're supposed to be? The cop is going to say, this is a crime?"

"Could you tell if anything was missing?"

"Well, I wondered. There was a bra I couldn't find. I wondered if he might have taken it. I guess they do, sometimes. I don't know."

"But you didn't have any concern about someone coming in?"

"No. Nothing. God, I had no idea."

"You were asleep?"

"Yes." Her voice was tiny.

He waited a moment for her to take up the narration. When she didn't, he asked, "What time did you go to bed, do you remember?"

"About, oh, about ten-thirty. I was really tired." Again she stopped.

"And the children?"

"They were asleep." Her knees were pressed tightly together, and she crossed her ankles, legs straight out and rigid in front of her.

"They didn't wake up, that you know of?"

"*No.*" She shuddered all over, as if shaking off an awful possibility.

"What was the first thing you were aware of? The first thing that made you realize he was in the apartment?"

"When he jumped on me."

"You were asleep when he jumped on you?"

"Yes."

"You were lying how?"

"On my side."

"What happened then?"

"He put his hand over my mouth."

"While you were on your side?"

"No, he pushed me over on my stomach."

"You didn't get any sort of look at him."

"No. He was behind me."

"And then?"

She took a long breath. "He stopped my nose, too. I couldn't breathe at all. He was leaning hard onto my back. He said, 'If you make a noise, I'll kill you.'"

"Could you describe his voice?"

"Oh, it was ... it can't have been his real voice. It was hollow, like air rushing. It was ... God. It was very low." She looked confused. She glanced at Lois. "I don't know." Again she shook her head. She stirred slightly in her chair. "I couldn't breathe. I couldn't breathe at all." Her voice grew tiny again. "I was *so scared*. Oh, God, I was *so scared.*"

Lois said, "It's okay, Jean. It's okay now." Jean looked up at her, and she nodded several times. "It's okay."

Gadek waited. When she seemed a little more collected he said, "Jean, this isn't a test. Nobody can remember everything that happens on an ordinary day, let alone ... This was two years ago. Just take your time, and if you can't remember, feel free to say so. Nobody's going to be upset."

She took another deep breath and met his eyes for the first time. "Okay," she said.

He took her all the way through it.

When I got home, Sara was standing in the pool of light around the kitchen table. Heather had been baby-sitting. Her homework was spread over the whole surface, largely overlaying the strata of newspapers from breakfast, the invisible place mats, and the scoured wood surface below all.

"I just walked in the door," said Sara, smiling her friendly smile. "I'm telling Heather about the movie."

It was a suspense movie. A *suspense* movie. I spend my evening listening to Jean Hayes and I come home to hear about a *suspense* movie. Jesus, it scared me just to hear the plot. I didn't need any more suspense in my life. I got out the scotch and ice, poured a healing measure, and went and sat at the table. I didn't listen to the discussion of the movie. I thought about a stately and reassuring piece that Sara and Melanie had played together. That's what I wanted, something stately and reassuring. I went into the other room and put on the closest record we had, a noble Rameau, and returned to my chair and my glass. My eye drifted over

Heather's books. Pre-calculus. The LaFollette campaign and the plight of farmers. *Candide*. The kitchen was a warm and friendly place, home's heart, seat of hospitality and learning. People nurture each other here, and study, and within their limitations they use their human understanding to advance and support each other.

Sara was still describing the movie, interrupting her narration to fill in details she had left out. Heather was nodding and smiling, bright, fascinated. John Marshall slumbered on the window seat and Robert Peel on Heather's lap. The Rameau softened and overlaid all—warm, rational, enlightened.

We were all reflected in the kitchen window, animated in the pool of golden light against the quiet shadows behind us.

It was what someone standing outside in the darkness of the garden would have seen.

Anyone could be out there, I thought, looking in. Watching.

My face was turned to the conversation, but my eyes strained at the glass.

I shifted my position in my chair enough so that I could feel the weight of my revolver in its holster. Reassured, I got up, stretched, and drifted around to the door.

I opened it and slipped out onto the steps.

There was nobody on the grass, but there were one or two places near the back fence, behind the apricot tree, that you couldn't see from the house. Someone could be standing there. If there *were* anyone there, he couldn't miss me coming across the lawn. Still, you have to know. I sauntered diagonally down, my left side turned to the fence so that without being too obvious I could keep my right hand inside the flap of my jacket, near the butt of my .38. In a moment I would be able to see the last corner. If there was someone there I could draw and jump straight ahead toward the fence, so as to be out of the light myself.

But there was no one there.

The fence, and the kids' toys. The shadows were merely vacant, merely dark. I stepped up on the lower fence rail and took a quick look on the other side. There was no one there that I could see. But the neighbors' rear porch lights weren't much to speak of. There were places I couldn't see. I moved along the fence, stepped up on the rail again, and peered. You couldn't tell. You just couldn't tell.

"Toby?" It was Sara, standing in the doorway.

"Yes, I'm here," I called back.

"What are you doing?"

"Nothing." I got down from the fence. It was probably all right. I couldn't search the whole block. I hadn't really seen anything. I hadn't seen anything at all.

"It's okay," I said. I started back up toward the house.

"Can you take Heather home?"

"Right."

She came down to the bottom of the steps and looked around for some explanation of my presence there. "Is everything okay?"

"Yes, yes, it's okay. I was . . . it's okay."

She whispered, "Are you sober, honey? Should I take her?"

"I'm sober. I'll take her."

On the way to the carriage house Heather said, "Mom says you're working on rape cases now."

"Yes," I said.

"Right around here."

"Yes."

"God," she said. "I don't know what I'd do if that happened to me."

I glanced over at her. She was gazing at the street, visualizing, I suppose, whatever "that" meant to her. I didn't know what particulars she knew at fifteen. I wanted to tell her that she didn't have anything to worry about, but of course a woman always has something to worry about. And living in the carriage house, I thought, she had a *lot* to worry about.

"Well," I said, "I . . ."

"God," she said, not listening. "I can't imagine it. God, I don't know *what* I'd do."

She had spent the whole week with her friend. They had come by briefly once or twice to pick up clothes, but they had not done anything about putting the place to rights, and when they came on Friday evening it was just as the prowler had left it. Now they made a game of it, whooping about the prowler's interest in the things they were rearranging, and inventing ribald jokes.

In the middle of the evening she suggested that she go downstairs and make them some tea. She noticed that her friend came right with her.

Her friend spent the night and stayed most of Saturday, but had a date for the evening. It bothered her to be alone, but she thought that you mustn't let these things run your life.

She went to bed at her usual time.

She must have been asleep for some time before he entered. There was no sound, no warning before he struck, leaping heavily onto her back as she slept and clamping her nose and mouth with his easy, practiced violence. She was instantly wide awake: this was him, the one who had been through the house, who had stood by her bed while she slept, the presence who had hung just behind her all these days. She struggled ineffectually for breath, writhing in the bed under his weight, trying to free her arms, trying desperately, first to resist, then simply to live. Her heart leapt wildly, and involuntarily she voided her bladder and bowels.

It cannot have bothered him. Maybe he liked it. In any case, it did not stop him.

The next day, Sunday, was Melanie's musical brunch. The group got together privately and informally all the time to play, but three or four times a year they liked to rehearse a program and perform it for family and friends. Sara had been putting in extra time on her viola, and looking forward to it. I drove to Melanie's to pick up Heather. My mind wasn't on it. Our guy's out here someplace, I kept thinking. I kept looking around each corner, jigged a block out of the way, went clean around a couple of blocks simply because I couldn't bear not to know who was on the other side.

"I'll be with you instanter," said Heather, opening the door. "I just have to cut the cake."

"No, no," said Melanie, a little hastily. "Don't keep Toby waiting. I'll get someone else to do it later."

I ferried Heather to our house. Today she was thinking about music rather than rape. She had sheet music and her clarinet with her.

"Are we depriving you?" I asked. "Would you rather be playing with the group?"

"Oh, no," she said. "I'm getting a little tired of all that Baroque stuff: I'm going to play some Meyer Kupferman for Adam and Joss. Do you know Meyer Kupferman's work?"

"No."

"It's very advanced," she said with satisfaction.

I dropped Heather off and drove back again with Sara, who was looking a little nervous.

The carriage house looked quite different with all the large furniture pushed to the walls. There was a circle of a dozen chairs and music stands in the middle of the room, and another dozen folding chairs in among the couches and easy chairs, wherever there was room. Walt had been non-committal when I conveyed Melanie's invitation, so I was surprised to see him already there. Punctuality isn't usually Walt's long suit. He looked in plain clothes as disheveled as he looked in uniform, except less heavily armed. Lots of corduroy. But you could tell that he'd made an effort to be presentable. He had a glass of punch in his hand and had been cornered by a young woman dressed in unrelieved black who was making some technical point about the evolution of the flute, which she insisted on calling "the *flauto traverso.*" There were two reedy young men with pimples who were almost at the point of blows over the theories of a violin maker who claimed to age the tone of his instruments with microwaves. Then Melanie, who had been trying to maneuver her way over to Walt but couldn't get through, said, "Well, ladies and gentlemen, shall we?"

Everyone sat down and began to tune and play scales and little bits of things. An efficient and important-looking young person threaded her way around, putting music on the stands.

Most of the chairs were filled. There were three or four spouses and a number of friends of varying degrees. There was a dignified fiftyish fellow in a three-piece suit who seemed to be in pursuit of the larger-busted of the two cel-

114

lists, and the aged mother of the bassoonist, who sat regally on the couch where she had been placed, holding an enormous red bandanna with which it was her custom to beat out the time. I found a place opposite Sara so I could watch her face while she played, which I have always delighted in doing. Walt settled in behind me, against the wall.

Soon they started. It was something by Handel, expansive and dignified. It didn't hold me for a moment. I found myself wondering what the streets of London must have looked like at the time this was written. Worse than my own city at the present day, far worse. And yet this was what he wrote. Didn't he notice the contrast? Didn't his audience notice? Were they just rising above it? Or perhaps this was their solace? I tried to listen more carefully. A little solace seemed like a good idea.

There was another Handel, then a Bach.

"Jesus," muttered Walt at the conclusion of the Bach. "These highbrow musicians have got staying power." But as it turned out, it was the break.

Melanie said, "Toby, you do the coffee so well, would you mind? Walt, perhaps you could help me with the cake."

"Sure," said Walt, suddenly on firm ground. "I understand cake."

I made the coffee. I thought, Gadek's right. We're missing something. I can't figure out how he gets in without anyone seeing him. He opens windows right in front of neighbors' windows, but no neighbor ever sees him or hears him. Unless he's got some other method of entry—if he had some way of getting keys, for example. I wonder if Gadek's considered that. He's always just walked out and left windows and doors standing open with pry marks all over them, but maybe it's so we'll think that's how he's doing it. Maybe he's doing something sly, and he doesn't want anyone to know what it is or how he does it, so he leaves a diversion. Or, of course, maybe he's just lucky. Just incredibly lucky. But I don't think that's it. He's so careful in every other respect, he wouldn't trust to luck.

The pimply young men were soliciting the young woman in black for her views on microwaves, but she kept guiding the conversation back to the *flauto traverso,* and they took their argument to another corner. Walt and Mike had struck up a lively argument about baseball stadium design. The fiftyish fellow and the larger-busted cellist stood by a window, deep in conversation. The smaller-busted cellist, looking disconsolate, had joined the main group around the refreshments.

Of course, there was that graduate student who saw him in his neighbor's garden and didn't do anything about it. So maybe our premise is wrong; maybe people *are* seeing him but they're not getting involved. *That's* a grim idea—that he might be nabbed any old time if we just got calls from people who have something to report. But hey, there's probably something to it. It happens all the time in Patrol. You do a neighborhood check after something's been reported, someone'll say, oh, yeah, I saw this-or-that, but I never thought of calling the police.

Surely it can't all be hanging on a thread of that sort. Not that it has any practical effect on us, one way or the other—we're certainly not going to sit around and wait.

Melanie was reassembling her forces, and I resumed my seat.

There was a Bach concerto, then a short piece by Corelli. Another Corelli.

Could that be it? Is the guy doing something tricky that he wants to keep to himself? Keys would work—what else is there? But what difference would it make? There are a thousand ways to get into a house, and even if we knew how he had done it in any one case, we couldn't very well use our knowledge against him. Even supposing you could alert the whole community about that danger, he'd just do something else. Maybe he's just secretive.

They seemed to be playing a Telemann.

The bandanna rose and fell sensitively. The fiftyish fellow slept with his hands crossed over his belly, his mouth slightly open.

There must be a lot of magical thinking about a guy like that. If he's an old con he must know how many different ways there are to trip yourself up. Being systematic is the way to avoid making mistakes when you're excited, but being systematic is also a way to get caught, because once you're regular you can be predicted. That's probably it: he assumes we're trying to outguess him, and he wants to give us as little as he can, whether it seems to matter or not.

Sara was deeply concentrated on the page of music in front of her, the slightest of smiles on her lips. She doesn't have a prime viola, but prime violas cost fabulous amounts. We went to a music fair once where there was a display in one of the practice rooms of fine stringed instruments for sale. She tried out one of the best violas. My ear isn't much, but even I could hear how much better it was. She played for a while and then stopped. "Dear," she said, running her fingers gently over the belly, "maybe we should sell the car." The dealer had been sitting across the room listening to her play. He smiled very sympathetically and said, "Sell the house."

We know he often makes an entry the day before and moves things. Even if he doesn't leave an unlocked window or door for himself, he could check things out and see where the easiest, quietest entry will be when he comes back to hit. My god, what if he's inside already? What if he does something slick, say, sneaks in when the victim is at work, hides out, and just waits? Sits in a closet or something. If he made an entry the day before he could find someplace to hide, and then he's right there. Now that's creepy. It'd mean staying hidden for several hours—I wonder if he'd do that.

Still Telemann. Melanie played her flute with slight swoops and inclinations of the body, as if it were a paddle and she negotiating some intricate current in the most delicate of canoes.

What can be going through his mind? He knows we're after him. Why doesn't he quit, or go start again in some other jurisdiction? Our city borders three others, and even if we all cooperated he could give himself a big advantage by just scattering his hits around. But perhaps this is the area he knows, and perhaps he figures he's better off exploiting a well-understood routine in an area where he has a maximum of knowledge and a minimum of surprises.

The phone in the kitchen rang once.

He doesn't want surprises. He doesn't have to make a big

mistake. A bit of luck falling our way. Any little thing would do it.

The earnest young person who had been distributing music approached.

"Mr. Parkman?" she whispered. "The phone is for you."

There were photos of Melanie's family on the mantle. I pressed past them on my way to the kitchen. Strong, confident faces, even the children. Automatically I thought of William's pamphlets and that earnest little girl. It seemed to be all I was capable of thinking about these days, menace and pedophiles.

"Hello."

"Toby? Leo. Sorry to bother you. The baby-sitter gave me the number. Look, we had another hit last night. Can you break loose from there?"

"Yes."

"Good." He gave me the address. I was going to miss the Fauré. I scribbled a note to Sara and gave it to the young person. From the kitchen door a narrow path led around the house to the driveway. I found Walt and Mike slouched on the back steps next to the garbage cans. Walt was expatiating on the genius of the interlocking fields of fire in the fortress designs of Vauban.

"What's up?" he said as I passed.

"Gadek called. We've got another hit. Not liking the music?"

"Oh, the music is fine," he said. "It's the musicians." He winked at Mike, who was charmed.

"They don't seem odder than most people," I said.

"That's it," he said. "That's it exactly. Somewhere I'm hoping to find a social circle made up of people who are less odd than most people."

That seemed to me a very inconsistent ambition for Walt, of all people, but there wasn't time to frame my thought gracefully, and I headed for the street. The engine sounded raucous when it started up in the Sunday quiet. I hoped they wouldn't hear it inside.

A large house on a cul-de-sac, beautiful grounds. We found Eddie already there, and he took us through.

"It was last night. Sometime afterward she went to a friend's place. The friend called this afternoon to report it, and Blondie went to meet them at the hospital. There's been a lot of cleanup, as you see—I presume by the victim. The bed's been stripped. This mess in the fireplace seems to be the bedding and some towels—it's not all burned. I fished around in the ashes"—he indicated some charred cloth samples lined up on the hearth—"that's sheet, blanket, that looks like a piece of nightgown or pajama, that's towel. It was pretty thorough destruction. There are stains on the rug, but even those have been scrubbed, so I doubt they're usable."

"We've got no details about the hit yet?"

"Not till Blondie gets back to us. We're working blind here. There's no point of entry that I can find, but most likely the victim will have closed it up before she left. When ID gets here I'll have him dust the bedroom and hall. I don't see much point doing more until we have some idea of where he might have been. It's a big house."

"I agree."

We were having this conversation in the bedroom doorway. It was pretty much like the last bedroom. The windows were all wide open—Eddie hadn't waited for ID to dust them. Gadek looked the place over in his usual, systematic way. ID was sure to find lots of prints, almost all of one person and thus, presumably, the victim's. There didn't look like anything new. Gadek didn't need to give Eddie much direction on a job like this, but while he gave it, I thought of children on the beach, straining the sand for pirate gold; they don't find any, but it could always be in the next bucketful, and they hate to give up.

11

On Monday morning the mood in Sex Crimes was flat. Saturday night's victim had scoured away the evidence on her body. The bed sheets and what was left of her nightgown she had burned in the fireplace. On Thursday workers arrived to recarpet the bedroom. On Friday she put the house up for sale, and by the following week she was in another state, with no intention of returning.

The only new item we gleaned from this case was that the neighborhood check had produced a report of a suspicious vehicle. It was described as a small, brown, two-door sedan of foreign manufacture, generally run-down in appearance, with no front license plate. It had been seen parked up the street from the victim's house late on the evening she had been visited, and again the next night. Each time it was gone in the morning. No driver had been seen. And, of course, we had no way of knowing whether there was any connection with the series.

There wasn't room for another desk in Sex Crimes, but we maneuvered a small table into place in front of the bookcase by the window, and Blondie cleaned her sweat clothes out of one of her drawers so that I had a place for my

papers. I brought in a picture of Sara and the kids. It felt
like home. My first job in my little nest was to make up an
information sheet on the brown car, a narrative with a picture of a similar vehicle. To do this, I took the DD Auto
Mug Book, with pictures of myriad makes, models, and
years, and went through it with the neighbor who had made
the observation. After considerable hesitation among several
rather different makes and models he declined to make a
definite choice, which was discouraging. The range of indeci-
sion was sufficiently wide that using a picture was more
likely to mislead than to inform. So I produced a sheet with
no picture, as close a description as we had, and a brief
narrative of the circumstances. The sheet was headlined
"Stop & Identify," and signed at the bottom "Gadek S-19."
I dropped off one copy of this at the sergeants' office, to be
read at roll call. I went to hang another on the squad room
pillar, which is right at the top of the stairs from the parking
lot to the squad room, just opposite the door to the sergeants' office and adjacent to the window where you get
your car keys and radio for each shift. Everybody in Patrol
spends a certain amount of time right there every day, and
so it is the natural place to hang all the little bulletins that
people ought to know about. There are flyers with photos
from bank surveillance cameras, and notices from Robbery
about stolen jewelry and silverware, often with drawings or
Polaroids stapled on. There are little narratives from Homicide and Robbery with mug shots of local bad actors, headlined "Stop & Identify" or "Arrest for Cause," depending.

One of these featured a color mug shot of a truculent-looking
individual, and the narrative said:

Hi, there! My name is Dennis Layton. I like to beat
people up. Three months ago I beat up my mother
[case number, date] but she dropped charges after I
spoke to her about it because she isn't tired of living
yet. Last month I beat up one of my drug-dealing/
pimp buddies [case number, date]. He hasn't died yet,
but he may, and so that mean Sergeant Petty in Homicide *really* wants to talk to me. I don't want to talk
to him, though, and that's why I'm avoiding the Strip,

which is where I usually hang out. But I'm dumb enough to show up there one of these nights, so I sure hope the west-end beat officers don't remember this mug shot and arrest me [warrant number] for assault with a deadly weapon, aggravated battery, possession of a handgun by a felon, concealed handgun (better be caaaaaaareful!) and, if I'm lucky, murder. Also, I'm usually good for possession of controlled substances, resisting arrest, and uncouth verbiage.

There were bad-check artists, runaways, missing persons. On this occasion there was a flyer from a nearby state featuring a snapshot of an anxious-looking three-year-old boy glancing hopefully up at the camera; after retailing a highly improbable kidnapping story given by the mother the text continued: "Both parents are longtime drug users and dealers. The possibility exists that the child was taken as collateral in a drug deal, or sold for drugs." Next to this was a poster announcing the Annual Police Department Pignic, with a droll illustration of a boar hog dressed in a uniform hat preparing to sink his knife and fork into a football. I hung my sheet in the space between these last two items.

"Ready for another interview?" said Gadek when I got back.

"Sure," I said.

"Your enthusiasm has limits," he said. It was a question.

"Well, what we got from dragging Jean Hayes through the whole goddamned thing again is that yes, our guy raped her, and he stole a bra. We got no other new fact."

"Y'mean the ratio of profit to pain?"

"Yes."

"I don't know," said Gadek. "We know his hits are very consistent, and I'm sure that one reason he keeps 'em that way is safety. He's got a system going. But maybe he wasn't so smooth two or three years ago. Going through it is obviously very painful for the victims, but it's not as if they don't think about it on their own."

"No, of course not."

"Remember, I told you it wouldn't be nice."

"Yes. I'm not ... well, I was watching her expression."

"It's like the tree that falls in the forest," he said. "Her expression is like that, even if you're not there to watch it."

"I suppose it is."

"In any case, we'd feel like a bunch of dumbbells if we found out later that the key was there all the time and we were just too nice to ask for it." He looked at me for a moment, and then he said, "Are you okay?"

"Yes. Yes, I'm okay," I said, and I meant it. "I can do this if I have to. I'm not afraid of grim choices, but I want to be sure I'm doing the right thing."

"Part of what makes these choices grim is that you don't always know whether they're the right choice or not. Is that hard enough for you? But think it through. There'll go on being victims until we get him. We make our best guess and give it a try. I'm sorry if it stirs up pain. But we can't just sit here. Right?"

"Right," I said.

"And we're it. Who else is going to do it?"

I thought about it. Who else was there? D'Honnencourt? Well, he was godlike, but I knew that Gadek was smarter than D'Honnencourt. Barry Dillon? Vanderloon? No. Protect the weak. Nail jerks. He was right. I felt better.

"I'm okay," I said.

He scratched his ear. "Some crimes just aren't solvable. Who knows, this may be one of them." He turned to the list.

"I think this next interview may be harder. This was Peter Tasso's case originally. He says she's real bitter. Apparently she didn't like cops much to begin with, and she's really down on them now. We'll just have to be gentle and persistent. You can do the talking this time. Trial by fire."

She didn't say yes, she didn't say no. We were on the phone for half an hour. She was bitter, she was fearful, she was hopeful. I wore her down. I reiterated the importance of it, I assured her, reassured her, waited, sympathized, repeated. At length she agreed to let us come that evening.

I spent the afternoon comparing the fingerprints that had been lifted from the scenes of the most recent hits with the unidentified prints from earlier cases. If we could find a match from two otherwise unrelated addresses we would have our guy's prints. Unfortunately, no two sets were even close.

Thinking to surprise and delight my family, I went home for dinner. They were surprised, and would have been delighted except that Sara was making scrambled eggs. I don't like eggs. She and the kids like them, and they're a treat they have sometimes when I'm gone. Their joke was that eating eggs was something naughty that the three of them got away with behind Dad's back. My being there spoiled that, and besides, I was almost completely distracted thinking about my interview. I fixed myself a hot dog and stared at the wall while family dinnertime floundered around me.

The woman lived not far from Gadek. He walked, and met me in front of her building. "You're doing it," he said. "Introduce us both, the way I did, but don't even look at me unless you need help. Keep her focus on you."

It took more than two hours, but we got through it. At one point she said, "Locks don't mean what they used to. The windows were latched and the doors were dead-bolted. It didn't stop him.

"I used to brush my teeth and think, did I lock up? And I'd run over it in my mind—yes, I locked the front door; yes, I locked the kitchen door; yes, I went around and checked the windows. I used to run through this just about every night because I didn't want to leave things to chance. I took myself seriously. It relaxed me. I'd think, well, I'm safe. It was a good feeling, and then I could just let go.

"I never lay my head on my pillow now without thinking, it may happen tonight, again, no matter what precautions I've taken.

"I think, so long as I'm awake and alert, I have a chance. I'm defenseless as soon as I close my eyes.

"You know that wonderful feeling when you lie back and just let your weariness take you, just drifting away? Not a care in the world, just close your eyes and disappear?

"Not for me. Never once since that night. For me, every time I close my eyes I'm putting myself at the mercy of— of whoever. Whoever. It's an act of faith, and I don't have faith anymore. Just closing my eyes is the hardest thing."

* * *

"You did a pretty good job," said Gadek afterward, "but don't be quite so friendly next time. You want to come across strong unless you can see that she's reacting badly to it. More often than not it makes victims feel secure when you're assured and a little remote. They can say these things to you because you're not a part of their regular life." He grinned. "And we learned something we didn't know before. That's progress."

We had learned that our guy had a scar about two inches long on his back just below the left shoulder blade, and that he had taken a camisole. It wasn't much, but it was something.

"You press on with the interviews," he said. "You've got the system. You can strike out on your own now. Just keep me up-to-date."

The phone rang several times before it was answered. "Hello?" A trim voice. She was forty-two, but she sounded younger.

"Could I speak to Claudia Murray, please?"

"This is she."

"Ms. Murray, this is Officer Parkman with the Police Department. I hope I haven't got you at an inconvenient time."

"No." Not so trim now. "This is all right."

I explained.

She said that if I really felt I had to, I could come right then. "If I think about it, I may change my mind."

I called home.

"Honey, I've got an interview. It'll be some time."

"Oh, *Toby*."

"She said I could come right now. I'm afraid she's going to change her mind."

"Oh ... okay, sweetie. Go do it."

"I'll be home as soon as I can."

"G'bye, already. I've got to feed the kids."

"G'bye."

"It was your night to cook, y'know."

"G'bye."

* * *

"Ms. Murray? I'm Officer Parkman."

"You could fool me." She pulled the door wide open and stepped back. "I wouldn't know a real badge from a fake."

"Thank you for seeing me so soon," I said, passing in. The front door opened right into the living room. On the coffee table was a tray with wine, two glasses, a plate with cheese and crackers.

She led the way in, gesturing toward the couch, when suddenly she stopped dead, turned on me and stamped violently.

"Do you know how this makes me feel?" she hissed. "Do you have *any idea* what it's like? First I get used like a piece of *dirt,* like I'm *nothing,* and I report that like a good citizen, and I have to tell some smarmy cop *all* about it, *all* about it. And then after three years, *three* years, a *new* cop calls up and *you* want to hear *all* about it, *all* over again! Do you have any *conception* ... to dredge it all up again? What it's *like?* Do ..." She shook all over. Between panting and sobbing she recovered her breath. Then, eyes fixed on the floor, she cried, "He did *EVERYTHING* to me. He omitted *NOTHING.* I never even *knew* ... I ... before that, I never *heard* of such things." She had sunk onto the floor, pushing against it with her hands and arms as if she would scrub away the carpet.

I wondered what Gadek would do.

She had stopped talking, and rocked back and forth on her hands and knees, slower and slower, until she stopped.

You can't just leave somebody like that. I sat down cross-legged against the wall and waited.

After a time she pulled herself up so that she was sitting on her feet.

"I ..." She looked around the room as if for inspiration. Then she looked near me and said, "I must have ... You took me by surprise. I ... I've tried not to think about it. I ... you don't ... not your fault, of course."

I said, "Ms. Murray, you don't have to talk about it, now or ever. I'm not here to make you talk about it." I stood up. "I'd leave right now, leave you in peace, but—"

"Peace."

"Look, let's talk about something else for a few minutes.

Why don't you sit down someplace comfortable, and we'll just chat about something? Or would you rather I just left?"

"I put out cheese and crackers," she said, as if, having exhausted shame, I'd set about triggering some vein of guilt. "And some wine. It's been open since yesterday, but it's not so bad." She got up off the floor. "Can you drink when you're working?" She started to lead the way into the living room. "Would you like a glass of wine?"

"Well, y'know," I said, "maybe I will. You're very kind."

We sat opposite each other. She began to put cheese on the crackers. Her hands trembled a little.

"Please pour," she said. I poured, and handed her a glass. She held it up, I held mine up. She sipped. She passed the plate, which trembled. I took a cracker, she took one, we ate them. She took another sip, holding the glass in both hands.

"Okay," she said. "Shoot."

She sat the whole time curled up in the corner of the couch, knees pulled up to her chest. She had by no means told the first officer all; there was much more. Once she got going she kept right on. She would interrupt sometimes with commentary, not as a way of refusing to face something but to break the tension for herself.

She said, "You know, it's hard for me to talk about this. I've never discussed such things with anyone. I've never put these words together like this."

At two or three places she held out her glass, and I replenished it for her, two or three fingers at a time. At one point she said, "You're not drinking your wine. That's all right. You're a nice man."

What she kept coming back to, a punctuation of the familiar, dreary tale, was that somehow she could have averted it. Something she could have done differently, precautions, classes in self-defense. Perhaps he had seen her in the street wearing something ... "Y'know, you make yourself vulnerable...."

"No," I said definitely. "You had nothing to do with it. It didn't matter what you wore or how you lived."

"No? Maybe you're right," she said without conviction. "Maybe it was just him, and nothing to do with me."

She picked up the thread again, but a minute or two later

she said, "It's like, if you leave the keys in your car, maybe you deserve to have it stolen. I mean, it's not right, but you make it possible."

"No, Claudia," I said. "It's not the same thing."

"No? Maybe not."

A few minutes later she stopped again. She had told it all, pretty much. I asked a few more questions, which she answered directly. I closed my notebook and we sat for a few minutes more, talking about indifferent things.

"I had a boyfriend then," she said. "A fiancé. We were planning to get married. Perhaps you didn't know that."

"No," I said. "I didn't."

"No," she said. "Well, I did. At first he was wonderful, very supportive. But he thought a lot about it, y'know? He brooded about it. What it was like. It came to be very important to him. He didn't know how to talk about it. He didn't know what to do, whether he ought to just be matter-of-fact or very solemn. So we didn't talk about it. He helped me move, and all that, he was very good, but the real questions he was afraid of making a mess of. It made him feel helpless. I could tell he wanted to know. Know what he made me do. And he could see that I realized that he was curious and wasn't responding.

"Maybe if he'd just said, tell me about it, and put his arm around me, well, maybe I could have just done it, and then it would have been done. But he was waiting for me, and I just couldn't say, make yourself comfy and I'll tell you what it's like to be raped. I just couldn't.

"We tried to have sex once or twice, but we were both thinking about it. We had a candlelight dinner, like we did before, and I thought everything was going to be okay. Then we went into the bedroom and undressed, and all I could think about was being raped. All the things . . . I don't know what *he* was thinking about. We couldn't talk about it.

"Anyway, after a while we broke up."

Then she said, quite dry-eyed, "Why did he do it?"

I looked up, surprised. Her eyes met mine firmly. It was not a rhetorical question. She really was asking me why our guy had raped her.

"Well, Claudia ..." It seemed such a naive question to ask a cop. Ask a philosopher. Ask a priest.

"How come?" she persisted. She really wanted me to tell her. I wondered what Gadek would say. There was an awkward silence.

Her eyes closed.

Not speaking to me, she whispered, "How come it had to happen at all?"

I said to Gadek, "It's not the interviews themselves I mind so much, but afterwards I have trouble taking the rest of life seriously."

"You're doing great," he said. "Put out the sign, will you? I've got a cool call."

I wasn't doing great. I was finally getting what these people went through, and how it had changed them. I was finally realizing what it was like for them, and then turned it around and got some conception of what it would be like if it happened to Melanie or Heather, or to Sara. If it happened to us.

I was getting scared, that's what it was. But you don't say to your wife, honey, I have formed in my mind a picture of this guy doing—whatever—to Jean or to Claudia, and I have substituted Heather's face or your face for Jean's or Claudia's, and I'm just about to flip out.

So these things didn't get said, and Sara didn't know much of what was on my mind. I preferred not to have these thoughts pinned down in language between us. She must have the same preference. I haven't asked her, and she hasn't told me. We never have discussed it.

12

I've invited Melanie and Walt for dinner on Thursday," Sara said. "Just the four of us. You and Walt are both off, Melanie can come, Heather can baby-sit."

"Did you tell them what you were doing?"

"Of course. They both seemed pleased. And if they can get past all the rumples and all the starch, they have a lot in common."

Melanie and Heather arrived together. Melanie was wearing what perhaps she supposed policemen's molls would wear—a rich black silk blouse with a ruffled front, and jeans far tighter than I would have thought she would stoop to, so to speak. Square dancing costume, you might call it. She looked great. Heather, carrying a pile of schoolbooks and far more modestly dressed, gave us a cheery greeting and trotted upstairs to spend the evening with Adam and Joss.

Walt arrived wearing what he had been wearing on Sunday, that being his fancy outfit. When I saw them together, each clearly aiming to please, I knew that Sara was pushing in the right direction. They really were hopeful. They kissed each other on the cheek and smiled.

Melanie was the more practiced in the art of oiling the social wheels, and she struck at once. By the time I had brought her "very light" gin and tonic she had Walt well into the narration of one of his recent arrests, an eccentric waving a machete on a downtown street whom Walt had persuaded to surrender by besting him in a contest of quotations from certain Jacobean revenge tragedies with which he was obsessed, and which Walt happened to have read. It was a funny story which Walt told well, and he capped it by declining to tell another, bringing the conversation determinedly around to Melanie's music. She responded with equal wit and restraint. Sara and I smiled and nodded and passed cheese and crackers. It was brilliant, but not easy. I pressed another beer on Walt and made Melanie's refill a bit stiffer than before, and it must have been a testament to the strain she was feeling that she didn't protest when she tasted it. After a bit they both relaxed a little, and the evening settled to a happier, more human level of discipline.

The conversation at dinner was warm and friendly. With the coffee I poured a new brandy made by a tiny California vintner, which the wine snobs of my acquaintance were then praising to the skies and which seemed to me to be, in fact, perfectly good. Melanie led the procession back to the living room in her tight pants, and Walt followed appreciatively. I wondered what Melanie and Heather had said to each other when they were heading out the door together with Mom thinly dipped, to all appearances, in indigo. But I didn't ask.

Sara was alert for any gentle management which the conversation might require. Among the subjects she was holding in reserve was the absurdity of plots in opera, among our musical friends a traditional topic consisting of the collegial exchange of examples, in the same way that baseball fans swap statistics. She thought this would be safe. She wasn't reckoning on Walt.

"Lordy, I do get sick of it," he said with considerable asperity when *Rigoletto* was mentioned. "Here's Rigoletto, your archetypal absurd father, trying to protect his daughter by locking her up. Of *course* he's going to lose in the end; who could be in any doubt about it? Shakespeare was constantly blathering about this stuff. Molière hardly wrote about anything else, for chrissake. It's been done. How could it touch anyone?"

"Oh, it touches me," said Melanie. "There, look at Sara and Toby nodding. You don't have a daughter, Walt. These archetypal absurd fathers aren't trying to do anything that any parent wouldn't do if they thought it would work."

"It's tempting to try, even then," said Sara.

"But that isn't how you actually live," said Walt. "You don't keep Heather locked up."

"By no means," I put in reflexively.

"The streets are full of weirdos," said Walt, widening his attack, "but you still let Joss go downtown by herself."

"Heather has to make her own way in the world," said Melanie, "and if I succeeded in locking her up"—and here she smiled resolutely in my direction—"if I *succeeded*, it would only mean that she wouldn't learn how to stand up for herself when she's on her own."

"That's nonsense," I said, fairly gently, "if we're talking about your windows. That's like saying that if you don't encourage her to loll around in bars, she'll never learn how to handle rowdies. Some possibilities you don't have to try out. Some ideas are demonstrably bad, even from a safe distance."

Sara said, "A little more coffee, any—"

"You're not being fair, Toby," said Melanie. "You're really not."

"Brandy?" said Sara. "Walt, a little—"

"There is some risk attached to how we live, Toby, I don't deny it. But there are benefits as well. Heather sees the world as a beckoning place, full of possibilities. She's not timorous about things. Mike—well, Mike is different, I don't know why. But one doesn't learn the finer things living in a fortress."

"Athens was a fortress," said Walt, his eye fixed on his glass while Sara replenished his brandy. "Thanks. Rome was. Paris was."

"I didn't mean it quite so literally, Walt," said Melanie in a tone noticeably softer. "These things are in the mind. But if we're being literal, people get bars and then can't escape fires. I got that dear dog for protection, after all, and he bit me on my own hearth rug. Some things you can't lock out."

"Look, I'm sorry," I said. "My fault. Shouldn't have brought it up."

"I do appreciate your concern," said Melanie a little stiffly. Then in a noticeably more friendly tone she added, "I understand you have a different perspective on these things."

I do *not* have a different perspective on these things. It's not a matter of perspective, it's a matter of not letting airy generalizations get confused with real life. But applying that same principle to the present situation I could see that I was beaten, and I said no more.

Sara plied the coffeepot. There was a general relaxing, a folding and unfolding of legs. Eye contact was resumed on a congenial footing.

"Where were we before ... ?" said Walt.

"Rigoletto," said Sara, taking the lead. "Opera certainly does seem like a plantation of old chestnuts sometimes. But as a metaphor for your archetypal parent's mental state, Rigoletto is just right."

"Rigoletto is a perfect metaphor for your archetypal victim, too," said Walt. "He's got something that someone else wants and no impressive way to protect it. It's the law of nature. Look at the birds and the bees, all eating each other as fast as they can. There's a spider on my back porch rail with a moth or something rolled up in a cocoon, and you know what's happening: the moth's alive, and the spider goes and sucks his juice when he's in the mood. Can you imagine that? And almost the worst thing about it is that I know what's happening, I know what's going on, and I don't do anything about it. It happens all over. The world is crawling with spiders, and most of 'em have a moth, and the ones that don't have one are trying to get one. If I clean up my porch so that I don't have to watch, that doesn't mean that it isn't going on; it just means I'm not watching."

"He's going to start blaming multinational corporations in a minute," I muttered. "I just know he is."

"Oh, I hope not," said Melanie. "I have a little oil stock." There was a considerable pause.

"I wonder if it's true," said Sara ruminatively.

"If what's true?"

133

"About the spider. Is the moth really alive? That would be terrible. But I wonder if it's really like that."

"I think it is," said Melanie.

"Everybody knows that," said Walt.

"Do they? I don't know it."

"We should look it up," I said. "Maybe it's in the encyclopedia." We had just bought an encyclopedia, and I thought everyone ought to get a lot of use out of it.

"Someone would have to get up," said Walt, looking helplessly toward the bookcase.

"And anyway, Toby, Walt was speaking about metaphors," said Melanie.

Jesus H. Christ, I thought. When is she going to tell him to relax his jungle instincts? But she never did. In fact, she seemed to be encouraging them.

At a decent hour Melanie thanked us very much for dinner, gathered up Heather, and departed. Walt lingered briefly and then went off himself, seeming preoccupied.

"I got the impression that he was going to drop by Melanie's on the way home," I said as we started in on the dishes.

"So did I," said Sara. "I call that a good day's work. That brandy's pretty good, too; maybe that had something to do with it."

At the beginning of May, Gadek said, "We're not getting anywhere eyeballing the crimes. There just isn't enough there to see. I think it's time we get on the street and try to run into him. He's doing 'em so fast now he must be on the street a lot. An awful lot. Blondie and Eddie are going to start on that, beginning tomorrow evening."

Gadek wanted to talk to us all at once, so the following afternoon I did niggly things in the office until Eddie and Blondie arrived at 6:00.

"Guys," he said, "we're changing focus. The basic approach is to examine a crime for evidence, and then on the basis of what you find you identify the responsible. But our guy keeps doing crimes, we've examined them till we're blue in the face, we don't get evidence that points to anybody, and we're not getting new stuff. If we can get hold of a bad guy and connect him to any one of these cases, then we've got him. But first we have to get hold of a bad guy.

"We know he is almost always inside his victim's place by midnight, and we're pretty sure he watches for a while before going in to hit—watches the pattern of the lights going out in the living room and then on in the bedroom and bathroom, then out in the bathroom, then the bedroom, for example. So it's just about certain that if he's going to hit he's in the target area by eleven-thirty at the latest. So we're going to start working the area in plainclothes from ten o'clock to two A.M. Obviously, we're looking for the guy himself, or anyone who might be the guy, anyone hanging around, cruising, whatever he might be doing to identify his next hit. He must be doing a lot of hanging around. We're also looking for vehicles that might be associated with the series, and anyone we can connect with them. License numbers, descriptions of occupants, and so on.

"We're also going to try for a direct interception of his person. It's reasonable to assume that he's at least occasionally heard or seen, and that the people who hear or see him at least occasionally call the cops. Burglary in progress, trespasser, Peeping Tom, suspicious noises, barking dog; anything of that sort that comes in from the target area we're going to be regarding as interesting calls. It could be our guy.

"We've all gone in on that sort of thing in Patrol. Somebody calls in with a suspicious circumstance, you roar on over there, walk around the house, talk to the resident, and leave. What else can you do? It's probably nothing, but if it was something you've got no way of finding out. The guy could be under a bush right behind you and you'd never know. You can't search the whole block every time somebody hears a twig snap.

"Well, we're pretty sure our guy's a con. He's got the complex sort of method that a guy doesn't figure out all by himself. He's educated, and prison is where you get that sort of education. And considering the range of his skills, it stands to reason that he knows how cops work this sort of call. So if he hears the cops coming he probably just hops over the fence into the next yard, ducks behind something, and waits till the beat man's done his little look-around. Then he gives us five minutes to leave, and the coast is clear.

"What we're going to do is this: we will be in the area in unmarked cars and on foot, looking innocent. We'll respond to any suspicious circumstance calls in our area, not directly to the location, but near: up the block, across the street, on the other side of the block, as seems best to each of you. We will then hide: get up a driveway, under a bush, whatever. Just disappear. Then the uniforms will come in. They're going to know you're there, but they're not going to know where you are, obviously. Try to stay out of their way. When they leave, we stay as we are for at least half an hour. If the call was connected with our man, and if the uniforms drive him into cover, then when they leave he should think it's cool, and out he pops, and there we are.

"We can't clear the area for this, 'cause God knows how long we'll be doing it, so we'll just have to coexist with Patrol routine.

"We're not waiting for calls to come in so that we can respond to them. This is an active detail. We're looking for anything that might be our guy or connected with him.

"If you see anything you'll have to make your own decision how to handle it. Jumping in is the last thing. Hang back and observe, if you can. If you need a stop made, get Patrol to do it unless it's an emergency.

"Remember this, guys: even if we had the right name, we probably couldn't wrap this up. We've got chemical evidence, we've got hair samples, we've got clothing fiber. But none of it's conclusive. A DNA match—which we'll get when we have a suspect—ought to be conclusive, but the courts won't accept that technology at face value yet. It's like the early days of fingerprints: you could *say* that no two people have the same prints, but there hadn't been enough prints taken to know that for a fact, and judges wouldn't buy a fingerprint ID on its own.

"So we need other connections. If we caught him in the act, obviously, that would clinch it. If one of his victims saw him and gave us an ID in a lineup, that'd be gold dust. Physical evidence establishing a connection is more likely: I assume that our guy has evidence in his possession, and it would sure help to get hold of it. Any proof that connects a body to a crime which is demonstrably our guy's is real important.

"What we *don't* want is to grab him and scare him without being able to hold him. All that'll do is send him home to get rid of everything. If you have Patrol make a stop, be sure they give some story. Then if we cut him loose, we're not burned. Don't grab him openly unless you're sure you can hang on to him at least long enough to get a search warrant.

"The most likely thing is that even if you see him, you won't know for sure that it's him. It'll just be some guy doing something that fits the MO. So you'll be dealing with something gray, and you'll have to use your head.

"We'll try this, starting at ten tonight, and see how it works. Eddie and Blondie, you'll start this off. We've never had a call within an hour of his leaving, so if we miss his entry we might as well go on home; still, we're going to do this until two and see what we come up with.

"Between now and ten, work on your other cases. I'll be working cases or coming out with you, depending. I'll leave a note on my desk about what I'm doing.

"Toby, you've got—what?—three more interviews?"

"Maybe a couple more than that. It depends on how much time you want me to spend coaxing."

"Well, do the ones you don't have to coax too much, and then let's review it. We're not getting the hoped-for avalanche of new evidence, and time is gold. We're putting a lot of chips on this one case, and we've got all our regular load, too. Oh, in your odd moments"—he smirked, and we all laughed—"in your odd movements" I want you to pursue that idea you had about house keys. Find out where some of the victims got 'em made. If they got 'em from their landlord, then find out where the landlord got 'em. Better yet, start with the landlords—maybe you won't have to contact the victims again at all. It's conceivable that this guy's a key maker or a locksmith or something, and he's just walking in and then leaving windows open to throw us off. I don't think so, but we ought to know for sure.

"Oh, and one more thing. Tomorrow the chief's going to

have a press conference to get the word out about the series. There's not a whole lot to expect from it, because there's no new advice to give, but maybe it'll make people more alert for a few days, and that'll be something gained."

I pursued the key idea, calling six landlords and two victims. It was a bust—no two people of the first eight I called had got their keys from the same source. We dropped it, although we did not drop the possibility that his entry methods were trickier than they seemed.

The chief had his press conference. He characterized the number of hits as being "possibly dozens," because he didn't want our guy to know what we knew or didn't know, but he hoped it would sound bad enough to get the word out. And that evening thirty reserve officers—the police equivalent of volunteer firemen—trudged through the target area and contacted every residence with ground-level access. They distributed leaflets describing the series, our guy's general method of operation, and basic safeguards. It all made a good splash in the local media for a day, but then, since there was nothing new to report, it disappeared from view.

Blondie and Eddie now began coming in at 6:00, doing what work they could on the routine caseload, and then heading out around 10:00 or 10:30 into the area our guy was working to prowl and look for things that didn't fit the normal pattern of a residential district at night.

They were armed with a list of vehicles to watch for, culled from reports of suspicious cars cruising, or mentioned in neighborhood checks and otherwise unaccounted for. There were only three promising items on the list: the dark foreign sedan from the most recent hit; a car described as a "large white four-door sedan" which the neighbor of a victim had reported as having been oddly parked when she walked her dog before bedtime on the night of the hit, and which was gone when she got up to give her baby its two-o'clock feeding; and an old pickup truck, primer gray, with its headlights in necelles alongside the hood and wooden stakes along the bed. This had been seen two or three days before a different attack, and the witness in this case remembered it because it had driven off in apparent haste when she came out her front door at dawn and looked at it. There was no license number for any of them, and no occupant had been seen.

It wasn't much of a list, but it gave Eddie and Blondie something to do besides simply looking for trouble.

I pressed on with my interviews, adding to the corpus of our guy's crimes but gleaning little new information. He had a one-inch-long raised scar on his left ring finger, hardly a rarity. There was nothing that might lead us to him.

And there was the suspense of waiting for new hits. There had been three in April, with about ten days between each. Now, in early May, we were due for another, and we all had a looming sensation of events about to burst on us.

"If he's being careful, one every week or ten days is probably all he can manage," said Gadek. "He's got to identify a victim, watch her, check her out. Presumably he's got other things to do, too. He must work. If he's a con he may be on probation, and he has to keep up appearances. It must be hard work to do a lot of hits. So if there's a gap, he may just be kicking back. He may not feel like working so hard. Or, of course, he may be hitting and they're just not reporting."

Melanie called me at home. She said, "Toby, rather an odd thing happened. Walt came by last night." There was just a hint of embarrassment in her voice, which amused me.

"Oh, well," I said.

"Yes," she said, sounding a little puzzled. "Mike was in the kitchen, and he and Walt got to talking about this and that."

"Oh," I said with a note of sympathy.

"Yes," she said. "Mike is quite taken with him. Walt is very easy with young people."

"He has those Explorers, you know."

"Yes. Well, they usually chat when Walt comes over. Anyway, Mike is writing a term paper on the social history of architecture. And it turned out that Walt was full of information about fortress design and the relation of archery skills to the size of windows in the medieval period."

"Oh, he's full of information," I said.

"I gathered he knew a lot about Jacobean revenge tragedies. I'm having trouble keeping up. Anyway, they had a very animated discussion."

"Mm," I said.

"Yes. Well, of course Mike was flattered by the attention. But then all of a sudden Walt asked him if he'd like to go *target shooting,* of all things, and Mike really looked very excited—of course, he tried not to, but he couldn't hide it— and he said he'd like to. And they set a date."

"Ah," I said.

"Well, then Mike said something rather fresh about leaving us to our own amusements, and went upstairs."

"Mm."

"I explained to Walt that Mike has never fired a gun, or even held one. I don't approve of shooting." Melanie sounded positively bewildered. "He listened, and then he told me that he liked Mike and they were going to do some male bonding, which Mike needed, living entirely among women. He was quite definite about it. I made a little joke about discriminating against women, and he said that if Heather—*Heather*—or I wanted to go shooting he would be delighted to take us another time, but this time he and Mike were going by themselves."

"I see," I said.

"Toby," she said uneasily, "all I know about male bonding is what you see at the tops of newspaper features that I don't read. Is it . . . I mean, is it all right?"

"All right?"

"I mean, there's nothing . . ."

"Ah," I said. "No. No, there's nothing to worry about."

"I mean, it's not that there's anything *wrong* with . . . but Mike is my son."

"Yes, that's true."

"It's all right then?"

"Yes. Quite all right."

"I'm glad," she said. "And shooting . . . ?"

"A fine, manly interest," I said.

"Ah," she said uncertainly.

*   *   *

I came to the end of the easy interviews and sat down with Gadek to consider next steps. All the victims who still lived in the area and were willing to talk had been seen. There remained the ones who lived locally and didn't want to talk.

"Nope," he said. "Let 'em lie if they're not willing. I don't think it's worth the effort. It's not as if we thought these people could tell us anything we haven't heard already. The guy is real careful—and real consistent. If we can catch him and connect him with fifty rapes, then there's really no point going for a hundred. Nothing more will happen to him."

He closed his eyes for a moment, and then he said in that different voice he sometimes used, "I'd like to connect them all. I think those women ought to have that sense of closure."

He scratched his ear. Then he said, "But we have so little to work with. That's not the best way to use it. I wish we had . . . well, we don't, and that's that." Then he perked up and said, "Toby, we're falling behind on our regular case-load. I've got a line on a friend of William's who seems to be trying to get another kiddie porn operation going. I'll give that to Eddie. He hasn't had much fun lately. Eddie and Blondie can take turns rotating back onto a daytime schedule, and you can concentrate on the street, starting Sunday. I'm worried that you're going to get fat sitting around the office all day."

Later that same night, Friday, the dry spell, if that is what it was, ended. The forty-first victim was a young woman living alone in a basement unit in a neighborhood that he had not struck for more than two years.

The victim was half in shock when he left at about 3:30. She went into the bathroom and began cleaning up, but she was in panic at the thought that he might come back. He had disabled her phone, of course, so she ran upstairs to get her landlord to call the police. She grabbed a wrap as she went out the door but she wasn't really focused on it and didn't get it very well fastened. When the landlord came bleary-eyed to the door he found his tenant on his front porch with her robe gaping open and some wild demand for him to call the police. He was half asleep himself. He'd always had the hots for her, and he thought this "emergency" was all just a ploy to get into his bed. He let her in, but when she reached for the phone he grabbed her and started pulling off her robe. She wasn't connecting very well either, but when she realized that he wasn't simply trying to calm her down, that he was trying to make her, she just completely flipped out. She began screaming and trying to get out again. She got the door open, still screaming. He kept trying to pull her back inside, at first because he thought that was the game she was playing, and then to keep her from waking up the whole neighborhood. But the neighborhood was already awake, and there were several calls to report a woman screaming in or in front of the house in question. There were cars close, and things got stabilized quickly, but it took an hour to sort out what had actually occurred.

Sergeant Draper called Gadek at around 5:00 A.M. on Saturday. Gadek called me, because although it was my day off, Eddie and Blondie had been on the street until 2:00. I met him at the scene at about 5:45. The beat man had taken the victim to the hospital, but Sergeant Draper came by and filled us in. We listened, conferred, and then I began the gathering process.

"There's no time like the present," said Gadek cheerfully. "Things dry up, they get stepped on. It only changes for the worse. So begin sorting things out. The ID tech comes on at eight, and you'll be first on his list." He scratched his ear. "I hope he's not expanding his area. We're overextended as things are." He went off to the hospital to take the narrative.

13

Saturday hadn't been much of a day off, but on Sunday I didn't have to report to work until 6:00 in the evening ("Please don't say 'eighteen-hundred hours' to me in my own kitchen," said Sara), so we took the kids into the hills for a picnic.

"I want to lie in the sun with my head in your lap," I said. "It's healing."

"You're not wounded just at present," she said, laughing. "You don't need to be healed. But the kids need to play Frisbee." It seemed, in fact, that they did need to play Frisbee, and we played quite vigorously for a while.

"Take off your sweatshirt, Dad," said Joss. "You're sweating." She burst into giggles.

"*Sweat*in' in a *sweat*shirt, *Dad, Dad,*" chanted Adam.

"Relax your jungle instincts and enjoy the day," called Sara. She burst into giggles, too.

I gave her a little warning shake of the head. I couldn't take it off. She came over.

"Honey, are you packing? For heaven's sake, it's a picnic. What's going on?"

"I don't know," I said. "I just stuck it in my belt."

*　　　*　　　*

143

In theory we got a dinner break in each shift, but dinner tended to get lost amid the whirl of events. Since I would have to be at the station by six on the nights I had street duty it seemed prudent to eat at five. In future, the kids could eat with me at five, or wait to eat with Sara. She's the better cook, but she doesn't often get dinner on the table before seven.

Once when I was a rookie I went around all night carrying a revolver I'd forgotten to load. When I got home I was taking my gear off and telling Sara about the night's excitement when I opened the cylinder to drop the cartridges out and nothing came—well, she had a fit. The next night she insisted on watching. This turned into a ritual, and we've done it that way ever since. We go to our bedroom and chat about anything other than crime or the law. We have three pistols: the long-barreled .38 revolver I carry when in uniform; the more compact .38 snub-nose I carry when working plainclothes; and the .22 magnum derringer I carry in either role. When they're not in use, we keep them in a metal lockbox in our bedroom closet. While we talk, I open the box and bring out all three guns. In the bookcase we keep a handful of hollow-point cartridges in a little oval wooden box, hand-painted in the old world by one of Sara's forebears. The contrast of the quaint container and its contents—hollow-points expand on impact and create ferocious wounds—seems symbolic of the defense of house and home, grim or droll according to our mood.

In DD I was working plainclothes, so Sara loaded the long-barreled revolver. The cartridges made an almost inaudible hiss as they slipped into the cylinder, with a soft little click when they were seated. The cylinder closed with a gentle snicking noise, and she put the pistol on top of the tall bookcase, where it was out of sight but easy to get at. She would keep it accessible until I came back. Sara learned to shoot after I was sworn—primarily, I think, to prove that she wasn't a snob. Without any macho complications in her attitude, she learned quickly, and does it rather well.

Then she passed me the box and watched me load the .38 snub-nose. It makes her feel secure to see me do it. It's as close as she gets to superstition.

Besides the .38s in the box there were some smaller .22 magnums, and with these I loaded the derringer I carry as a backup weapon, and put it in the hip pocket of my jeans. Every cop's nightmare is to be disarmed in a tussle and watch helpless while some gloating jerk points your own weapon at you and opens fire. Hence a backup gun—a poor second chance, but something instead of nothing.

There was a melodramatic aspect to all this, of course, but I was leaving my family to chase a rapist who watched his victims to make sure they would be alone. Our house was well inside his working area. He had never hit a house with a resident man, except by mistake. He might make another mistake. Or he might know, somehow, that I was a cop who was working shifts during his chosen hours, and decide to play a little joke. A man who would rape forty women, Sara would say brightly, is not a man to be trusted.

Sara could be cheerful, but more and more I began to think how easily something might go wrong—it happens all the time. She doesn't carry the pistol around with her everywhere. If he got into the house, she might not be able to get back to it. She's not a big girl. It would be no contest.

On the way to work that day I noticed the cover of the regional free paper, *Shout*. This was a periodical notable for the unbuttoned nature of its classified sex ads and the virulence and ungenerosity of its editorial content. Sexual license and political bluenosing seem to be an irresistible combination. I don't know why that should be so. The cover showed a dark shadow falling across a voluptuous sleeping woman, and the headline said, SEVEN VICTIMS—AND WHERE ARE THE COPS?

The article was as bad as the cover. It was about a woman who worked at a rape counseling center. The counselors had begun comparing notes. They found a pattern and decided that they had no fewer than seven victims who had all been raped by the same man. Our guy, in fact. They called a press conference. Only *Shout* sent a reporter, but it was bloody. All sorts of charges were made. This being a radical group, the idea was that men don't object to the rape of women and keep it all hushed up—something like that. Our press officer (described as "a Country & Western vision in polyester and sideburns") was quoted as saying that the police were aware of the series, and referred to the chief's recent press conference on the subject, but would have no further comment. Gadek was not mentioned, nor was the leaflet detail. There was a good deal of misinformation in the article and, fortunately, a great deal of omission. There was also a lot that would certainly give us grief in the future, all sorts of details about the rapes themselves—our guy's sexual tastes, his perversities—which it could help nobody to know but would make police work a great deal trickier. Taking it all in all, I thought it was a bad development.

Blondie thought it was a good thing.

"It'll make people more conscious," she said. "Maybe they'll lock up better."

"It'll make *him* more conscious," I said. "And locks don't stop him, apparently."

"Maybe folks'll keep their eyes open."

"Perhaps."

"And maybe it'll unstick some more money from somewhere and we can get some more people."

Blondie and I divided the target area into northern and southern halves, hers and mine. For the most part, we would just prowl around and see what we could find. If there were any hot calls for us to respond to, she would always cover from the north and I from the south, even if we had to circle around to get into position. That way we wouldn't be tripping over each other. We appointed a rendezvous for midnight.

I drove north from the station into the target area. I was wearing jeans and a field jacket bulky enough to conceal my snub-nose .38, a dozen extra cartridges, the .22 derringer, a radio equipped with an earplug rather than a speaker (for silence), a flashlight, handcuffs, a small dispenser of tear gas, badge, and notebook. I had sewn a couple of large, stout pockets inside under the armpits to help accommodate all this.

My first night on the street was not altogether novel. You do a certain amount of prowling in Patrol, in the quiet periods between calls. But Patrol officers get lots of calls, and most of their time is spent responding to something or other. Although Patrol cars are solo they are typically concentrated at any dangerous moment, and the experienced ear gleans from the almost continuous radio traffic a vivid sense of what all the different members of the watch are doing. The shape of your working day is frequent comings and goings, meetings and partings. You lead a teeming tenementlike life without privacy, passive almost to the point of being without personal volition, always called away to some new emergency. You are glued to your car, which for the shift is nested with your gear. Getting mobile, staying mobile, staying in touch, are the Patrol officer's first principles. And you will find yourself in one of those unsettlingly quiet moments which fall in the middle of the busiest night, suddenly gunning your black-and-white down the street for no reason at all, like a horse pawing at the gate, waiting for the gun.

A Patrol car is a noisy place. The window is rolled down so you can hear what's going on ("You can always tell who won't make it past probation," Sergeant D'Honnencourt had intoned at orientation. "It's the one who rides around trying to be a cop with the window rolled up: a contradiction in terms"). The heater fan is roaring, like as not, in the middle of the night, and the radio is turned up loud enough to be heard over everything else. By contrast, the corner where I began walking was silent at a quarter past ten. I put the earpiece in my ear and turned on my radio. It was a tiny, personal sound. The radio traffic seemed disconnected from me: whatever trouble 42 and 131 got into with their drunks in the street, I wouldn't be flying across town to succor them. After twenty minutes, the cackle, which in a black-and-white seems like the breath of life, became a background noise. The silence of the nighttime street muffled it, the sound of my footsteps in my open ear drowned it out.

Now and then a passing car, carefully noted. Mostly, silence.

And to be looking for one man.

Not racing to a succession of hot calls, not looking loosely for whatever suspicious or questionable observation might obtrude itself, but to be looking only for one man of unknown appearance.

After half an hour it began to seem very personal. The department, the watch, my platoon, which I visualize as a tight cluster of cars roaring through the gate of the yard and striking out into the city like a pulse of blood from the heart, warm, pressured, busy—the Constitution, the Supreme Court, the sergeants' office—it all faded into the tiny hum in my ear. They're not involved.

Here am I; where is he?

So quiet on the street, nothing to distract, nothing to take away from my personal contest with this guy. What's he thinking tonight, right now? What's in his mind? I began to wonder what he would look like from a distance, how he would move.

At this next corner, turn right? Or left? What if he's one, and I take the other? The guy's human, he's visible to the eye. He comes into the area in a car or on foot, he watches from somewhere. He slips plastic into doors that aren't dead-bolted, he's a champ at windows. But he has to stand right there to do these things. So he can be seen. If he's hitting tonight, he's got to be around. He's hit this early; hell, it's almost eleven-thirty—he's usually in by this time.

I found myself walking faster, to cover more ground, and then for no specific reason stopping, listening, waiting to hear—something. But I didn't.

At midnight I met Blondie in the parking garage of a small building right between our areas. We had no business, but Blondie was my friend, and I was Blondie's friend. Our guy could be almost anybody on the street. It was pleasant to spend fifteen minutes with someone you know you can trust.

"I've been thinking," she said. "If we're right that he's a con, it might explain some of the cruelty. Rape in prison is all about dominance and revenge. Of course that's against other men, but that's part of the point, part of what's degrading about it."

"You mean to treat a man like a woman," I said.

"Yes. Now we won't go into what that says about the way men think of women, 'cause I try not to think about things like that while I'm armed."

"A good choice," I said.

"But it's an attitude he could bring back to life outside."

Out of our old habit from Patrol, we stood facing each other a trifle obliquely, looking over each other's left shoulder so that no one could approach us unseen. The garage echoed, so we whispered, as if we were the guilty ones.

I ran into Walt passing through the squad room.

"I'm sorry we don't get to do dinner break these days," I said.

"Yeah, I am, too. I miss Sara's casseroles. No, really."

"Yes. Well, I hope you're getting some cooking other than your own."

He gave me a considering glance, then looked away.

"Yeah, well, as a matter of fact, I've been dropping by Melanie's."

"Ah. Really?"

"Yeah, as a matter of fact." He scratched his chin thoughtfully. "She said that since she was right on my beat and all, it made sense, y'know."

"And?"

"Well, she *is* right on my beat."

"True. Very true. She is." We nodded sagely. She *was,* after all, on Walt's beat. Then I said, "How'd the shooting go with Mike?"

He smiled happily.

"Pretty well. Really pretty well. He'll make a good shot if he can relax. I started him out on tin cans at short range, y'know, a lot of noise and visible results. He liked it. He likes me. It's a pretty flattering feeling."

I thought I would spare him Melanie's reservations. I said, "Well, that's great."

"Yeah," he said. "God*dam,* he's an anxious kid. Not to talk to, y'know, but when he *does* something. He's gotta be an ace, right from the get-go."

"You may be right," I said. "I've never seen him do anything. Still, it's nice if the two of you hit it off."

"Yeah," he said. "It really is."

And then, because the conversation seemed to be flagging, and Sara would want to know all the details, I said, "Good cook. Melanie, I mean."

Stan Washburn

"Yeah," he said, and looked vague. One of Walt's endearing characteristics is that he doesn't discuss his love life if there is anything to discuss. I inferred from his brevity that their love was prosperous.

"Good," I said. "Glad to hear it."

"Yeah," he said. "Good. Good."

"Good."

14

The story in *Shout* was making waves in City Hall. Stories like that can become issues. The mayor was up for reelection in the fall, and she was worried. Three activist groups announced a community meeting whose purpose would doubtless be to denounce the cops. It would be a lively evening for the press officer, who would have to attend.

Gadek was pleased.

"This is eating us up. What we've gotta have is a task force to work on the series and nothing else. Half a dozen people."

"It doesn't seem likely," I said. "You barely got me, let alone half a dozen."

"Things change," he said. "Politics. If there's pressure, maybe the brass will be more receptive. I'll go talk to the lieutenant again."

Perhaps the brass were in a receptive mood. No doubt they were getting pressure from above as well as suggestions from below. But whatever their reasons, they moved quickly. Two weeks after the *Shout* article, word came down that a task force would form. It would be dedicated to the series and nothing else. But by a quirk of seniority it was not Gadek who was to command it, but Barry Dillon.

"What?" said Blondie.

"You're kidding," said Sara.

Sergeant D'Honnencourt was seen at his desk with his eyes closed and one hand pressed to his temples as if he had a headache. But of course he might have been thinking about something else.

"I have the greatest respect for Barry," I overheard Sergeant Vanderloon saying on the phone, "but his own mother wouldn't have said he was equal to this. Any pecking order that gives this responsibility to Barry in preference to Leo has something wrong with it, by definition." This seemed to be the general opinion. But from the tone of voice people used you could tell that it was a mistake that wasn't going to be unmade.

Gadek and Eddie were to remain in Sex Crimes. Blondie and I were assigned to the task force.

"I'm sorry you won't be doing this," I told Gadek.

"I am, too," he said. "But I'll be around. I'm not running it, but I'll be in the picture."

"Leo, do you think Barry . . ."

"Yes. You work as hard for him as you have for me. If you all do that, Barry'll do just fine."

Walt and Melanie and Sara and I sat in the garden that weekend and drank espressos and discussed the whole thing several times. Walt took the view that things will be done sloppily and for the wrong reasons, and we shouldn't get all het up about it. Sara thought that the right thing was being done, although in the wrong way and for the wrong reasons, and that that was better than the right thing not being done at all. Melanie and I maintained that people and institutions ought to act for the right reasons, and not because the mayor wanted another term. We didn't settle it.

Walt and Melanie certainly seemed to be making progress. They didn't do much billing and cooing, but increasingly they seemed to speak in the multilevel shorthand which people use who spend a lot of time talking to each other. Walt and Mike had gone shooting again. They returned grubby and happy, Melanie said, amused. She seemed almost reconciled to their activities; at all events, she told Sara how delighted she was that Mike had a man to look up to, rather than his father.

The task force was given its own office on the third floor of the Hall of Justice. There was a large, cheerful room with several windows and a vista of treetops. There were six desks around the walls, and in the center a conference table. There was a place for a secretary by the door, a private office, and a windowless interview room.

Apart from Barry, Blondie, and me, there were three new people: Myron Fry, Patty Dwornenscheck, and Charlie Footer. I knew Fry from the Magician detail, and Patty from Patrol. Footer I knew only by reputation: he was regarded as a brilliant investigator, but without practical judgment.

"Have you ever talked to Footer?" I asked Patty as we headed up the stairs for our first meeting.

"Nah, but I've heard stories."

"He sounds like a very odd duck," I said.

"We're talking about his personal life, right?" said Patty. "There are tales, Parkman. There are tales. He glommed onto Miranda Pocock almost the first time she walked into the squad room. She was real impressed and went out with him. She had trouble describing him, but she was using Sherlock Holmes and Attila as comparisons. They had a couple of drinks before dinner, and when he wasn't trying to run his hand up under her skirt he was making puns on her name. He said *his* cock wasn't so po—that's the one she could remember. She broke down and took a taxi home, and the entrée hadn't even come yet."

"Great," I said.

"Well, c'mon, Parkman," said Patty. "Don't be such a prig. Everybody says he's a super detective. And he isn't going to come on to *you*. At least, from what Miranda said you wouldn't think so."

We were ordered for 6:00 P.M. It was just like roll call, except that our table was shrunk. Barry sat at the head, but instead of the Daily Bulletin he fingered a sheaf of miscellaneous papers. His face was a little flushed, and he looked nervous.

"Guys, I'm easy to get along with," he said. "All I ask

is"—and here, with a broad smile, he hesitated—"that you bust your butts."

Clearly, he had rehearsed this speech. We all chuckled politely.

"Because if we don't nail this guy, the chief will bust mine."

Another pause, another chuckle, slightly smaller. But that was it. Apparently he had felt some introduction to be in order, and had managed to come up with those two lines. He turned to the papers in his hand with evident relief.

There were housekeeping matters, schedules of hours and days off. For the most part, we would be working nights.

Then he turned to our work. He had made copies of Gadek's charts and pinned them to the walls of the interview room. We all crowded in and followed while he ran over the background of the series, pointing here and there. It was fascinating to watch Footer. He was wound like a spring, sitting or standing, one leg or the other jittering unceasingly from the ball of the foot, listening to the briefing. His eyes would dart around and batten on whoever was speaking while his head angled around less abruptly and stopped with one ear or the other tilted a little forward. Sometimes he smiled suddenly for no apparent reason and then glanced around as if he felt he'd betrayed his train of thought and wanted to know if anyone had noticed. Once our eyes met; he grinned, nodded toward Patty's fanny, and pantomimed giving it a pinch.

Barry's presentation was reassuring; he had studied the cases one by one and knew them pretty well. He talked for an hour, a little stiff, like a student reciting, but full of detail and anecdote. It wasn't new information for Blondie and me, but it was for the others. Several times he flattered the two of us by asking for more information.

"I'm just the new kid on the block," he said, laughing. "If you want to know something, come to these two. But you'll all know it soon enough."

When he was done with the background he said, "Now, people, the question is how we're gonna nail this guy." But it wasn't a question, the way he said it. It was a statement, and he looked truly happy and relaxed for the first time since he had come into the room.

We trooped back to the table. I thought, He can't help being nervous. It's not like Patrol; it's his first independent command. But operations he knows like the back of his hand. He ought to be all right.

"We're going to add a new approach to our street work," said Barry, "and try to find his car. This is Leo's idea—he didn't have the people. Now we do.

"It's just about certain that if he's going to hit he's in the area by eleven-thirty at the latest. Assuming he drives, there's no reason why he should park far from where he hits. So on the nights he hits, his car should be somewhere in our target area. What we're going to do is drive up and down every street in the area and tape-record the license number and description of each and every car, beginning at midnight each and every night. If we get a report of a hit, we quick go back and rerecord every license, and see who was on the first tape but isn't on the second one. A fair number of cars may have been taken out, especially if we don't get the report in until people start leaving for work in the morning. But most of 'em ought to check out pretty easily. The cars that aren't registered in the area are the ones we're interested in."

"Won't that take all night?" asked Fry.

"No," said Barry. "Leo tried it. If two people do it, it ought to take about forty-five minutes.

"While you're waiting for calls, you'll cruise. You know what you're looking for. Blondie and Myron will be a team, covering the north half of the area. Toby and Patty, you two will cover the south. Charlie will be covering for anyone who can't make a shift, and when he isn't covering he'll be running down whatever leads we've got going, and working day or night as necessary."

"Or both," said Footer.

"Or both," said Barry. "I'll be overseeing and working with Charlie, on flex hours.

"We have some new concerns to bear in mind when we're on the street. From now on, we're going to assume that he's listening in on the police band. Just assume that every word you say on the air is said right to him. If you need a stop made, go over to Channel One. Ask for cover and give the location. The desk knows who you are, and they'll send in uniforms. To anyone listening in on our frequency it'll sound like a routine stop-and-cover situation. Again, make every effort not to go near the stop yourselves. We don't want every creep in the city to know that there's a plainclothes operation going in that area. Word gets around. We don't want to burn this operation.

"If our guy's smart he's gonna pick up on the fact that Patrol isn't using Channel Two. He's gonna know that means that Two is reserved for a special detail and there's something going on. It could be a dope bust or a hooker bust or God knows what that has nothing to do with him, but he knows we're after him. He's got a guilty conscience and he's going to worry that if there's any special unit on the street, it's devoted to him. So be *very* circumspect on the air. Don't say *anything* on the air that can wait until you can say it face-to-face. Never mention the task force, or the fact that there are plainclothes units on the street. Never mention street names or addresses or any landmarks that would give away the area we're working. He obviously knows the area like the back of his hand, and he'll pick up on real subtle stuff, so don't think you can get away with being clever.

"Never mention the series. Never say, 'I can't talk on the air,' because he'll wonder what it is that you can't say. The less air traffic the better. Questions? Oh yes, Blondie and Myron will do the first recording tonight. Blondie do east-west streets, Myron do north-south. After that, we'll switch off. When we get calls, Blondie and Myron will cover north and east; Toby and Patty will cover south and west. Now, questions?"

There were detail questions, but it was all pretty clear. When we broke up I went around the table and introduced myself to Charlie Footer. He shook my hand, said he'd heard good things about me and he was glad we'd be working together. I was flattered. He grinned nervously.

There was a pause. He looked at the floor, then at me, grinned again, looked at the floor again. Then, seizing on a conversational inspiration, he said, "Hey, y'know what a woman is?"

"Well, I . . ."

"A life-support system for a cunt!" He smiled, suddenly, brilliantly, and scanned my face keenly for indices of delight.

"Ah." I temporized. "Well, ah . . ." But fortunately Barry shooed us away to the street.

Patty was taking no chances. Her 9-mm automatic was in her belt holster, she had a snub-nose .38 in a shoulder holster, a lipstick-size tear gas in her jeans, and a lead-loaded sap in her jacket. I had my snub-nose .38 and my usual .22 magnum derringer and tear gas, but I thought the sap was putting on the ritz, and I gave her a bad time about it. We also had to carry flashlights, handcuffs, daybooks, and radios. We counted ourselves lucky that the nights get chilly, and it looks normal to wear a jacket bulky enough to conceal all the lumps.

We took my car, a nondescript station wagon. I had folded down the back seat and put several pieces of baby furniture in the back. This was a device calculated to convey innocent preoccupation. When as a trainee (and therefore an unfamiliar face) I had been sent out to buy dope and prostitutes I had used it to great advantage in disarming their suspicions. Perhaps dopers and hookers don't associate cops with children. Or perhaps experience leads them to think that any family man must naturally be hooked on vice.

We drove to the center of our cruising area and parked. We had decided that a moonstruck couple would be the most disarming cover. Patty took my arm in a chummy way and we sauntered up and down the streets. We went a long block west, two short blocks south, then two long blocks east, and so on. This way we were never more than two blocks or so away from our car, in case we had to go mobile in a hurry. When we finished this square we would drive two long blocks west and start again.

We were looking for cars on our list, or any cars that seemed to be cruising—any car, in other words, which didn't seem to have some clear errand; anyone hanging around, or sitting in a parked car, or doing any work that seemed

157

Stan Washburn

improbable or inappropriate and that might therefore be a
cover for hanging around. Anyone working on a car who
didn't have an obvious connection with a residence, again,
because it might be a ruse. Any pedestrian who appeared
more than once. Any pedestrian who seemed to be paying
unusual attention to the houses, or who simply seemed more
alert than pedestrians usually seem. Or anything else that
seemed to us not right.

If there was something we wanted to observe we would
stop wherever we were and lounge, pretending to be in conversation. Lovers can do what they like without exciting suspicion. We could sit on steps and walls, lean against
telephone poles or trees, or simply embrace in the open if
that would give us the best view. We agreed that since
women are less threatening to men, I would turn my back
and Patty would surveil over my shoulder.

We found little to observe. Between 11:00 and 2:00 there
isn't much to see on the street, and what there is really grabs
your attention. Cars seemed merely intent on getting from
place to place. Pedestrians passed us, intent on exercise or
business, self-absorbed. There was no suspicious activity, and
little activity of any kind.

Shortly after midnight we saw Blondie moving slowly
along the street in a clean green sedan, recording license
numbers. She had to drive the length of each street twice,
recording the numbers on one side at each pass. It seemed
painfully slow, and although you couldn't tell exactly what
she was doing, she was clearly doing something that had to
do with being attentive to cars.

A few minutes later Fry passed at right angles. He seemed
just as obvious. I didn't like it. You didn't need a very long
nose to know that something was going on.

"Jeez, Parkman," said Patty, the third time we saw Fry,
"let's hang a sign on him: 'Your Tax Dollars At Work.' "

We passed Walt, whose beat it was, ticketing a fireplug
violation.

"What gives?" Patty said. "Did somebody call a parade?
It was all so quiet ten minutes ago. Suddenly the place is
up to the eyeballs in cops. Our guy's a nut, but he's not
stupid. He's gonna take one look at all this and go home."

But a moment later we rounded a corner and found ourselves following a serious subject. You couldn't miss it, the way he was moving. He was walking slowly and irregularly up the street, peering up each driveway with great attention. Once or twice he walked several steps up driveways, then retreated to the street. He didn't linger under streetlamps, and he definitely liked bushes and hedges.

"D'ya see his elbow?" Patty murmured, pulling herself in close beside me. He carried his right arm close to his side, and from time to time he made a little rubbing motion with his elbow against his waist.

"Yes, I see it." It's a habit people fall into who are carrying a concealed pistol: they rub it with their elbow to make sure it's still there. They think they're being sly because they don't put their hand on it.

The man was staring up another driveway. Clearly, in a moment he was going to look back down the street. I stepped in front of Patty and pulled her up to me. You couldn't see her eyes at all in the shadow of her hair.

"Just in time. He's looking back. He's staring at us. Okay, he's going on up the driveway. No, he's coming back down. He's stopped. He's looking again. He's going up to the house again. He's standing in the shadow by the corner of the driveway. He's waiting for us to clear out."

We couldn't stand there all night. I eased up. I'd never quite registered before how well-built she was.

"Let's go past," she said steadily.

"Okay, let's." We strolled slowly up the street, with Patty on the curb side so she would have an excuse to look toward the houses.

"He's right where he was," she breathed as we passed.

"When we get a couple of doors on, pretend to tie your shoe. I'll stand in front of you, and you can call the desk for a stop."

"Jeez, Parkman, why don't we get out of sight and then come back? We might get something."

"He's seen us. If we come back he'll make us. And if he goes any farther up the driveway we can't see him anyway. We may lose him altogether."

"Okay," she whispered, and then in a normal voice, loud

on the quiet street, "Oh, jeez, my lace is broken." She knelt down. I stopped between her and the subject. She fished under her jacket and came up with the microphone of her radio. It took one hand to use the radio, and clearly she couldn't do lace-tying business.

"Here," I said out loud, "let me." I knelt beside her and fiddled with her shoe.

Burrowing in her coat she said, "Control, 62." She called for cover on the stop of a suspicious individual, and gave the address. It was worded in the standard form of a Patrol officer who is about to make the stop herself and simply wants backup.

"62, Control. Acknowledge. Any car to cover?"

There was a scratchy bit of transmission as several cars answered up. Everyone knew that 62 was doing whatever was being done, and wanted to get in on it.

"37, I'm close."

"37, take it. 118, were you in there?"

"118, that's affirmative."

"Okay, 118, why don't you drift over that way too. ETA?"
"Three blocks."

It wouldn't be long, and we wanted to be out of sight. We concluded the shoe-tying business and strolled on a little more briskly. We were half a block up the street when the first Patrol car ghosted past us, Able Miyasaki coasting in with his engine turned off and his lights out.

There was a large bush on the parking strip across the street. We sauntered hurriedly across and watched from behind it as Miyasaki's car pulled up two doors short of the house, its brakes quite loud in the silence. The door flew open. We couldn't see the subject from where we were, but clearly he and Miyasaki had seen each other, because the car's searchlight suddenly shone up the driveway. Miyasaki stepped out into the street.

"You in the driveway!" he bellowed. "Step out here right now!"

There was a roaring and screeching audible for blocks as the other car, Henry Lomus, burst around the corner, high beams on, engine revving, and seeing the stop in progress lurched to a halt diagonally across the street so that its lights also shone up the driveway and illuminated several lawns. Lomus left his engine running as he jumped out, and his car radio turned up high. Both were plainly audible up and down the street. Lights began to come on in neighboring houses.

"Keep your hands out where I can see them!" Miyasaki was still several yards away from the subject, who had come back to the corner of the house. Lomus sprinted up onto the lawn to take him from the flank.

"You! Straighten out your right hand! I can't hear you! Straighten out your right hand! Stop right there! Hey!" The man was lurching forward. *"Police! Stop right there."*

Lomus and Miyasaki had both drawn, crouching slightly, holding their automatics in two-handed grips. Miyasaki quickly stepped forward to the street side of a parked car and took cover behind it. Lomus retreated a bit, but there was no cover for him. The man stopped, squinting hard into the lights, looking back and forth between Lomus and Miyasaki.

"Lie down!" bellowed Miyasaki. *"Put your hands in front of you and lie down."*

Patty and I were sprinting back across and down the street in case we were needed. The man began to lie down. Suddenly the porch light came on, the door opened, and a middle-aged couple stepped out into the blaze of headlights. They were above the man, but they were directly in Miyasaki's line of fire.

"Police!" he shouted without changing his aim. *"Get back inside! Right now!"* The couple looked bewildered.

"You on the porch! Get inside! You will be shot!" The man turned and collided with the woman. For a moment they looked at each other. Then they looked again at the street and went inside.

The man had never got flatter than his hands and knees, and now he was getting back up. Patty whispered into her mike, but her transmission thundered out from Lomus's car, *"Control, 62, we'll take two more."* We hovered just outside the pools of light, ready to intervene, but Miyasaki was doing very well.

"You! Lie down flat! Down flat! Put your hands out in front of you!"

The street was lighting up. Windows were filling with heads.

He was down flat now. Miyasaki and Lomus were advancing, weapons forward.

"Cars on 62's stop. Neighbors report subject has two accomplices hiding in the bushes just east of there. 17, 45, 19, copy? Man and woman in dark clothes is all I've got."

"17 copy. I'm close."

"Jeez, Parkman," murmured Patty. "That's us. We'd better blow outta here."

"Just a sec," I said. "Till Miyasaki has him."

Miyasaki got the man in a wristlock as I spoke and was slipping over and behind him as he lay prone; Lomus stood covering. They were firmly in control. It was time to slip away, but there was the roar of engines from up the street, the screech of brakes, and Walt, much too good an officer not to see us in the shadows, and not quite omniscient enough to know who we were, had got us in his searchlight.

"17, I've got the other two just east of the stop. I'll"—he recognized us—*"Oh shit."*

"Oh, Jeez."

"S-16 to all cars." It was Sergeant Bridey. "Unprofessional language on the air will not be tolerated. 17, see me when you're mobile."

Miyasaki was extracting a long wrecker's bar from the man's sleeve.

Walt came over to us.

"I guess you guys want to get out of this."

"ASAP, but cool."

"Right. Let me frisk you." A growing cordon of neighbors watched with interest while he passed his hands deftly over our many weapons and put us in the backseat cage. There were now five cars dumped higgledy-piggledy over the street, doors open, lights on, engines idling, radios blaring. Walt backed hastily up to the corner, turned into the side street, and returned us to our car. It was blissfully quiet.

"You detectives have all the fun," he said. "I never get to do anything hush-hush." He chortled a deep chortle.

"Thanks, pal." I smiled. "Enjoy your chat with Sergeant Bridey."

"Shi—"

"Thanks again, Walt," said Patty. "It's been real. We gotta run."

As soon as we were mobile we cruised back past the stop. The whole neighborhood was in the street. Lomus was talking to the residents of the house. The man was in Miyasaki's cage car. Miyasaki was holding the wrecking bar and a large revolver. At the other end of the block we could see Fry's car stopped in the street. He was still recording license plates, and he couldn't get past.

"I don't think that's our guy," I said.

"Nah—crude operator. But it was a righteous stop. He was sure up to something."

"Let's check in with Blondie." I waited for a hole in the air traffic. "122, 93. Location to meet?"

"93, 122, the usual."

"What's 'the usual'?"

"The rear parking lot of the supermarket. It's convenient to both halves of the area. The market's open twenty-four hours, so there are always cars in the lot, and a couple more don't attract attention."

"Jeez, Parkman. Us gumshoes know all the tricks."

Blondie was parked in the middle of a dimly lit corner of the lot when we arrived. I pulled in next to her, facing the opposite way.

"That sounded really neat on the air," she said. "That sounded really unobtrusive. And the two accomplices that Walt got ... ?"

"That was us. We were keeping an eye on Miyasaki and Lomus."

"Well, live and learn. But if we bust twice as many cops as crooks each night I predict a quick death for this whole operation."

"Y'know," I said, "I just noticed—the way we're parked."

"Yes?"

"Like cops. Any con would know that two cars parked like this is cops."

We both started up, parked properly a couple of spaces

163

apart, got out, and lounged against Blondie's car. "So what did you think about this citizen you got?"

"Not our guy," I said.

"No way," said Patty. "Bumbling around. Not a smooth operator. We were right behind him and he didn't see us until he'd already started to make his move."

"Also, he was looking for an opportunity. Our guy would be doing some unobtrusive surveillance, or he'd be moving on something he'd already thought out, but he wouldn't be . . ."

"He wouldn't be bumbling," said Patty.

"Doesn't sound terrific," said Blondie, "but after I finish recording my streets I'm going to go on in and hang around while they book him. We may be able to eliminate him right off the bat, and then we won't have to worry about him."

The supermarket's security guard had noticed us, and he approached warily. He was a rent-a-cop. The ancient .38 on his hip was probably rusted solid, and he didn't want trouble. "This parking lot is for the convenience of our customers," he said sternly from a distance of about fifty feet. "I'm going to have to ask you ladies and gentlemen to move on." He sounded tough—you had to give him credit.

"It's not an evening of triumph," sighed Blondie. "We're moving, Officer," she called to him. We departed.

It was only 12:45. We drove a little way west, parked, and started walking again.

"Y'know what I like about this task force, Parkman?" said Patty happily. "All those years I've spent clutching my purse and walking down the middle of the street at night, scared to death I was going to run into some criminal. Now I'm all set. Now I'd love to run into 'em." She did a couple of little skipping steps. "Now it's their turn to worry. They don't like it, they can stay home and watch TV like everybody else."

I dreamt that night that Sara and Adam and Joss were hiding in a pit in open woods outside the city. They were talking and laughing out loud. Our guy was looking for them, but he couldn't find them in the pit. I was terrified that he would hear them, but they seemed entirely unconscious of the danger. At length he came to the verge of the pit and stood there for some time, peering down toward them. The shadows at the bottom were almost palpable, so that although it was not deep it was very dark. He couldn't make them out. Finally he turned away, prowling back and forth while the woods rang with their laughter. Occasionally he would stop suddenly and tip one ear forward, and each time I would think, He's heard them. He knows where they are.

15

We had hoped that the community meeting would get the word out in a way that the chief's press conference and the leafleting and the *Shout* article had not. But the organizers were interested primarily in the opportunity to share a microphone and communicate their fear and hatred of one thing or another. Their interest in the rape series lay in its utility as a symbol of a wider social decay rather than in any significance it might have in its own right. They devoted themselves to attacking The System on a broad front. Colorful speakers performed gleefully for the cameras. Our guy was not there to be photographed, at least so far as anyone knew.

For most of the news media the story was not the rape series or the rapist but the meeting itself: one of those droll sociopolitical happenings which occasionally convulse college towns. One of the area late-evening news programs gave the story thirty seconds and devoted most of that time to snippets of wild-eyed enthusiasts denouncing police-raper conspiracies. The newspapers ran brief stories on inside pages next day. The series itself, the immediate fact that there was this nut running around, that women should be careful, tended to get lost.

But there was an exception. Ivy Dobbins, field reporter for one of the local news programs in attendance, produced an account in which the visuals were accompanied by a voice-over summarizing what was known of the series, and even included a very brief shot of the press officer at a pre-meeting interview describing the formation and purposes of the task force. The following morning she called the task force office and spoke to Barry, who dashed out immediately afterward and got his hair cut. That afternoon Ivy appeared with a two-man camera crew and interviewed him at some length. The evening news gave this story a minute, and the late news two minutes.

We were all astonished. Barry was transformed. The camera imbued his habitual slouch with the latent violence of a compressed spring. His gaze, in life hearty but unfixed, assumed a mysterious air, veiled and questing. His utilitarian speech, neatly edited into sound bites, conveyed a folksy charm. Detective Sergeant Barry Dillon, everyman's cop, it was clear, would always get his man.

In the middle of all this excitement, just before midnight on June 12, the Saturday night after the community meeting, our guy entered an open window in a ground-floor rear apartment in the center of the target area. The occupant was a single, childless woman. Afterward, she cleaned herself and the apartment completely, destroying all evidence. She called to report the attack late Sunday afternoon. The subsequent interview yielded nothing new to advance the investigation. But the media was agog, and came back in strength to cover the new hit.

They had found in Barry the personality, the photographic object, without which facts scarcely exist. Barry spent the whole morning Monday briefing a small group of print reporters. He lunched with the producer of the news program which had slighted the community meeting story, and spent a good portion of the afternoon with their crew taping a long feature. The next day was much the same, and the next. The story blossomed.

And not the story only. Within a week, Barry and Ivy were meeting frequently "to discuss the case." They both worked odd hours, and she began appearing in the office in the middle of the night when the other reporters weren't around. They were seen driving off together in his car.

It seemed almost too delicious. Barry and Ivy, an American Dream: humble-but-ruggedly-handsome cop and beautiful-but-accessible media celebrity join hands across the teeming urban wilderness.

Ivy made Barry her media protégé. Ivy knew every reporter, print or electronic, who might be interested in our business. She gave Barry excellent advice. She saw to it that he understood all the personalities, and guided his introduction to the important individuals. She instructed him in the pressures and problems of each medium so that he could appear to best advantage in each. She helped him decide what to say and how to say it, what not to say, and how to avoid saying it. She taught him the etiquette of the media, so that he would not give offense by apparent favoritism or detectable manipulation. When Barry wasn't lunching with some other reporter he was lunching with her, disappearing for two or three hours at a time, still "discussing the case." Barry regarded these excursions as arising from the chief's admonition to stay on the right side of the press, and there was certainly no faulting that facet of operations.

There were one or two features or follow-ups a week on almost every station as June passed into July. It was great fun while it lasted. All the stations ran much the same sort of stuff, but Ivy's was the best. She saw to it that her crew shot plenty of the most glamorous sort of background footage, and she made sure that the station used it. Her pieces were full of serious-looking officers of both sexes and all races in earnest conference over fat sheaves of reports, or stepping purposefully to their cars, or pods of black-and-whites debouching irresistibly from the station parking lot and whizzing off into the night. To look at it you would have thought that no officer in our department ever smiled, or pondered, or dawdled, or stood still, or did anything whatever for more than two seconds in a row. Everything was in motion all the time. Her voice-over was redolent of urgency and importance: *"This* is what is *happening,"* it seemed to say. "It is told to you in the voice of a *beautiful woman. You can trust this voice. This* is what is being done on your behalf, so far as I can reveal it. Ivy is on *your* side."

Her reports always closed with a half-figure shot of herself on location, her fabulous mane perhaps slightly tousled by the wind, her color glorious even in the wash of the television lights, her clothes just so, her lovely cleavage just tastefully hinted at, her expression devoted, her voice earnest. *"I am on the spot,"* she seemed to say. *"You are seeing with the eyes of a beautiful woman."*

Barry was much featured in these pieces. The camera didn't flit over him quite so quickly as it did over the rest of us, sometimes lingering for several consecutive sentences. It gave the impression of someone at the still center of things, where people aren't always on the run, and where a train of thought can last for five or even six seconds. Not that it was ever permitted to be dull. Maybe the camera angle, worshipfully low, would make the moment striking; or the way the view zoomed in and out so that if he was motionless the viewer was always in motion. It was star treatment, and everyone knew it. We were all impressed.

Mike had mentioned to Heather that Walt was taking him shooting again. Heather asked if she could come, and Mike, rather to his credit, since he might have been possessive, asked Walt, who said yes. Heather told Joss and Adam, who asked if *they* could come. Heather asked Walt. Walt wasn't sure about that, so he asked me. I said that if the kids were coming, maybe I'd better come, too. Walt told Melanie that as long as Heather was going to learn to shoot, why didn't she? Melanie said she'd come if Sara would. So we figured on a picnic. In a light moment I mentioned it to Gadek, who said we should pull our camping gear together, make it a weekend, and come to his hideaway; there was an old gravel pit in the woods nearby, great for shooting. I told Barry, who liked to know whether he could get ahold of his people in emergencies.

"Great, Parkman," he said. "I'll loan you a little twenty-two I've got. Good for the small fry and the ladies. Every American should know how to shoot," he added, giving me several thumps on the shoulders.

"Ah," I said. "Well . . ."

"*Absolutely*. Gotta defend our Constitution. Remember, Parkman," he said, prodding me heavily on the chest, "when bare is outlawed, only outlaws will have bare arms." He grinned, and winked hugely.

To reach Gadek's hideaway you took the Interstate into the mountains, then secondary county roads, paved and unpaved, and finally a dirt access track which petered out at the margin of a little meadow. The cabin was on the uphill side where the forest began again. The view across the meadow was to a considerable wooded mountain spur a mile or so away, and the bustling upper reaches of a handsome river which was hazily visible in the distance.

Gadek's and Walt's cars were there when we arrived, almost hidden in the trees near the cabin.

"O *disgrace*," said Joss, drawing the back of her hand over her forehead. "We're last."

You could see the tracks through the grass where they had passed. I followed them, jouncing over the uneven ground.

"We started late," I said. "I didn't get to bed till three."

"Slowcoach Dad," said Adam happily.

"Gotta sleep, gotta eat," said Sara. "A slave to your appetites, dragging the rest of us down. '*Three Meals a Day: My Husband's Terrible Obsession.*'"

"I noticed you ate all your hash browns at that greasy spoon," I said.

"And bacon," said Joss. "We all saw you eating bacon. Sulfate city."

"I'm devoted to greasy, crusted potatoes," she said brazenly. "You knew it when you married me. It's too late to start complaining now."

"I think a mother ought to set a good example," said Joss. "And anyway, *I* didn't marry you."

"I was too young," said Adam.

"I defy you all," said Sara.

We passed from the bright sun into the dappled shadow among the firs. I stopped by the other cars. We got out. Heather and Mike burst suddenly, silently, out of the bushes close at hand and swept past us, each wordlessly catching up one of our children and bounding off with them into the forest on the other side. Shrieks of surprise and joy rang in the trees and faded into the distance.

"Well!" said Sara, looking after them. "So much for parenthood. Let's see who's at home."

The cabin was a single room with a bathroom at the back, a modern wood-burning stove in the middle, a double-decker bunk bed on one side, a stove and sink on the other, a round table with four chairs at the front. It was perfectly clear that there was nobody at home.

"I suppose they've gone for a walk," I said.

"Let's us, too," said Sara. "We can put our tent up later."

"I wonder what Leo does with guns?" I said, looking around the room.

"Won't they be safe locked in the car?" said Sara.

"I'm just a city boy," I said. "I don't know what passes for safe in the back of beyond." You hate to be separated from your weapons. We had the large .38, my snub-nose, and Barry's .22. After some hesitation I got out the snub-nose with its holster and put it inside my waistband. I pulled out my shirttails so that all that was visible was a slight bulge. Then we headed into the forest.

We hadn't gone far before we met the others coming back.

"Hello!" called Melanie from some distance.

"Finally made it," said Walt, a little nearer.

"Planning to make a lot of busts?" said Gadek at about fifty feet, pointing to my waist.

"I understand Melanie was bringing her teenagers," I said. "I wanted to keep things under control."

"Oh, I've been doing fine with chairs and whips," said Walt.

"What are you talking about?" said Melanie, who hadn't noticed my waist. Walt explained. "Oh, dear," she said. "I can see I have a great deal to learn about observation."

"Well," said Gadek. "I'm heading back to civilization. I showed Walt where to hide the key when you take off. The deer come out onto the meadow at the end of the day, and if there isn't a lot of noise they'll come right up to the cabin."

*   *   *

Mike was firing Walt's automatic. He had picked up something of Walt's romantic style, feet well apart, leaning low and forward, left hand back and the pistol punched forward with the arm straight. Walt made this posture loose and athletic. Mike gave an anxious edge to it, driving his head forward in little thrusts with each shot, tightening his mouth and narrowing his eyes. He was shooting at six tin cans lined up on a log about twenty feet away. He fired in nervous pairs of shots with a little pause between pairs. He hit three cans with six shots, which was creditable. There was a ripple of applause from the bleachers, another log a few feet behind him.

"Hey, great!" called Walt, and then murmured to me, "See how tight he is? Everything's a big deal to him." He called out, "Set 'em up and go again. How many rounds do you have left?"

"Uh ... it's eight," said Mike, setting the safety on the automatic and starting forward.

"Keep track," called Walt. "Always know how many you've got left."

"Weren't things a big deal to you when you were that age?" I said.

"Not like that," said Walt, watching Mike set the cans back on the log. "He's very well-mannered and polite, really a nice kid. Smart, too, smart as hell. But he's scared to death of screwing up. Just a sec."

Mike was coming back to the firing point. Walt ambled forward and murmured, "Okay, did you feel how tight you were that last time? Relax. Don't think so much. Just keep your eye on the can you're going to hit and let the rest take care of itself." When he came back to me he said softly, "Too many people watching, especially when one of 'em is his mom. We shouldn't've done it this way."

Mike slipped off the safety, dropped into his crouch and fired three bursts of two. He was no looser. He hit two cans.

"Great!" called Walt.

"I'm getting worse," said Mike, looking distressed.

"Nah," said Walt, going forward. "It's hard. Now, how many have you got left?"

"Uh, two," said Mike pretty quickly.

"Right. Hit that can on the right, and then someone else can have a turn."

Mike looked over at the four standing cans. Awkwardly, because he was thoroughly self-conscious by now, he crouched and fired. One shot struck a shower of splinters off the log just below the can in question, but the other was a clean miss. He handed the warm pistol over to Walt with a glance of shame.

"God*dam,*" said Walt to me a moment later, when Mike had drifted away. "We were making progress, too."

"Well, practice makes perfect," said Melanie doubtfully.

"You shoot so *well,*" said Heather, who wasn't dumb, going over to Mike. I could hear his murmured denial. "Well, you saw *me* shoot," she said, but this was a misstep because she had done better than he did on his first outing, and he shook his head. Falling back on uncritical admiration, she put her arm over his shoulder and said, "You're my *favorite* brother," and got a shy smile out of him.

Adam and Joss took another turn, with Sara and me standing close behind them. Barry's .22 made a flat popping sound in the open air which didn't cover the "sprong" as the cans were hit or the cheerful rattle as they bounced away across the gravel.

Sara took a turn to keep her hand in, firing the long-barreled .38 at close range, but quite fast. On her third six she hit five cans.

"Go, *Mom!*" yelled Adam and Joss.

"*Wow,*" said Heather.

"Perhaps we should go back," said Melanie when Sara was done. "It's getting rather late. We were talking about having some music tonight, but I'm afraid our ears will be ringing too badly."

"It'll pass," I said, gathering up equipment.

"You're so *deadly,*" Joss was telling Adam. "If you came near me and I were a bag of old tin cans I would just totally *hide.*"

"Mike and I'll gather up all this mess," said Walt. "We'll catch you up."

"I'll help," said Sara.

"No," said Walt cheerfully, giving her a little shake of the head. "We'll do it."

We started down the hill through the woods. Joss had her arm over Adam's shoulder.

"You're *murderous*," she was saying. "*Homicidal.* I bet every barn door in the state is trying to wiggle off its hinges and get down flat." He giggled with pleasure.

"Shucks," he said.

"You're a *killer*," she persisted. "After dinner, will you take my turn doing dishes?"

"No," he said. "I'm a *smart* killer."

From behind us came an even succession of six shots.

"They seem to have gotten distracted from their cleaning up," said Melanie.

Two shots, rather slowly. Then two more. Then two more, and two more so that the last four were almost evenly spaced.

Good for Walt, I thought. Not wasting any time.

A long, fairly slow succession of fourteen reports, in which the pairs were almost indistinguishable.

"I liked shooting more than I thought I would," Heather was saying to Sara and me. And then, lowering her voice, "I *never* thought Mom would let us do it."

"Like *thunder*," Joss was saying. "Like *lightning*."

"I'm not doin' your dishes," said Adam stoutly.

"Like *dynamite*."

Heather thought it was time for a change of subject.

"I'm gonna tickle you guys *unmerciful*," she called, and charged. Adam and Joss yelped and pelted off down the path, hotly pursued.

Melanie joined us.

"Shooting is really very absorbing," she said. I had coached her, and she fired in my style, rather erect and motionless. "But do you think about what it means? Learning to shoot *people?*"

"Yes," I said. "I think about that a lot."

"Doesn't it upset you?"

"Yes, but not as much as having someone shoot me. I've never fired my gun on the street, but I've had it out several times. I practice quite a lot, and I have reasonable grounds to suppose that if it comes to shooting I'll be better at it than the other guy. I hope it's true. But whether it's true or not, bad guys can see that I'm confident, so they don't make the experiment."

"You're going to say next that weakness begs for trouble."

"Now he doesn't have to," said Sara, to head off my saying more.

Six reports, regular as the strokes of a grandfather clock. Good for Walt, I thought.

The path narrowed, and we fell into single file, Sara and Melanie in front and me bringing up the rear.

"I don't think you ever met Mike and Heather's father, did you, Sara?"

"No."

"Well, he had all the surface you could want, and none of the insides. What I wanted to replace him was someone with a surface just like his who would actually be a man, too. But I never found anyone like that. And now here is Walt, who ... well, I don't know whether he has no surface, or whether I'm just looking at the wrong parts. But he thinks all the important things, and he acts on what he thinks. He bewilders me completely."

"The best brains are supposed to have the most convoluted surfaces," Sara said.

"Do they? Well, maybe they do. If you had told me six months ago that I would be standing out in some gravel pit watching a man very dear to me teach my children how to shoot pistols ... But he teaches beautifully, don't you think so? He makes it seem so simple, even if it isn't. He's very patient with Mike, who doesn't quite seem to get it."

"Mike's coming along very well," I called out from behind, too positively.

"Walt tells me I'm too hard on him," she said, hiking her voice up a little to include me, "and it seems you agree, Toby. But I don't think I've done such a bad job bringing him up so far. And he's not going to be weak like his father."

Stan Washburn

We reached the clearing with the cabin and the scattering of tents. I started a fire in the stone-lined pit near the steps. We moved leisurely around preparing dinner while the sun settled toward the west and each successive string of reports, softened by the distance and mellowed by the accumulated echoes, passed gently over us.

16

We had all come to the task force expecting brisk, loud
leadership, a series of energetic frontal assaults on targets
of opportunity: not cerebral, and not necessarily well-
directed, but in any event full of movement and activity.
From Barry's perspective it might have felt very much that
way. He was constantly in motion himself, always dashing
off to some meeting or interview, and when he was in the
office he was besieged with myriad inescapable housekeeping duties. But by the end of the day he had seldom got
around to the case itself, and we found ourselves increasingly without direction. All the pieces were present: the
street details worked the operations mandated for them,
Footer and odd assistants pursued leads as they were developed and followed each new possibility out to its seemingly
inevitable dead end. All the strings led to Barry, but Barry
mostly wasn't there. The task force, barely launched, was
already adrift.

What was going on was that Barry was floundering, completely out of his depth. You didn't need to be an adminis-
trator to see it. He was an uncomplicated man who had a
very good grasp of a Patrol officer's skills. From this firm
base he had advanced to a tenuous hold on a sergeant's

administrative and teaching responsibilities, which he ac-
quitted mainly on the strength of his technical mastery, his
diligence, and his reflexive honesty. Now he had an independent command of experienced peers with a suddenly visible
and politically charged case as its entire reason for being
and sole standard of success. The wave of publicity had
lofted him, for no reason that he could see, to considerable
prominence. The politics of it—assessing who the players
were, their interests, their requirements—was all a mystery
to him. Indeed, he didn't even recognize that there were
elements there that he ought to understand, and didn't, unless it was pointed out to him.

In the normal course of operations Barry would have received a great deal of support and supervision from the
chain of command. But the brass knew a good thing when
they saw it. They were perfectly well acquainted with Barry's
strengths and weaknesses, but this sudden media success,
scarcely more accountable to them than to him, made them
wonder if he weren't more subtle than they had supposed.
The series, a swelling embarrassment, had become a positive
political asset. The task force was a quasi-secret operation
anyway, and there was a conscientious disinclination to med-
dle. They left Barry alone, unsupported and unsupervised.

And so he kept his chin high and advanced, as from childhood he had always done, in simplicity of heart, meeting life's
challenges as they presented themselves to his blinkered vision,
one by one. The span of his mind didn't cover half his
responsibilities. Perhaps if anyone had sat him down to make
a list in priority order, and then made him stick to it, all would
have been well. But nobody did. His maxim was that you deal
with the first thing in front of you, and then when that's done
you deal with the next. The most pressing claimant for his attention was Ivy, and as it turned out, he never got done with her.

It isn't fair to blame Ivy. The series story had moved her
from being merely one of a number of pretty faces on the
tube to considerable prominence in the area media. The
series was a rich vein, and she meant to explore its full social
significance. Of course, to do this she needed a great deal
more information than was necessary to make up the little
stories she put on the air. She kept showing up at the task

force office, sometimes with her camera crew in tow, more often, as time passed, by herself, to "study the case."

Ivy was gracious and charming to all of us, but it was Barry who had intrigued her.

"You go on about her," said Sara. "She fascinates you."

"Yes, I suppose she does."

"Beware, dear."

"You don't flatter me. You have nothing to worry about."

"No? She's so gorgeous."

"No doubt. But leaving her mind entirely out of the question for the moment, I can tell you that her cup size is just the same as yours."

"Omigod. They must really be getting on. I presume you got her cup size from Barry, rather than from her?"

"Yes, dear."

"I didn't know you knew *my* cup size."

"Well, the subject of cup sizes has been a feature of my police career almost from the beginning, and it seems like an affectation, once the question is mooted—Joss, I've asked you more than once to say hello when you come into a room. Really, honey, it's very rude—"

"I'm always in the way," said our daughter, world-weary. "And I bet you won't tell me what 'mooted' means, either."

"Oh, yes I will," I said, and I did.

On June 24 our guy entered an in-law unit in the rear of a large house. We never did figure out how entrance was made in that case. The occupant was a high school student who was living semiemancipated from her elderly parents upstairs. She woke up to find him in the room, and she got off one scream before he was on her. Apparently he didn't think anyone would have heard it, because it didn't stop him. She didn't report until morning. During the neighborhood check it turned out that a person next door had, in fact, heard the scream but assumed that it was someone having a nightmare.

The task force secretary was Marcia Gold. She was a veteran of DD. She liked me because I understood that she made the place run, and treated her like a player.

"We're bustling," she said when I came in. "Myron's got someone who claims to have a hot tip." Fry had just hung up, and was scribbling notes on his pad.

I stepped into Barry's office, tapping carefully on the door before entering. I felt lucky to find him—by the time I got to work at 6:00 he was often out of the office. Fry entered right behind me.

"Goddam, form a line," he said cheerfully, waving to chairs. "Marcia says you've got a nut informant."

"Marcia's probably on the money," said Fry, "but it's a problem tip."

"Okay. Let's hear it."

"Okay." He began to run down his notes. "The guy's name is Wesley Hunter. He's—"

"Who?"

"Wesley Hunter." Fry ran off the date of birth, Social Security, address, occupation.

"The hell," said Barry.

"The hell?" said Fry.

"The hell. I know Wesley Hunter. He's not our guy. Not even close." He was incredulous.

"Very probably not," Fry said. "But this informant—"

"What informant?"

"Her name's Polly Rhine. She's—"

"I know who Polly Rhine is," said Barry. "She's a nut. She wanted Wes to marry her, and he wouldn't, and she's had a grudge ever since." He looked like someone who had been mildly but unaccountably insulted.

"Clearly, there's a grudge."

"You bet there is. I've known Wes since he was a kid. I used to date his sister. I've taken Wes boar hunting almost every year since . . . well, a long time. You ever hunt boar, Myron? Have you, Toby? I mean, pistol hunting?"

"No."

"No."

"Great sport. Anyway, Wes was going to be a cop. Only he couldn't put up with all the regimentation. Didn't want to cut his hair, that whole bit. It didn't bother me."

"Well, she says . . ."

Barry let Fry talk, but he was only half listening. He was

revolving refutations in his mind's ear. It was an odd situation. I wondered what Gadek would do.

"There's one real problem," Fry said.

"Yeah?"

"She knows that you're a friend of Hunter's. And she knows that you're in charge here. She thinks that's why we're not moving on the guy."

Barry almost spit. He threw up his arms and said, "Christ, that's horsepukky. I'd arrest my mother if I thought she was doing this stuff." I believed him. "For another thing, if she thinks I'm protecting him, why's she calling the task force? Why isn't she calling the FBI or something?"

"Well, it doesn't make much sense," said Fry. "But there isn't anything very convincing about the whole thing." He ran his finger down his pad. "Essentially, she asserts that Hunter is our guy, and that she knows it and we know it. She says it isn't her business to prove it, it's our business. She won't give me details, she says we know them already. She says we can go ahead and bust him or she can go to the media."

Barry smiled a thin smile.

"I'm working on that," he said. "I think we can handle the media."

"So that's where it is," said Fry. "She won't let me come and talk to her in person. She says she'll call back when she feels like talking to me, and find out what we're doing about it."

"Okay, Myron, look," said Barry. "This is what you do. It's a waste of time, but this is what you do. This shit she's given you, well, run with it, do what you usually would with it. But I'm telling you, it's a waste of time."

"Well, I don't see much to run with, but I can start a records check. Maybe Footer can do something with it."

"Do what you think is called for. And knock off a memo, what she said about me, and get it to Lieutenant Bloom. So there won't be any horsepukky about a cover-up. Do that now, before you hit the street tonight."

"Okay," said Fry, and he left. Barry glanced at his watch.

"Right," I said. "Now, I've got questions on some other

stuff." I hefted a sheaf of papers. "We've been taking all these samples, and the evidence locker isn't—"

"Okay, look, Toby," he said. "It's getting late."

"Late?" I said, surprised, looking at my watch. It was 6:48.

"Yeah, well, it's getting late," he said happily. It didn't seem late to me, since I had just come on at 6:00, and would be on the street until after 2:00 A.M.

He winked at me. "I've got a date with Ivy," he announced in a conspiratorial half whisper. "She's making dinner at her apartment."

"Ah, uh, well," I said, "that must be fairly soon."

"At seven," he said.

I was thinking, he's going off to have dinner in the middle of the working day? But of course, lots of people have dinner at 7:00 in the evening, as Sara had lately reminded me in a tone of grievance when I had told her I would have to eat at 5:00.

"My grandfather—not the Turk, the other one—said, you should never keep a lady waiting." He grinned lasciviously.

Barry's dirty-mindedness was so innocent that you could easily be embarrassed, but you couldn't be offended. I said, "I guess television is turning out to be a warm medium." He laughed, delighted.

"So I gotta get out of here." He began gathering papers into his briefcase. "Myron's tip is definitely a waste of time. Wes has always been a little rough," he said ruminatively. "But he isn't our guy."

"And the samples? Gadek thought—"

"That's what Service Division is for. They know about this stuff. C'mon, Toby, read the general orders."

And off he went.

"Well god*dam*," I said softly, staring after him and holding my papers.

Blondie called in sick, and after a discussion we decided that Fry should stay in the office with Footer to do gumshoe work while Patty and I split the target area between us, working solo. All this was really Barry's decision to make, but of course Barry wasn't there.

I spent the first part of the street shift walking my lonely quadrant without the slightest excitement or interest. The midnight-to-1:00- A.M. hour I spent taping the north-south streets. Usually I did the east-west streets, but Patty also usually did east-west, so we flipped, and I lost.

After a few times, taping wasn't so bad. Partly one got better at it, just the mechanics of rattling off the time as you pass each intersection, phonetic alphabet reading of the license plate, and the basic vehicle descriptions: "At oh-oh-twenty-three hours, Oak west from Forest, a red VW bug George-Edward-Adam-six-five-eight, white Ford wagon William-Nora-William-six-zero-nine, brown Datsun pickup one-Charles-seven-seven-zero-two-eight," and so forth. But after a few nights you got to know some of the regular cars, and you didn't have to mention them. After a couple of weeks you could leave out most and rip right along. But if you had to do the unaccustomed direction, then it was like starting all over again. You had to do all the cars. When cars are parked close together it's hard to see their plates, and sometimes you'd have to stop and shine a flashlight in between two cars to get a look. Sometimes you'd have to back up and make another pass. And you can never go faster than a walk. It's pretty obtrusive.

Residents spotted me and called the police to report a suspicious vehicle cruising down the street. This had happened before. What we did was to tell the dispatchers who receive the initial calls from the public what cars would be out each night: we gave them descriptions and license numbers. When they got a report from a citizen they were just to say, right, we'll be out right away, and then forget the whole thing. This worked pretty well, with lapses, until this night, when I aroused the suspicions of *dumb* residents. They gave Dispatch the wrong make of car, they muddled the license number, and, under streetlights, they got the color wrong as well.

Their report didn't correspond to anything on the task force list, so Dispatch thought they had something. They gave it to Control as a priority item, and Control put it out. Patrol was having a slow night. No fewer than four cars busted me. Alertly correcting for the color mistake and discounting the vehicle ID, and not recognizing the car, but knowing suspicious conduct when they saw it, they boxed me from both directions in midblock, roof lights flickering and spotlights blasting. It was a very pretty piece of Patrol work.

It was Sergeant Bridey who approached my driver's side window.

"Oh, Jehoshaphat, it's Parkman," he said when he saw my face. He canceled the stop. The lights cut off and the patrol cars pulled out just as the neighbors began to appear on their front porches.

"Really, Parkman," said Bridey. "We've done this before. We need to refine what we're doing here. You detectives are so smart, I wish you could think of something."

The following day Barry called me into his office on some trifling excuse. Clearly, he wanted to confide. Bette, Pauletta, Elaine, Maya, and now Ivy. We slipped into it. One minute we were talking about our problems with Patrol, and the next we were talking about Ivy's bosom. There didn't seem to be a moment when I could gracefully say, golly, gotta run, or, Barry, I was hoping we could make progress on catching the rapist who is our reason for being here. He wouldn't have held it against me if I had, but he would have been disappointed. You didn't disappoint Barry lightly. In his personal capacity he elicited strong protective reactions even from those junior to him in years and rank. He sounded lonely as well as boastful. Anyway, I didn't stop him.

Dinner, Barry told me, was candlelit, the music lush, and Ivy not overdressed. To hear him tell it I was reminded of the overstuffed interiors in the advertising supplements that come with the Sunday papers, but perhaps I was only being jealous. After dinner they took the bottle and retired to the living room. They hadn't got very far with the wine before she got up.

"I'll be right back." she said.

She was gone only a few minutes. When she reappeared she was wearing even less than before; she smiled at him, wiggled, smiled again, and was gone. Barry bounded off the couch and into the hallway. The bathroom was on the right, and opposite it the bedroom. There was a small red lamp burning on the dresser. Ivy was on the bed, lying on her stomach, pretending to be asleep. Barry chuckled. Okay, he thought. He undressed by the door as quietly as he could. Then he tiptoed across the room and jumped lightly onto her.

"This is it," he whispered in a mock-angry tone. "I've been lusting for you and now I'm gonna have you. Don't try to make a noise."

"Oh, please don't," whispered Ivy with mock desperation, wiggling her bottom. "Oh, please spare me."

I don't know which astonished me more, that Barry would tell me such things or that there seemed to be no significance for him in the fact that this rather early sexual encounter with Ivy had been a mock rape. I'm not a symbolic thinker, but it's hard to miss something like that. No doubt if I had pointed this out to him he would have been astonished in his turn. He would have pointed out that it was *not* rape. Sex is sex and rape is rape. He knew right from wrong. So long as you stayed on the proper side of that division, he wasn't much concerned with implications. He knew where he was; he would find out where he was going when he got there.

In any case, I didn't point it out to him. There was a time early on in our acquaintanceship when I worried that Barry would notice that I wasn't matching his confidences with confidences of my own. I had worried what I would say if he were to turn to me and say, hey, Toby, what's *Sara's* cup size, and how about a few racy anecdotes from *your* sex life? But he never did. Apparently he confided not to create closeness but because in his mind something not imparted seemed scarcely to have happened.

The days passed, and still he would talk about it. Either at the time or later, after he left the department, he told or hinted everything.

And it got crazier. A few days after their first fling, Ivy suggested that it might be possible to, y'know, *learn* something about the series by, well, *reenacting* something similar to the series. She had been thinking about this, and she laid it out at some length. She had in mind a reconstruction of our guy's point of view, an insight into—it got rather muddled. Why not try?

Why not?

He was to hide somewhere in the apartment, just like our guy. She would go out, come in, take a bath, go to bed—her usual late-evening routine. He would pounce at the appropriate time. She would not look for him, but she would not avoid doing whatever she would normally do, going into closets, that sort of thing. She laid it out in considerable detail, rather tensely.

Barry had a high degree of intellectual passivity. Although he had a close understanding of a wide range of criminal methods, he had never attempted to re-create the mental process of a criminal. If she had proposed a plan for raiding a drug dealer, or if she had tried to give him a false address, he would have been all alert attention. As it was, he listened to what she had to say, and, well, shouldn't you always try to please a lady?

Barry had the key to her apartment, so the entry wasn't a problem. He and Ivy had agreed that she shouldn't know exactly when their little reenactment was going to occur, so he picked an evening when he knew she would be working late. He arrived in plenty of time to make a leisurely reconnaissance of her apartment. After examining the few doors which he had never had occasion to open before, he decided that the pantry closet/wine cellar was the most spacious cubby available to him. Her indefinite schedule meant that he would be hiding for at least an hour, and he didn't want to be uncomfortable as well as bored. He got a pillow off the couch, selected a women's magazine off the coffee table (for the skin), found a flashlight in one kitchen drawer and the corkscrew in another, secured a glass, and made a nest for himself. When he heard her key in the lock he closed the door.

Of course it was all very well to say that Ivy wouldn't know when this was going to happen, but she knew it would be soon, and she tingled with a delightful sense of mystery every time she put her key in the door. She anticipated the brooding sense of menace, that vague feeling of presence that seemed to be an early, albeit unrecognized, sign of our guy's imminent attack. She thought of what minute tokens of entry there might be which she, the alert and trained observer, might be able to pick out. But naturally she hadn't been in the apartment for ten seconds before she noticed the missing couch pillow and the gap in her fan of magazines. And when she adhered to her invariable routine upon coming home late, went to the pantry closet to make a nightcap, opened the door and found Barry, slouched on the cushion among the mineral waters and designer pastas, with a glass of a particularly choice Cotes du Rhône (the newly opened bottle beside him on the floor) and a flashlight with which he was scanning a layout of naughty lingerie, she could not contain herself. What in God's name was he thinking of? Did he call this hiding? How was he supposed to get insights into a rapist's mind by drinking and reading smut? If Barry had been more witty, and perhaps differently placed, he might have replied, a great deal, but as it was he simply looked sheepish while she let off steam.

The mood was spoiled, and the evening might have been a serious failure, except that Barry was repentant, if not altogether comprehending, and Ivy wanted very much to patch things over; she wanted to proceed. And so after some cooling off and mutual peacemaking efforts she went out again for half an hour.

He concealed himself more seriously this time, and Ivy found no sign of him when she came back, or as she moved around the place, getting her drink, settling down. It was no novelty for her to undress in the presence of men, but knowing that there was a man there somewhere, without knowing where, gave her as her last garments came off a feeling of conscious nakedness that she had not experienced for a long time. Filling the bath was nerve-racking—the roar of the water covered all other sounds, and she found herself simply unable to stand at the vanity with her back, so bare from neck to heel, toward the door. The mirror steamed as quickly as she wiped it off, depriving her of even a partial view into the room behind her.

In the tub, at least, she had her back to something solid. She found herself absurdly reluctant to leave it.

She had more than half-expected him to leap out of concealment at some point in this process; when he did not, and the time she had been in the apartment lengthened to an hour, to ninety minutes, she felt the tension increasing. She made no sort of search for him. She told herself that she didn't want to spoil the fun, but immediately she had to admit that she would not have dared. It was too frightening to think of opening a closet and Barry's bursting out at her with a maniacal expression—so she imagined it—on his face. Somewhere he was waiting for her; it sounded different than it had. It was not the anticipation she had felt immediately after returning, when she flinched involuntarily from every door she passed as she moved about, but a more active and general sensation of menace. Once or twice it got so strong that to reassure herself she whispered aloud, "It's only Barry, after all." She pretended to read for a few minutes, but she was straining to hear any sound that would give some notice of his approach. Finally she turned out the light, and pretended to sleep, lying on her stomach, eyes not quite closed, face toward the door, straining to hear.

She had no warning: she felt the loom of him behind her, between the wall and the bed; she began to turn, but in that half second he was on her, pinning her.

The sex part of it was much as it usually was with them, except that he did all the choosing, and ordered rather than asking. It was familiar but it was different. It excited her a great deal.

Afterward Barry flatly refused to tell her where he had been hiding or how he had managed to get so close before she was aware of him, large as he was, alert as she was. He could see plainly enough that a mystery was more tantalizing than a technical explanation. For Ivy this feat of stealth lent him a whole new fascination. She could not figure out how he had done it.

Unremarkably for Barry, revealingly for her, neither of them noticed that they never once raised the subject of what they might have learned about our man's mind from their little "experiment." Ivy's focus was locked on her own experience; Barry merely noticed that she had been very ardent, and that his own enjoyment was proportionately great. That was enough for both of them. Ivy had loved it and wanted to go farther with it another time.

I couldn't believe that Barry was telling me these things. For the commander of a rape task force to admit to forming such fantasies, let alone acting them out—well, goodness gracious. He thought it was funny. It didn't bother him a bit, so far as it had gone. But there was a note of caution. Far less directly than was usual for him, he gave me to understand that next time Ivy wanted the whole thing to be less calculated, more "real." And she wanted the sex to get farther out. Even Barry sounded a little cautious about it.

"She's in trouble," said Sara when I told her this. "That kid has a screw loose."

"As it were." I laughed. Usually she would have laughed too, but this time she didn't.

"It's not funny," she said. "She's got her wires crossed somewhere pretty deep." Then she gave me a long, level look and said, "Toby, all this is no more than I would have thought of Barry. He's never been my favorite. But will you be shocked or offended if I ask if this is *your* fantasy, too? Because it certainly isn't mine, and I hope you haven't got your heart set on trying it."

Well, now that she mentioned it, I could see that I had been so engrossed in recollecting all the details of what he had told me, and so absorbed in re-creating the locker room manner of his telling, that I hadn't inserted anything in the way of reassuring editorial comment. In fact, I had no desire to rape my best friend, the mother of my children, the companion, as I sincerely hope, of my old age. I told her so, and she was pleased to hear it. But disavowing it brought on a great wave of affection, which the alchemy of the evening hour and the quiet house converted almost instantaneously into a great burst of lust. We hurried upstairs, took a quick shower together, and jumped into bed.

17

On the third of July he entered a first-floor room in an old house which had been cut up into small apartments. He appeared to have used wire on the latch of a window which was screened from the street by bushes. The occupant was the manager of a small, chic clothing store, seldom home before 8:00. As soon as she opened the door she knew that something was different, and she thought she knew what it was. Nothing seemed to be missing, and her immediate suspicion was not of burglars but of her landlord. In the two months she had lived there he had been very nosy. His apartment was right across the hall, and he often left his front door ajar. It would be easy for him to know when she was out. He had a key; all he had to do was come in and look around.

The suspicion grew almost immediately to conviction as it formed in her mind. She marched across the hall to confront him, but he was out. She steamed about it while she prepared her dinner. She was just sitting down to eat when she heard the front door open and close. She darted out into the hall. It was he; she confronted him. He denied it, but not convincingly. She warned him, threatened to call the police, and stumped back behind her own door. The out-

190

burst relieved her feelings. She relaxed as she ate. By the time she was through she felt altogether better, proud of having stood up for herself and handling an alarming situation on her own.

She was still feeling good at bedtime. She put the chain on the hall door, which she didn't usually give herself the trouble of doing, and felt much more secure. She lay in bed with the lights out, listening to the radio. It was still playing when she drifted off. It was still playing when he came in, and when he left two hours later.

She reported on July 6, three days cold. There was no evidence to be had from her person, of course, after three days of bathing, but there was a thread to pick up. When the announcement of the hit reached the Daily Bulletin on the evening of July 6, officers were requested to forward the record of any stops they had made or encounters they might have had in or near the target area on the night of July 3–4. Five items came in.

Three were "stop cards," index card–size field records of noncriminal contacts that officers had had with a citizen for one reason or another. We could eliminate these: one was a stop on a drunk: the officer, when contacted, was quite sure that the man had, in fact, been almost insensible. Moreover, he described him as skinny, flabby, and generally in very poor physical condition. That wouldn't be our guy. The other two cards were on two young men who were probably in the area for nefarious purposes but who were too young, unless you posited that our guy had started the series at the age of ten.

The other two items were traffic citations. The first was a speeding ticket written on the arterial that forms the western boundary of the target area. The driver's license information showed him to be on the young side, overweight, and with poor eyesight—all probable eliminations.

The second ticket had been written two blocks south of the target area, which is why our street detail hadn't been alerted to it at the time. The vehicle was traveling directly away from the victim's neighborhood. The time was about right: 2:35 A.M. The officer, Lindy Webb, had made the stop because the vehicle, traveling without lights, had whipped through a stop sign right in front of her. It had taken her two blocks of pursuit to get close enough to put her roof lights on, and it took the driver another two blocks to decide whether he was going to stop or run. The physical description of the vehicle's lone occupant was right on the money, the age was close enough, and the name was Wesley Hunter.

Lindy forwarded a copy of the citation together with a memo describing the circumstances. Footer looked at it and whistled. Fry was in the office, and Footer passed it to him. Fry looked at it and whistled.

"Anybody seen Barry?" said Footer, and laughed. "He ain't gonna like this at all."

"No," said Fry, shaking his head. "Barry won't like this at all."

"But I bet it isn't our guy," said Blondie, skimming the memo. "This guy drives like he's in the circus. Our guy is smooth. He wouldn't make himself conspicuous like that."

"Maybe," said Patty. "But let's look at him. He oughta be worth a little time."

"Time's awasting," said Blondie.

"Shit," said Barry, looking at it. "I can't believe this. This is crazy. What's the matter with Lindy, is it her period or something? She got two cover cars? What's the big deal?"

"I'd have taken three," said Fry. "C'mon, Barry. I know he's your friend, but he's got some pretty peculiar habits."

"Aw, Christ, Myron." Barry thrust his arm down the back of his neck and scratched vigorously. He looked unhappy. "Haven't you ever forgotten to turn your lights on?"

"Yes, for a block or two. But I don't blow stop signs like that, or go through blind intersections at forty miles an hour. And I yield for emergency vehicles."

"Hell, he stopped," said Barry without conviction.

"Two blocks. Two long blocks. Barry, if you'd been Lindy you'd have been all over this guy."

This was hard for Barry, because we were all there for the weekly meeting, we had all read Lindy's memo and citation, and we all wanted to go to work on Hunter without further delay. I'm sure we all hoped it didn't pan out, for

Barry's sake, since Hunter was his friend, but friendship doesn't close the question. You can't pick up a news item about the arrest of some criminal lunatic without finding a sidebar in which his mother says that he was the most affectionate boy, and all the neighbors recount instances of his thoughtfulness to old folks and children. " 'Such terrible things they say about my good Adolf,' says Hitler's mother." Don't tell me about it.

So it was five to one, not counting Marcia, who didn't sit with us at the table but who voted with her eyebrows from her desk. Six to one.

"Okay," said Barry. "Look, I'm not saying we're not going to do anything about it. I'm saying we're wasting our time. Wes isn't our guy. But hey, hey, we'll run with it. Myron, you've been onto him for a week, since Polly the Bitch Rhine fingered him. Why don't you lay it out now so we all know what we've got?"

"Right," said Fry, reaching behind him to his desk and lofting a thin manila folder which he opened in front of him. "Wesley Hunter hasn't got much on record. He's been arrested three times on various disturbance complaints, all of them involving girlfriends, all of them dropped. He was arrested two years ago on a battery complaint. The victim was Polly Rhine—"

"Bitch," murmured Barry.

"That was dismissed by the D.A. He's never done jail time."

"Our guy's done jail time," said Footer firmly, jittering one leg. "Our guy's a con."

"That's our assumption," said Fry.

"He's a con," said Footer.

"Wes is no con," said Barry. "He's a little wild, but he's no con."

"Then he ain't our guy."

"Hunter's car doesn't come near anything on our list of suspicious vehicles," continued Fry. "It's a black GT, according to the citation. That's a pretty conspicuous car. We should eyeball it and see if any of us remember seeing it in the target area. Apart from that, we don't have anything. He isn't very promising, in my view—"

"Our guy's a con. If he ain't a con he ain't our guy."

"I told you."

"—but he also isn't eliminated."

"Okay, Myron," said Barry. "He's your meat. You work on him. You and Charlie. And let's keep this clean; I want you to knock off a short memo to the lieutenant every couple of days about what you're doing and what you're finding. I don't want anyone to be able to say I'm sitting on any asshole except my own." He laughed happily, and with various degrees of enthusiasm we all laughed with him.

"And now, if we've wasted enough time, I've got two single-spaced pages of bullbleep here from Administrative Division about the new vacation schedules, and I want you to listen closely." He began to read, and he was pretty well along in it when Marcia, whose habit it was to pick up the phone halfway through its first ring, laid an eloquent finger on the Hold button and said, "Barry, it's Ivy Dobbins for you on line one. She says it's urgent."

Barry passed the vacation order to Fry, who took up the reading where Barry had abandoned it. Barry had gone into his office and pushed the door to, but it had not closed completely. His hushed tenor whispered under Fry's firm baritone.

When Fry came to the end at the bottom of the second page, he stopped. He had no further business himself; it was Barry's meeting. He glanced over at the inside office door, from which Barry's murmurs occasionally issued. He settled his eyes on the table, folded his hands, and composed himself to wait. All six of us, five at the table and Marcia at her desk, sat quietly, stared straight ahead, and waited while the tone, if not most of the exact words, of Barry's passion drifted out to us.

We heard him hang up. A moment later he appeared in the door and beckoned to Fry. They were in consultation for a minute or two. When they emerged, Fry returned to the table and Barry headed for the stairs.

"Barry asked me to finish this tonight," said Fry unhappily. "He says he's got things to do." Footer snickered, and Blondie laughed outright. Everyone had some sort of reaction of the cynical amusement variety.

"I wonder what he's got to do," said Patty acidly, which was unlike her.

Footer made an *O* with forefinger and thumb, and ran his other forefinger vigorously back and forth through it. For once, no one seemed to think that this was out of line.

"Well, I don't grudge him his luck," said Blondie, "but I wish he'd do his work. I've been waiting for a chance to talk to him since yesterday. Have we got a commander or haven't we?"

"Blondie's got a point," I said.

Patty said, "I came in at two o'clock today 'cause he asked me to do some eliminations, and he wasn't here and hadn't left any instructions. Jeez, how many times can you clean your gun? I've wasted half a day."

For a minute or two there was a buzz around the table, with everyone throwing out little instances of disorganization attributable to Barry's neglect. Fry looked grave.

"Look, guys," he said at last. "We all seem to feel the same way about this." He looked around the table, and everyone nodded. "Maybe someone had better have a little chat with him."

"You're senior," said Footer, jittering his foot at a great rate. "You're it." Fry had been Barry's training officer when Barry was sworn.

"Okay," said Fry. "I'm it. I'll talk to him as soon as I can." He glanced around the table for concurrence. "In the meantime, let's not fall to pieces around here. We're a little disorganized, but we know why we're here. Let's do the best we can, eh?" He said this like a kindly uncle, which, I suppose, was what we all needed at that point. He was quite right; we did know why we were there. We stopped bitching and sat up a bit straighter. Fry pulled the sheaf of announcements over and began.

It was all routine stuff, but we all voluntarily sat still and listened, more or less, and made notes of things that concerned us. Fry was solid, slightly graying, and he had a sergeant's voice, firm and confident. He had internalized the rhythm of the roll call long years before. He had the lingo and the droll turns of speech. He summarized some arcane revision of the Regs, and then, putting the paper aside and giving it a reassuring little pat, said, "For the benefit of those to whom this appertains, it'll be on the bulletin board to peruse at leisure," saying it "pahrooooose" and "leeeeee-sure."

It was ten healing minutes.

"Okay," he said, "so much for that. Now for police work. We're going to take a look at Hunter. Charlie, you've been on all day? You go home. Blondie, you and I are going to spend—let's see, it's ten past seven—the first part of the evening on the phone. Hunter hasn't got much of a record, but it's the sort of record that only a real jerk accumulates, and I bet there's more to know about him. So we'll put in some calls to our colleagues in other parts of DD and see what they know. And some of the retired people, too. I bet we can find out more."

"Barry's so straight," I said. "I'm having trouble making out how he and Hunter could be such buddies."

"Well, they've known each other a long time," said Fry. "Loyalty's important to Barry. And besides," he continued, with the slight hesitancy of one making a painful concession, "and besides, he doesn't always sweat the small stuff."

Nobody laughed. It wasn't funny. Fry had put his finger on what troubled us all about Barry. In our little corner of the world cops are people who sweat the small stuff. There was a brief, glum pause while we pondered Barry's fall from grace. Then Fry picked it up again, and said, "What'd be great would be to get something we can send to the lab, to see if we can eliminate him on a chemical test. Blood, saliva—a cigarette butt is enough, if we can get it fresh. Well, maybe we'll luck out.

"Parkman, you go sit on his car tonight and see what you can see. Don't get burned, that's the first thing. But if he drives, see if you can follow him.

"Dwornenscheck, I asked Barry about those eliminations. They're in a file on his desk. Marcia, do you know ... Marcia'll show you. It's delivery men, utility installers, that sort of thing. Do those till ten. Then we'll hit the street, except maybe Parkman, if he's onto something hot.

"Questions? Questions that I can answer, at any rate?"

He smiled firmly. "Okay, go do it." And off we went to do it, moving faster, feeling better.

Wesley Hunter lived in a little vine-covered stucco bungalow with his mother, who had white hair (I discovered in the course of watching the place) and who doubtless considered her son, who was in his forties, a fine boy. The house was in the middle of a long block of similar bungalows. His car, a gleaming black GT with a scoop for the carburetor and a spoiler fin for the trunk lid, was parked in a garage at the rear end of the driveway. When I cruised past I could see the car and its owner, the one being polished lovingly by the other.

It was a very conspicuous car. I was sure I'd never seen it in the target area, and everyone else would be able to say to a certainty whether they had or not.

I was driving my little station wagon. I found a parking place at the corner where I could see the house. In early July it was still broad daylight at 7:45, so there were no shadows to disappear in, and I couldn't very well pretend to be asleep. I tried to look as if I were waiting for someone, and whenever anyone came near I would glance at my watch and then glower impatiently up and down the street. I relied on the playpen and high chair in the back to provide their usual emotional camouflage.

Dusk.

Twilight.

Darkness.

At about 9:30 Hunter's car backed suddenly into the street and roared off in the opposite direction. He wasn't showing lights. I started up immediately and hastened after him, but my station wagon was no match for his GT. By the time I reached the end of the block he was out of sight. I fished the microphone out of my jacket and raised Fry.

"79, 93."

"Go ahead, 93."

"He's out. Northbound at high speed when last seen. I'm loose. You want me back at my spot, or come to you?"

"Why don't you hang on your spot, 93, and see what happens."

"Check. 93 out."

I returned to my spot and waited for Hunter to come home to his mother, but he didn't. Around 11:00 Fry called me to the target area to resume street routine.

About 12:30 I cruised past Hunter's place. The garage door was closed, so presumably he was home in bed. I went past again at about 2:00, before calling it a night, and found no change.

"Blondie and I spent a couple of hours on the phones," said Fry when we were back in the office. "There's a lot of information that never finds its way onto paper. We got a lot of new stuff about Hunter, going back years. All the DD people past and present know about him. But it's all just like the stuff we had already. We knew he was a jerk, and now we know he's a thoroughgoing jerk. But nothing to make him a rapist, and nothing to help us get a handle on him. The way he drives, I don't think trying to follow him is going to do much good. Tomorrow I'll think of something else."

But next day Fry had not thought of something else.

"I don't know what to do that we're not doing," he said. "Barry isn't around."

"Have you hashed it over with Gadek?" I asked.

"What could he suggest?" said Fry. He sounded puzzled.

"I don't know. That's why I'd ask him."

Fry stared at me for a moment, not offended, not challenging, but looking to see what he could see. Finally he said, "That's not the way I work, Toby. Gadek's got his job, I've got mine. For now, what we're going to do is, we're going to keep an eye out for Hunter's GT in the target area."

"I'd go sit on him," said Gadek. "Get to him when he's not in his car. Does he work? Find out. See what you can think of. How you get near someone depends on what they do and where they do it. Find out what you can, and after that, use your wits."

"How do I sell this to Fry?"

"First, you don't tell him you've talked to me, unless he

asks. Second, you don't try to sell him a program that has uncertain pieces, because that's what he doesn't like. Fry's a good guy and a first-rate beat cop, but there's a reason he's not a detective. What he's been trained for, what he's done in the past, he's great at. But he doesn't like novelty, and he doesn't like to go out on limbs. So don't make him. Just tell him you'd like to find out if Hunter works, and where; basic stuff. Then when you've figured out the next step, get him to approve the next step. And so on. One step at a time."

"Baby him along."

"Baby, nothing. Toby, don't get cocky with him. A lot of stuff has landed on him that he never bargained for. He's not the right guy for the position he's in, but he's the one who's in it. You may run up against your own limitations someday."

"Do I get cocky, Leo?"

He laughed.

"It's just a word to the wise," he said.

18

We were sitting on the back steps with the morning sunshine and our breakfast while Adam and Joss prospected for dinosaur bones in the bottom of the garden and disagreed about the division of the spoils.

"So now you know he's a housepainter," said Sara. "Now what?"

"Now I want to find out what job he's on just at present," I said. There was a weed in a pot of geraniums by my elbow, and I began digging at it with my spoon. "It shouldn't be hard. The contractor he works for is pretty small beans. They can't have a lot of jobs going at once. I don't want to just call the contractor up and ask, because word would probably get back to him. But it shouldn't be too hard." My weed yielded, but I had seen another in the next pot and I hunched down a step.

"The contractor has a couple of pickups and a corner of a warehouse in the industrial area. I presume his painters go there at the beginning of the day, get their gear, and go to their jobs. My thought would be to go hang around on Monday morning. If Hunter comes there and takes out a truck, then all I have to do is follow him."

"And then?" She began weeding the pots on the other side of the steps.

"Then we'll see. I don't know what the next step is. Monday and Tuesday are Fry's days off. If I think of something I don't want to take it straight to Barry, because he may shoot it down. But he won't say no to Fry. So on Wednesday we'll talk about it."

"I love hearing about the fine points of administration in the civil service," she said, and told me a bit of lubricious gossip about two of the partners in her firm.

There was a gap in the conversation, and then she said, "What would the Founding Fathers have thought if they had known that the front-line defenders of their heritage would be Barry Dillon and Charlie Footer?"

"From what I know about their period, they would have felt right at home."

"I hope you're right," she said glumly.

"Pass me the knife, would you?" I said. "This one's kind of deep."

It was at about this time that I had the first occurrence of what was to be a recurrent dream. I dreamt that I was in the woods outside of town, near the pit where our guy had been searching for Sara and the kids. This time, I was searching for him. It was very dark. I moved silently about through the trees, one hand extended in front of me, feeling my way with my feet. Sometimes I knew that he must be very close. Sometimes I could hear his breathing and feel the loom of him just beyond the reach of my arm.

The painting contractor's business was on a street of warehouses and light industry. There was a fair amount of traffic coming and going. There were no curbs, and a polyglot collection of vehicles was parked haphazardly over the margins. It was simple to find an inconspicuous spot half a block back.

Just before 8:00 the black GT appeared, moving, as always, much too fast. It darted into the parking area beside the contractor's warehouse, and Hunter emerged. He popped the trunk lid, fished out overalls, and put them on. Then he went inside. Ten minutes later he came out with several other men. They divided themselves among the two pickups and pulled out into the street.

Fortunately, Hunter wasn't driving. Whoever was driving was in no tearing rush, and there was no problem following. Both trucks drove to a commercial building in the center of the business district. There was scaffolding along one of the outside walls above a narrow driveway to the rear. The contractor and three of his painters went inside the building while Hunter and another man began passing buckets and equipment up onto the scaffolding, preparing to work.

I hastened to the Hall of Justice, three blocks away. Barry wasn't there, so that wasn't an obstacle. I called Fry. He wasn't answering. I knew he had parents out of town, and he often stayed with them on his days off. Gadek was somewhere out of the building, return indefinite. But Footer was in the office, and I explained the situation.

"It's a great setup," I said. "It's downtown, so there's lots of foot traffic, and we could hang around without being obvious. He's up on the scaffold, so he's easy to watch and nobody has to get too close to him. Running along the driveway there's a hedge, and on the other side of the hedge there's a parking lot for the bank next door. It'd be easy to hang out in the parking lot. Then if he throws down a butt, or spits, or drops some gum—whatever he lets go of that's got saliva on it—we just sidle in, scoop it up, and whip it off to the lab."

Footer was senior to me by six years. In the absence of a superior rank, the senior officer makes the decision. He listened carefully, left ear turned slightly forward, right foot jittering at a great rate.

"Hmm," he said. He'd got in trouble many times for jumping at things. "Oughta run it by Barry. Or Fry'll be back on Wednesday. Good to talk to him."

"But we've got time pressure," I said. "They've done all the patching and priming on the wall. The finish coat won't take more than a day. If his next job is indoors or on a house or something it'll be a lot harder to get near him. This is perfect now. It'll only get worse."

"Hmm," he said, for the sake of form. "Let's do it. Couple of bums. Got some old clothes? Run home. How quick can you be back?"

"Half an hour."

"Do it. I'll meet you here. Let's go." We hustled for the stairs.

In less than half an hour we were back. Footer's old clothes were more than old: they were patched and worn through the patches, and filthy, if not actually greasy, on every layer. Mine were not nearly so repellent.

"Ready in a mo," said Footer, and snatched up a phone. He dialed the bank whose parking lot we proposed to lurk in. He asked for the manager.

"Ah, yes," he said gravely. "This is Detective Footer with the Police Department. We are investigating a major felony case, and we will need to have two of our undercover agents working in your parking lot this morning. I'm calling so that we can coordinate our activities with your security people. . . . Ah, yes, well I'm afraid I'm not at liberty to divulge that at this time. . . . Yes, there will be two. They will be dressed like street people." He described us and our clothes. The manager promised that there would be no interference.

Next he called Patrol and had Dispatch notify the downtown beat officers that we would be working the bank.

Then we headed for the street.

Hunter was an energetic worker, faster than his companion, but so far as I could tell, doing a better job. He seemed entirely focused on his roller and the wall, getting the irregularities of the surface, laying a rich, smooth coat. He never took a moment to look around. I was pretty sure he hadn't noticed that Footer and I were anywhere near him. This was discouraging in itself, because I assumed that our guy would be a wary one, keeping an eye peeled, whatever else he might be doing. What I was watching here seemed to me suspiciously like honest work.

Nor, so far as I could see, did he have any bad habits that involved discarding saliva. The other painter on the platform smoked like a chimney and rained butts down into the driveway; when he wasn't smoking, or even when he was, he chewed gum, exhausted pieces of which he tossed periodically into the hedge between us. He blew his nose a lot, and let the breeze take the tissues where it would. He spat. Hunter painted smoothly away, seeming, at least in comparison of personal habits, like a highly genteel individual.

Footer was sitting on the base of a light standard between two parked cars close to the hedge. He had a bottle of wino wine in his hand. He was right where Hunter would drop or spit if he were dropping or spitting. Being cleaner, and therefore less alarming, I was at the edge of the lot, next to the street. There was a little plaza here with benches, where I lounged.

At midmorning the painters came out of the building and down from the scaffold, and ambled over to the plaza, as we had hoped they might. I lurked, watching for anything Hunter might leave behind. When they were done they all left butts and paper cups behind, except for Hunter, who, in addition to all his other categories of self-denial, apparently didn't drink coffee. He had a little package of cough drops which he kept in his cheek until they were small, and finally chewed and swallowed.

By lunchtime they had covered a large portion of the wall. The contractor came out of the building at noon, followed by his crew, and called the scaffold workers down to join them. They all gathered again on the benches. Nobody looked twice at me, and Hunter was the least conscious of the lot. He seemed to pay no attention to his surroundings. There are ways and ways of looking innocent when you're not, but the fact is that if you want to look around, then you have to look, however well you disguise your purpose, and if he had regarded himself either as predator or prey I was sure I would have caught him out.

Of course, if he made us when we first arrived, this could all be an act. In that case, he wouldn't have to look, because he already knows what there is to see. I didn't think this was the case, but it keeps your mind alive.

I had high hopes of his lunch. They were disappointed. I watched like a hawk, but there was simply no accessible saliva. We lounged away the afternoon while they finished the wall. Their afternoon break gave us nothing. We watched them disassemble the scaffold. Finally they loaded up their trucks and drove away. Footer ambled stiffly over.

"Fucked, Parkman," he said. Then he added, "It's too bad he isn't a woman. I could have seen right up her skirts from where I was sitting."

But by the time we got back to the office he was more sanguine.

"He's got a couple of warrants out," he said. "I checked. Traffic stuff. They can't have been in the computer when Lindy made her stop, or she'd have served 'em. We can pick him up on those anytime. Bring him in to the jail. We oughta be able to get something without him knowing." He looked at the floor. Then suddenly he smiled and looked up and said, "Hey, Parkman. Didja ever hear the one about the candlemaker and the nun?"

I hadn't, and he told me. It was actually sort of funny. But then we came back to the warrant idea, and kicked it around.

We would try to stop Hunter on a traffic violation on his way home from work on Friday afternoon so that he couldn't go before a judge until Monday morning. This meant that unless he could make bail he would be ours for the weekend, and it would be pitiful if we couldn't get a bit of his saliva in the course of sixty hours.

"Christ, you're gonna throw him in the slammer for three days just to get some spit?" said Barry when we told him. "Isn't that pretty heavy? He's got things to do, you know. He's in a bowling league."

But it was six to one again, and he said, "Well, screw it. Go ahead. I just hope I don't run into him between now and then."

"Good," said Fry. "We'll do it Friday. Uniforms for you and me. I'll go downstairs this evening and arrange a couple of patrol cars."

We would do this ourselves, rather than simply having Patrol do it, because if Hunter were our guy, and if he guessed what was happening, he could be expected to be dangerous. It wasn't fair to send a couple of beat officers into such a situation without warning them, and we couldn't warn them without everyone in the department knowing what we were doing and who we were after. Naturally, everyone would know that the task force had taken out two patrol cars, but they would only know that we were up to something, not what we were up to.

Barry walked in just in time for roll call. Except for the TV interview, he had spent most of the day in the office returning phone calls and pushing paper, Marcia had told us. She thought he looked worried.

The meeting was perfunctory. He didn't ask for updates or give directions. It was a bizarre situation.

Early enough on Friday afternoon I was waiting in a marked radar unit under cover of a little jig in the road. At the risk of showing some black fender I parked so that I could see the road in my side mirror and get a good shot with the radar gun. Fry, in another marked car, was positioned several blocks ahead, ready to cover me if the stop went as planned, or to intercept and box Hunter in if he decided to run.

He certainly didn't drive like someone trying to avoid notice. He was flying when he came into sight, and he handled the jig by pulling way over into the oncoming lane to make almost a straight line of it. The limit was twenty-five miles per hour. My radar said fifty-three. He saw me and braked hard to drop his speed, but it was too late. I shot out behind him and hit him with the roof lights. He pulled over at once. I called in that I was making a routine stop, and the location. This was Fry's signal to move in to the nearest cross street and stand by. We had decided that it would be suspicious if Fry showed up too soon, so we settled that I would make the initial part of the stop by myself.

The tricky part about making the arrest itself was that we were dealing with a man in connection with numerous series-related felonies, but the warrants were traffic violations, infractions. If we were busting him openly for felonies we'd do it with multiple cars, shotguns, loudspeakers, the whole nine yards—much safer for everyone concerned. Obviously, that would tip our hand. The car stop process for infractions is much more respectful of the citizen, and much more dangerous for the officer. Our principal protection would be that he would assume that we had no more in mind than the warrants, and that he wouldn't think that was worth major resistance.

I strolled up to his car, feeling like a target, forcing the fingers of my right hand not to curl around the butt of my revolver. I got his license, told him his speed, and strolled back to my car to write out the citation. Fry arrived after the proper interval, and together, looking, we hoped, professional but bored, we got him out of his car.

I said, "Mr. Hunter, you have three outstanding warrants for your arrest. I'm going to have to take you in."

"Aw, shit, man." He was pretty phlegmatic. "Well, make sure you lock up my car. God, you cops are a pain."

Fry locked Hunter's car and slipped the keys into his pocket. Then together we walked him toward my car.

A small car pulled up on the opposite side of the street. It was brightly polished. Its chrome wheelcovers glinted. Even the tires were polished. It was driven by a young woman who looked much like the car. Hunter looked over at her. Without changing expression he called out,

"Got some chicken-shit warrants. Pull some bread together, okay?"

She nodded and pulled away.

We put him in the front seat and belted him in. I thought it was about as smooth and light as a bust could be, and I think Fry thought so too.

But I had a sinking feeling that this was going to be another of those disappointing days. This chippie was bad luck. If she came up with the bail quickly it would reduce his time in custody and our hopes of collecting his saliva.

The jailer was in on what we wanted—there didn't seem to be any way to avoid it. Hunter had spent several nights in this very jail and knew what the routine was.

Booking went smoothly. We had a box of tissues on the booking desk in case he needed to sneeze or cough, but he didn't. He used his phone call to let his mother know what had happened and to arrange for her to see that his car was not left in the industrial area overnight. It didn't sound to me like a criminal mastermind at work.

Having seen Hunter into his cell, my job as arresting officer was done. I stayed in uniform, however, in case we needed to have any further contact with him. We convened in the task force office and tried to plan the evening's work. It was Patty's day off; I would have to stay in the office, and Footer had been working all day. That left Blondie and Fry for the street detail, and Fry wanted to stay around in case of any developments with Hunter, so it looked like Blondie by herself.

Our next hope was for dinner. After he ate he would have no place to put the paper napkin except back on his tray. But when the jailer went around the occupied cells to pick up the trays he found Hunter's untouched. I didn't blame him: it was some sort of TV dinner. You don't get hungry enough in one afternoon to eat that stuff. But breakfast, although much the same, might find him more receptive.

At 7:00, Footer went home.

We passed the evening in the office pursuing the driest paper leads.

At 10:00, Blondie departed for the street.

At 10:15 the front desk called up: Hunter's girlfriend was here to bail him out.

"Oh, Jesus."

Fry just shook his head.

I went out to the front counter to see if there were any nits I could pick with the bail, but everything was in order, and soon he and his girlfriend had departed.

Gloomily, I headed back to the office. Fry passed me, dashing down the stairs.

"Change and get your car," he called over his shoulder. "We've got a hit going down right now, and Blondie's the only one on the street."

19

She had gone to bed at her usual time, but she had a sore tooth, and it hurt enough to keep her awake. After tossing and turning for a while she got up to get some aspirin from the bathroom. The bathroom door was open. The bathroom window was directly opposite the neighbor's back porch light, and the light cast the shadow of the sash and curtains on the opposite side of the hall. As she came to the bedroom door she saw, dimly but quite distinctly, that the sash was up. She saw the shadow of a man beginning to lift himself in through the window.

She screamed. Still screaming, she grabbed up her purse from the foot of the bed and dragged out the key chain and whistle. She sounded peal after peal. The shadow had disappeared at the first sound but she did not stop blowing. Holding the whistle to her lips and blowing frantically, she raced around the room, turning on all the lights. She threw open her bedroom window. She seized the phone and dialed the emergency number.

It rang and rang.

All the lines were lit up, and there were only two dispatchers. They answered as quickly as they could. All the calls were from around the same intersection: screaming and a

209

whistle blowing. One of the dispatchers put out a hot call alert, giving what they had: "For cars in the north end . . ." She gave the intersection and glanced at the other dispatcher for a more specific location, but he shook his head. "Woman screaming and whistle blowing. Several calls. Exact location unknown. More to follow." She turned again to the phones, cutting short the callers who had no new information. It was almost three minutes before the intended victim's call got through.

The intruder ran immediately. As we later pieced it together, he ran west through the block, crossed the first street, went through the second block, crossed another street, and disappeared into the third block. Someone in this third block heard him in his backyard, climbing the fence. He called, but his report was "a funny noise," and the Communication Center was still getting calls about the screaming woman. The dispatcher hadn't even time to take his name. She told him to call back in half an hour.

Our tactic of response was based on the assumption that the alarm had not been raised and that we could get into position before our guy realized that he had been noticed. This was not that sort of call, but Blondie did the best she could, on the off chance that he might not have run immediately, or might have been delayed in getting out of the block; even bad guys sometimes twist an ankle or fall off a fence. With the location of occurrence given as an intersection, she was faced with responding to any of four blocks. She found a spot half a block to the west and settled in within three or four minutes, but he was gone long before she was in position. Fry was in the vicinity in ten minutes or so, I a little longer. It was much too late to hope for an interception. We recorded license numbers on the chance that he had parked nearby and then left his car behind when he fled on foot. But it didn't pan out.

And there was trouble, for Barry, at any rate.

Lieutenant Bloom happened to be in his office working late on his division budget. When the call went down he heard it on his monitor and he thought it would be a good opportunity to observe how the task force handled these things. He didn't rush out into the street, but he followed our transmissions. You didn't need to be a lieutenant to realize that everyone was out of position, the response much too slow to accomplish anything, and the whole exercise seemingly leaderless. When the cover broke he called us all in like children who have somehow escaped from supervision.

Where was Barry? He was never around during the day—Bloom had assumed he was working nights. Why were two out of three of us in the HOJ instead of in the target area? Who was Wesley Hunter? What on earth was going on?

Marcia said, "Toby, do you have any idea where Barry is?"

"No, of course not."

"He hasn't been in at all today. Lieutenant Bloom's been trying to get ahold of him, among others. I can only cover for him so often."

Barry appeared, looking grim. He whipped the messages off his spindle and disappeared into his office, closing the door. A minute later he reappeared and said, "Toby, everything's standard tonight. You run roll call. I got things to do." He was looking harried.

"Right," I said, but he had already closed the door.

Fry appeared.

"Is Barry around?" he asked Marcia. He hadn't forgotten his promise to have a little chat.

"Yes and no," she said. Fry made a face. He went to the door and knocked. There was a noise beyond, and he disappeared, closing the door behind him. A moment later the door opened again, and I heard Barry saying, "Yeah, a little while. I'll let you know. Close the door, willya?"

"What's going on in there?" I asked. Fry looked displeased and shook his head.

"I dunno," he said. "He said I could talk to him later. He isn't doing anything hot—at least, not about the case."

"Well, there's a number of things—"

"Yeah. Well, stick around. You can have him when I'm done with him."

After an hour or so Barry came to the door and called Fry in. Fry rose from his desk looking suddenly very senior and responsible. Barry noticed the expression on his face and looked surprised.

"Leave the door open," he said, but Fry closed it.

They were closeted for the better part of an hour. When Fry came out he was looking just as stern as he had when he went in. He tossed his head toward the door and returned silently to his work. I went in.

Barry was sitting behind his desk doing something with a fingernail. He looked edgy and unhappy. He said, "Okay, what's up?" But he didn't look at me.

I had a lot of stuff. All the press coverage was bringing in a constant trickle of tips, and the ones that couldn't be discounted on their face had to be run down. We assumed that last night's attempt was by our guy, but of course we weren't sure; Hunter was still in custody at that time, so did we drop him or keep working on him? The street details were always coming up with odd bits of information that weren't getting dealt with. Who was to do it all? Who was to do what?

It wasn't my job to tell him all this—it wasn't anyone's. It was Barry's job to know it already, to be up on it all the time. It was embarrassing to have to call his attention to it. Finally he interrupted me and said, "Look, Toby, what're you bringing all this to me for? You've got it, you know what to do with it. You're a big boy now, I shouldn't have to wipe your nose for you." His eyes met mine momentarily and then wandered.

"No. But what we've got here is full-time work for someone for weeks. Footer can't keep up with it. It means taking someone off the street to do it—or more, if you want it done quick. We can't make that decision."

"No problem. You're it. You come off the street and do it. Type up the order and bring it to me." He glanced at his watch. "I gotta meet someone. So listen, Toby." His voice sounded distant. "You guys oughta be able to keep busy. If you've got something hot, go for it. You don't need me to tell you that. I'm here every day—if you've got a question, ask it. But I can't do everything." He looked quite puzzled and unhappy. "I'm doing my part, keeping the press at bay."

Fry didn't look up when I came out, and I went back to

my desk. I looked at the street schedule. If you took me out of it altogether the ends wouldn't meet. I went back to Barry's office. He was sitting, fidgeting, not working.

"Look, Barry, I don't think this is going to work." I held up the schedule. "I think—"

"Shit, Toby," he shouted. "Will you stop fuckin' whining all the time? What's the matter with you? *Just take care of it.* That's my order. *You* take care of it. *You* decide. *You* do it. Now clear out."

I was already out. I hadn't got farther in than the door, and I backed clear. Fry and Marcia were staring. Barry suddenly emerged, locked his door, and stalked out without a word or a look to anyone.

I turned to Fry.

"Do you know what in hell's going on?" I said. I was stunned. I had been lectured, patronized, chilled, and ignored at various times by my superiors, but I'd never been sworn at. I didn't like it.

"Yeah, more or less," he said glumly. "All of a sudden he isn't getting on so well with Ivy. She may be going off the reservation."

It was all too true. Whatever it was between them, suddenly it had cooled. Barry didn't talk about that part of it. He didn't seem to understand what was happening.

Thinking back, I had the impression that Ivy hadn't been around much during the last few days. Of course, I worked odd hours and I might not know, but Marcia said I was right. And she also said that the last time Ivy had been in the office she had been very cool and professional, which was a change. Barry, on the other hand, was in the office more and more in the days following Fry's little chat, but he was even less attentive to business than before. Marcia said that he had begun to call up reporters who, in the previous weeks, had always called him. He had nothing to give them; he just wanted contact.

Cops are very insular, and although we had all been flattered by the media attention, we were offended that Barry should have chosen glamour in preference to his duty and his real friends. It was impossible not to feel a proper reassertion of the natural order of things when his affairs began to totter.

Patty said, "The real world's a rough place. He should have stayed with us."

Then Ivy did a public thing. She had already shot footage for a review of the series. There was some footage of Barry just before the interview began, including one of him picking his nose with his finger. Ivy reedited the piece, including this shot, and renarrated the whole thing. There was a strong suggestion that the task force was floundering and that innocent women would continue to suffer because of *bumbling*—and this over the shot of Barry dabbing his nose with his finger—*bumbling at the top*.

A bolt of lightning went through the media community. This had been Ivy's story, and everyone had followed her lead. It was common knowledge that she was pretty friendly with the commander of the task force, but so what? And now—a revolution. If *Ivy* had doubts . . . The phone began to ring again. Voices formerly friendly were redolent of skepticism. What *was* the vaunted task force doing, exactly? Why *wasn't* it getting results? When *would* an arrest be made? When would innocent women be *safe* again? *What was wrong with the command?*

Barry was no politician. Finesse was not in his repertoire. Got a brick wall? Punch it. Didn't crack? Punch it again. Unluckily, these were not the requisite virtues at such a moment.

Then the second shoe dropped. Polly Rhine called a reporter and told him her story. The rapist's identity was known to the police, she said, but they were doing nothing because he was a buddy of Sergeant Dillon's. Women were being victimized because Dillon refused to act. Now the department was engaged in a cover-up.

Two weeks before, most reporters would have thought long and hard before printing such a tale. Not now. The reporter had a sensational scoop, and he made the most of it. The rest of the media hastened to interview Rhine and add whatever tidbits had escaped their colleague. She was a striking individual with a loud, clear voice. She made great quips. She was made for TV.

The mayor promised an investigation. The city manager called in the chief and told him to clean it up, and quick.

Barry was summoned to the chief's office. Captain Claypool and Lieutenant Bloom were already there. They had a long chat.

Early in the evening of July 22, the Communication Center received an emergency call for an ambulance in the southwestern corner of the target area. The caller was hard to understand, highly excited. The task force was still in the office. It was unclear whether there was something still in progress, so Patrol responded to cover the ambulance.

She was the forty-fifth victim, a woman of nearly seventy. Both her elbows were sprained, one wrist broken, and both eardrums burst. After he left her she had lain helpless for the rest of the night and the following day until a neighbor, quite by chance, came by to return a borrowed magazine and found the front door ajar.

Blondie and I spent most of the following morning doing the interview, which was grim. The tantalizing thing about it was that we both were sure that she had seen him.

"She was in the living room, wide awake, when he came in," Blondie said to Gadek.

"She all but said that she had seen him," I said. "She all but said it several times, but then she would clam up and look away. He threatened her."

"She believed it, too," said Blondie. "Poor old lady, living by herself. She believed every word."

"We pressed as hard as we thought we could, but it was no go," I said. "We came back to it a couple of times and tried different approaches. It was really hard on her, and so we dropped it."

"Maybe she'll change her mind later," said Blondie. "I'll keep in touch with her." Blondie did go back, twice, but the victim wouldn't speak about it. And about three weeks after the hit she had a stroke and never spoke again.

"Well," said Blondie, "it's something new. This is the first time we know of that he hasn't just run off when someone sees him."

* * *

Marcia looked tired when I came into the office next day for roll call. She was transcribing the narrative report for the old lady. I nodded.

"There are things I could have lived and died without knowing," she said. Then she looked around and said, "Barry is gone."

"So?" I said. "He's—"

"No, that's not what I meant."

Gadek and Lieutenant Bloom strode into the room and across to the table. Everyone broke up their conversations and sat down. I seemed to be the last to know.

"Are we all here?" said Bloom in his "we'd better be" tone of voice. "Good. As you've heard, there was another attack in this series last night, and I won't keep you longer than necessary. But I have some administrative matters.

"Number one. You have perhaps been aware that Sergeant Dillon has been overstressed of late."

Charlie Footer guffawed, glancing around the table for partners in his amusement. Luckily for everyone else, we noticed Bloom's face before joining in. Seven stony stares froze Footer into silence.

"At the suggestion of the chief," continued Bloom, "Barry has taken some long-overdue vacation and compensatory overtime. We expect him back in about six weeks, at which time he will be given a new assignment."

There wasn't a sound.

"With Barry out of action, the chief has approved my recommendation and appointed Sergeant Gadek as commander of the task force. I think you've all worked with Leo, and have the same confidence in him that I do, and that the chief does. Usually these transfers take place with some notice, but in this case Leo's appointment is effective immediately.

"Let me just say a word about the atmosphere you're working in. I'm talking about politics and the press, if there's any difference." A chuckle. "For your information, the press officer is now the only member of the department who is authorized to talk about your work. You have no comment. You have no comment about why you have no comment.

Refer any questions politely but firmly to the press officer. Is that clear? Good.

"People, for a long time the press ignored this series. Then we had great press, for which we're grateful, but which didn't mean that we were doing a better job than we were doing. Now we're getting terrible press, but that doesn't mean that we're doing a worse job than we're doing. It means that politicians and the media aren't in the same business we're in.

"They say that good actors never read their reviews. Try to follow that example. Try not to pay attention. Do your job, for professional reasons. Let the media do what they do, and on Judgment Day"—he hesitated, and got a chuckle—"we'll know who was right. It can wait till then. Leo, it's all yours." He left the room.

Gadek said, "We know he isn't going to hit tonight—he's never done two nights in a row—so the street detail's canceled. The first thing I want to do is to find out where the case is and what each of you is doing. I can see what's on the walls and Marcia can show me the files, but before you go tonight I want to spend a few minutes with each of you so I'll have a sense of where we're at. Toby and Blondie handled this morning at the hospital. I'll start with them so they can get home."

Gadek spent the first night and day of his new command catching up on the paper that the case had generated during the six weeks since the task force had formed. The second night he spent on the street with the detail, familiarizing himself with what we were doing, how we worked as a group, and how each individual functioned. The second day he posted a new schedule which put us all on a rotating basis so that none of us spent more than three days in a row on the street, and all of us had a packet of eliminations and investigations to be responsible for. He met with each of us at least once a week to go over our packet and review progress.

Wesley Hunter had wound up in my packet.

"He's not our guy," said Gadek, "but this Polly Rhine is going around making speeches saying we're protecting him

217

because he's Barry's friend. I hate to waste the time, but we need a positive elimination."

I explained our difficulties.

"Well, it was a good try. But if sneaky doesn't work, try direct. Go knock on his door, explain the situation, tell him if he cooperates we'll be off his back."

This had the brilliance of simplicity. I went that very evening and found Hunter polishing his GT in the driveway and enjoying the lingering July twilight with two under-dressed lady friends. I explained matters. You never know how people will react to this sort of thing: Sir, we suspect that you are a violent and sadistic serial rapist and I would like you to chew on this piece of gauze and then spit it into this vial.

Outrage? Violence?

He laughed hugely, not because it was such an outland-ishly inappropriate calumny that nobody could take it seri-ously but because he regarded it as a professional compliment to his cocksmanship. He could scarcely have been more forthcoming with me, in a large, patronizing way, and I came away five minutes later with a prime saliva sample.

Unfortunately, when the lab analysis came back, he wasn't eliminated: he fell into the same 20 percent of the male population as our guy.

"Go back," said Gadek calmly, "and explain about the test. Tell him you want a sample of his pubic hair for com-parison—*that* should clear things up."

"What if it doesn't, Leo? What if he *is* our guy?"

"Then I'm going to feel like a first-rate ass, because he'll go and dump whatever evidence he's holding and we've spoiled our best chance at holding him." He laughed, and then he said, "But of course, it's your name on all this paper."

Back I went. Again I found him in front with his car and several friends of both sexes. The men had beer bellies and loud voices, the women very tight pants and done hair.

Hunter declined to be taken aside, and everyone gathered around to hear what the cop had to say. My explanation that the test had not eliminated him raised a great swell of jocularity, with the men congratulating him on his enterprise and the women saying that nobody who'd dated him could doubt it for a minute, and so on. This continued for some time, with Hunter enjoying it more than anybody else. When they'd exhausted the immediate comic possibilities of serial rape and had come to some sort of order, I explained that the next layer of analysis was a hair comparison, and for that I wanted a sample of his pubic hair. Another burst of laughter, and on the crest of it Hunter reached paradingly into his pants and yanked, coming up with a pretty good yield; hastily I produced my specimen bottle, secured my samples, and left these innocents to their noisy pleasures.

In due course, the lab comparison of hair samples removed Hunter from contention. Gadek provided copies to the press officer, and the intimations of an insider vanished from all but the most intransigent press venues.

Barry called me at home a couple of times in the weeks following his departure. We had some beers together. He reminisced, mostly about Ivy. I told him how the task force was getting on. He listened, at first with a general professional interest, but increasingly with discomfort and even a penitential manner. I think it became clear to him, listening to what Gadek was doing, what he should have done himself. And he could have done it, more or less, if he'd kept his wits about him. Once or twice he said something vague about having learned a few things and how he would do things differently when he came back.

By an ironic coincidence, the day I received the lab report eliminating Hunter was also the day we heard that Barry had resigned from the department for good. There was a family business somewhere, people said. He'd had enough of police work and he was going to go into whatever-it-was. I don't know what changed his mind, because I never saw him privately after he made the decision to quit.

He threw himself a little going-away party at a bar that cops frequent, and among a number of others he invited me. He didn't invite Gadek, or Fry. He told us, individually and in groups, loudly and repeatedly, that he wasn't going to miss it. I went to the party intending to tell him that I was sorry he was leaving, but that didn't seem to fit the occasion, so I joined with the others in congratulating him on his escape.

A week later he went shooting with a couple of friends. They all got rather drunk, and one of them dropped his rifle. It went off and Barry was hit in the thigh. It needn't have been a fatal wound, but the friend who knew first aid stumbled off to call for help, and the one who remained didn't know what to do. By the time help arrived it was too late.

Fry said it was a tragic ending for an unlucky man. Footer said it was a clown's end for a clown. Taking Barry all in all I had to agree with Fry, of course, but if you left personal sympathies out of the question there was a lot to be said for Footer's point of view.

August brought us no reports of new attacks. Every night the street detail diligently plied its routine. We arrested a burglar, a peeper, an exhibitionist, two vandals, and an abusive ex-husband in defiance of a cease-and-desist order, all of whom blundered into our clutches; but not our guy.

At the end of August, Melanie gave a little off-to-college party for Mike. There were family friends and several of Mike's contemporaries of both sexes. Walt was there. Mike made a point of bringing his friends to Walt to be introduced and shoot the breeze. Walt was mixing street stories with references to Suetonius and Dickens in a very engaging way. Mike's friends were much taken with him, and Mike was clearly pleased as punch.

In early September it had been six weeks without a report, and the brass inquired whether Gadek might not be able to spring a couple of his people for other duties. He showed them his docket of leads assigned but not yet completed, the list of leads still unassigned, and the log of current tips to be investigated. They told him to press on.

By October the media had largely lost interest in our work, either its success or its failure. The press officer was closemouthed and not photogenic, so there was little to report except the bare facts. Publicity dwindled to a trickle, and our flow of new tips along with it. But the tips we got were more substantial ones. Although there was usually some element of animus or personality to be considered, there was usually also some observation, some pattern of behavior that suggested a possible involvement. Often these things were secondhand: "somebody I know" had suspicions about a friend or co-worker. The somebody wouldn't call, but the third party would. These things had to be approached carefully even if they were long shots. Until you write off a possibility you have to treat it as if it's the key to everything. If word gets back to the subject that he's being investigated, it gives him every opportunity to cover himself, destroy any evidence he may be holding, or simply disappear.

Gadek's system of parceling out these investigations meant that we each had a few in one stage or another of resolution. Each of us met with him at least once a week to go over our whole packet case by case.

"What's up?" I said to Gadek in the middle of October. "The last hit was on July twenty-second."

"It's happened before," he said. "Maybe they're not reporting. Maybe he's on vacation."

"Maybe he's died of old age."

"Could be. Now, this tip about the parks department worker—how're you coming on that one?"

On November 14, an insurance agent returned unexpectedly to her apartment in the middle of the day. She had brought work home the night before, forgotten to take it to the office, and now she was coming back for it. She was astonished to find her large sliding kitchen window standing wide open.

The window was about four feet above the ground. Outside was a strip of ground five feet wide that ran all around the building, bounded by an ivy-covered fence, very secluded. She looked out. There was no one there. She closed the window and locked it, got her papers, and went back to the office.

As we pieced it together afterward, he had just come in. He was probably in the kitchen closet, right behind her, while she was dealing with the window. After she left, he spent most of the day there.

That night he came back, a little after midnight. He was there for more than three hours. When he left, he ordered her not to move for an hour, he might hang around to check, blah blah blah, but when he went out the window he slipped and fell. He grabbed the curtain to try to save himself, pulled down the rod, kicked over the chair he had climbed on, and fell anyway. It made a lot of noise. The victim heard it and knew what it meant—that he wasn't standing right over her, ready to beat her if she moved. She got one eye partly clear of the tape and made a run for it, bursting out her front door into the hallway screaming at the top of her lungs. It woke the other tenants on the ground floor, and they started calling the police in a big way. They were *all* calling, in fact, and none of them dared to open their doors to see what was happening. The victim was terrified that he was going to come storming back in after her, and she began running up and down the hall, pounding on doors, first this one and then that, screaming to be let in. That just reduced the neighbors to jelly, and they told the dispatchers that someone was being murdered—multiple reports of murder in progress. Patrol went straight in, major response. The task force was in good position, but of course we were last to arrive, and of course he was gone before we got there. It was a close shave for him, but he got away.

Blondie and I went to the hospital to take the narrative while Patty did the rerecording. He had taken a bracelet from her. We got a description and made a careful note of it. If ever we got a bad guy and did a search, it would be a very identifiable piece.

The license plate inventory was negative. We had been recording licenses for more than five months, and this was our first chance to try the license rerecording on a fresh hit.

"I wonder if there's something we're not getting," said Gadek. "If he's driving, you'd think we'd have picked up his car. I can't believe he's walking into the area and never running into our detail. But what could we not be getting? What else is there?"

"Maybe he's parking farther away than we've been assuming, and then moving through blocks instead of on the street," I said.

"That's a high-risk way for him to get around," he said. "You can act innocent on the street, but if you're in somebody's backyard at midnight it's hard to pretend you're looking for your tennis ball. He's always been very conservative, so far as we've known for certain how he works."

"Lucky?"

"That may be it. You hate to think it comes down to that, but maybe it does. He's got all the advantages. He doesn't have to make any move he doesn't think is safe. He's got a good system, and he's sticking to it. But sooner or later he'll make a wrong choice, or something won't go the way it always has. Nothing goes in a straight line for very long." He scratched his ear. "I'd really love to wrap this up. I haven't been sleeping very well."

At roll call Gadek said, "Sooner or later we're going to lay our hands on a suspect. When that day comes, we may not have anything very tight to hold him on. If he blunders into the middle of the street detail we might well pick him up for trespassing or peeping or something equally dinky, and he's going to bail out like a shot unless we have a good story to tell the judge. We'll have to have warrants for a search of his car and residence so he can't get home to sanitize them. We want to be ready.

"I'm taking Charlie Footer off the street detail altogether. He's going to work full-time and put together a draft warrant and supporting documents: all the souvenirs our guy's taken, anything we suspect he might be holding that would link him to the series. So that when the time comes, all we have to do is fill in a name and wake up a judge."

Later, I said, "Leo, are you starting work on the warrant to keep our spirits up, or do you think something is going to change?"

He didn't miss a beat. He said, "I get up every morning assuming that we're going to get this guy today. I hope you do, too. Are you getting tired, Toby?"

"No. I just like to know what's in front of me."

"You know what's on my mind. Y'know, there's such a

thing as making things more complicated than they need to be."

I was the only member of the group who lived with a spouse and children, and the consensus was that I should have December 24 and 25 off. At about 11:00 on Christmas Eve, the whole street detail—Fry, Patty, Blondie, and Gadek—came by our house on the way to their quadrants and stood in the front yard and sang carols amidst much hilarity. The kids were asleep. Sara and I had gone to bed early to catch up on our marriage. We had to scramble into our bathrobes and rush to the window with happy smiles, but it was hard to be irritated.

"Maybe they'll pick him up tonight," I said as we got undressed again. "That's what I'd call Christmas."

"Wouldn't you be disappointed if you weren't in on it?" she asked.

"Not tonight," I said. "Not if they get him tonight."

Walt said, "Mike's home for Christmas vacation. I dunno, Tobe. College is killing him. He'll tell me, but he won't tell Melanie, and he won't let me tell her. He says there are things you don't tell his mother, and not being able to do things is one of them. I can't talk him around. That kid just makes things harder than they need to be."

"It's in the bone," I said. "It's not something you decide."

On January fifth, a cashier in a restaurant reported that she had been raped on the fourth. I went to take the narrative. She was very cool, very matter-of-fact, except that when I would ask her quite straightforward questions she would stare at me for long moments before answering, as if trying to reconcile her newfound reality with mine. There are the people who've gone through this sort of thing, and then there are the people who haven't.

20

Oh, wait, just a moment," said Marcia brightly. "Here's Officer Parkman. Will you hold, please?" She punched the hold button. "En garde," she said. "Tipster on three."

"Righteous?"

"You're the detective," she said primly. "She's angling. She wants me to drop stuff she can use."

I picked up the phone on my desk. "Parkman."

The voice on the other end was masterful.

"Now, are you a real cop, or another secretary or something?"

"I'm a real cop. What can I do for you?"

"Well, I know who your rapist is." It was very strong, the way she said it. If Marcia hadn't set me up I'd have had a real jolt. She was very intense.

"Who is it?"

"It's my ex—my *former* gentleman friend. It's Henry Dorn."

"And your name is . . . ?

"Beatrice Malley."

"Okay, Ms. Malley." I was taking notes and trying not to sound preoccupied when I spoke. "And you said the person we want is Henry Dorn?"

"That's what I said."

"And what makes you think our rapist is Henry Dorn?"

"What makes me *think*? I don't *think*. I *know*. I *know* who it is. Look, if *you* don't want to know, just say so. Just say so. I've got things to do. I don't need this what do I *think*. I don't need it."

"Really, Ms. Malley. Please excuse me. I didn't mean to sound skeptical. Please tell me what you know."

There are lots of things to bear in mind when listening to the tales of informants, and one is that they often don't tell their tales very well. You could tell in two minutes that Beatrice Malley was a very difficult woman who had been mortally aggrieved by this fellow Dorn. Her thinking was partial and disorganized. Listening to her was tedious. But all of this didn't mean that she didn't know something that could be useful or even crucial to us. Sprinkled among the many topics she covered were such verifiable facts as his having served time for burglary, which was an element in Gadek's profile of our guy. On a more subjective level, she cited several instances of personal cruelty and malignity.

People came and went in the office. I scarcely noticed. I talked with Beatrice Malley for upwards of an hour. If half of what she was saying was true, he was a stinker of the first water. His arrest record was interesting, if true, because burglars sometimes do a bit of rape as a recreation. Henry Dorn sounded great.

Nevertheless, I wasn't getting excited. It was interesting but general. I wasn't hearing anything to link him to these particular rapes. And obviously there were yellow lights.

The first yellow light was that she clearly hated this guy with a passion. That might be very natural if he was, in fact, our guy, but it was a problem. Everyone has a point of view that you have to discover and allow for, but the stronger that point of view is, the more careful you have to be. Our guy is hateful, but many men are hateful without being our guy.

And she wasn't a reliable reporter of fact. She inferred from circumstance and from her assumptions about Dorn's attitude and motives that he had done certain things, and then stated her conviction as fact.

226

And she wasn't telling me anything factual that she couldn't have read in *Shout*. That article had mentioned several features of our guy's standard routine, and she was describing them, but she wasn't giving me anything else. *Shout*'s informants didn't have perfect or complete information; there was all sorts of ripe stuff that the article didn't include. If she had mentioned any of that, I'd have been panting. But she hadn't, and I wasn't.

And she wasn't giving me any hard connection with any crime. What we had, if her facts checked out, was a real bad actor with appropriate predilections, someone who might prove to be, but was not yet proven, the one we wanted.

What Malley was proposing was that she work with us on the investigation, consider it case by case, and by her intimate knowledge of Dorn's life establish his culpability. This was clearly a fantasy for her: all the detectives with their papers and reports sitting around in a circle throwing out mysterious circumstances, and she in the center of all, weaving her enemy into the pattern, giving it shape and substance, while all the detectives earnestly copied down her information.

Every informant has a motive, some disinterested, some not. The desire to be of consequence, to be central to some famous event, is a common one. It's a less repellent motive than hatred, but it's no more likely to promote truthfulness.

I declined, politely, to make Malley a principal in the investigation. You don't give informants facts that they don't know already. If they're accurate and disinterested, their information will correspond in some way with what you know already, and they don't need to know what you know. If you give a sincere informant a new fact, he will fold it into his story unconsciously and think it's his own. A liar will do the same thing consciously. Either way, the truth gets lost.

At length we ground to some sort of standstill. It was a dignity issue with her. She was giving me stuff, and I wasn't giving her anything. I tried to deal with this by citing "regulations," and by complimenting her on her civic-mindedness. This didn't satisfy her, but she didn't stop talking, either.

It was all very unsatisfactory, but I couldn't write her off. I made an appointment to meet with her the following day.

Marcia said, "Well, that must have sounded better to you than it did to me."

"No, probably not. But hey, what do I know? I'm just a bureaucrat."

"Now, Toby," said Gadek, laying down a map he was annotating. "Marcia said you had an informant on the horn. She sure seemed to know how to talk. What did she have?"

"I don't know. She's not a nut. Certainly another vengeful ex. Perhaps a real tip." I summarized what Beatrice Malley had to say about Henry Dorn.

"It rings a bell," said Gadek, when I mentioned the name. "Wasn't he a burglar? Years ago, right after I joined. Seems to me he went down for a lot of burgs."

"That's what she says. Basically her formula is burglar plus class-A jerk. But she's soft on details. I'm going to see her tomorrow."

"Okay. You wantta do that alone or take someone?"

"I'd like to take someone. She's big on dignity, and she sounds lonely. I think a little Mutt-and-Jeff action might work very well with her."

"Fine." He looked at the schedule. "Take Myron. Don't get fancy. If she takes a shine to one of you, use it, but don't jerk her around."

"I'll be gentle."

"Keep me posted."

Next day, as appointed, Fry and I arrived at Beatrice Malley's to see what substantial dirt she might have to throw on Henry Dorn. We agreed between us that he would be sympathetic and I would be skeptical: Mutt and Jeff. He and I hadn't worked together enough to run this device on a very sophisticated level, but even crudely done it works. A person unsure of his position will ally himself with a friendly interviewer against an unfriendly one, and he'll make his alliance valuable by rewarding his "friend" with information and cooperation.

We defend the liberties of our nation by imposing on the simple with these paltry manipulations. Well, why not?

Malley lived in the best building in a bad neighborhood, in a penthouse which shared the top floor with the communal laundry room. Her furnishings were cheap and grandiose. There would have been a certain rough justice in likening her to her furnishings. She was lonely, needy, bitter, imaginative, intelligent, aimless. A dangerous person.

Fry took charge. He asked her to recapitulate what she had told me, by which device we would know if she told her story the same way twice. She did, more or less. Then he asked her various friendly questions about details, and listened respectfully to her interminable answers.

Then I began to question some of her assertions: what she knew, how she knew it, what was her observation, what was her inference, what was gossip. I began with polite skepticism and became by degrees less polite and more skeptical. Frequently Fry would interject himself, and rephrase my questions in a less pointed manner. She fell in with it, attaching herself to him and answering his questions, rejecting mine and rebuking me. We were there for three hours before Fry raised an interrogatory eyebrow and I nodded.

Outside, we compared notes. She had no single fact about the series not previously published; she had nothing to connect Henry Dorn with any crime. He had been a burglar, he took precautions against being followed, he kept irregular hours. On the question of her own state of mind, we were divided: I was inclined to think that in her ignorance she sincerely believed that this miasma constituted proof of his guilt; Fry was inclined to doubt that even she believed it.

But we both agreed that Dorn was worth putting on the list of names to check out. The fact that she hadn't implicated him didn't eliminate him. On his face, he was a very promising individual. We reported this to Gadek.

"We both think he's a worthwhile name," Fry said. "We'd be interested if we had the bare facts without her as a complication."

Gadek said, "I agree. Let's start looking for the usual quick eliminations. Fry, you'll have to work on that before street time. A couple of days ought to give you a pretty clear idea whether he's worth going on with. Let's just hope we don't have any emergencies."

Early that evening a woman called the office to report that her best friend had been raped six days before, on February first. The victim couldn't pull herself together to call, but she would talk, according to the friend. Everyone now had experience in taking these things, and bodies were short, so Gadek sent Patty by herself to take the interview. She was back in a couple of hours. It was, in fact, our guy. There was one novelty: he told the victim that he had a knife, and to prove it gave her several superficial but very scary stab wounds on her shoulders and upper chest. She let Patty see the wounds and make a diagram of their location in her report, but she absolutely refused to be photographed.

"She was scared out of her gourd," said Patty. "He threatened to come back if she told. She won't even see a shrink."

"He's trying out a new turn-on, cutting her." said Gadek. "It's going to get worse."

At roll call that night Gadek showed us a new map of the target area.

"You can see—the red dots are last year, yellow this year—he's working more to the north than he did. I suppose he's extending his trolling activities out from the areas he knows, and after he's been around a new street for a while and gotten comfortable with it, then he'll hit. But he's also working the older areas too—here, here, here. So the whole thing is getting bigger, and we'll have to expand. Let's say three blocks north, to here, in addition to what we've got already. It's your call when you're on the street, but if it were me I'd push well north—really jam the northeast corner. That's the direction he's tending in, and I think that's where he'll hit next. If he hits southwest, of course, then you'll be way off position."

That night there were no fewer than four reports from the target area.

The first call was a suspicious person seen skulking by a bush in front of the house opposite the reporting party. That came in at about 10:30, from a block almost at the southwest corner. Of course we were all jammed up in the northeast, so our response was slow. When we were all concealed and Patrol went in they found that the suspicious person was a bundle of garden debris put out for collection.

The second call, received at 10:56, was to report a suspicious noise, perhaps someone climbing the caller's back fence, in the northeast corner. We dashed back to our cars, crossed to the opposite corner, and settled in. Patrol responded, found nothing, and left. This was a low-hope operation, since there was only one suspicious noise without any recurrence or anything seen, but it was the best we had going. We waited.

The third call, at 12:12, reported a man seen at the window of a neighbor's house, still there as the reporting party spoke. Occupant of the house reported to be a single woman living alone. The location was in the west. We broke our low-hope cover, pelted back down to the new call, and settled into a tight pattern. As we approached, Dispatch put out updates: the man was working on the lock of the window; he had it open; he was going in. Patrol decided not to wait, and responded before we were fully in place. They found the single woman on the front porch; she had lost her key, and her boyfriend had cheated a window to let her in.

We had to get our recording done, Blondie for east-west and me for north-south, so we went directly from call number three to the beginning of our first street and started in. The fourth call came in at 12:22: a woman reporting that someone was in her house, downstairs. It was the west again. Patty and Fry had never left the west after the last call. They'd found a quiet place to sit down and chew the fat. So they were right on the spot. Blondie and I were a little longer. Patrol dashed in. Two uniforms found an open window and were in like a flash. A moment later the front door burst open and a real burglar, not our guy but a real criminal and not just some boyfriend or bag of dead leaves, came flying out with a stereo amplifier in his arms and his pockets full of the household silver. He was busted with great satisfaction by seven uniforms from the night shift while our people looked on from their hiding places.

And then a mistake was made.

A woman on the same street called to report a man standing in her neighbor's backyard across the street from the burglary. The dispatcher was green, and confusing the way street numbers work—odd on one side, even on the other—got confused about what side of the street the woman was calling from and thought that she was reporting one of the task force people getting up from his hiding place behind the victim's house. Instead of reporting the call to Control and letting him verify that the report was of a police officer, the dispatcher simply reassured the caller and forgot about it.

It was our guy.

We had a dozen cops within twenty-five yards of him.

The burglar was put in a car and whisked away; the beat officer took the beginning of his report and then went off to the HOJ to finish it; the other uniforms dispersed to their beats; Blondie and I returned to our taping; and Fry and Patty to their quadrants. In fifteen minutes the street was as quiet as before.

The woman who had called watched the police leave. The man was still there, almost invisible between two bushes. She wondered if he could really be a cop, when all the others had left. But the dispatcher had sounded so definite.

She went off for a minute, and when she came back and looked again, the man was nowhere to be seen.

He was in the neighbor's house, prowling the ground floor, disabling the phone. At around 1:00 he went upstairs. He left sometime around 3:00. The victim called for an ambulance at 3:16. Patrol responded and called Gadek at 3:25. Gadek came back in by himself and rerecorded the area, then went to the hospital. This victim had the same random constellation of stab wounds as the last.

The neighborhood check came up with the ignored caller but nothing else. The transcript of the rerecording was identical to the first: not one vehicle had left the area between about 12:30 and 4:15. There was no other new evidence.

When the dispatcher found out what had happened, he walked out of the building and never came back.

It was a heartbreaker all around. A real heartbreaker. It all could have been over. It was the first time it had occurred to me in any sort of immediate way that after ten months there really might be an end: no more nights trudging around the streets, no more recording those damned license plates, no more gumshoeing useless leads to their certain, useless ends. No more drip-drip-drip of interviews and reports, each adding nothing except a substantial sum to the balance of revealed human misery.

Deliverance seemed for a moment so real as it blossomed in the imagination that when, a moment later, reality intruded again I needed a space to remember which was which.

At roll call next day, Gadek was upbeat. He reminded us that it wasn't our fault. We'd done just what we were supposed to do. These things happen. We'd probably been that close before without knowing about it. Well, luck had run his way then, and it would run ours another time. If we did our jobs, we'd be there when it happened.

What else could he say?

Abruptly, for the first time, really, Sara found the whole thing beginning to tell on her. What really made it all threatening to her was that I was coming home with names of suspects. Wesley Hunter I hadn't taken very seriously, but still he was a personality. Henry Dorn was looming larger in all our thoughts as the quick and easy screenings failed to eliminate him. He had been resident in the area the whole period of the series, so far as we could tell; his age was on the high end for this sort of crime, but not out of the question; his local criminal history, so far as it had been researched, was just what we'd expected to find. He was a name, an individual. I talked about him as a person, not a shadow.

She stopped joking about my leaving my family in danger. She began to ask more questions about how he worked, how much we really knew about his pattern. She commented several times about how these things are progressive: wherever these people start, they just get worse, and of course this was exactly what was happening. You can't depend on past experience. She laid a lot of emphasis on that. You don't know.

Stan Washburn

Sara couldn't avoid feeling, as it were, a personal relationship with this man. And it was not inconceivable that he was aware of us and felt a personal relationship with us. She had taken this possibility pretty lightly before, but she didn't now. What better revenge for him? What better new thrill?

21

There was no action at all for several nights. Then it came with a rush: a miss, and then a hit.

The miss was barely fifty yards from our house. The intended victim was armed and let off six shots at him. Sara, working at the kitchen table, heard the reports. One of the bullets the woman fired struck our house. We didn't know it at the time; I found it later when I was painting the trim over our bedroom window: a rough hole, and the base of the bullet visible half an inch into the wood. I left it where I found it. It's there now.

She was a student, living on the ground floor of a big old house divided into apartments. She had come home the day before and thought that something was strange about the place. She thought that somebody had been there—things were not the way they had been. Our guy had been through and prepped the place. She was concerned, but she was not a meticulous housekeeper and it was hard to put her finger on it. And it might have been one of her friends looking for a book or something—they didn't have keys, but she didn't always lock her door. She didn't really think it through. But as she was looking around she found a window latch unfastened. It was a side window, right beside the fireplace.

The chimney outside hid the window from the street, and the woodpile was right under it—a perfect ladder. She latched the window and didn't think anything more about it.

That night she went to bed before 11:00 as usual, but she had things on her mind and she couldn't sleep. Her habit when she couldn't sleep was to go sit by the window in the living room and watch the cars go by on her street. It relaxed her. She didn't turn on any lights, she just sat in the dark.

At about 11:30 something distracted her from the street. In the window behind her there was a man standing, visible from the chest up. She could see him only in dim silhouette against the little porch light on the next house. He was pressing upward on the sash, which, since she had locked it, was not giving.

Now, she happened to have a .38 revolver, but it was stuck in a slit in a big throw pillow she kept on the bed, and to get to it she had to go right past that window; they would have been five feet apart. And while the part of the room by the front window was in shadow, the part by the bedroom door was lit by the porch light: he couldn't miss seeing her go past. She thought, well, she would run past and get the gun before he could climb in the window, but then it occurred to her that maybe this is the one who went through the place during the day. Maybe the gun wouldn't be in the pillow.

She considered jumping out one of the front windows and running for it, but the windows stuck and made a lot of noise, and she wasn't sure she could open one far enough anyway. And where would she run? He only had to come around the corner of the house and he'd be on her.

Now he'd gotten a piece of bent wire through the space between the upper and lower sashes, and he was working the latch around.

She said later that he was very, very quiet; if she had not seen him, she would never have known he was there.

The latch was almost around.

There were voices outside, next door. It was her neighbors coming home. The guy sank down on the woodpile, blending in with it and with the shadows against the side of the house.

She could just see the back of his head and his shoulder over the windowsill.

She was barefoot and quiet; she was into the bedroom as fast as she could move. The pistol was still in the pillow, and she had the phone.

The neighbors went inside and closed their door. The guy rose smoothly up again and resumed work on the latch.

She was trying to dial 911 but she couldn't read the buttons in the dark, she couldn't remember which they were, and she didn't dare go near the doorway to get light from the window where he was. But 9 had to be one in the right-hand row, and she tapped away. Finally she succeeded, and she'd just told the dispatcher that someone was trying to break into her apartment, and the address, when he lifted the sash and put a leg in.

She opened fire from where she was in the bedroom, a distance of about ten feet.

She'd never fired a pistol at night, and she wasn't expecting the flash. It blinded her, and the report deafened her. She couldn't see or hear, and she was panicked that he was going to tumble in and grab her. She just started firing blind, traversing from left to right and holding up and down, in case he was sliding at her across the floor. Plaster fell, glass splintered. She emptied the gun. There was a box of cartridges in the pillow, and she was frantically groping for it when her vision began to come back and she could see that he wasn't in the room. She reloaded and waited with her back to the wall, facing the window, until the first cop started hammering on her door.

There was a bullet hole in the window frame about four feet above the floor. That would have been her first shot, the only one she really aimed—it must have come very, very close. One shot took out an ashtray and a framed picture of her boyfriend on the mantelpiece and lodged in the wall. Another went through the front window, one was in the floor just outside the bedroom door, and two were unaccounted for—probably gone through the windows.

The dispatcher was putting out a "burglary in progress" when she started shooting, with the pistol in one hand and the phone in the other.

I heard the shots plainly, less than a block away, and I was almost in position; I started running.

The dispatcher was almost deafened by the reports, but she kept the details coming: "Cars responding to the burg, responsible is described as male, unknown race, average height and build, dark clothing, nothing further. Unknown direction of flight."

Half a block from the scene I found some bushes by a church wall that gave me a view of the south and west sides of the block in question. Since the location of occurrence was toward the south end of the block, the responsible would probably have fled south and then east or west. He had not come south or west, because he would have run right into me. He might have gone north, although that was less likely because he would have to run the length of the block without turning a corner; he might have gone east. I didn't think he could have driven out, because I would have heard a car starting up anywhere in my quadrant.

Or he might not have gotten clear so quickly, heard the approach of the first cars and just gone to ground. As the first patrol car flew past I pulled the mike of my radio out of the depths of my field jacket and was just pressing the transmission button when Blondie's number came on the air.

"Control, 122. I'm just north. Nothing this way." If she was that close, she would have heard a car starting in her direction, too. This was looking hot. I broadcast, "Control, 93. Nothing south or west. He may still be in the block."

"Copy, 122, 93. Cars responding, we want a block cover. Responsible may still be at the scene. Answer up when you have spots."

"117, I've got the southwest corner." At the word, a patrol car gunned hard up the block and screeched to a halt across the middle of the intersection in front of me so as to have the same view I did.

"16, northeast corner."

"Okay, 117, 16, hold your spots. Cars at the scene?"

"58."

"104."

"Copy 58 and 104 at the scene. Make contact with the reporting party and advise."

For a few minutes nothing moved, but the night, which minutes before had been so quiet, pulsed with the presence of virtually every mobile patrol unit in the city. Their engines idled loudly in the quiet streets and their radios were plainly audible through the rolled-down windows, broadcasting the progress and tactics of the response for the benefit of anyone, good or bad, who had ears.

"Control, 104."

"104."

"We have some sort of attempted entry. The resident opened fire before he got in. There's no blood or other sign that she hit him. Nothing further."

"Okay, 104. It's your case. S-5, are you close?"

"S-5, that's affirmative."

"S-5, why don't you hook up with 104 and decide if you want to sweep the block. If you do, advise how many units you'll need."

"Stand by."

Another wait. I began to wish I'd picked a more comfortable bush.

"Control, S-5."

"S-5."

"We're going to sweep. Corner units will hold their posts. 104 will stay with the reporting party. I've got 58 with me, and I'll need three more."

"Check, S-5, I can give you three, but we'll be completely flat in the south end."

"Well, we'll break somebody loose if we have to, but this looks good here."

"Check. Cars 67, 3, and 160, rendezvous with S-5 at the south end of the block."

The assigned cars appeared immediately. Too late for the initial rush in, they had been hanging close and hoping for a bit of the action. Sergeant D'Honnencourt's car, plain black without insignia on the door, and with a red searchlight instead of roof lights, rolled serenely into the street and double-parked close to my intersection. The three rookies hurtled at unnecessary speed around the corner to the east and jerked into line behind him. 58 hustled around the corner on foot.

D'Honnencourt formed his four people into a line along the block with himself in the center. Then together they disappeared up driveways and into the first row of backyards. When they were all up to the first row of fences, and each could see at least his neighbor in the line, they would climb over and search the next yards, always being careful not to leave a hole so the fugitive could slip between them into the part already searched. So they would proceed through the whole block, climbing fences, peering into crawl spaces, opening sheds and garages, shining flashlights into cars in driveways. If insurmountable obstacles were encountered, the line would have to hold while whoever was affected went out to the street, up the next driveway, and into the new advanced position.

Residents of the four streets affected were aroused by the shots, the screeching of tires, the roaring engines, the blaring radios, and now the chatter of the sweep. They began to peer out of windows and appear on porches and in backyards, only to be ordered urgently back behind lock and key.

I really had nothing to do while the sweep lasted. I thought it would be nice to drop in on Sara in the next block and visit for half an hour. She would have heard all this commotion. She could see it from our bedroom window. She might be anxious. Hell, *I* might be anxious. Howsoever, she was there and I was here.

I wondered whether I should bring an air cushion with me next time, but decided that it would probably make too much noise inflating it.

There was very little radio traffic. Everyone in town was here and had an assignment. Whatever calls for service were coming in to the station were not being assigned. Nobody was getting cleared for dinner break, or getting a case number, or announcing arrival at a call, or availability for service. For long minutes the only sound was the idling cars.

A sweep is a slow business.

After forty-five minutes Control came on the air.

"S-5, Control."

"S-5."

"How're you coming?"

"Another ten or fifteen minutes."

"Okay. We're holding some calls."

"I'll let you know."

"Check."

The patrolman at the corner spot in front of me had no idea that I was there. He was a very junior rookie whom I knew only slightly, but he seemed very steady. He was watching two streets, waiting for the subject to break out of the block under search and try to get away. He waited and watched, his head shifting back and forth.

If the subject had been a poor hider, or unlucky, the sweep might well have had him. But perhaps he slipped in behind a pile of wood and lay with his face down so that even when a light passed over him the officer holding it did not realize that he was looking at a man. Or he could have crept into an unlocked crawl space under a house and slid far, far back behind the center foundations, or behind the heating unit, where he could not be seen. He might have gotten up a tree, and been lying along a branch while the search passed slowly underneath him. Or on the low roof of a garage overgrown with masses of bougainvillea or trumpet vine, invisible except from above. There are a great number of hiding places in a block if you are knowledgeable and bold—or lucky. But in any case they didn't find him.

"Control, S-5."

"Go ahead, S-5."

"We've drawn a blank. You can have everybody here. I'm going around to check in with 104 at the scene."

"Check, S-5. Pull the corner cover?"

"Pull everyone."

"Check, S-5. For 117 and 16. Start over towards Low-Class Liquors. Details to follow. 58?"

"58."

There was no time for exasperation or the luxurious relaxation of tension. Other business had accumulated around the city, some of it urgent. Control unloaded his backlog in a flurry of assignments. The corner spots gunned off up the street, and the sweepers jogged back along the sidewalk to their cars and hastened away.

104 was done with his report before the sweep was finished. He lingered only long enough to help the young

woman pack an overnight bag. By the time D'Honnencourt arrived they had secured the place as best they could with its shot-out windows. A friend arrived to take her away to spend the rest of the night, 104 announced that he was clear, was assigned, and departed. D'Honnencourt appeared, walking briskly down the block to his car, which stood in silent grandeur in the street. He had watched me working many times when I was not aware of him. Now I was watching him, and he was unaware. I had an anxious moment; I thought that in his supposed solitude he might do something un-D'Honnencourt-like: pick his nose or scratch his crotch. But he did not. He prepared for his departure from that lonely street as if the whole night shift had been lined up to watch him do it, and drove away.

The neighborhood fell quiet again.

Patrol doesn't give DD welfare checks. You have to look after your own. Blondie was concealed somewhere to the north. It would be nice to find out just where we were. I waited for a hole in the radio traffic and slipped in hurriedly.

"122, 93, go to 2." And then, switching over to Channel 2, "122, 93?" There was a double click in response. Someone, presumably Blondie, had clicked her mike twice, meaning that she could not talk. It might mean that she had something hot going, but more likely it meant that she had taken up a spot close to a house or some other place where she would attract attention by speaking out loud.

I waited for a moment. Then I said, "122, 93, I'm going back to 1." Another double click. She would be switching back too. It was important that we both be on the same channel, whichever one it was, and if we weren't going to be doing much talking it was desirable to be on Channel 1 so that we could keep half an ear on what everyone else was doing, what Patrol units were in our area, and what they were up to.

I examined my watch as best I could, turning it this way and that, trying to catch the light. So far as I could tell, it was a few minutes after 1:00. I started to rub my legs and do stretching exercises. I had been under that bush for a long time, and it would be a pity if he came out and I couldn't chase him because my legs were asleep.

It was very quiet, and nothing moved.

If our man was there, and if Gadek was right, he ought to be coming out pretty soon. The chances were, moreover, that he would come out at my end of the block, unless he had moved along north attempting to avoid the sweep.

As 1:30 approached I began to despair. He would be wise to give the residents close to his hiding place plenty of time to get back to sleep, but he ought to be moving soon.

At 2:30 I tried again to raise Blondie. I got the two clicks again.

At 3:30 the radio was very quiet, as it usually is at that hour.

"93, 122, go to 2." I switched channels. "93?"

"Go ahead, 122."

"Let's wrap this up. I don't think he's in there." Blondie's voice sounded tired and discouraged.

"I agree. Meet at the usual?"

"Five minutes."

"Check."

When I got there Blondie was waiting in her car.

"I came in from the north," she said. "I was just a couple of blocks away. I knew there was a nice fenced yard at the northeast intersection and I was going to go in there. Right at the intersection there was a white, full-sized four-door sedan, right off the list of suspicious vehicles, parked facing the wrong way. Beautiful, and right in front of my yard. I got the plate number and settled down.

"Man, it looked good to me. I thought our guy'd come bombing out of there and hop into this car and we'd have it all wrapped up."

"And instead?"

"And instead I get no fewer than seven juveniles, all drunk, who come out of a house opposite to watch the commotion. Then they decide to go for a drive. Turns out the car belongs to one of them. Great. There goes my neat closure. And those seven kids in a car would probably be the most dangerous thing going on in town all night, mad rapists included. But just then D'Honnencourt pulls into the intersection. I stood up behind my fence, got his attention,

243

and pointed out these kids. He didn't have time to bust 'em. He lifted the driver's keys and told 'em all to walk.''

The rest of her night had been much the same, with people hanging around. Her end of the block had been as busy and sociable as mine was quiet.

And our guy?

"I don't know, Toby,'' she said. "It looked good to me. It sure looked good to me.''

The joke around the station the next day was that we should all chip in and give this chick some shooting lessons, 'cause she's got the balls, and all she needs is technique.

Vanderloon said, "Tell the young lady to shoot low at night. always shoot low at night.'' To do her justice she was right on for elevation, just a little off for line. Of course, she sent wild shots flying all over the neighborhood, too, but I suppose that's the price we pay.

Gadek was not discouraged. "It was a good try. Next time do it just the same way. I don't know if he was there or not, but one of these times he will be, unless he gets scared off. We learned something this time, though,'' he added, "assuming that this actually was our guy and not just some burglar. And that's what the girl said about his working on the latch with the wire and how quiet he was. He's technically very strong. But he doesn't have some mysterious device. He doesn't walk through walls.'' He laughed. "I'd begun to wonder.''

Fry laughed, too. "He must be feeling like a dumb shit. A lucky dumb shit. It's funny to think about it.'' He chuckled. Then the smile faded and he said, "Of course he's just going to take it out on the next one. She'll pay. He'll see that she pays for all the laughing.''

Four nights later he raped a woman on the other side of the same block, a mother with two children, four and six. He saw to it that she, at any rate, had nothing to laugh about. He woke her up in the usual way, taped her eyes, stripped her, and slapped her around till she was bloody. He had a stocking mask which he put on. Then he pushed her, sightless and naked, smeared with blood, into the children's' room.

He turned on the light, and made her call the children to wake them. Of course they were terrified. He made her threaten to beat them if they didn't keep quiet.

Then he raped her, with occasional intermissions to make the little cuts on her back and breasts, and he made the children watch the whole thing from beginning to end. From beginning to end.

She was the fiftieth known victim. I didn't talk to her myself. Blondie and Leo took the report. They were pretty quiet when they came back. The nurses at the hospital told them that the victim was frantic to see her children and comfort them, but she couldn't meet their eyes; she would begin to shudder and mumble and they would start to howl, and they would have to be separated again.

It was my area, and I was nearby for most of the evening. I walked right past the end of the street while it was going on. There was no way I could have known, of course, and nobody blamed me, and I didn't blame myself, exactly. But you think about it. How could you not? It was a block from our house, where Sara was sleeping, where Adam and Joss were sleeping.

I had the next night off. Sara and I spent most of the evening catching up, and among other things I told her pretty much everything about it: the kids, the whole thing. I didn't meet her eyes, I just told. What I really wanted was to have her hold me while I talked. I don't know why I didn't suggest it.

22

The following day, the kids decided to wait and have dinner with Sara. I made them hot chocolate to tide them over. I warmed some leftovers for myself, standing at the kitchen counter by the big window watching the sky darken with the late afternoon. There was a little breeze. Treetops stirred slightly. The light faded into a paleness, the shadows seeming to rise up against it and swallow it.

I took my plate to the kitchen table and ate facing the window. The kids took their chocolate to the window seat and curled up on the cushions. They pulled an afghan over their heads and shoulders like a tent. They held their cups luxuriously with both hands just in front of their faces, sipping slowly. They began to extemporize a fairy tale suitable for the dying of the day, about an ogre who dwelt in a hovel in the deepest part of the woods at the bottom of the garden, and who would dart out onto the twilight meadows to snatch those who were tardy in returning to the safety of their firesides. I ate in silence, watching the sky fade, charmed with the notion of a fireside which would be proof against an ogre.

Sara came home just as I was finishing. The kitchen light was on, but the rest of the house was dark. She went around pulling down shades and turning on lights, moving hurriedly, as if someone were arriving right behind her and she wanted the place to look inviting. But it seemed that nobody was. I got my coffee and her wine, and went upstairs to change. When she came into the bedroom she said, "After this, please turn on the lights and close the curtains before I get home."

"What?"

"Every night. I hate to come up to the house when it's dark. It's as if something had happened."

This was unlike her, and so I said, "Sure."

She went to the lockbox in the closet and got out the guns.

"Let's be quick," she said. "I don't want to leave the kids alone downstairs."

I looked at her. "*Has* something happened?" I asked.

"I guess I've finally gotten fed up," she said. She was whipping the cartridges into her revolver, *slap, slap, slap*. "After all these months. I don't like it a bit."

"Don't like what?"

"Any of it. You out there and us here. Us up here and the kids downstairs. I'm worried. I worry about it all the time now. I've been thinking about that poor woman and her children. I haven't been able to get that out of my mind all day. I just don't know what I'd do. I worry about going to sleep. I think, so long as I'm awake, so long as I'm armed, I'm alert, nothing much can go wrong. But of course he doesn't come in when people are awake. He comes in when they're sleeping.

"Of course, it's hard on you too, but you're doing something. You're looking for trouble. You're looking for him. You're the last thing he wants to meet up with. But I'm not." She ran her hand through her hair distractedly. "He's looking for the likes of me. He'd like to meet up with me." She was holding her revolver, not as I hold mine, like a thunderbolt, but as if it were something that could float. "It's just really punched my button, all of a sudden.

"And right now," she said, getting up, "I'm worried about the kids. I don't want to leave the kids alone. Please, just do it and let's go down." She passed over my snub-nose in a peremptory manner and dropped some cartridges into my other hand. I loaded and holstered. She was hovering with the derringer. I loaded that and put it in my pocket. She laid her pistol on top of the bookcase, said "Okay," and headed for the stairs. She was almost running.

The kids were still in the window seat when we came into the kitchen. The wind was higher now, and the gusts rattled the windows all around the house. It was dark, but against the city glow you could see the trees whipping around in a pretty lively fashion.

"It's wild," said Joss.

"It's neat," said Adam.

Sara and I sat at the table, sipping and watching the view through the window. I reached over and took her hand. She took mine in both of hers and pressed it. It made me feel very big and tough.

"It's okay," I whispered. I smiled, which reassures me when she does it. "We'll be fine."

"Promise?" she whispered back. Her lips were almost motionless. Her eyes were on the lashing branches against the skyline.

"We'll be fine."

"Promise," she said. I looked at her.

"Sara, nothing is different. Nothing has changed since yesterday."

"Promise."

"Okay. I promise. It'll be okay. We'll all be okay. That's why you have a husband: to make sure that everything turns out okay."

She closed her eyes for a moment and whispered, "Silly as that is, it makes me feel better." She leaned over and kissed me.

"There's nothing silly about it," I said. "That's the deal with a husband: you have to do more laundry, but you don't ever have to worry." I can't say that she looked much more peaceful than she had before, but she gave me credit for trying, and kissed me again.

There was a stir from the window seat, and Adam murmured, "Don't look now. They're doing *mush stuff*."

"Oh no!" whispered Joss, pretty loud. "Oh no! Quick! The blanket! We have to guard ourselves against mush stuff!" They pulled the blanket over their heads and rolled around on the window seat, whispering "Mush stuff! Look out for mush stuff!" pretty loud.

It was time for me to go. I got up, grabbed them both together in a great bear hug, and peeling back the blanket remorselessly planted a resounding buss on each shrinking cheek. Then I kissed Sara again, for pleasure as well as luck, and headed for the door.

She stood behind the closed door for a minute, listening to the footsteps on the porch, and a moment later the sound of the car pulling away. When it was gone, she turned back into the hall.

Perhaps it was the wind playing over the house in gusts, rattling first this window and then that one, and dragging bush and branch across shingled wall and roof, that struck her with a newfound sensation of the largeness and complexity of the house. It is not, in fact, a very large house, but it is more than you can keep under your eye at any one time. All the ways someone can get into such a house, if he is determined and knows what he is doing. All the places you have to turn your back to as you go from room to room. All the closets, all the corners behind things, all the little nooks and crannies.

Just behind her, the front door creaked a little.

She leaned back against it, to assure herself that it was not moving.

She thought, It's perfectly reasonable to be worried. But I'm taking steps. He can't make himself invisible. He's a man. When she thought of him as "a man" she held several meanings in her mind simultaneously, but the principal one was: Bullets will stop him. She was steady as she walked, at first slowly but quicker with each step, up the stairs. She was almost running by the time she reached the bedroom door. She paused a moment to listen: she could hear Adam in the kitchen saying something, and Joss's reply—not the words, but their tone of voice. All was well there, but it seemed to her that she could hear the windows all around the ground floor creaking, as if something were straining the sashes upward against the locks.

It was crazy. It was as if her ears had suddenly developed an extraordinary sensitivity.

She thought she could hear him.

She thought she could hear him moving outside the house.

She wanted to run down again to Adam and Joss, but she wanted her pistol. She whipped it down off the bookcase, snapped it open to reassure herself that it was fully loaded, closed it, and hurried down the stairs.

At the landing she paused to draw the shade aside and look along that side of the house.

There was no one there.

In the hall she put the pistol in her briefcase under some files. Then, almost running until she was at the kitchen door, she carried the briefcase to the kitchen and put it on the counter near the stove.

She talked to Adam and Joss while she made dinner.

It was beginning to rain, scattered drops at first and then harder, a steady pattering over the roof and the porch outside.

The three of them ate at the table. She sat so that she was facing the hallway into the rest of the house and the door to the back steps was to her right. No one could get into the room faster than she could get to the briefcase. She chatted as cheerfully as she was able, but she had to keep pausing to listen, trying to hear past the rain. As often as she looked at one or other of the kids she would run her eye down the hall again and glance out through the back door at the porch.

"Is someone coming?" said Joss, who had noticed this.

"No," she said. "Nobody's coming." She couldn't hear anything right then. "It's the storm."

"Sing out if you see the ogre," said Adam with relish.

"I will." She laughed, in spite of herself. "Trust me, I will."

The three of them did the dishes after dinner, and then she brought the briefcase to the table and laid out her evening's work. Adam started to his room to get the model airplane he was working on. She was almost going to stop him, but she let him go, suddenly tense. Joss curled up on the window seat with a book.

She waited at the table, holding her pen, listening to Adam, who was in a whimsical mood, mount the stairs in little rushes of three steps: clump clump *clump,* pause; clump clump *clump,* pause. His bedroom was above the kitchen, and she could hear him faintly as he moved around overhead, gathering what he needed. A few footsteps as he crossed the room, then a brief silence, then a few more. She would certainly be able to tell if anything was wrong, if he was alarmed.

"Mom," said Joss, "what's the half of a griffin that isn't eagle?"

"Shhh," she said. "Just a sec." Adam was moving toward the stairs.

"Mom?"

"I'm thinking," she said. He was coming down the stairs steadily, so as not to drop his work board with all the parts spread out on it. He was in the hall. Now she could see him.

"It's half lion," she said, relaxing a little.

She made notes for a will, a prenuptial agreement, and the division of property in a divorce. But she looked around every few moments. From time to time she thought she could hear sounds which wind or scratching branches would not account for. The kids did not know that she had the pistol there at the table, and she did not want to alarm them by producing it and going to see what was making the sounds. On the other hand, it made no sense to investigate unarmed. At least where she was she could not be taken by surprise, or from the rear. She pressed down the papers in the briefcase hard enough to feel the shape of the revolver under them, to be sure that it was there and how it lay. She sat and listened until she was pretty sure that he was not there.

Bedtime was the tricky part. She could not very well bring her briefcase upstairs and carry it around. She doubted that she could get through the bedtime story without somebody feeling the pistol if she had it in her waistband. Still, that seemed like the best plan. And if they noticed it, well, she could make something up. So when they went upstairs she lingered till they had left the room and then slipped it into her waist in the middle of her back. She pulled the tails of her blouse down over it. It seemed like a pretty big lump.

It wasn't until she had completed this process that she remembered that of course anyone standing in the garden would have seen her do it and know that she was armed.

She pressed her face to the glass of the door, shading her face with her hands. Of course, there was nobody to be seen, but of course she couldn't see the whole garden. She thought of taking a flashlight out to look, and instantly discarded the idea. She couldn't search the whole block, and anyway, it would mean leaving the house.

She hurried upstairs. There was an urgency to keep them under her eye such as she had not felt since they were quite young.

She read to them in Adam's bed, careful to settle herself against a pillow before they were ready so that she would not have to turn her back to them close-up. Adam tried to put an arm around her, and she had to say quickly, "No, honey, that's not comfortable."

After each paragraph she listened for a moment. John Marshall had curled up in Adam's lap and gone to sleep, but Robert Peel had taken an Egyptian pose, sentinel-like, on the bedside table, facing the door. He awakened in her an absurd feeling of gratitude and common purpose.

When they were done with the story she sent Joss off to bed, waiting until she had left the room before getting up. She tucked Adam in and turned off his light.

Joss was allowed to read for half an hour before lights-out. When she went to tuck her in, Joss said, "Mom, is everything okay?"

"Yes, of course," she said.

" 'Cause you keep looking around all the time, as if someone was late or something."

"It's fine," she said. "The rain makes me nervous because the roof is old, and we're hoping we won't need to replace it for a couple more years."

Joss gave her a level look.

"Is Dad okay?"

"Honey, of course he is. He's probably working inside

252

until ten. Perhaps it'll have stopped raining by then." Joss was still looking. "Really, Joss. I'm worried about the roof."

"Would you tell me?"

"Yes, dear."

"Promise?"

"I promise."

There was a pause.

"Well?" said Joss.

"There's nothing to tell, cupcake," she said. "The question has been asked and answered. The rain always makes me jumpy. Good night." She got up. She couldn't possibly walk backward to the door, so she tried to stand as straight as possible, and hoped her blouse would billow out enough to cover the lump. At the door she turned back as she always did, and said again, "Good night, honey." Joss was sitting just as she had been, watching her, but saying nothing. She couldn't tell whether Joss had seen or not.

She went down the stairs. At the bottom she drew the pistol from her waistband and held it firmly, drawing the slack from the trigger as she went from window to window, trying each lock with her free hand, examining the sashes to see if there were any misalignments that might indicate that someone had been trying to force them. There was nothing that she could find.

She went back to the kitchen table. She picked up the notes on the property division.

There were several trees close to the house large enough to climb. If he got up one of them he could go in an upstairs window.

He would be between her and the kids.

She swept the papers into the briefcase and took it quickly upstairs to the bedroom. Joss was still reading. She slipped the pistol back into her waistband, this time in front, and pulled the blouse down over it again. She checked the locks on the windows in Adam's room and both bathrooms. She would check Joss's room later.

All evening she alternated brief bouts of work on the papers spread out over the bed and prowls through the upstairs. Once she went down to the kitchen for a snack, but she couldn't bear to be out of sight of the staircase. He might get past her. She abandoned the snack idea and re-treated quickly back upstairs.

She piled the pillows up against the headboard and leaned back against them. From there she could not see the top of the stairs, but she could see Joss's door and most of Adam's. He could not get into those rooms from the stairs without her seeing him. She glanced at the clock: it was 11:20. She thought about the detail on the street somewhere near. She turned again to her work.

Rain and wind died away to stillness.

Then she heard him.

He was there. He was in the house.

Had she been dozing? Somehow he had gotten in without her hearing him, and now he was in the hallway by the foot of the stairs. She could hear him as he placed his foot on the bottom step, hear as he leaned forward to let it take the weight of his body, very cautiously, very silently. She could hear him starting up. Her fear had left her; the foreboding, the unremitting alertness, had worn her, but now, in the actual moment, her mind was lucid and untroubled. The thing to do was to slip the pistol from her waist and step quickly to the door; from there she would have a clear shot down the stairs. It did not matter if he heard her moving, because it would be too late for him. The thing was to move fast.

But her body would not move at all.

When she started to lift a leg to slip off the bed she found that she could barely shift it on the coverlet. It was all she could do to drag her hand along her stomach toward the pistol. Her arms and legs were past weakness, as if her blood had drained away.

She could not pull the pistol loose from her waistband.

She could not get up.

He would pause in his ascent every couple of steps, to listen. She could hear his breathing clearly.

Perhaps he could hear her as clearly as she heard him. He would hear her breath coming faster as she tugged feebly at the butt of the pistol. He would hear her wrist passing faintly across the fabric of her blouse, her feet stirring help-lessly among the papers. She was frightened now, almost panicked. He would hear her quickening pulse, hear her breathe.

He was almost at the top.

She bolted suddenly to her feet, yanked the revolver from her waist and jumped to the doorway, her legs hard, her grip hard and her arm extended firmly, thrusting the heavy muzzle forward like a thunderbolt.

There was no one on the stairs.

She stared down into the hall, the muzzle traversing a little, following her eyes. There was nothing.

Her forehead ran with sweat, her back was soaked. Her hands were shaking. Her legs would barely support her. The weight of the pistol sank her arm slowly to her side. She leaned against the door frame, breathing heavily and waiting for her strength.

The clock said 1:15.

There was the phone.

She dialed the task force office, which she had never done before. There was no one in the office, and a dispatcher in the Communication Center picked up the line. She didn't know him. She explained who she was and asked him to get a message to her husband to call home. He told her to wait and put her on hold. A moment later he was back on the line. Her husband was on the street. There was some sort of cover going down, and only emergency transmissions were possible. It might be some time.

She called Walt. The phone rang and rang, and finally she hung up.

She sat down on the bed again and tried to focus on her work.

She noticed the clock. It was 1:48. Soon after that she must have drifted off again. She was going outside just at dawn, feeling happy and confident. It was a bright spring morning, the sky yellow and blue, the earth rich and sweet-smelling, the light striking like justice into every dark place. Everything is fine, someone was telling her. Nothing can go wrong now. She felt a great wave of relief. She believed it. It was a dream.

It was a sound that woke her. Not a house sound, but a voice. Almost a hiss.

He was in the room.

He was wearing a stocking mask so that his face seemed merely a dark mass, the nose and ears pressed flat, the eyes and mouth like pits.

In front of him, cramping both arms just above the elbows, he held Joss.

Joss was naked. Her eyes were taped. Blood ran from her nose into her mouth and around her lips, down her chin and neck and spattered over her chest. There were broad smears of blood on her belly and thighs where she had tried to clear her mouth with her hands and then wiped them.

He was forcing Joss toward the bed. She was disoriented, trying to feel her way with her feet, turning her head this way and that, trying to see or hear. Her mouth opened and closed, bright with blood.

She heard herself say aloud, "My *God,* she's only *nine.*"

The mass of his face broadened across the middle. She heard the hiss again. She couldn't distinguish the words. Her ears sang, she felt her face engorged. But she saw Joss's mouth open again, saw her lips form the word, "Mom?"

She wasn't weak now. She could move. She would shoot. Joss was so tiny, he couldn't hide behind her. She would step right up to them and fire past Joss. She could almost hear the discharges thundering in that small room, one after another, again and again, like some great pulse, as she rent his body with the shattering hollow-points.

She heaved herself suddenly upright, her eyes fixed on his, slipping her hand to her waist.

The pistol was not there.

She slapped the bed frantically all around her.

"*My God!*" she screamed, starting wildly to her knees. "*Where is it?*" In a frenzy she upended the briefcase and scattered the papers, yanking the folds of the coverlet, jerking away the pillows.

She stopped.

I was three feet from the bed. I was just coming out of the bathroom.

"*Jesus,* honey," I said, frozen. I'd never seen such a look on anyone's face. Wild rage and a bottomless fright.

For a long moment we stared at each other.

I knew perfectly well what she had been looking for: when I came in I took the pistol from beside her, unloaded it, and put it away. I didn't want to get shot by mistake. It seems to have been a good idea.

"My *God,* Sara."

My tough, competent, cerebral wife began shaking from head to toe. The bed was torn to pieces. The contents of her briefcase were scattered around, tumbled and crumpled. Her face gleamed with sweat, her hair was plastered to her head, mascara smeared down one cheek. She was a mess. I sat down on the bed and pulled her in to me. She clung. I held her for some time. I was still feeling big and tough.

After a while I asked her if she'd like a dram of something, and she nodded. I went downstairs and poured two glasses of scotch.

When I came back up the stairs she was coming slowly out of the doorway of Joss's room, arms folded tight, biting her lip. I put a glass in her hand there at the top of the stairs. She drank a good deal of it on the spot.

When we went back into the bedroom she sat down on the very edge of a chair in the corner, leaning forward, knees pressed together and her free arm pressed tightly in beside her as if she were very cold. I picked up the briefcase and began gathering the papers. Usually I sit and she tidies. She finished her whiskey while I straightened up the room and remade the bed. When it was done, she came over and traded glasses with me.

She said, "Hold me while I tell you."

The next day before I went to work I trimmed the branches of the trees near the house until the second story was completely inaccessible. We agreed that I would make every effort to call every night, sometime around eleven, just so we could hear each other's voice. We agreed that I would call from the Hall of Justice as I was leaving for home, even if that meant waking her up, to make sure that she wouldn't shoot me in her sleep. Beyond that, what could we do?

23

It is impossible to know what was on his mind. He had never purposely gone into a place with two adult women in it. He might have thought that Heather was younger than she was, or that she would be out of the way for some reason—or that Melanie would be out of the way. Nobody knows what he was thinking.

Melanie had to be away from early Wednesday morning to Saturday morning. Heather wanted to stay in the carriage house by herself, but Melanie vetoed that. They procured her an invitation to stay with a friend who went to her school. Her visit began Tuesday afternoon.

Melanie came home from work early Tuesday evening.

She spent the evening alternately cooking (so that there would be some easy meals in the freezer when she got back), packing, and watching the evening news. She cleaned, and changed the sheets.

As she moved around the house she noticed, of course, that things were out of order. Some of the books in the bookcases were pulled out a little, some pushed back. Her flute case had been nudged slightly, and there was a Vivaldi concerto on the top of the pile of music, and she knew that she had most recently practiced a Handel. Clearly, this was

Heather's revenge. They had had rather a set-to over the weekend about whether Heather was old enough to stay by herself that had led to a brisk discussion of telephone abuse, curfews, Melanie's blindness to contemporary culture, and kindred topics. At one point, standards of housekeeping had come into the conversation. No doubt Heather and her friend (who had a car) had come by after school and done all this. They had turned the spice jars so that instead of the labels all facing the front they were a few degrees this way or that. They had even gone through her clothes—she would have to speak to Heather about that, that was simply an intrusion—and done such things as rehanging three or four blouses and jackets on the bar so that they faced right instead of left.

And a silk blouse, one she particularly liked, was missing.

This disturbed Melanie. You do *not* go into your mother's clothes, and you most *certainly* do not walk off with her things, even as a joke. She was on the point of calling Heather at her friend's house and demanding an explanation, but her second thought was that this was an important event. If Heather was feeling rebellious enough to do all this, they needed to have a substantial talk, or more than one, and that would have to wait until they were under the same roof again. That would be better. She would wait.

What was happening to her children? She had taught them to be responsible and independent, and suddenly they seemed to be collapsing. Mike's calls and letters from college had been so confident in the fall, and then they had acquired a more tentative air as the year progressed. At the end of Christmas vacation he had seemed reluctant to go back. She had said something about pulling himself together, and Walt had told her quite sharply to lighten up—where had *that* come from? It was almost as if Walt knew more than she did, more than he was telling. Then when Mike had called on Sunday he had been terribly blue. His confidence, his resolution, seemed suddenly to have failed him. He had made a joking remark that she should not be surprised if he turned up on her doorstep one of these days, only she did not think he was joking.

And now Heather. Everything had been so smooth before.

She was packed, the cooking was done, the house tidied. It was only nine o'clock. She laid out three Telemann trios which a friend had mentioned. After a diligent series of technical exercises, she began to work through the trios.

The living room felt stuffy, and she opened the casement nearest her. The windows were, as ever, defiantly uncurtained, and when occasionally her eye left her music she could see in the glass the reflection of the lamplit room, the foliage of the closest ferns and bushes, and the darkness beyond that. This had always seemed to her a romantic progression of view, from the gold of the hearth to the mysteries of the night. But this evening, uncharacteristically troubled, she wished the room were cozier. Soon after she opened the casement she got up again and closed it. The little forged catch was as elegant as ever, but this evening she could not help noticing that it really had very slight purchase on the opposite frame.

"Perhaps Toby is right," she said aloud. Well, it would have to wait until she got back.

It was not long before eleven when she felt that she had Telemann well in hand. She put her flute carefully away, closed the music, arranged the three thin folios attractively on the music stand, and turned off the light.

Upstairs, she performed her customary ablutions. She changed into pajamas. There was an excellent radio in her bedroom, invariably tuned to the most serious classical music station. While she was preparing for bed she listened with some concentration.

It was just 11:30, her usual hour, when she turned out the light.

It was just 6:30, her usual hour, when the alarm rang.

She bathed and dressed quickly, placing the last necessaries in the suitcase as soon as she was done using them.

By 7:45 she was on her way to the airport.

Friday was my day off. It was not a good one. Sara left for work at 8:00, and I drove the kids' carpool to school at 8:30. I came home and worked in the garden for an hour.

In the middle of the morning the sun came out through the overcast like a blessing thrown away. I made a cup of espresso and sat tensely in the gentle sunshine to drink it.

Everything threatened. My mind snatched at things but couldn't grasp them. Never anything resolved, never anything fixed, everything revolving.

I made rather an elaborate lunch of spaghetti with chopped garlic and tomato and some leftover salmon. I put it all on a tray with a cloth napkin and a glass of wine, and ate it in the garden with my book propped up against a brick. I thought, graceful outside, graceful inside, but it didn't work. It was a very pretty ritual, but I couldn't follow what I was reading, I got sauce on my shirt, and I spilled the wine.

Melanie's flight was due in before 6:00 in the morning, and the airporter would drop her at her door around 7:00. Walt knew this, and he had planned, as a theatrical demonstration of his love, to let himself into the carriage house and lay a lavish champagne breakfast to greet her when she came in the door. Heather's presence had been a considerable inhibition to their love life, but he knew that Heather wasn't expected home until dinnertime. He did not have a key, but he had inspected the casements, and he knew that thirty seconds with his pocketknife would remove that barrier.

And so the dawn found Walt hurrying up the driveway into the almost nocturnal gloom of Melanie's driveway carrying a picnic cooler and a large paper shopping bag. He laid them silently by the front door and slipped around to the side.

He found one of the casements unpinned, removed, and leaning against the wall among the ferns and sorrel.

He studied this for a moment, and then, faster and more quietly than he had come, he hastened back down the driveway to the street. His pistol was in the trunk of his car: covered by the raised lid from the alarmable gaze of any neighbors who might be watching, he drew back the slide and chambered the first round in the magazine. He stuck the pistol into his belt, closed the trunk as quietly as he could, and hastened back up the driveway.

He slipped off the safety catch, passed the corner of the house, slowed, and then, with great precaution, leaned around the frame of the open window.

Dawn is an unlikely hour to catch a burglar in action. He will have come earlier, when people are asleep, or later, when they are at work. Still, you never know.

Walt put a leg in, then the other, scanning the dark living room, the muzzle of his automatic following his eyes, and straining to hear whatever there might be to be heard.

It was a rubbing sound, upstairs.

And with the rubbing, an irregular gasping: someone out of breath, or sobbing, or both.

It is a very good rule at these moments not to be drawn to the first thing you notice, because it may not be the most important thing. While the noise continued upstairs, Walt made a swift circuit of the ground floor: living room, kitchen, pantry, and bathroom. When he was pretty sure that there would be no major surprises in his immediate vicinity, he considered calling the station for reinforcements. He hesitated about this. What *could* be going on? The window suggested burglar, but the hour was against it. And the sounds were against it. When a burglar works, what you hear are rapid footfalls and drawers opening quick quick quick, dumping-out noises and sorting noises. These were not burglary sounds.

Could it be Heather? With Melanie gone, could she have imported some pimply swain to enjoy in privacy? But why the window? Why not use her key? And surely she would know that her mother was due back in an hour. More likely it would be some friend of Heather's who had heard that the place would be unoccupied and was putting it to the obvious use. But it didn't sound like passion, or any activity associated with passion.

There was probably some discreditable although relatively innocent explanation, but the prudent thing would be to call for reinforcements. Melanie wouldn't like a fuss, especially if this turned out to be something to do with Heather. Still, better safe than sorry.

He found the phone in the kitchen, but it was dead. He pulled gently on the wire and soon came to the end, loose from the wall.

Teen passion seemed less and less likely. He was beginning to think he knew what this meant. It looked like our guy.

But it didn't sound like rape any more than passion. What could be going on up there?

Advance or retreat?

With some precaution he approached the bottom of the narrow stairs. He leaned into the stairwell and looked up. There was nothing to see, but the rubbing sound was louder, and there was a cry, almost a shriek, treble, brief, subdued, before the breathing resumed. Then suddenly a scramble, a clanking metallic sound, and footsteps right overhead. Water running in the bathtub.

He started up the stairs, climbing sideways so as to keep his face and the muzzle of his pistol directed upward. When he reached the landing the water stopped running, and he froze. It was very dark on the landing, and he did not think he could be seen unless someone suspected his presence.

There was a light in the bathroom, which was directly above the first flight of stairs, and another in one of the rooms. It was not Melanie's, which was to the right. Mike's sleeping porch, then, to the left, opposite the bathroom, or Heather's room, a few steps beyond that.

The footsteps again, the light dimming for a moment as someone passed through the bathroom doorway, and again at the bedroom. Then the rubbing resumed.

Walt was sure by now that he had only one direction to worry about. Whatever was going on was happening to the left. He moved more confidently now, more quickly. The action was in the sleeping porch. The hall from the doorway to the bathroom opposite was slopped with water. It was two steps from the head of the stairs to the sleeping porch door. Transferring the pistol to his left hand to keep it in front of him, he peered around the frame.

It was Mike.

He was facing away from the door on his hands and knees. He had a bucket beside him, scrubbing at the floor with a brush held in his left hand while he held his right awkwardly beside him. The nightstand was overturned. The lamp had been set upright on the floor. A crumpled piece of broad tape, with many strands of hair adherent, lay next to it. The bed had been stripped, and the sheets and blankets, stained and foul, huddled onto the floor in the corner. The mattress had a plastic cover, which he had partly cleaned.

He looked as if he had just gotten out of the shower, hair wild and uncombed, but he was by no means clean. Both wrists were bruised and blotchy, and his right wrist was swollen. His lip was cut and showed evidence of recent bleeding. He was wearing a T-shirt and jeans, splashed with water. The back of the shirt had a scattering of small bloodstains. Without quite meaning to, Walt stepped out into the doorway.

"My God," he said aloud.

Mike screamed and jerked to his feet, plunging back against the far wall, jamming against it as if he would fly right through the planks. Again and again he sprang back against the paneling until he focused on Walt's face and recognized him. Instantly the panic was supplanted by fury.

"Get out!" he screamed. *"Get the fuck out of here!"*

"Mike, for—"

"Out! Get *out*! *Who the fuck told you you could come in here?"* He was wild, He was dancing on the tumbled bedclothes. But he was not approaching; he was staying right by the wall, turned more than halfway into it, leaning into it as if he still was expecting it to yield, yelling over his shoulder.

"Out!"

Walt pulled one step back out of the doorway, glanced into Heather's room and down the hall at Melanie's door. He did not like to leave a closed door behind him, but he was pretty sure they were alone.

"How long has he been gone?" he said. Mike stopped raving, but he didn't answer. His breathing fell back into the tight gasp that Walt had heard from downstairs.

"Mike," he said firmly. "This is me, Walt. Now c'mon." And then, more gently, "It was him, right? It was Toby's guy." Mike's eyes ran across the ceiling and around the walls. They ran across the floor. He passed his good hand over his mouth, where his lip had begun to bleed again.

"Oh God," was all he could say. "Oh God."

Walt consulted his watch. Melanie was due in forty-five minutes. He could picture the scene: Mike explaining to his mother that he had been raped, explaining what had been done to him. He could see their faces. It was not a pretty image.

Perhaps, he thought, there had been other men among the victims. If so, they weren't talking. He wondered if *he* would.

If the victim were just anyone, Walt would have pressed on with the investigation, on principle. But this was Mike, and the question wasn't such a simple one. The task force was often coming up with no useful new information, even out of fresh crime scenes, and this one was hopelessly compromised for evidence. Mike had not got it clean, but he had pretty well spoiled whatever was there. Any profit there might be in reporting seemed greatly outweighed by the cost.

And this was *Mike.*

"C'mon," Walt said. He thumbed the safety on his pistol to uncock it, and stuck it into his waistband.

"C'mon," he said again. "I'll help you." He pulled off his jacket and rolled up his sleeves. "We've got time." And then, because Mike was not following him, he added, "Melanie never has to know."

For a long moment Mike stared at him.

"Mike," he said. "It'll be between us. I promise you." He didn't cross into the room; he left that space between them. "You won't tell, I won't tell, nobody'll know. Only for crissake," he said, turning to the room, "we gotta make tracks."

He took up a sponge from the bucket and set to work on the mattress cover. Mike watched him swooping up and down between the bucket and the mattress. He worked very fast.

Perhaps it was possible. Perhaps it could be done.

Soon they were both hard at it.

They threw open all the windows. They gathered the fouled linen together with Mike's luggage and put it by the door. One of the blankets had a bad stain near one end, but they scrubbed it pretty clean, dried it with Heather's hair dryer, and when they remade the bed they put that spot underneath and on the bottom.

They cleaned the place as best they could, scrubbing the floor, setting the furniture to rights and rearranging things. They used towels from the laundry hamper to dry the floor, and then worked over it with the hair dryer. They cleaned the bathroom.

Mike was working pretty well, but his mind was clearly in two places. Once or twice he suddenly slowed to a stop, and once, seeing something not in the room he jolted backward and let out that little cry. Whenever Walt saw him slowing down he would give him a shake or an avuncular thump on the shoulder and say, "Hey! C'mon! We've got things to do!"

This is not what cops are supposed to do, he thought. I hope I'm doin' the right thing. But he kept moving.

When the upstairs was clean and orderly they went down. As quickly as possible Walt walked Mike through everything he had done since arriving early the previous evening. He had sat in that chair and listened to some music, had two bottles of beer, made a sandwich, looked at magazines, played the piano. They retraced his steps around the ground floor, plumping pillows, putting away records, closing the piano, rearranging the magazines, wiping off the kitchen counter with a paper towel so that Melanie wouldn't find the sponge damp after an absence of three days.

The phone and the window they left untouched.

With five minutes to spare they loaded Mike's things into Walt's car—unobserved, so far as Walt could tell, by the neighbors—and drove to Walt's apartment. There was no concealing Mike's injuries, so he would have to stay at Walt's until they were better. No one would know that Mike had been home.

Walt pushed Mike in the front door and drove hastily back to Melanie's. It was ten minutes past seven, but she had not arrived. He ran next door to a neighbor's and called the police. Then he went back to the carriage house and waited for everyone to show up.

24

Gadek didn't get the call until after eight. He woke up Charlie Footer, who had Friday night off, and told him to hustle out and rerecord the license numbers of all cars within a two-block radius of the scene. Then he called me. He said that our guy had apparently attempted a hit, but nobody was home. He gave me the address. It was the carriage house.

"I'll tell you later," I said to Sara, and went for my gear.

"Yea, Dad," called the kids as I ran out to the street.

When we arrived there were a couple of patrol cars and the ID van parked in front. Curious neighbors stood on their porches. Uniforms passed from door to door doing the neighborhood check.

We went up the driveway to the carriage house. Melanie's suitcase was sitting outside the front door next to a cooler and a paper bag. The ID tech was dusting the casement.

Melanie was at the big table with Walt, looked scared. Her face was pale, and you could see the four faint marks where the dog had bitten her.

I introduced Gadek. She explained that she had come home to find Walt waiting, the place swarming with police, and all this—she waved at the window and indicated the disabled phone.

Walt explained how he had come to surprise Melanie with breakfast, found the window open, and called from a neighbor's. When the first Patrol unit had come they had searched the place together. All he could figure was that our guy had cased it at the beginning of the week and gone in last night, not realizing that nobody was at home.

"My God, Toby," she said. "My *God*. What if . . . Heather wanted to stay by herself while I was gone, and I wouldn't let her. How . . ."

"Well," I said, "it just goes to show that sometimes fate lets us down light. It's a fine stroke of luck." What I felt like saying was, sometimes we get away with stuff we don't deserve to get away with, but she didn't need chastening. She was chastened already. I gave myself a little pat on the back for not rubbing it in.

We asked her about premonitory indications, and she told us about the way the house had been gone through and how she had attributed it to Heather. As she spoke she kept shaking her head. Gadek said, "Okay if we look around?"

She nodded several times.

"Yes, of course. Whatever you like. I looked around with Walt. The only thing I can find missing is a silk blouse and some bedding."

"Bedding?" Gadek raised an eyebrow and glanced at me.

"From the linen closet. Two plain single sheets, and I think a pillowcase. I don't notice anything else."

"Bedding," said Gadek. "Okay, there's a novelty. C'mon, Toby, let's see what we can see."

The wire to the kitchen phone had been pulled straight out.

"He must be awfully strong in the arms to do that quietly," I said. I was going to add that he must have felt like a damn fool when he got done prepping the place so carefully and stealthily and then went upstairs and found nobody home; but I remembered what happened the last time he looked like a fool, and superstitiously I refrained from saying it.

The place looked like a housekeeping magazine. Melanie

clearly belonged to that category of traveler who likes to come home to the ideal environment. We poked briefly into each room. The upstairs was neat as a pin.

The ID tech came up to announce the usual total failure to find likely prints and departed. We followed him.

Out in the street again Gadek said, "Well, that wasn't very exciting. But good luck for your friend. That's the first time we know of that he's scored a clean miss."

Footer pulled up, his recorder beside him on the front seat.

"I wish we'd got this a couple of hours ago," he said. "It'd be worse if it wasn't Saturday, but there are still going to be a lot of cars missing from this second list."

When we got back to the station I called Sara and told her about Melanie's lucky escape.

"Maybe we'd better have her and Heather stay with us for a few days," she said, "till they can decide what they want to do."

"I was half expecting Walt to offer to put them up," I said. "He didn't. But he *did* seem very protective—very alert."

There were thirty-two cars missing from the second list, but it wasn't nearly as difficult to sort things out as one might suppose. An aide ran a registration query for each plate through the Department of Motor Vehicles and brought the printout up to the office. All but seven of the missing cars were registered to addresses in the immediate neighborhood and could be tentatively discounted. Of the seven remaining, three had out-of-state plates which would have to be checked later but presumably belonged to recent arrivals in the neighborhood.

This left us with four to concentrate on, cars registered in the state but not in that neighborhood. They might be residents who hadn't reregistered at the new address, they might be people visiting for the evening who had then gone home, or they might be our guy.

The first car, a late-model foreign sedan, was registered

to one Yvonne Liman at an address across town. The phone book listed her, and also a Joan Liman three doors down the street from Melanie. Probably a family visit, therefore, and easy to check.

The second car, a ten-year-old mid-sized sedan, was registered to one Katherine White at an address in a poorer neighborhood across town. The phone book listed her at that same address. This was a go-slow, then, since there was no immediate suggestion of a reason for the vehicle's presence in the area.

The third came back to a three-year-old camper van registered in another part of the state. But the description on the previous night's tape of the vehicle carrying that number was "blue two-door sedan." This was a go-slow.

The fourth came back to a late-model sports car registered to one Richard Loring in a stranger city. The phone book had no Richard Loring, but Information had a new listing under that name at an address within a block of the scene. Probably a new arrival, and again, easy to check.

Gadek passed this list to Patty and said, "How would you handle that?" She looked uncomfortable and said, "Well, jeez, Leo. I guess numbers one and four, I'd go by and ask 'em where their car was last night and who was driving it, and see if it checked out the way it seems.

"The camper could be an error in transcribing the recording, or an error in reading the plate. Or it could be a stolen plate. I guess I'd check and see if the plate's reported stolen. If not, listen to the tape again to see whether the typist heard what Charlie dictated. If *that's* correct, then I suppose he could have made a mistake and just described the wrong vehicle—you get kind of groggy reading numbers block after block. So I'd call that camper's home jurisdiction and ask them to see if it's there and where it's been. If it was here last night at midnight it could be home by now if it was driven straight through. If the camper checks out okay, then Charlie probably made some error in reading the number, and so I'd make a list of similar numbers and run them through DMV and see if we get one that comes back to a blue two-door.

"Number two, since we have a name I guess I'd do a file

check on Katherine White, and then go ask her where the car was."

"Right. You're it. The two easy ones we can do later. I'll give those to somebody on the street detail. Toby, why don't you start the checks on number three while Patty's doing her file check. Then the two of you go and talk to her."

"Jeez, Parkman," said Patty. It was her first independent action. She looked delighted and headed for the stairs.

Since the street tape was in the office, I began with that. It was not terribly clear; it was a cheap recorder and a cheap mike, there was wind noise from the window and engine noise, and Charlie was speaking as fast as he could. But it was clear enough, and there was no error in transcription: it was 982 OOT.

Next I called down to Records and asked for a stolen check. The aide ran it while I waited. She confirmed the registration description as a camper van, and that it had not been reported stolen since the thirty-two numbers had been run some hours before.

Next, I phoned the camper's home jurisdiction, a small rural town. The dispatcher connected me with the solitary on-duty officer. I explained that the camper's number had come up in connection with a major felony, that we suspected a mistake, and that we'd appreciate a verification of the vehicle's whereabouts over the past twelve hours. I would have preferred, obviously, not to have said so much; but you have to let a colleague know what he might be getting into. He said he thought he knew the van and he would check it out and get back to me. He sounded relaxed.

Then I began to put together a list of similar plate numbers. License plates are tricky little devils, especially at night. Dirt, irregular illumination, reflection, fading, interference by bent fenders and misaligned plate frames—all these factors can mislead, quite apart from ordinary human error, transposing, misspeaking, that sort of thing. Combine a couple of these conditions and the results can be pretty far afield. Numbers are more subject to verbal error than to misreading. Letters are a problem: O and Q get confused with each other and with zero; L, F, and E; I, J, and T; G and C; U and V; Z and 2. Some of these misreadings seemed likely, given the number that Charlie had recorded, and I began to list new possibilities.

"Katherine White has a history," said Patty when she came back a little later. "She has three convictions for shoplifting, two for soliciting an act of prostitution, two for passing bad checks, and one for battery. Several for disturbing the peace, which are probably plea-bargains for solicitation charges. More recently she's been working for the High Class Escort Service. The most recent arrest was a year ago, which was for bad checks. She did six months, and she's on probation."

"Well," I said. "Let's listen carefully to what she says." The phone rang. It was my bucolic colleague. The camper van in question had been in a mechanic's tender care for the previous three days. He had gone himself to see its pieces strewn about over the workbench. It could not have been in our city the previous night.

We dropped off my list of similar numbers in Records for the aide to run through DMV during breaks in other business, and proceeded to Katherine White's. A large stucco apartment building with open balcony breezeways. Patty rang. A woman opened the door and visibly shrank back when she saw our badges.

"Katherine White?" said Patty.

"Yes," she said with great reluctance. We knew it already, because Patty had her mug shot in her pocket.

"May we come in?" said Patty, gesturing unobtrusively to the neighbors who were beginning to come out onto the balconies to watch the cops. The woman stepped back, we entered, she closed the door. A pretty woman, still young but aging fast. An interior suggestive of irregular fortune: a fancy stereo and expensive glass coffee table, and a cheap, ratty couch-and-chair set. A grubby shag rug. A bedroom, door ajar; bathroom; kitchenette. I walked past her and glanced around the bedroom and bathroom, which were unoccupied. You always want to know who's at home.

"Miz White," Patty said in a firm, not unsympathetic voice, "We had a problem in the north end of town last night, and we're looking into it. Your car was seen in the area." I came around the other side of her so that she stood between us.

Perhaps she turned a little away from us, perhaps she sank her head a little into her shoulders, arms folded tight across her chest; she seemed to withdraw into a deep place. Even her eyes, still open and flitting back and forth between the two of us, seemed to occlude.

Patty waited a moment for an answer, and then said, "Were you driving your car last night?"

Her fear was pitiful. Whatever her car had been up to last night, it was no good, and she knew it; but whatever it was, she had thought it was safe. She had no story prepared, no glib excuses. She was not quick, she was not inventive. Some people can come up with plausible lies on the spur of the moment and with a broad smile. If you haven't got them dead to rights you'll never jerk it out of them with surprise. But Katherine White was not one of these. She was frozen like a bird staring into the eyes of a snake—two snakes.

Finally Patty said, "Miz White, the best thing you can do is come clean and tell us what was going on last night."

She seemed to be shriveling before our eyes. Patty's voice was firm but reasonable. "Now you can see we didn't come here for nothing. The best thing for you now is to tell us the truth."

"You're on probation, Miz White," I said, less sympathetically. Her eyes left us for the first time, jerking around the room, looking for something else. She had not expected us to come.

"You don't want to go back to prison," said Patty, like a kind aunt.

Eyes on the floor she spat out, "I don't know anything about it."

Having said this she looked back at us in turn, half defiant, half despairing. We stood there a long moment.

"Katherine, you know that's not true," Patty said. "And what's more, we know it, and we can prove it." Her eyes fell again. She was sweating, and her knees trembled.

"Think again," said Patty.

Finally she burst out, "Well, what're you playing with me for? Go ahead and bust me, if you know about it. Go ahead,

if he's told you. You're going to do it, go ahead and do it."
She was shaking now, her knees trembling so they could
scarcely support her, still not moving her feet, but pivoting
back and forth between us, arms folded tight, eyes big,
bright, sweat standing on her brow.

"We don't want to arrest you," said Patty, firm, sympathetic. "We want to know what you know about it. We'd
rather not arrest you."

She looked sharply at Patty.

"Not arrest me?" She was shaking her head. "You're not
going to arrest me?"

"I can't promise," said Patty. "I don't want to. I'll help
you if I can. But you have to be straight with me. You're
not being straight with me."

She was staring hard into Patty's face, trying to read what
was hidden there. Very carefully, making no movement with
my upper body, I edged backward out of her line of view
so that she would have no distraction from Patty.

"I think you'd better tell me," said Patty. "Okay?"

She didn't answer, but she gave a little shrug.

"Okay," said Patty. "Tell me."

"Okay," she said, and shrugged again. "He's an old customer. He used to call High Class. Then I gave him my
number so he could call me here, save a few bucks." And
that, apparently, was it. She had been in the neighborhood
turning a trick. Unless, of course, she was suddenly a lot
cagier than she had been a few minutes ago. Patty was staring at her, which sometimes works if you don't know what
to ask next, because the person you're asking knows, and
will sometimes just blurt it out.

Finally, since that approach was unproductive, she said,
"Who else has been driving your car?" There was a look of
surprise, but it was incomprehension.

"Nobody," she said, quite clearly. "I don't let anybody
drive my car."

"But other people have keys," said Patty, casting afresh.

"No," she said, still surprised, still trying to figure out
Patty's motive for this assertion.

"Katherine. You started out lying to us. Don't you do
it again."

"I wasn't . . . I'm not lying now. I don't let anyone drive my car."

"Okay, if that's what you're telling me." Patty took out her daybook, turned it to a fresh page, and gave it to her. "Here. I want this in your handwriting. The guy's name, address, phone number. Right there."

"You know it already."

"I want it in your handwriting. And I don't want to waste the rest of the afternoon. You just do what you're told and I'll let you off this time."

She sucked in her breath hard.

"That's a promise. But only if you cooperate."

She wrote. Patty reclaimed the book and read the information carefully.

"What name does this Thomas Abbott know you by?"

"Crystal."

"Are you sure?"

"At High Class I've always been Crystal."

Patty added this information to the sheet and returned the book to her pocket.

"I'm going to talk to him. If this doesn't check out, then I'll be back for you."

There was no reaction. It would check out, most likely.

"Don't try to warn him," said Patty. "We'll know."

"I won't." And then, almost pleading, "You're not going to tell High Class?"

"No, I won't tell High Class."

"That I was cutting 'em out?"

"No, I won't tell them."

"I don't want to lose my teeth."

"I won't tell 'em. If you lose your teeth—*when* you lose your teeth—it won't be because of me." Patty stopped with her hand on the doorknob. "Listen. If you want to get out of the business, and keep your teeth, you call me and I'll help you."

"I'm okay," she said, looking at the floor.

"Can you remember me? Patty Dwornenscheck, Badge 62."

"I'm okay." But she looked at Patty a little sideways, and with a more complex suspicion.

"You can get out of this if you want to. Can you remember? Badge 62."

The neighbors were waiting for us when we came out. Opinions were clearly divided. Some, especially the younger men, watched us down the stairs with hard looks. But one woman's voice was clearly audible up and down the courtyard: "I'm *glad* to see the cops. The cops are welcome here, anytime."

When we were back in the car Patty said, "I always have to say I'll help 'em. Hookers, dopers, you name it. Jeez, it's a waste of time. They don't call, but it least I've tried."

"It didn't take very much time," I said. I thought it was quixotic, but so what? "I think we ought to talk to this Thomas Abbott and make sure about it," I said, "but I believed her."

"So did I," said Patty. "Poor little whore."

"Not romantic."

"Abbott. Thomas T. Abbott." An apartment in a big old house.

"It's not far. Let's go see if he's home."

"Howzabout you handle it?" said Patty. "I'm talked out."

Thomas T. Abbott was home. We showed him our badges and asked if we could speak to him. He blanched and drew himself up in the doorway.

"I don't know, Officers," he said. "I don't know whether I want to speak with you or not. What do you want?"

Pompous bozos bring out the bully in me, and I have to struggle against it. I took a deep breath and said in the voice which is the equivalent of a firm handshake, friendly but muscular, "Mr. Abbott, I am Officer Parkman, and this is Officer Dwornenscheck. We're engaged in an investigation of some importance, and I'm given to understand that you have information which would be helpful to us. If you could spare us a few minutes, it would be a great help."

He squinted at us. "Well, I'm pretty busy," he said. "Pretty busy. Why don't you call my office, and you can see me there? I think that would be better." He didn't sniff, exactly, but he came close.

"We're under some time pressure."

"I see," he said. He leaned against the door frame with

a negligent air. He was really pretty cool. "Well? What do you want to know?"

I thought that what we needed was to rearrange the social ascendancy. There was a couple approaching the door to their own apartment just down the hall. I hiked my voice up a bit.

"We understand that last night you employed the services of a prostitute named Crystal, who—"

"Come in, come in," he murmured, jumping back. We came in. "That is, not that I admit ... I mean, I don't know ..."

"Mr. Abbott," I said, still a good deal louder than necessary, "is this true or not? Did you employ a prostitute named Crystal last night?"

He was goggling at me.

"Well, I ... I don't ..." He pulled himself up again. "I want to talk to my lawyer. I want to know—"

"Mr. Abbott," I said, "I'm not here to arrest you for that. I'm not interested in your sex life. I've got other fish to fry. I have my own reasons for wanting to know whether Crystal was here last night. And since I'm not proposing to arrest you, your attorney is beside the point, isn't he? But if you lie to me, I'll arrest you for obstructing an officer. And I'll throw in soliciting an act of prostitution just to make it more fun for the newspapers. Get the picture?"

"Well, eh ..."

"What time did you call her last night?"

"Well, I ..."

The guy really was driving me frantic. I pulled my handcuffs out from my belt and slapped them in the palm of my left hand. They made a chinking noise.

"About eleven-thirty," he said quickly.

"Good. About eleven-thirty. And what time did she get here?"

"About twenty minutes later. Before midnight."

"And what was she wearing?"

"Wearing?"

"Yes. She was wearing clothes when she arrived, I suppose?"

"Well, I don't know. Some sort of coat, I think."

"Just a coat?"

"No, not just a coat."

"What else? Please think about it."

"Oh, a blouse, y'know, and a skirt."

"What sort of skirt?"

"Oh, well, short, you know."

"Loose, tight?"

"Tight."

"Kind of tight, or very tight?"

"Very tight."

"Shoes?"

"Shoes?"

"Yes, Mr. Abbott. Was Crystal wearing shoes when she came in?"

"Well, of course."

"What sort of shoes?"

He swallowed. "Y'know, heels."

"High heels?"

"Yes."

"Very high?"

He swallowed again. "Yes."

"And how long did she stay?"

He looked decidedly chagrined. He said, "Oh, I couldn't say, exactly. A while."

"How long, exactly?"

"Oh." He glanced at Patty. "About ten minutes."

"Ten minutes."

"About that."

"Not much less than that, I suppose."

"No."

He was looking pretty secondhand. I couldn't resist. I said, "You're sure."

He stared at me, working his jaws.

"Are you not sure?" I said, raising an eyebrow. "Might it have been a good deal less than ten minutes?"

"No!" he spat out.

" 'No' it wasn't, or 'No' you're not sure?"

"No it wasn't." I began to wonder if I wasn't indulging myself too much. We had what we needed. White had been there barely long enough for Charlie to tape her license

number, but at just the right time. When he had crossed the nearest intersection he had given the time as three minutes past midnight. She had been there at the same time, and she couldn't have walked the distance from her apartment in less than half an hour wearing a *very* tight skirt and *very* high heels. So we could discount the possibility that she had walked while somebody else used her car. Of course she might have gotten a ride with someone, or taken a taxi, or driven another car, or jogged over and changed her shoes outside, but I doubted it.

"Well, Mr. Abbott," I said, "I think that just about wraps it up for the present. If we have any more questions, we'll get back to you."

The poor man could only stand there grinding his teeth.

"Thanks, Mr. Abbott," said Patty with a bright smile, and we let ourselves out.

"Jeez, Parkman," Patty said when we were in the street. "I used to worry that you were too nice."

"Was I too hard on that clown?"

"Oh, no. That's the way to deal with jerks."

So Katherine White's car was eliminated—for the moment, at any rate. When we got to the station we went by Records. The aide had run the variations on the camper van's plate, and we got a long printout. Most of the vehicles were nothing like our "dark blue two-door sedan," but there were two two-doors on the list. One was registered in a stranger city some distance off, but the other was local. Its number was 982 OQT.

"Let's go eyeball it," said Patty. We cruised past the address on the registration, a small apartment building with all its parking in a row by the street. The car wasn't there, nor, so far as we could see, in the vicinity.

"We'll try again later," she said.

We went back to the station. Gadek had come in.

"Now what do you do?" he asked Patty.

"I was going to run a file check on the registered owner of this local car, to see if there's anything interesting, and make a few phone calls to see if the other car is still living where it's registered."

"Right. Do that. And Toby, maybe you should go home

and get some rest. Fry's called in sick, and I'm going to want you on the street tonight."

Walt had made a quick decision at the carriage house that reporting would cost Mike more than it would benefit society. The physical evidence was gone; beyond that, there could only be what Mike could tell. It takes time to find out what a victim has observed, and there had not been any time. But Walt knew that forty-some victims had been able to contribute very little, and these were victims who had made the decision to report, to cooperate, to talk about it.

Once Walt had tried to take a report in the hospital from a young man, barely an adult, who had been raped by older prisoners in the jail. There was no doubt about what happened: the jailer walked in on it. What alerted the jailer was the sound of the laughter.

The kid wouldn't talk to Walt, or respond to a question. His eyes never moved. He lay perfectly still in the bed. His legs were tight together, his arms pressed into his body. The only movements he made were as if to make himself smaller.

This experience made a deep impression on Walt.

With Mike there was no present physical emergency. Walt did not think that Mike's wrist was broken. Wherever he had been bleeding, he seemed to have stopped. If there looked to be an ongoing problem, they could go to some clinic in a stranger city, give a false name. Walt took a deep breath, put his customary professional reflexes on the back burner, and set himself to being the friend that Mike required.

He began by establishing a bluff, bonhomous tone between them which both recognized as slightly false, but which gave them almost the advantage of having a third party present, a stranger who could be uncharacteristically frank and bossy when those qualities were needed. They spread a sleeping bag in a corner of the living room and found a place in the hall closet for Mike's clothes. Walt explained the intricacies of the stereo. He said, "Hey, tiger, I bet you know how to handle the refrigerator." Mike just nodded.

Walt made a mental survey of the liquor supply so that

he would be able to detect any serious problems in that area. He put first aid materials on the vanity in the bathroom and gave Mike a few pointers in caring for his cuts. He had to go to work soon, he explained, but he would pick up pizza or something and come by on his dinner break. Until then, he thought that perhaps Mike should stay put.

Mike was compliant, moving around the apartment settling in, listening and nodding, but he was coming out of the initial shock. His mind was fluttering here and there, without power or control. He did not meet Walt's eyes.

Goddam, Walt thought as he left. *This isn't gonna be easy.*

The house was full of refugees when I got home. Sara had moved Melanie into Joss's room while Heather and Joss bedded down on the floor in Adam's.

"It's only till Monday," said Sara. "Melanie's got a realtor friend who has an apartment they can take for a month while they get sorted out. I'm sorry it isn't longer. It's nice to have more people in the house."

Walt had helped them bring their things over, and then he said he wasn't feeling terribly well and thought he ought to go home.

"Poor man," said Melanie, "I think he was more upset about it all than he wanted to show. He seemed very preoccupied all morning."

I took a cup of coffee into the garden and sat very still. Robert Peel came and sat in my lap, and John Marshall sat under the chair. Heather was playing advanced music on her clarinet. It was hard to follow, but soulful.

I thought about Katherine White, and what she was like, and what Crystal was like. I thought about Patty. I even thought about Thomas T. Abbott.

I thought about Melanie and her incredible luck. I thought about Heather, so full of life, and what she had been spared, and how grateful I was that nobody I cared for had been put through what he put his victims through. I began to think about Sara and Joss, and put the idea aside even before it formed in my mind.

25

While I was sitting very still, Patty was running a file check on the registered owner of the blue two-door. This citizen, Leonora Hart, had arrests for petty crimes. It wasn't much. But there was a property receipt from her last arrest, and it caught Patty's eye. Leonora Hart's personal belongings had been released to her brother, Henry Dorn.

"Bingo," said Patty. She hurried off to find Gadek, taking the stairs two at a time.

At roll call Gadek came as usual to the head of the table, snapped his notebook down, extracted a mug shot from the outside pocket, and held it up.

"Guys," he said, "this is Henry Dorn."

A guarded, intelligent face.

We stared, fascinated.

For a long minute nothing was said. It could be a red herring, of course; there were a thousand ways he could be eliminated as a possibility, just on the basis of records, without further investigation. You always have to be careful not to get too excited about a line of inquiry, because it can blind you to other possibilities. But this one smelled right. You could feel that tightness in Gadek, in all of us.

"He did time for a major series of burgs," said Gadek. "He was implicated in at least one rape, but not charged. This goes to the front burner," said Gadek. "We'll have Blondie, Myron, Charlie and Toby on the street tonight.

"Patty and I will expedite putting together a history on Dorn this evening. We didn't get very far, before.

"Charlie, before you hit the street, get Dorn's prints from the booking records and do a rough comparison with our file of unidentified prints. If you get anything close, take it to Emery in Records for confirmation.

"Blondie, Myron, spend the time between now and street time cataloging Dorn's cases, and make a complete set of the reports. Be sure and check the cross-references in the narratives.

"Patty, you go out to the big slammer tomorrow first thing and look through his prison records.

"It turns out that Leonora Hart has two cars registered in her name, the blue two-door and an older, brown sedan." Everyone copied the descriptions and plate numbers. "The brown sedan might be the vehicle that was seen in the vicinity in connection with number forty. Dorn probably uses them both.

"Toby, I want you to cruise by his place and his sister's place as soon as we break from here, have another look for the blue two-door and the brown sedan. If you don't find 'em, then make a pass by those addresses every hour until we pin down where those cars are. If you find 'em, see if you can sit on 'em. But don't get burned." He leaned forward in his chair, ran his hand over the papers and slapped it down.

"By jiminy," he said happily, "maybe things are beginning to run our way." He glanced around the table, eager and alert.

"Questions? Let's go." There was a general rush for the stairs.

I cruised past Leonora's place without result. Then I worked the streets for two blocks in each direction on the theory that Dorn and his sister might belong to that school of criminal who doesn't want to be followed home and therefore never parks close to where they live. Nothing.

Then I went past the address we had for Dorn. It was another apartment, but with the parking underneath and not readily visible from the street. He occupied apartment number eight, on the first floor above the parking level. The apartments opened onto open breezeways, but there was a solid facade on the street end which blocked any view of the apartment door or windows. This was an inconvenience.

Then I cruised the neighborhood. Nothing. Back to the station.

The print comparison had bombed in twenty minutes. This didn't eliminate Dorn, but it would have been very neat to have had a match.

Footer was establishing a "Dorn wall" in the locked conference room, where copies of all new information were to be posted. I went in to see how it was coming. In the middle of the wall, just at eye level, was Dorn's mug shot.

Our guy? I stared at it. The abstraction suddenly personal.

We all spent time studying that wall the first night, and increasing amounts of time every day as the initial flood of easily obtained information accumulated there.

I returned to the two addresses every hour or so through the evening while the rest of the task force tapped inquiries into computer nets, rummaged files, quizzed the senior aide in Records, telephoned irritable off-duty detectives, and quickly built a respectable pile of paper in the conference room, which Footer cataloged and posted on the wall, according to its nature.

Nine o'clock seemed late enough. I parked a block from Dorn's apartment and walked slowly past. The garage was dark and hard to see into, which was perfect for me, but the security light over the entrance was the brightest thing in sight. It spilled out over the sidewalk and illuminated not only the garage entrance but the walkways on either side. One of these doubtless led to a rear entrance, but they were just as conspicuous as the front way.

Well, sometimes you just have to be bold. I strolled around the block to my car, slouched a bit in the seat, and steering onto Dorn's street with a slight but noticeable weaving motion, drove right into the garage. I drove all the way to the back. There were twelve parking slots, each with an apartment number painted on the wall. Neither car was there, and the slot for number eight was unoccupied. However, there was a large, fat man.

"Hey!" he shouted. "No guest parking in here. Park in the street." He was really quite rude. I slurred my voice a bit and called back, "Y'know, I think I'm in th' wrong place," and backed out, weaving widely.

At 10:00, the street detail departed for the target area. This time we had a focus. We had a name, a face, and two cars to watch for.

At 11:00 I found the blue two-door. It was half a block from his apartment, parked near a corner and pretty well illuminated by a streetlight. I permitted myself one slow pass to get a good look. 982 OQT. The rear license plate frame partially covered the plate, making the Q look like O. That was what had misled Footer when he was taping.

Half a block farther away was a fairly long parking space on the side of the street opposite the blue two-door. I got right into the middle of it so my view wouldn't be blocked by any bigger car parking behind me, and settled down. I was facing away. I rearranged the mirrors, the outside door mirror to show me the car, and the inside rearview the other way to show me the sidewalk and just a bit of the car behind me. I locked the doors, scrunched into a corner of the seat, and reported in. Gadek was still in the office, so I raised him.

"S-19, 93."

"93, go to 2." It was Patty's voice. She would be monitoring the radio and taking calls for whoever was in the office. I switched over to 2, and said, "S-19, you there?"

"Go ahead, 93." That was Gadek's voice.

"S-19, I'm going to be tied up here for a bit."

"Okay, 93." His voice sounded hard and excited to me, but perhaps that was just because I knew what he usually sounded like. "Need any help?"

"Negative."

"Okay. Advise."

"Check. 93 out." I folded my arms and pretended to be asleep. These things can go on for a long time, and you can't just sit there. The neighbors notice. I didn't want word to pass around that undercover cops were working in the neighborhood. Or, of course, they might call the cops, and we'd have another of these depressing little scenes of Patrol busting DD.

I thought, there's no point doing this past two A.M.

There he was, crossing the street to his car. He looked like his mug shot, heavy for his size, compact. He moved smoothy and loosely for a man his age. When he opened the door the interior light didn't go on. He backed into the intersection, turned north, and drove off.

I had waited to start my engine until he had started his, so he wouldn't hear me on the quiet street. As soon as he was out of sight I pulled out, drove quickly to the end of the block and turned north. I accelerated pretty hard up the block, restrained principally by the possibility that he might have turned west, and that if he had he would pass right in front of me, and I didn't want to be conspicuous. There was a stop sign at the next corner. I stopped, and glanced east as I pulled forward. The blue two-door was stopped partway across the intersection. He was waiting to see what traffic was moving around him. I didn't think he could have seen me when he first got into his car, and so presumably this was just standard procedure for him: drive a block or two and then wait to see if anyone is coming after you. Tailing on a parallel street is a common technique, and by stopping so that he could see in all four directions he could spot anyone moving with him. Now he had seen my car, the first mover since he pulled away. He'd remember, and if he saw it again any time soon he'd know something was up.

Goddam, I thought. This guy is going to be tough.

Footer was in charge of the street detail, and I raised him. "32, 93."

"Go ahead, 93."

"Meet at the usual?"

"Check."

I took the next couple of blocks pretty carefully in case he should pop out again, but he didn't. Then I drove like mad northward into the target area. When I got to the market Footer was waiting.

"He's out, and heading this way."

"Where did you see him last?"

"One block from his place. He's very cagey. I couldn't tail him. All I can suggest is to cruise westward into the area and try to pick him up as he comes in from the other end."

"If he was coming behind you he'll be in by now," said Footer. "I'll call Blondie and Fry here and let 'em know, and then we'll work westward. You take off and try to pick him while he's still moving."

"He got a good look at this car. I don't dare show it to him again."

"Okay, let's trade. Take mine. Let's get this show on the road."

We hustled to each other's cars, and I pushed off to the west. Footer came on the air, summoning Blondie and Fry to "the usual."

I took the first couple of blocks pretty fast, and then slowed to a sedate pace. I didn't know where he was or where he was going. If I saw him, I wanted to be going slowly enough so that I would have time to judge his direction and speed. Also I wanted to look up and down each side street for his car; he could perfectly well have come in and parked by this time.

Or, of course, he could perfectly well have been going out for cigarettes, too. The fact that he started north didn't necessarily mean that he was bent on crime. For all I knew, he was back home by now curled up with an improving book. Well, I thought, perhaps we'll find out. If not tonight, then some night soon.

We worked the area until two. Much of the time I spent in the southwestern quadrant of my territory, parked just back from a corner, window down, listening for cars in the quiet and watching the streets up and down. Several times I saw small, dark cars moving, and hurried around to get a look at them. Once I intercepted Blondie in this way.

Around midnight I stopped at a gas station and called Sara, who told me in a determined tone of voice that all was well.

At one o'clock I cruised past his apartment, without result. Now that I knew which space belonged to number eight I could see from the street that it was vacant.

At 2:00 Footer called us in. I cruised past again. The blue two-door was in the same parking place on the street where I had seen it before.

Patty had gone home, but Gadek was still at the station when we got in. He listened carefully to what I had observed, eyes fixed on some point in the back of my head.

"Well, that's interesting," he said. "Dorn's going to be a tough nut. Let's think about it, and we'll work something out tomorrow. And I'd love to find that brown sedan. We've never seen it."

"Melanie is going to figure out that you're not in school," said Walt. "I think you ought to call her up, tell her you're taking some time out, you're okay, you need a little vacation. You can call her again in a week or two."

"Okay, Walt," said Mike. He was slouched into a corner of the couch. He didn't move.

"She's gonna want to know all about it," said Walt, "what can be done, and all that. You'll have to put her off. Can you handle that?"

"I guess," said Mike, but he was flat.

"Tell you what," said Walt. "We won't call. We'll write. That way we can make sure we send just the right message. Is there somebody reliable you know at school who we could send a letter to, who could mail it from school so it'd have the right postmark?"

Mike thought about this.

"Yeah, I guess," he said.

"Okay," said Walt. "You have paper? A pen? Write."

"Okay," said Mike, but he didn't move.

"Mike?"

"Do we have to do it right now?" said Mike.

Walt thought, is this what being a mother is like? No wonder women look older than their husbands. He said "Mike, did they make you read Herodotus in school?"

"A bit," Mike said. "The famous bits."

"Yeah, well, there's a story in Herodotus about these two guys who both want to be king of Persia. And they agree that they'll line up their horses before dawn, and whoever's horse whinnies first when he sees the sun rise, that guy's king. Remember this part? No. So they go out of town to some nice, picturesque spot where the view is good and there's no smog. They point their stallions toward the dawn and wait. Now, one of 'em has a handler who's given this whole thing some thought. Before they left town he went and rubbed his hand on a mare's pussy. So he's holding the bridle of his boss's stallion, and when the first sliver of the sun comes up over the horizon he passes his hand in front of the stallion's nose, who promptly whinnies, and the smart handler's boss becomes king. Now, do you know why I'm telling you this?"

"No."

"Because it teaches us that we gotta hustle. Here's the paper. Write."

The letter had to be brief, reassuring, and firm. Walt suggested the points which ought to be covered, and Mike paraphrased them, but when they read it over it sounded like a kidnapper's ransom note. They tried again. They made several drafts before Walt was satisfied. Then Mike wrote a cover note to his friend, enclosed his note to Melanie, and Walt put the whole production in the mail.

"Now listen, tiger, you need something to do," said Walt when the letter was out of the way. He plopped down on the other end of the couch and stuck his feet up on the coffee table. "You can't just sit here and think glum thoughts. Have you got some reading you want to do? I've got Herodotus here, y'know, if you'd like to finish it."

But not even the prospect of Herodotus would enliven Mike.

"I'm off tomorrow," said Walt. "Let's drive up the coast and have hamburgers somewhere. You need to get out of this place for a while."

"Okay, Walt," said Mike.

Walt thought, this is like digging a ditch. More was needed.

"And I'm gonna set you up with a shrink. You got some stuff you gotta talk out."

"Okay, Walt."

A pause stretched into a silent minute. Walt dragged his feet off the coffee table and put them on the floor. He settled his elbows on his knees. He rubbed his nose. Mike did not move.

Walt had dealt with several women who had been raped. Each reacted to what had happened in her own way, but none of them denied the central fact as Mike seemed to be doing. Perhaps it isn't simply that he's a man, Walt thought. No doubt there are women who can't admit it, either. The ones who don't report. Perhaps Mike just happens to fall into the category of people who can't admit to themselves that what happened actually happened, that it can't be undone somehow, or reinterpreted in some benign way. Perhaps it just happens that all men fall into that category.

But Walt thought that some progress ought to be made. "I know it's tough, Mike," he said at last. "It really is. But it wasn't your fault."

He scratched self-consciously. This was dangerous ground. He said, "It doesn't make you less of a guy."

Mike did not speak or move, except to close his eyes. A moment later he was crying, holding himself as rigid as he could to hide it, tight in his corner of the couch. Walt watched him. They were just out of arm's reach of each other, a long distance apart. Walt thought, Heather would put her arms around him and say "You're my favorite brother." That's what he needs. I wonder if I'm doing the right thing. God*dam*.

After Sara went to work on Monday, I helped Melanie and Heather move over to their temporary apartment. I'm not partial to houseguests, but it had actually been a jolly weekend, considering, and they seemed in a sense like reinforcements. We would have liked them to stay.

At roll call Gadek said, "You'll be glad to hear that Patty called an hour ago. She's getting all sorts of good stuff from the prison records, and she'll be back late tonight.

"We're changing the focus of the operation. Dorn's the best thing we've got going and we're going to put all our chips on him until he's eliminated or busted.

"First, I need more investigating time in the office. Charlie, you're coming inside on a permanent basis. I've seen the captain about getting overtime help from Patrol and else-where. You'll supervise them task by task and coordinate all investigations.

"The street detail is going to focus on Dorn rather than on the target area. From what Toby's observed, it's clear that the guy's real savvy and real careful.

"Here's what we'll do. Toby, sit on his car. When he moves, put out the direction and sit tight. Give him a min-ute. That should let him go to the intersection and wait, and then go on. Then follow him. Try to get square behind him so you don't have to worry about his turning into you and burning you.

"Blondie, Myron, and I will be spread across the southern border of the target area. He ought to pass near one or the other of us. That one will try to pick up a loose tail from Toby, and the others will angle in.

"The object is to tail him and nab him in the act of entry. If we can, we'll let Patrol do it. If that doesn't work out we'll jump him and hope for the best. If it rains as much as it looks like it's going to, vehicle traffic will be down and foot traffic just about nil. That's just going to make us stick out more. You'll have to be cagey."

It only rains when you have work to do. I found a space nearly a full block down from the car and on the same side of the street. It wasn't terrific, but it was all there was. Obvi-ously you can't run your windshield wipers when you're parked, and the glass fogged, so visibility was poor. I left my window down, which helped, but of course I got pretty wet.

Dorn came out to his car around 10:00. He pulled out and went straight east. When he was two blocks away I pulled out and started after him. After two more blocks he turned south. I speeded up. When I reached the street where he'd turned he was a block and a half away, still going south, but I no sooner made the corner than he turned west. When I made it to *that* corner he was nowhere to be seen.

Well, he had to have turned north or south, and north was what I was worried about, so I went west one block and turned north. There he was, two blocks ahead.

He would by this time have seen a car turn after him each

time he turned on the usually quiet streets. I couldn't stay on him without making the situation clear. It might be clear to him already. I turned off at the next corner, parked, and, since there was no good hiding place near, walked slowly up the sidewalk. In a minute he appeared, coming around the corner ahead of me. He gave me no more than a glance, but when he saw my car he slowed, then drove on around the corner. I kept walking, and sure enough, he appeared again. This time he was coming from the opposite direction, making another pass to see if a driver had appeared and the car had started off again. When he drew up to it he stopped in the middle of the street, got out, came around and looked in to see if there were anyone scrunched down in the seat. Finding that there wasn't, he got back in his car, turned north again, and disappeared.

But he was perfectly capable of coming back again, either right away or at some later time that night. If he did come back, he should find that car. I kept on walking through the wet and fished out my mike.

"S-19, 93."

"93."

"I've had to drop off. The last I saw of him he was heading your way."

"Okay," said Gadek at roll call. "We'll try a split tail. He's seen Toby a couple of times, so Blondie'll spot on the car tonight. Toby, take a spot three blocks east. I'll be three blocks north. Myron, you'll be in the center of the target area. When he moves, Blondie, don't follow him. Just put out his direction and wait. If he's coming into our area he'll come within sight of either Toby or me. Whoever sees him, put out his direction and get in behind him for a few blocks if possible. Once we're moving, Blondie, you try to parallel on one side, and whoever else is disengaged parallel from the other. If he turns, the one he turns toward picks up the tail, and the others try to parallel. Nobody follow close, and nobody follow for long, especially on side streets. Oh, and guys, nobody use the car Toby had last night."

"Okay, S-19, he's coming to his car."

"Check, 122. 93 copy?"

"93 copy."

"He's starting north."

"He's passing me, still heading north. 122 and 93 get moving. I'm going to get in behind."

"He's turning east. 93, that's you."

"I've got him. Still east."

"He's turning north. 122, you there?

"Negative. I'm stuck at a red."

"93, S-19, make the turn, stay with him."

"Check."

"S-19, 93, he's turning east on a westbound one-way. I'll cut east when I can."

"He's just come past me moving south."

"Anybody got him?"

"S-19, 122, he's just come past me moving west."

"He's circling. 93, 122, go west and north and wait for him. 79, hold where you are."

"79 copy."

But that was the last we saw of him that night.

26

Gadek and Patty at first, and eventually all of us, gathered Dorn's history in bits and pieces from various files in our own department, from the records of adjacent jurisdictions, from prison records. We spent hours on the phone with retired detectives who remembered Dorn and who added recollections not found in reports. Over the third week in February the pieces came together.

Dorn had started his criminal career as a juvenile. At that period of his life he worked during the day, when the occupants were out. His first burglary arrest was at seventeen. A brief period of detention gave him the opportunity to pick up some pointers from more experienced colleagues so that he was smarter and more effective when he returned to the street and to his chosen line of work.

In his early twenties he was arrested again for burglary, convicted, and sent to prison. This was the pattern of the next twenty-five years.

He married once, and was soon divorced. He was implicated in various assaults, usually against women. Sometimes these were his live-in girlfriends, sometimes not. Once he was arrested. Charges were always dropped—sometimes, presumably, because of fear, but usually because he moved in a world of weak and fearful people to whom a beating is by no means the darkest possibility.

At some point he began to add hot prowls—nighttime entries while the residents slept. He confided to a prison informer that he liked to go into bedrooms. He liked to stand in the room, often right beside the bed, and watch the sleepers. If he found a couple together he would linger, sometimes for hours, hoping to see sexual activity. This might have been the period of his first rapes, probably opportunistic embellishments when a prowl revealed a lone female occupant. He was suspected in several attacks, but never directly connected with any of them.

His last arrest was in connection with a long series of hot prowl burglaries. He pled guilty to six counts, and as part of the agreement he helped the police close their files on the rest of the series, which numbered upwards of two hundred cases. This time he served four years. He was forty-nine and a tough old con when he got out, less than a month before our guy's first known hit.

The next day, February 23, I cruised by Dorn's apartment on my way in to the station in the late afternoon. Space number eight was vacant, as always, the customary corner spot was occupied by another car, and I couldn't find the blue two-door anywhere. I checked regularly throughout the evening, and couldn't find hide nor hair of it. In consequence of this the street detail, which had been prepared to try another split tail, did its usual loose cover in the target area. We responded to an "unknown man in backyard" call at 11:30, sat in various uncomfortable places until 1:00 A.M., but came up empty.

When we came in at 2:00 A.M. there was a note from Gadek, who had been in the office until 1:00, that he would check for Dorn's car first thing in the morning. At 7:15 the next morning Sara woke me: it was Gadek on the phone.

"It's here, where it always is. Come on down and sit on it. Then we'll know where it is. I'm going in to the office. It won't move in the next forty-five minutes. And the brown sedan's finally turned up—it's in front of Leonora's apartment."

He was quite right. It didn't move until three in the afternoon. I had eaten my sandwiches, drunk my coffee, filled the paper cup twice and carefully poured the contents out onto the street when at 3:30 or so Dorn appeared, got in, and drove away to the west. I followed carefully, but this time he went straight to a one-way street, turned up it the wrong way, and drove at least two blocks. I don't know how many because I didn't wait to see. I tried a parallel to the north, and lost him.

I went back to spot on the apartment, but he didn't reappear. Fry came a little after 4:00 to relieve me, thank God, and I went home, done for the day. Fry had no luck at all: he sat until 10:00 without anything, then went to join the area cover. There was no action, no Dorn, nothing. The detail recorded license plates, and apart from that there was nothing to do.

But the next morning at 4:10 A.M. I got a call from Patrol.

"We have a hit in your series, reported about twenty minutes ago. Gadek said to call you."

"Great. I'll be right there." I rattled down the receiver and started pulling on my clothes.

"Toby?"

"Another hit." She didn't say anything. She lay with her eyes closed, listening to the sound of my dressing, the hiss of the cartridges as they slipped into the cylinder, the faint click as they were seated.

The victim was an actress, Abbi Beshouri. Not a famous actress, but well-known locally. The attacker came from some unknown quarter, unseen. She had come home from a party at 12:30 and gone to bed not long after. He probably attacked around 1:30 and was gone by 3:00. She called around 3:45, as soon as she could get her wits together. She had done nothing, not even washed. She wrapped herself in a sheet, and in that condition was taken by ambulance to the hospital where a rich trove of physical evidence was collected.

When I reached the station at 4:30 Gadek sent me out immediately to rerecord license numbers. If Dorn was our guy this seemed a waste of time, because neither I nor Fry, who had done the recordings at midnight, would have missed the blue two-door. But of course he might have another car, or access to another, or Dorn might not be our guy—it might be somebody else altogether.

I was back in the station with the tapes by 5:30. The aide in Service Division was drafted to begin the transcription, and another was awakened and called in to assist. But for all our trouble, we got nothing useful from the comparison of the two lists. Perhaps he couldn't find a parking place nearby.

Blondie came in from the hospital shortly before 9:00. She had done the whole interview, got the whole thing.

"This is one tough lady," she said, shaking her head. "She's called a news conference."

Beshouri appeared punctually. She looked like hell in the bright light. Her left eye was swollen and discolored, and she had several other bruises on her face. One wrist was swollen, and both were discolored. She had chosen a low-cut sundress for this occasion, to display the bruises and the constellation of stab wounds, deeper and more numerous than before, across her chest.

"I'm doing this now because I think it ought to be done, and if I think about it I may not have the courage." She spoke quickly and untheatrically, but boldly, with a firm, full voice. "I am the fifty-first reported victim of this man. I don't want another soul to have to go through what I have gone through. I don't want there to be a number fifty-two."

Her introductory remarks made the national news programs. Her appeals for information and cooperation were extensively covered locally. Most of what she had to say about the attack itself couldn't be repeated either on TV or in print, but the summaries given by reporters, clearly sobered by what they had heard, were powerful.

We were all huddled around the TV in the office.

"Jeez," said Patty.

"Brave lady," said Gadek.

"Man," said Blondie, "I hope she doesn't regret it."

* * *

On February 26, Myron and Charlie were in the office when Marcia said that there was a woman in the DD waiting room downstairs who wanted to speak to someone from the task force. Myron went down and took her to an interview room. Her name was Julia Frome. She had been to the community meeting the previous July, and had been following the accounts in the media ever since.

She said that she had been raped just three years before. She was sure that it was by this same man.

She had never reported it. He had threatened her and told her he would know if she did. She believed him. She was coming forward now, not because she was less frightened, but because she had to. The public account of the young actress had shocked her, it was just like what had happened to her. It was like going through it all over again. She wanted to make a report. No rush—she supposed we must be busy, and she'd waited three years.

Myron was a warm and tactful individual. Gently he led her into her account. She had not been talking for more than a few minutes before he was convinced that the responsible had, in fact, been our guy. She was the fifty-second known victim.

"It was pretty bad," she said. "It was pretty bad. That poor girl wasn't acting when she was describing it. But y'know what I remember, what I think about?"

"What?" said Myron.

"It was the expression on his face. It was . . ." Myron felt all his muscles go tight at once. "It was *mean*."

"Excuse me," he said. He couldn't wait. "Excuse me. You're describing his expression—you mean you saw his face?"

"Oh, yes."

"But you said your eyes were taped."

"Yes, he taped them. But I have a skin problem, I get zits—see." She indicated several blemishes. "It's better now than it was then. I was using this antibiotic lotion on my zits. I'd put it on at bedtime. Greasy stuff. I'd put a lot on this cheek. The tape didn't stick there. It pulled away and so I could see down pretty well. I saw his face a lot."

"How good a look did you get?"

"A very good look. Too good. I've been seeing that face in my mind's eye, sleeping and waking, all this time."

The next question was almost too big to come right out with.

"Could you identify him?" asked Fry. "Would you know him if you saw him again?"

"Oh, yes," she said, firmly, frightened. "I know that face. I'm never going to get that face out of my mind."

"Julie Frome," Gadek mused. "I've heard that name before."

"It rings a bell," I said, "but I don't remember which one."

"It's in this case," said Blondie. "Somewhere that name appears."

"Oh God," murmured Fry. "I smell trouble. Footer will remember."

"It's his day off," said Gadek. "It'll come. We all remember it. We'll think about it. It'll pop out in the next day or two. While we're thinking about it, let's get a photo lineup organized. Myron, that's for you. Do it today, if you can."

A photo lineup can be a tricky thing.

There are various mistakes that can predispose a witness to select one picture rather than another. Any picture that is different than the others: bigger, for example, or a different shape, or in color when the others are black-and-white or vice versa, or a different pose, or an expression that stands out from the others. Or the way the photos are presented, with one out of line. Or more of a close-up, so that the face appears bigger even though the photo itself is the same size and shape as the others. The eye picks up any of these hints and says, ah, *that's* the one they started with, and then they added all these others. So all of these factors have to be neutral, or the identification may be useless.

Fry met with Julia Frome that afternoon. He explained that he was going to show her a group of pictures, one of which might be the man who had attacked her. When he showed her the pictures, she should look at them all. Her attacker might not even be among them, and she shouldn't pick any unless she was sure.

And having said this he opened the folder of twelve mugs and laid it on the table in front of her. She hissed a little breath and placed her finger without hesitation on Henry Dorn.

"That's him," she said.

"Take your time," said Fry. "There's no rush."

"No need to rush," she said. "No need in the world. That's him. There's no doubt in my mind."

"He looks a lot like this one," said Fry, tapping the mug of a small-time pimp/junkie with his pen.

"Yes," said she. "He looks a lot like a lot of folks. But it's only this one here."

Bingo! thought Fry.

At roll call that same day, Gadek said, "You've all heard that we got a positive on Dorn. We could be very close to wrapping this thing up, and when the moment comes we'll want to move fast. So let me review our status on this thing so we're all operating from the same assumptions. I've been in close touch with Jaime Reyes in the D.A.'s office, so I'm secure on the legal angle of all this.

"We have a unique crime series going, and we have a bad guy who we're pretty sure is the responsible. What we didn't have until this afternoon is a firm connection between the series and the bad guy. We're in a much better position now, but it's not tight yet: a three-year-old ID isn't great, and we're still scratching our heads about where we've heard of Julia Frome before. That may matter.

"We've got chemical analysis that will eliminate all but about three percent of the male population, but that's not conclusive. We've got the scar on his back, the scar on his hand, the missing tooth, the general physical description. None of that is conclusive. Taken all together it's promising, but each piece comes from a different case. What it means is, you have to convince a jury that the same guy did all these rapes, because they're so similar; *and* then that small bits of evidence from the different cases each point to Dorn; *and* that all the evidence taken together incriminates him beyond a reasonable doubt. That's going to be the hard part.

We know Dorn is our guy, because you don't get all these indicators pointing to some innocent citizen. But it takes a jury to convict, and of course the district attorney's office is going to be thinking about what it'll look like to a jury.

"It would be very nice if, in addition to what we already have in evidence, we could catch Dorn in possession of physical evidence, like souvenirs. Our guy's usually taken something from each victim, very often clothing. Some bad guys like to take trophies to commemorate a hit, and they take things to keep. Some like to use women's clothing to masturbate in and then discard. So he may have been throwing these things away as he goes along, or he may have been keeping them. If he's been keeping them, and if we can identify specific objects as having belonged to specific victims, then we'll have him. But what it means is that we can't give him any indication that we're onto him. If he suspects that he's the focus of an investigation before he's actually taken into custody he'll get rid of anything he's holding, and we'll be a lot weaker.

"Myron, I want you to work with Charlie and bring the draft search warrant up to date. List all the souvenirs we'll be looking for, the blood and saliva samples we'll want to take from him, photos of scars, the whole thing. Summarize the connection with him. We'll want to search his apartment, his sister's apartment, any storage areas—there are storage lockers in the garage of his building, we'll have to check on hers—and both cars. Update it whenever we get any new information. What we want is to have it constantly ready to fill in his name and drop it in front of a judge when we're ready to move, because we may want to move fast.

"And guys, I hate to do it to ya, but we're going to have to start sitting on Dorn pretty much around the clock. I'll try to get us some help for inside work, but however that goes we're going into a very busy time."

That night Gadek arranged for a sergeant to make a pass every hour through the night, and to call him at home if there was anything to report. Neither the blue nor the brown car moved, and there was no sign of Dorn.

*   *   *

At one time or another during the night every single one of us woke up remembering that Julia Frome's name appeared in a list of women who had corresponded with Dorn in prison. She had written to Dorn, and he had written to her, according to the logs. She had visited him in prison. It seemed highly improbable that she would have failed to recognize him, if, as she maintained, she had seen him. We turned on our bedside lights and made notes on our pads.

It came to me at 4:30 in the morning, and since I couldn't go back to sleep after that I was at the station at 5:30. Blondie was there already, with the relevant papers spread out in front of her. Gadek appeared at 5:40, and Fry at 6:10. Only Patty was able to go quietly back to sleep, arise at her usual time, shower, eat breakfast, drink home-brewed coffee, glance at the paper, and appear trim and rosy at 7:30.

"Frome is on the jail correspondence list," she announced as she walked through the door.

We glowered at her.

"Oh, jeez," she said.

Footer arrived, fresh from his day off.

"Who's Julia Frome?" we chorused.

"She visited Dorn in the slammer," he said. "What's up?"

"I believe she was raped," said Fry, "and that it was our guy. There's no doubt in my mind. She gave me a lot of detail that hasn't been in the papers, and she was convincing."

"Well," Gadek said, "there are lies and lies. If she's telling the wrong sort, it blows our one solid connection between Dorn and the series."

"If she's lying, she's not lying about everything," said Fry.

"Let's find out," said Gadek. "Myron, Toby, you're it. Don't be tougher than you have to be, but pin it down. We have to know. If Dorn isn't our guy we're giving the real responsible a free ride."

It was still only 7:45. We called her. She hadn't left for work yet and would see us right then and go to work late.

A small stucco house, trim and well-maintained.

Fry's interviews tended to be short. He believed in going straight at things, shaking things loose. He declined coffee for both of us, and said, "Julia, when you came in to the office you described the attack very fully, and I believe what you said. But let me lay out my problem, and you tell me what I ought to make of it."

Her face clouded slightly, and she turned away from him just a little. I thought, she's dirty.

"You told me that you saw his face several times, very clearly, during the attack. Isn't that true?"

"Yes."

"And you said that you'd be able to remember his face because you'd had such a good look, right?"

"That's what I said."

"Julia, you didn't tell me that you knew him before the attack."

She sat frozen for a long moment, staring at Fry.

"You didn't mention knowing him before, did you?"

She glanced at me, finding no comfort, and back at Fry. Then she looked at the floor, the walls, the ceiling, the floor again, and said, "No."

"You did know him."

She answered in a tired, distant voice, "Yes."

"What's his name?"

"You know his name."

"I want you to tell me."

She almost spit it out: "His name is Henry Dorn."

"At the time of the rape, did you see his face?"

"No."

"The tape slipping, you made that up?"

She nodded. I felt my stomach sink. This was disaster.

"Why don't you tell me about it now." Fry's voice was sympathetic, but there was no question mark.

She waved a hand heavily in the air.

"Oh, what difference does it make." There was no question mark here, either.

"It makes a big difference, Julia."

She waved in dismissal again. She shook her head, eyes on the floor, her jaws working.

"Julia, I'm going to tell you what's on my mind, and then you decide what you're going to do. I believe that you were raped. I don't believe that you lied about that." She raised her eyes to his and stirred a little in her chair. "And I believe that the man who did it was the same man who raped all those other women. But I know that you tried to conceal the fact that you knew the man you've accused. And you lied about seeing him. I have to know why you did that. Was it because you had some grudge against Dorn, and you want to get revenge by blaming all these rapes on him?"

She had been meeting Fry's eyes as he spoke, and she was shaking her head vehemently before he had finished.

"No," she said. "No, he's the one. I didn't lie about that."

"Julia, I have to know. If we arrest Dorn, and he's not the one, then we do a terrible injustice to him and to all the other victims. Because the real rapist goes free. There's no justice in that."

"No," she said again. "It was him. It was Henry Dorn."

"Okay," he said. "Tell me."

She stirred again, and said, "Okay. Okay. Here's what it was. I knew a guy who had a friend in prison. He talked about him a lot—how interesting he was. I was lonely. Then I got a letter from him—the guy I knew had given him my name."

"When was this?"

"Oh, six, seven years ago."

"Okay."

"Well, it was Henry. He wrote back. He wrote real well, real smooth. So we wrote back and forth, and one time he said, why don't I come and visit him? Well, it wasn't far, so I did. I guess I was stupid. I liked him. He was real relaxed, real amiable. Not like what you'd expect, not like the other cons I saw there. I went several times, and then he said he was getting out and he wanted to see me."

"Did you want to see him?"

"Yeah, I guess I did. Anyway, I didn't see how I could say no, so I said, sure."

"And he came?"

"Yeah, he came. He called about a week after he got out. He came over. We couldn't go out because he was on parole and he wasn't supposed to drink, so we just stayed in my apartment. I was kind of tense about it, but he was real nice, he didn't push or anything. He left early. The next time he came it was pretty much the same. I guess I stopped worrying about him." She glanced around. "Well, then we started having fights, and I told him he couldn't come any more. He got . . ."

"Just a sec, just a sec. What were you fighting about?" The waving gesture.

"Oh, it doesn't matter."

"It matters. Julia. You have to tell me what happened." She had lost eye contact.

"Okay, okay." Her voice had dropped. She sagged all over. These things take different people different ways. She had spoken of the rape itself with comparative calm. It was her betrayal that caused her the deepest shame. That was the hardest thing for her to talk about.

She had been disarmed by his manners and his intelligence. They had gone to bed on his third visit, and begun what she had regarded as a serious affair. Some things had puzzled her: he had wanted to borrow her car on several occasions, saying that something was wrong with his own. He asked her to store some boxes for him, which he brought heavily taped shut. She became aware that he was lying about various things. Sometimes his surface slipped, and she was disturbed by the glimpses she had of him. Finally she confronted him about his untruthfulness. They had several ugly scenes. She broke off their relationship, deeply frightened of him. She changed addresses and got a new, unlisted telephone. She heard no more from him.

It was about a year later that she was attacked.

She was sure it was Dorn. She didn't actually see him. She invented the slipping tape because she thought she wouldn't be believed otherwise. She thought that if she admitted knowing Dorn before, she would be written off as a disgruntled former girlfriend.

"Boy oh boy," said Gadek when we told him. "It looked so good, too."

"She was certainly raped by our guy," said Fry, "and she's probably right that it was Dorn. But she didn't see him, and she lied. We can't use her to put the two together. That's the end of that."

"It sets us back," said Gadek. "It sets us back in a big way."

*　*　*

Mike was pretty drunk when Walt got home shortly before midnight. This had happened before, and Walt didn't like it. Physically, Mike was almost back to par, so long as you didn't see him without his shirt. But seeing the shrink seemed to have unstoppered him, and emotionally he was reeling.

He was crying. He said, "God, I jus' came out of the bathroom and *bang!* There he was. I don't know. I . . ."

"Look at this," said Walt. "Mike, you've drunk half the bottle. This isn't gonna fly, buddy."

"I jus' came out, and *bang!*"

"Hey! Mike! I said you're drinking too much. *You're not listening.*" He clapped a large, avuncular arm over Mike's shoulders. *"You gotta learn to listen."*

"What's the decision point?" I asked Gadek. "When have you got enough to move?"

"When you think it's enough to convince a jury, and when you don't think you're likely to get more by waiting. We've had a long, long series without much in the way of incriminating evidence. At this rate, we'll have a lot more victims before we have enough to be safe. But if we jump too soon, we won't have enough to convict." He exhaled. "It's just one of those iffy decisions."

For three days and nights Dorn didn't appear to move. During this time Footer completed the assembly of the arrest and search warrants, and Gadek and Reyes spent long hours in the conference room reviewing the status of the case. Reyes vetoed an arrest on the basis of what we had, especially with the collapse of Frome's positive ID. We hoped for more connecting evidence when we searched Dorn's place, but it was no more than a hope.

On the fourth day Dorn emerged from his apartment at about 9:00 P.M. and walked east, then north. He cut through parking garages and vacant lots. He hopped fences. It was impossible to follow him through blocks without either losing him or being spotted. I radioed the office that he was moving, and drove a series of loops in advance of what I took his route to be. Then I parked and waited. When he appeared I watched his route and made another loop. Blondie, Gadek, and Fry hastened out from the office. I saw him enter a large garage, and moved around to the other side. Within minutes the others had formed a loose cordon around the area. That was the last we saw of him. Shortly before midnight, still on foot, he was seen approaching his apartment from the west.

"Well, it explains some things," said Gadek. "We've been assuming that he's in the same place as his cars. It means that we're going to have to spot on his place all the time. Car checks won't make it."

On the fifth day Dorn took the brown car in the early afternoon and drove west. Blondie tailed him for several blocks. He curled north, then east, heading for the target area. Gadek and Footer scrambled from the office. By the time they reached the area Blondie had dropped off and lost him, but they cruised, and found the brown car parked on a side street. Gadek spotted on the car itself, and Blondie and Footer took spots a block away, one to the northeast and the other to the northwest.

They assumed that he was at some stage of preparing an entry, and it was possible that they might see him coming back from it to the car. It was not impossible that they might see him coming out of the residence itself.

One of the blocks that Footer had under observation from his corner spot had several large shrubs and untrimmed trees planted on the parking strip so that he couldn't see far up the sidewalk. It was down this street that Dorn appeared at about 4:30, a familiar figure now, compact and alert. He passed quite near Footer without seeming to notice him, and returned to his car. He drove away southward, and a few minutes later Blondie reported that both cars were parked in their usual places.

27

Sometimes things just work out.

Gadek hastened to Footer's spot as soon as Dorn was out of sight. They walked quickly up the block to the point where Footer had first seen Dorn coming down the sidewalk.

"Now," Gadek said, "if all my assumptions about him are on the money, he'll have parked his car within two blocks of the place he intended to hit. It'll be in this block. You didn't see him cross the street, so it'll be on this side. It'll be a place with ground-floor access. We oughta be looking at it." They looked. There were three houses and a small apartment building with three ground-floor units at that end of the block. Any of them would fit.

"Okay," said Gadek. "It'll be one with a woman living alone, or with small children. You try the apartment building. I'll start at that house."

Fifteen minutes later they were in the street again. Most of the residents weren't home, but from those who were they had learned that all three houses had men, in one status or another, in residence. Of the apartments, one was occupied by a couple, one by a single man, and the last was vacant.

"Okay. Let's go up to the corner, and see what we can

see there." There were several possible units around the corner or across the street. Blondie returned from seeing Dorn home, and they divided them up three ways. They started knocking on doors just before 5:00.

It was at the other end of the block that the sole resident of a small, one-and-a-half-story cottage came home just after 5:30. She went out the kitchen door to empty the garbage, and noticed that some flowerpots had been moved from the picnic table by the back door, just below the kitchen window. When she went back inside she checked the window and discovered that it was unlocked.

She had been to her neighborhood Crimewatch meetings, and she had received one of the informational leaflets that the reserve officers had distributed. She knew a suspicious circumstance when she saw one. She went straight out the back door and over the fence to a neighbor's, and called the police from there. She said she was afraid someone was in her house. Two Patrol officers responded and searched the place, finding nothing. They accompanied the resident back to the cottage and went through it with her very carefully. She could find nothing missing, but it didn't seem right to her; she was sure that someone had gone all through the house. One of the officers was a rookie named Grimes. He had put in some overtime on the task force, knew our guy's pattern, and appreciated the possibilities. He called the task force office at about 6:30 and spoke to Fry. Fry raised Gadek on the radio. The whole task force was out on the street by this time, working its way slowly outward from the first, most likely, group of houses.

Gadek walked quickly up the block to the cottage and walked through it with Grimes. Clearly, this was where Dorn had been.

Gadek had dreamed of such a situation: our guy sets up a house, comes back at night, goes through at least the first part of his ritual, comes to the bedroom, and finds—cops. Connect him to the series via MO, chemical and physical evidence—prints, DNA, hair and fiber comparisons—get a warrant for a squeaky-clean search of his residence for property known to have been taken from earlier hits—you got him. Get a body in the act, everything else follows. It's the detective's wet dream.

Our guy usually struck between midnight and 1:00, but it had been as early as 10:00. Nobody knew how long he might be inside the victim's home before making himself known, and he almost certainly watched the place for a while before entering. Say an hour. So everything should be in place by 9:00. Make it safe, say 8:30. So there was almost two hours to put it all together.

Gadek explained the situation to the resident. After hearing him she abandoned any intention she might have had of staying there herself, and she readily consented to the occupation of the cottage by as many cops as could be squeezed in. She was a fairly tall, fairly robust blonde, similar in size and general appearance to Patty Dwornenscheck. Patty was summoned to the cottage, and the rest of the task force called in from the street to the station. Whatever organization needed to be done would be done there. Gadek wanted to avoid making a commotion outside. He hastened back to the office himself, while Patty grilled the resident on her usual evening routine, what lights she had on and when she turned them off, which curtains she closed and which she left open, her bedtime—anything that might be visible or audible from outside.

Footer was to remain in the station, where he would have radio and telephone communication with everyone on the street and inside. Blondie was to go sit on Dorn. Fry, Patty, and Gadek would suffice to occupy the place. I was to find someplace in front where I could get a clear view of the street, and preferably the cross street as well. Grimes reported a clear view of the rear of the house from the neighbor's across the fence, and that the neighbor had volunteered permission to use an upstairs bedroom for that purpose. Gadek gave this post to Grimes. This was an improvisation, but it would be valuable to have an outside view of the rear area where, most likely, entrance would actually be made.

Vice canceled a hooker bust and promised to have two two-person undercover cars in the area by 9:30 for close backup. Patrol promised two uniform units at a greater distance by the same time. All units connected with the setup to be on Channel 2, and all others to be informed that Channel 2 was to be kept clear until further notice.

With radios, flashlights, tear gas, two thermos bottles and some sandwiches, Gadek and Fry piled into Fry's camper and arrived at the house at 8:15.

Grimes and the resident were still there. She was tense but friendly, quickly packing an overnight bag. Her car was to remain in the driveway, and an aide was dispatched from the station with a spare key to pick up Grimes's patrol car from just up the street, deliver the shotgun to Grimes and transport the resident to stay with friends. She had laid out for Dwornenscheck a lumberman's plaid shirt, which she often wore in the evening, and jeans.

Presently they departed, she to her refuge and Grimes to the observation post opposite.

Grimes had a perfect view of the back of the cottage. I had found a spot for my car just across the intersection and across the street. Whichever way he came, up either street or through the block, those inside the house would have advance warning.

The question of fields of fire was Gadek's first concern. Nine-millimeter pistols would penetrate walls: with bad luck, several walls. When he entered, our guy would undoubtedly go around the ground floor before going upstairs; this meant that everyone in the house would have to be upstairs. At the top was a landing with three doors: the bathroom directly opposite the stairs; the bedroom, to the front; and a small spare room opposite the bedroom.

There were no good solutions here; the best command of the stairs and the bedroom was from the bathroom, but that door was always left open. Our guy was systematic in studying his victims and Gadek had to assume that any deviation from routine would alarm him. He might abort his approach, or if he did not he would be more wary and harder to take. The spare room had a view of the landing and a slice of the bedroom if its door were left open, but it was ordinarily kept closed. In any case, fire from any room into any other meant that only a window or a single exterior wall stood between the target and the houses on either side, or across the street or the backyard. And if the group were divided among the two rooms they would simply be shooting at each other.

"Of course, so far as we know, he doesn't carry a gun," said Gadek, "so we may be able to take him without any shooting. That'd be nice."

It was almost 8:30.

At the Hall of Justice the chief and the Patrol and DD captains reviewed the situation with the watch commander, a lieutenant. They discussed evacuating the neighboring houses as a safety precaution, and rejected it as impractical. They discussed canceling the setup as excessively hazardous to the neighborhood, and decided to proceed. Aware of the curiosity of Patrol officers they declared the whole target area out of bounds unless explicitly ordered. The press officer was paged and recalled to the station. The city manager was informed, and he called the mayor. The mayor set her aides to calling favored reporters and everyone else who might be flattered by being in the know.

Patty and Fry busied themselves making a dummy out of the resident's clothing to put in the bed. If life was sweet, our guy would get all the way into the room and jump it before they took him.

He would certainly check out the spare room before entering the bedroom, so nobody could be concealed there. Fry would be in the narrow space between the dresser and the wall. Gadek and Patty would be in the closet beside the bed. The closet door was normally closed, but it would be left open. By the time he was far enough into the room to notice, it would be too late for him to retreat. Or at any rate, that's what they thought.

Grimes waited in the dark bedroom, sitting back from the window, in shadow. The lower sash was fully open, so as not to impede his view or his fire. His shotgun lay across the bed beside him, its muzzle resting on the chest of a large teddy bear. Before opening the window he had chambered a round, which made a loud clack-clash sound, and added another shell to the magazine: a total of five. At the distance across the two backyards—about thirty yards—the nine heavy buckshot pellets from each blast would spread about thirty inches. Aiming at the chest, Grimes could count on four or five hits with each shot.

It was still probably too early to expect any action, but this was the most uncertain part of the setup; if our guy watched the house for any period of time before entering, where would it be from? Not from the street in front, probably, where there was little evening pedestrian traffic and he would be conspicuous. Where then? Grimes expected him to appear in the victim's driveway, to come around the rear of the house, climb on the table and enter through the window. That's what he would do himself, he decided.

A very likely scenario would be that he would come from either side of the block into one or another of these backyards and do his surveillance from some convenient place in the middle of the block. There were lots of these.

There was a garbage can two yards over that looked a lot like a crouching man, and several bits of fence and wild rosebushes near it that were so dark that a person moving in front of them would probably be lighter.

If our guy were to come along the driveway of the house to the east, he would be behind a six-foot plank fence and invisible until he climbed it; he would be very visible then, but the warning would be very brief.

For the most part the nearby fences were low and easy to climb, yards were grassy and open, without many obstructions. But there was a garage two doors to the west, and a large tree next to it that cast a profound shadow. Opposite that was a large lemon bush which offered little cover but cast a confusing dappled shadow from the nearest porch light.

Considering only the rear of the cottage, Grimes's position was a commanding one. But the farther around to either side he looked, the less perfect his view was. Trees and bushes close to the houses on either side meant that he could see little to the immediate right and left. If our guy came up the driveway of the house he was in, Grimes would have no way of knowing until he was halfway across the yard.

It was a nervous thought.

His hostess, Mrs. Bertram, had two grown children, the younger a son just Grimes's age, living out of state. Her heart warmed to this earnest young man, and she insisted on providing him with a dinner such as she would have served her own boy, large enough for several ordinary people. It covered a TV table in front of him. Grimes lived alone, and home cooking was a rare pleasure for him. While his eyes ran ceaselessly over the fences and shrubbery he worked his way steadily through the meal.

It wasn't until he had finished, about 9:30, that he felt the first pang of fear.

He seemed very alone.

In his patrol car Grimes might spend an hour or more on a quiet night without seeing another officer, but he was accustomed to the almost continual background of radio chatter of the night shift. If, as sometimes happened, this traffic fell silent for a few minutes, every rookie would begin to experience a most unpleasant feeling of isolation, as if everyone else had silently locked up the station and gone home. Looked at reasonably, this suggested an inconceivable practical joke, but the quiet air had a threatening aura, and after quite a short time someone would ask for a time check, or a radio check, or advise Control of some trivial road hazard.

On special assignments there was no routine radio traffic. Channel 2 had been dead for more than an hour. He wanted to break the silence, but he could think of nothing to say. A radio check would be comforting, but he knew he had clear radio contact with the house because he had reported himself to Gadek when he was settled by his window, and the battery was fresh. So a radio check was out. A time check was ridiculous: even if there were anything wrong with his watch, which there was not, he knew perfectly well that he would be sitting there until something happened or until Gadek called him in. Time was irrelevant.

Two doors down a door opened and a man came down the steps to the woodpile at the bottom. He took several pieces and went back inside. This suggested a topic, and Grimes took up his microphone.

"S-19, 57." Brief as it was, Gadek heard the tension in Grimes's voice. And all over town, in the station where every monitor was tuned to Channel 2, and in every patrol car where the car radio was on 1 but every portable radio was on 2, each listener heard it and paused in what they were doing.

In my car up the street, looking innocuous slumped in the corner of the seat, I could hear his tightness and I thought, Grimes has got something.

"Go ahead, 57." Gadek's voice was always brisk, but you could hear the eagerness. Grimes heard it, and realized that he had made a mistake. He had made contact; the isolation was broken; it was all he needed. But he had to go on. Trying to sound brisk he said, "S-19, I'm getting some people coming into the yards here, and I can't always tell right away if they belong. Do you want to hear about possibles, or just when I'm sure?"

It was pretty lame. One of the dispatchers said, "Why doesn't he just ask for a time check?" and the others nodded. Downstairs, Sergeant Bridey raised an eyebrow at Sergeant D'Honnencourt—they regarded Grimes as a red-hot, but capable of development; this surprised them. Comment was unnecessary, and they returned to red penciling the reports submitted by their night shift fledglings. Out in the cars the beat officers smiled or grimaced according to their inclination, and in the locker rooms where they were preparing for the change of shift Grimes's fellow rookies paused in their various states of dress and looked at one another uncertainly. "It's just when he's sure, right?" said one, and they began to discuss it among themselves.

Gadek hesitated before answering. He saw his mistake. He didn't know Grimes. He had given him the observation position because he was on the spot, and to reward him for having recognized the importance of the original call and acting promptly.

Still, he didn't want to start rearranging things now. Everyone gets nerves. It was a second or two late that he said, "Just tell me when you've got a hot one, 57."

"I don't blame him," said one rookie in the locker room. "I'd be worried about it."

Sergeant D'Honnencourt said, "Now I'm worried," and Sergeant Bridey nodded.

Feeling stupid, Grimes clicked his microphone button to acknowledge Gadek's reply, and after that Channel 2 fell silent for some time.

Gadek laid his radio down on the bed. He considered calling in someone to hold the observation post with Grimes, but that was almost as bad as replacing him outright. No, he thought, let him stick it out.

Downstairs, Patty was pretending to watch TV. She was dressed in the resident's plaid shirt with untucked tails, and jeans. Her hair was down. She had her 9-mm automatic stuck in the waistband in back, her derringer stuck down the elastic of a big woolly sock, her radio under a pillow on the couch beside her.

There were two windows in the room, one overlooking the street, the other, behind her, the driveway. Both were low enough for someone standing outside to see in. Both had blinds, but they were not normally closed. In training, great emphasis had been given to the importance of having your back to something solid; officers were taught to park with the back of the car against a wall if they were going to sit and write reports or do anything which might distract them from the rearview mirror. She had internalized all of this, and she was profoundly uncomfortable sitting with her back to windows through which someone might be watching her. It's just creepy, she thought. I wonder how she can stand it. It was a continual temptation to turn her head and look.

The resident liked the TV loud, which our guy might know, and might be counting on for cover in his approach or entry; the effect was that if, for some reason, he should alter his usual pattern and come after her in the living room she would not be able to hear him. She had taken a large double-frame photograph from a bookcase and placed it on the television. It was disposed so that the reflection in one of the panes showed her the window behind her, and the other the hallway into the kitchen. Her eyes were fixed on these.

Patty had been on the street for more than three years. She was proud of being a cop, but she was not planning to be one forever. She was working on her master's degree; in two more years she would be gone. She had progressed from the novice stage through the confident-cautious stage to the veteran-cautious stage without ever passing through the cocky stage. She admired Gadek, and trusted him. She trusted Fry. She knew more than she cared to know about what our guy did to women. During her service she had found that she was plenty brave enough. She was delighted to be there. She hoped he would come. She hoped she would have some major role in arresting him or, if it came to it, in killing him. The 9-mm prodded reassuringly into her back, and the derringer weighted her ankle.

But courage doesn't cover all the bases. Things go wrong, sometimes. It happens so fast. She was taking nothing for granted. She was deeply concentrated. Her eyes moved back and forth between the dim reflections in the two panes of glass, and the bright images just below flickered by unheeded and almost unnoticed.

Soon it would be time to turn off the lights and move upstairs. She would have her back to a wall there. That would be better.

In the street I stretched and wiggled, trying to keep the circulation going without moving noticeably. A big elm blocked the street lamp completely so that I was in heavy shadow. There was no way anyone could see me. But the elm also threw the sidewalk behind me into shadow, so that even though I had turned my rearview mirror around to cover my back, I wouldn't see him if he came up behind me.

Gadek and Fry sat on pillows on the floor, leaning against the bed.

Blondie sat in her car singing to herself, very softly. She was almost a block away from the blue two-door, but it was near a streetlight, and there was no way she could miss anyone approaching it. The brown car was in shadow, but closer. There would be no mistake.

Grimes heard the voices in the hall, downstairs. Through the closed bedroom door he could only hear that there was a disagreement between Mrs. Bertram and a man. At first they were almost inaudible, more felt through the floor than heard, but they grew louder. Soon he heard footsteps coming up, the hall light clicked and cast a line of yellow under the door, and then the door opened suddenly, flooding the room with light.

"Close that door!" whispered Grimes fiercely, and he sprang past the man who had entered and closed it sharply. "Gotta keep it closed," he whispered. He could barely see who he was talking to: a large man, presumably Mr. Bertram.

"Now wait a minute," said the man in a loud, normal voice. "This is my house." He reached for the door. Grimes pressed it shut.

"You can't open it with that light on," he hissed. "Someone can see it from all over."

"Now look here, young man," said Mr. Bertram, pointedly refraining from lowering his voice. "This is my house. I have just returned from a long day of work to find that my house has been occupied by the police and that this might be dangerous." He had been looking around the room. "Look at this," he cried, stepping to the bed. "What the hell's a shotgun doing on my daughter's bed? You're going to have a gunfight in my daughter's bedroom?" Miss Bertram, age twenty-six, had not inhabited the room for eight years. "That's smart. That's really smart."

"Mr. Bertram," began Grimes.

"I swear to God I don't know what Cheryl was thinking of."

Mr. Bertram went on in this vein for some time. Grimes's night shift hours meant that the people he came in contact with were usually either victims or criminals. He understood his role with respect to each of these categories. He was not experienced at sweet-talking citizens to whom he stood in no clear relationship. Reflexively he tried authority. This was a blunder with an indignant homeowner almost twice his age, as Mr. Bertram gave him to know, at some length.

Every minute or two there would be a car. Blondie would warn us when he moved, so it was unlikely to be him, but you never know. We hadn't been watching him so long that we could really be sure we knew his pattern. He might borrow a car sometimes, and show up in something we'd never seen before. I watched each one carefully as it approached, on general principles. From time to time I ran my hand over the butt of my revolver. Once I took it out, opened the cylinder, and ran my fingertip over the ends of the cartridges, just to be sure they were all there.

With hitherto untapped resources of diplomacy Grimes had backed off trying to overawe Mr. Bertram and ventured on a flattering appeal to the responsible citizen who, at great cost and risk to himself, supports by his courage and vision the desperate struggle of good against evil. He was delighted to find that this was right on the money. He plied this new avenue earnestly, careful to adopt the very slight inclination of the head which implies respect without subordination, the slight hesitancy in tone which seemed to submit the most banal truisms for the approval of Mr. Bertram's higher judgment and experience. And Mr. Bertram, once he had got the taste of this gratifying theme, responded by paraphrasing Grimes's speeches and repeating them, with a considerable augmentation of prolixity, as his own insights.

There was a brief transmission audible in Grimes's earpiece. He wasn't familiar with Blondie's voice, and he was focused on Mr. Bertram, but he did take in her report that Dorn had taken the blue car and started off to the east.

Grimes redoubled his efforts. Mr. Bertram recollected that his dinner was waiting for him, and after pummeling on the bedroom door until Mrs. Bertram could be made to understand that he wanted the hall light put out, and she had, he seized Grimes's hand in his own, shook it firmly, and slipped out of the room.

Grimes was deeply satisfied with his diplomacy. "I'm learning," he muttered happily as he stepped back to his chair. But as he settled into it he found a puzzling sight across the way: the patio of the target house was deserted and unchanged, but the porch light was out and the kitchen window was partially open.

"Fuckin' *idiot!*" Grimes gasped, and snatched at his radio. The coiled cord tangled in the top button of his jacket and the microphone slipped through his fingers and bounced around his knees. He bent quickly to recover it, struck his head heavily on the bookcase beside the bed, stepped backward and stumbled over the desk chair. It was some moments before he had recovered himself and found the microphone.

"S-19, 57," he whispered.

"57."

"The kitchen window's open and the light's out."

Fry said afterward that he'd never seen Gadek look quite so astonished. He said, "Check, 57. You keep your eyes open." All over town the beat men thought, what the *hell's* going on there? In the sergeants' office, D'Honnencourt glanced at Bridey, and both shook their heads.

Gadek turned back to Patty, who had come upstairs to say that the porch light was out and that she'd reached out the kitchen window to remove the old bulb, but she couldn't find a new one.

"Keep looking, Patty," he said. "It'd be better to replace it. We can't come downstairs to help. Look in the pantry. That's where I keep mine."

"S-19, 122."

"Go, 122."

"He's shaken me off, but he's circling. Last seen heading north."

"Check, 122. Stand off to the south."

"Check."

It was just 10:25.

He lived two miles away. Even if he doubled the distance with circling, he'd be coming in very short order, if he was coming. My stomach felt heavy, my arms and legs heavy. I felt I wasn't up to this sort of thing. They need somebody more experienced—it's crazy to have me here. Fear, is what it was. Very unpleasant.

This could really be it. Now, if he's going to take a spot, where will he take it? There was very little moving on the street.

From the west, headlights moving sedately up the street towards me. I watched incuriously, sinking down out of a sense of professional consistency rather than any concern about being seen. There was only one man in town I didn't want to know I was there. The car slowed a good deal toward the middle of the block, drifted more and more slowly past the cottage, and finally stopped at the crosswalk in the full glare of the streetlight. It was the blue two-door.

Jesus H. Christ, he'd driven right up to the front door.

"S-19, 93. He's in front. He's just driven past."

"Check, 93. Advise."

The blue car pulled through the intersection and moved slowly up the block. There was a space halfway up, and there he slipped in. Staying low, I could turn in the seat and watch him. There was just enough light for me to see the door open and close; the interior light didn't go on. He was crossing to my side of the street, and as he reached the line of parked cars I lost sight of him. He must be coming down the sidewalk behind me. I settled against the doorpost as low as I could be and still see out. It was very dark under that elm.

It seems we both had noticed this.

He was right beside my car.

He was leaning on it.

This was where he was spotting on the cottage: under my elm tree, leaning on my car. If the window had been open I could have turned my head and bitten him on the ass.

It's out of the question to giggle in such circumstances.

After a few moments he stepped slowly forward and sat on the front fender. It was a run-down Vice car, and the springs were none of the best. The front sagged noticeably. He shifted a little and then was motionless. He was deeply focused on the cottage.

"93, S-19." It boomed in my earpiece. I've never been convinced at such moments that something that sounds so

loud to me can't be heard by all the world. But he didn't
stir or turn his head. I clicked my mike button twice.

"93, he's near you in front? Two for yes, three for no."

I clicked twice.

"Check."

I couldn't see my watch.

After a long time the downstairs lights began to flick off
in the cottage. The glow from the TV continued briefly, then
it went off, too. There was a faint glow from the light on
the stairs. Then upstairs the bedroom light came on, and the
bathroom. There was a faint shadow passing back and forth
over the blinds as someone walked about in the bedroom.

He shifted on the fender, and the whole car bobbed
slightly.

A car came into the intersection and turned up, its headlights sweeping across us and filling the tree shadow. It lit
him head to toe, lounging nonchalantly, face unobtrusively
averted. It lit me from the nose up, lurking behind him. The
lights passed on and for a moment I could see very little.

The bathroom light went out. The main bedroom light
went out. There was a soft glow, perhaps from the bedside
lamp, which continued for perhaps twenty minutes. Then it,
too, went out, and the cottage was dark.

For another ten minutes we stayed just as we were, me
inside, slumped down against the doorpost, and him outside,
sitting on the fender. Slowly he heaved himself up and
walked a few feet off, glancing around but mostly watching
the cottage. Then, decisively, he turned and walked quickly
back up the sidewalk and out of my field of vision. A moment later he appeared in my mirror, crossing the street
farther up the block where the light was dimmest and the
shadows most extensive. He was coming down the sidewalk
on the other side. I slipped the mike out of my field jacket.

"S-19, 93, he's coming."

"Check."

He slowed as he reached the intersection, and walked
straightforwardly across it. Once under the trees on the
other side he was almost in front of the cottage. I could just
make him out, standing by a bush, watching the place up
close. He was very skillful, moving innocently when he was

moving, and when he stopped, standing right next to something where the light was bad, almost disappearing.

But he didn't go any nearer. And after a couple of minutes he came back across the intersection, up the block, and across the street again.

"S-19, 93, he's coming back to me again."

"Check."

He loomed at my right. He passed the car and stood again at the edge of the tree shadow. Then he came back and sat on the fender, but soon he was on his feet again walking out to the edge of the tree shadow, back to the car, back and forth. He was giving her time to get to sleep.

You don't get this sort of chance to watch a bad guy in action.

Increasingly he was drawn to the edge of the shadow. He would sit on the fender for a moment and then pace back and forth, and then stand out there for several moments.

He was sitting on the fender when the next car came. It entered the intersection and turned up. Just as the lights swept over us, illuminating him from head to toe and me from the nose up, he turned his back to them and faced me. We were eyeball to eyeball, five feet apart. The car passed; he was a silhouette, I was invisible. But he had seen me. The whole thing was burned.

For a bare moment he hesitated. Then he broke into a sprint, straight as an arrow out into the street, straight to his car. I lurched behind the wheel and started up, holding the mike in my left hand.

"S-19, 93, we're burned. He's running." I pulled hard into the intersection and hung a U-turn, tires squealing.

"S-5, S-19. S-5, are you there?"

He was starting up, pulling out. I was too late to block him into his space.

"S-5, we're burned. Move in."

"S-5, 93, we're eastbound. Blue two-door sedan, nine-eight-two Ocean Queen Tom. He's turning south." He was picking up speed. He was really flying.

"17, 118, 67, 160, move in."

"S-5, 93, turning west." I had the faster car, and no difficulty staying with him, but we were reaching truly dangerous speeds, flashing down the narrow residential streets. I fiddled with the volume control of my radio, trying to get it up so I could hear it. The night was suddenly full of noise. I shouted out the intersections as we shot through them. A long block behind me appeared the flickering red-and-blue roof lights of the first of the uniform cover—we'd got outside the cordon far, far faster than expected.

"S-5 to cars in the west end, move in. Answer up."

"37."

"3."

"104."

"93, S-5, advise."

"93, still westbound, crossing the tracks." He was slowing for nothing now, running flat out. We were reaching sixty on the straights.

Time was against him. The flickering lights behind us were solid now, and gaining. If he rolled it or wrapped it around a tree or smashed himself on another car, he was lost. And soon he would be boxed in. It's a small city, and he was running out of room. He might be able to make it to the freeway, but he couldn't hope to outrun patrol cars in his clunker. If he could just get clear of me, make himself a little room, he could hope to ditch his car and escape on foot.

Clearly, that was his intention. He was running along the margin of a neighborhood of small houses, a warren of gardens and fences. Once into that his chances were excellent. Careening wildly and almost losing it, he hurled his car down one of the back streets, and in the middle of the first block slammed on the brakes. Smoke billowed from the tires, the rear wheels broke loose and he skidded almost halfway around, facing me as I braked madly right behind him. My brakes weren't as good as his: he was slowing, his car still sliding backward along the curb, when I ran into him squarely over the passenger door and just at right angles. Jammed together, we slithered a few yards farther and fetched up hard against the back of a large pickup truck. Metal crumpled and glass flew. He was jammed on both sides.

We were face-to-face, six feet apart. I drew, held my revolver up sideways so that he could see me cock the hammer, and laid it straight on his face.

There was a moment of apparently perfect silence, and then the first black-and-whites sirened up. Then all. The street filled. Radios boomed, high beams and searchlights blasted everything with brilliant light.

The first uniforms had slipped out behind their open doors and leveled their shotguns on the fugitive in the best felony-stop style.

"You in the vehicle!" shouted the first, his voice cracking slightly, pronouncing it *"vee-*hicle." *"Get your hands up where I can see 'em! Higher! Palms open!"* Latecomers had dashed around to the sidewalk and taken up positions behind trees and on the other side of the pickup. Eight or ten shotguns and automatic pistols were leveled at his one visible part, his head; eight or ten adrenaline-pumped fingers rested on as many light triggers.

Things can go wrong, of course, but I was blessed if I could see how he could get out of this one.

I caught a glimpse of his face. It was just like his mug shot: guarded, alert.

His eyes were right on me.

I thought, he's not caving in. In the middle of all this he's still thinking.

This son of a bitch is *dangerous.*

I was impressed. I had thought that after all these months of chasing, lurking, waiting, plotting, hoping, that when we finally had our hands on him he couldn't possibly measure up to it all, that there would be a great sense of anticlimax. It wasn't like that a bit. He wasn't beaten yet. This guy was impressive.

Sergeant D'Honnencourt appeared and took command.

With considerable precaution my car was backed away to clear his passenger door, which, after some delay to locate a proper instrument, was levered open from the outside. Then, under the gaping barrels of three selected shotgunners, and without lowering his hands out of sight, Henry Dorn was compelled to slide out of his car and flatten himself on the street.

Gadek had been watching the extraction from across the

street. Now he hurried out to confer with D'Honnencourt and me.

"I'm heading for the on-call judge to set his bail and sign the search warrants. Toby, you can start booking him on this chase. Take your time. We don't want him to get in his phone call before we're ready to serve the search warrants. We don't want the evidence to start disappearing before we can get to it. We don't know how much his sister knows, or somebody else might know. And just in case we get delayed," he said to D'Honnencourt, "can you put uniforms on his place and his sister's? Warrants on the way. Nobody leaves. Can you manage it?"

"Yes, Leo," said D'Honnencourt, "I think so."

"Got it?" he said to me.

"Right."

"Good. It's in your hands. I'm off to wake up a judge."

28

It was only a little past midnight when we got back to the station. Dorn was brought in by two Patrol officers and taken straight to the jail. Fry called down to the sergeants' office with the addresses of Dorn's and Leonora's apartments. D'Honnencourt instructed four cars to meet him a couple of blocks from Leonora Hart's apartment, a back door/front door cover for both places. He gave them their instructions and saw them in position.

I piled up all the charges I could think of from the chase, and we began a leisurely booking. If all went well, Gadek should be back before we were anywhere near done, but we wanted a margin. Sometimes on-call judges turn out not to be where they say they'll be, and then you have to scramble. In any case, there are judges, and then there are judges. Tonight's on-call judge could be difficult. If he wanted to debate the warrants at length, it would be a long night.

I dawdled, I went to the bathroom. But we got to the phone call without any word from Gadek.

He used his phone call to call his sister, inform her that he was in jail, and order her to put together the bail for the charges from the chase. He made the call with me standing beside him. He was very cool. He was playing the cards he

327

had as best he could. He wasn't giving anything away. The game wasn't over.

The jailer searched him very carefully before putting him in a cell. There was nothing of evidentiary value except for a small, very sharp pocketknife such as our guy might well have used to cut his victims.

For the moment there was nothing further to be done about securing Dorn, and so I went down to the office. Blondie, Patty, and Fry were there.

The mood was unsettled. We hadn't gone and busted him before now because Reyes wasn't satisfied that there was a chargeable case. We really had no more evidence that evening than we'd had that afternoon. He'd never set foot in the cottage or even left the sidewalk. There was the chase, but that doesn't prove anything about the series. The reason for setting up the cottage had been to establish a better connection between Dorn and the series. We'd missed it, and we certainly weren't going to have another opportunity. Our best remaining chance to clinch the case would be if we could serve the search warrant before Dorn or anyone else had a chance to clean up. We might get something good and conclusive. Then we'd have him. Failing that—well, it didn't bear thinking about. He might still walk.

We were tired. Patty and I were the only ones who had not been working since 7:30 that morning, and it had been a wearing evening. Still, as soon as Gadek reappeared with the warrant we would be off, and the thought kept everyone keyed up.

The phone rang. I answered. It was Gadek.

"We got it. The judge has set bail at a million dollars. We'll be there in ten minutes. Call Reyes at home. Get him out of bed. We want him with us when we go in."

"Right. D'Honnencourt's put uniforms on both apartments."

"Outstanding. See you shortly."

It was 2:45 when Gadek arrived. He detailed Footer to take Dorn to the hospital for the collection of blood and saliva samples, and then to photograph him for scars. Patty and me he sent to Leonora's apartment to begin the search of that premises while he and Blondie tackled Dorn's. Reyes he took with him.

The rookie in front of Leonora's apartment said that she had come out in a great rush shortly after 1:00, carrying a cardboard box. She saw uniforms and took the box back inside. She tried the back door, with the same result. Around 1:30 she emerged again, and he informed her that if she tried to leave she would be arrested. Intimidated, she went back inside. I complimented this enterprising young man on his good work and told him that there was now a search warrant for the car, so nobody should approach it.

It was almost 3:00 when we thundered on the door.

The door opened a crack.

"Miz Hart, I'm Officer Parkman," I said, holding up my badge. "You're aware that your brother has just been arrested. We'd like to look around for some missing possessions." It never hurts to try to get permission, because if you get it your discoveries are admissible in court even if there should be a flaw in the search warrant.

She looked really unhappy to see us, but opened the door and stood back. She had not been to bed. There were several boxes piled up by the front door.

Patty and I brought in our cartons of evidence bags, catalog forms, and tape recorders, and put them down.

"Miz Hart, this is Officer Dwornenscheck. I take it it's okay with you if we search for certain missing property in your apartment?"

Poor weak, ignorant woman. She didn't know what to say or do. She looked at Patty for advice.

Patty said, "We just want to look for some stuff. We'll try not to bother you."

She looked more confused than ever. Finally she said, "Well, okay."

"Thank you," I said.

"Thanks," said Patty. "I believe your brother has stored some things here?" She indicated the pile of cartons by the door. "Is there more?"

Poor Leonora wasn't equipped for this. She said, "Yeah. There's more in the bedroom closet."

"Great," said Patty, beaming like a sister. "Could you show me?"

We went into the bedroom. There was a considerable pile of loose odds and ends on the floor of the closet.

"All that?" said Patty.

"Yeah."

"And is there more?"

"Just a few things in the bureau."

"Could you show me?" Leonora led Patty to the bureau and opened a drawer filled with loose articles of women's clothing. That might be exciting, if we could connect any of them to specific victims. But they might be innocently obtained, or they might be stolen from unreported victims, or we might simply be unable to prove a connection. So we remained calm.

"Golly, Leonora," said Patty. "What was Henry doing with all these women's clothes?" Leonora looked away.

"I don't know," she said.

"Where'd he get it all?"

"I don't know. He said he bought it."

"Bought it?"

"Yeah, you know, like at thrift stores."

"Bought old women's clothes? What for?" Leonora looked away again. She sighed. She seemed to have her thoughts fastened on some other, brighter place than this one.

"I don't know," she said. "I don't ask Henry questions." She had a bruise high on one cheek and another on her forehead. Several days old by the look of them.

"That's all he has?" said Patty.

A nod.

"Look, sometimes things get mixed up. Would you mind if I looked through the rest of these drawers?"

"That's just my stuff in there," said Leonora.

"Yeah, but y'know. Could I look?"

A nod.

"Great," said Patty, and started opening drawers. These appeared much neater and more homogenous than the collections identified hitherto as Dorn's. Patty was certainly more primed than I was to distinguish between Leonora's possessions and Dorn's, and I would have been glad to leave her there and get started on the pile in the living room, but Patty was on the floor with her nose in the bureau, Leonora was standing up behind her, and I didn't altogether like to leave them alone together. Leonora didn't look violent, but you never know. Instead, I took some evidence bags and started on the pile in the closet floor. I took every woman's garment, which was the bulk of it. I took all papers not of an obviously routine personal nature. All of this went into paper bags marked with date, time, address, where found ("bedroom closet"), and my badge number. I took the few items of male clothing. I looked around for anything else that might have been overlooked, always saying, "D'ya mind if I look here?" or "Okay to open this box?" But there didn't seem to be anything more.

When I had dealt with the closet and Patty had gone through the rest of the room with Leonora, I got out my tape recorder, dictated the date, time, address, and intoned:

Officer T. Parkman, badge number ninety-three, and Officer P. Dwornenscheck, badge number sixty-two, made contact with Leonora Hart at that time and location and obtained her consent to search the residence for any and all items belonging to her brother, Henry Dorn. The following items one through ten were found in the bedroom closet and identified by Leonora Hart as the property of Henry Dorn.

Bags one through nine miscellaneous woman's clothing found in a pile.
Bag ten:

    a. A fourteen-page typewritten list of names, addresses, ages of women.
    b. A slip of green paper three by six inches, torn from an envelope with the name and address of one Nancy Lebell.
    c. A three-by-five-inch piece of white paper with the name and address of one Grace Williams.
    d. A three-by-five index card with the name and address of Sheila Cox.

    e. A three-by-five index card with the name and
       address of Gloria Dade.
    f. A black three-ring binder titled MY PRISON
       FRIENDS filled in with names and addresses of
       men.
    g. A bundle of twelve letters fastened with a rubber
       band and addressed to Henry Dorn in prison
       from Julia Frome.

We went through the place item by item, each item taken
being related to the categories of stolen possessions or personal items of evidentiary value specified in the warrant.

It was nearly 5:00 before we were done with the bedroom.
Leonora made us all coffee. I felt like a heel to drink it, but
I drank it.

Having exhausted the bedroom and eliminated the bathroom and kitchen, and determined that there was no access
from the apartment to any crawl space above or below, we
moved on to the living room.

"What have you got of Henry's that isn't here?" said
Patty as brightly as she still could.

"Nothing," said Leonora. "That's everything. But he told
me I shouldn't let anyone see that stuff." Her unease grew
as we got closer and closer to opening those boxes.

"Well, we've seen all that other stuff," said Patty, waving
to the bags lined up by the door.

"I dunno," said Leonora, who was clearly confused by the
situation and bleary from lack of sleep. "Maybe you
shouldn't look at those. He told me not to let anyone look
at those." She passed her fingertips over the bruise on her
cheek.

"Well, Leonora, you told us we could look for his stuff,"
said Patty.

"Yeah, but he told me I shouldn't let anyone see it. I
don't want you to look at this stuff," she said with some
decision.

She had crossed back over the line of consent, and we
had to notice it.

"Well, Leonora, let me explain," said Patty. She pulled
the warrant out of her jacket. "We have a search warrant

for this stuff. See, signed by the judge. That means we can look at whatever we want. I'm afraid you have to let us see it. Here." She fished about in another pocket. "Here's a copy for you, so you can read it."

Leonora accepted the copy with a leaden face. She was beaten, and she knew it.

"Henry won't like it," she said. She didn't quite understand what had happened, but she could see that sooner or later she would have to account to Henry. She sank into the couch and buried her head in her arms.

I dictated:

> At oh-five-ten hours Leonora Hart withdrew her consent to search Henry Dorn's possessions. At that time she was shown the original search warrant for her residence and provided with a copy.

We took papers, letters, a copy of a police report in a long-past case, bed sheets, clothing, photographs, a pillowcase with flowers on it, some watches, some jewelry, vehicle registration certificates, several license plates, a good deal of marijuana, and on and on and on. We took anything that might connect Dorn with one of the victims. Written materials might establish some connection. Clothing might be identifiable as theirs through marks or labels or chemical analysis or traces of hair or fiber attached to them. We went around with scissors and cut fiber samples from the carpets, and brushed fuzz off the couch and chairs.

We were done with the apartment by 9:30 in the morning. I raised Gadek on the air, and he came over. He made a brisk tour, ran his eye over the catalog, and poked into the boxes.

"Well, looks good. We're going to be some time at Dorn's place. You haven't done the storage locker in the garage, I take it?"

"No."

"No. And you're looking pretty fagged. Well, so are we. I called the lieutenant, and he's going to get us some relief over. Be here any time. You can leave the locker and the brown car to them. All this stuff goes to the evidence room and gets put into the personal hand of Sergeant Wren. He's cleared a bay for us so there'll be no risk of mixing it with stuff from other cases. If he isn't there, wait till he gets back. Got it?"

"Right."

"Right. Then you two can go home and get some sleep. Since we're all on this sleep cycle we'll start again at six this evening and see what sense we can make of all this."

And he stepped briskly off.

Gadek always kept up appearances, but I had the distinct impression that he was worried. We certainly hadn't come up with any bombshells at Leonora's place. If they weren't doing any better at the other apartment we were going to be in a very iffy situation.

Sergeant Terrazas was having a slow day in Homicide, so it was he who showed up to relieve us soon after Gadek left. We showed him the locker. D'Honnencourt had had the brown sedan towed to the impound yard, and it could be examined there, along with the wreck of the blue two-door.

"Okay," said Terrazas. "I think I've got the picture. Why don't you two go get some sleep? You look like hell."

"That's what guys always say in the morning," said Patty, and smiled sweetly.

Sergeant Wren was well organized. He had cleared one of the small cell-like storage bays and hung a tarp around it so that nothing could fall in or out through the wire mesh partitions. He had vacuumed it. Nothing would be in it except what we put there.

"I've got a padlock with a different key than the others bays," he said as we stacked our boxes in a pile and scribbled Leonora's address on the outside of each one. "I'm keeping one, and Leo will have the other."

"It looks great," we said.

"You two look like hell," he said.

"Maybe we should get some sleep," said Patty. "Maybe that would help."

"That's certainly what I would do," he said.

* * *

# INTENT TO HARM

No one was at the office. Before leaving, Footer had posted his warrant return on the Dorn wall:

> The following are the items taken from the person of Henry Dorn while in the custody of Ofc. Charles Footer #32 at Memorial Hospital. Date. 0330 hours.
> A. One red-capped vial of blood, drawn from the person of Henry Dorn.
> B. One saliva sample, taken from Henry Dorn by having him chew on white cotton gauze.
> C. One saliva sample, taken from Henry Dorn by having him drool into a vial.
> D. Head hair, obtained from Dorn by combing through his hair.
> E. Various head hair, obtained by cutting samples of Dorn's hair from four different locations on his head.
> F. Pubic hair, obtained by cutting samples of Dorn's pubic hair from four different locations on his pubic region.
> G. Pubic hair obtained by combing the pubic region.
>
> This concludes all the items taken from Henry Dorn's person.

We read this gloomily. The burst of excitement was long gone. It was unlikely that there was anything conclusive in all of this. We were both too tired to think it through, but not quite so tired that we couldn't believe that we would have seen it if it had been there. The only thing to do was go home and rest up.

We signed out and headed for the door.

"It's been a long day, Patty," I said.

She pulled me over and hugged me. I hugged her back. Male cops don't hug. It was nice. Patty and I had been through some times together.

"You're okay, Parkman," she said.

"You're a grand girl, Patty," I said.

She was very well built.

335

It was one of those unexpected moments.

We hugged again. We headed for our respective homes.

I wouldn't have minded a hug from Sara, too, but of course nobody was there at 11:30 in the morning. I turned on a hot shower and stood under it for some time. Whoever invented hot running water did a good day's work. And while I stood there it occurred to me that the last time I had eaten was an early dinner the day before. No wonder I was feeling a bit down. There were some excellent leftovers available. I ate them all, and had a beer with them.

Really, perhaps things weren't so bad. I wrote a note to Sara:

> Our guy's in Stony Lonesome. I'm in bed.
> Please wake and feed at 5:00. Gotta be back at
> 6:00
> XX
> T. Parkman

and left it on the kitchen counter.

It was the alarm clock which woke me, and when I went downstairs I found another note:

> I remember you. We're at Melanie's.
> It's Heather's birthday. But I crept in and
> admired
> your slumbering magnificence
> and would have kissed you, had I dared.
> Dinner's in the oven keeping warm.
> XX
> Ms. S. Parkman
> P.S. Toby, I'm glad he's in Stony Lonesome.
> I'm so proud of you I can't tell you.
> You really believed in this.
> God, *I* believed in this.
> The kids say "Yea Dad!"
> XXX
> Ms. S.

29

We came to the 6:00 meeting facing radically changed lives. The routine of the last year was suddenly broken off. We wouldn't be hustling out for street detail at 10:00, and recording license numbers, and skulking in the underbrush. We wouldn't be waiting with that sense of pumped-up helplessness for the report of the next hit.

Gadek came in with Jaime Reyes just before 6:00.

The chief and Captain Claypool came in just after 6:00.

The chief said, "I don't want to interrupt you. I know this thing's not over yet and you still have a lot to do. But we've been following your work downstairs, and admiring it. And of course we're very glad to hear about the events of last night. I've been getting calls about it all day. You may have seen the initial news coverage. Very positive. So go on and wrap it up, but I had to mark this milestone."

Captain Claypool smiled collegially and said, "Yes, and we're going to offer to settle your overtime claims by hiring a plane and sending you all to Monte Carlo for a few weeks."

Everybody laughed. It was boilerplate stuff, but they meant it sincerely, and we were all glad they had come to say it.

"Well," said Gadek when they had gone, "to work. We've got some tasks.

"First, the samples that Footer had the pleasure of taking last night from Henry Dorn's person have gone to the crime lab for analysis. They could eliminate him as a suspect, but I don't expect that to happen. They won't convict him, either, unfortunately, because blood types and DNA aren't definitive for evidentiary purposes. We need other connections, too.

"With that in mind, we've taken, as you know, a mountain of stuff from those two apartments and two cars. It all has to be sorted and milked for whatever value it may have. Guys, I won't kid you. I didn't see any smoking guns in what we took. My Christmas list had things like lists of victim's names with dates, or souvenirs with labels, or something like that. That would have been delightful and easy. But I guess Santa missed our chimney this year. Now, there may well be something there that doesn't pop out at us, and that's what we're looking for. The more solid connections between Dorn and individual victims, the better.

"Our learned colleague here from the D.A.'s office"—indicating Reyes—"will be overseeing our efforts. Whatever suggestions he makes, observe them with the utmost—the *utmost*—care."

"Yeah, ladies and gentlemen," said Reyes with a broad and rather inappropriate smile, "we're not fat on evidence in this case, and we don't want to lose anything we've got. So care is the watchword. Speed isn't so important now. He's in the jug, and he's probably going to stay. He doesn't have a million dollars. His attorney is trying to get bail reduced. I don't think the judge will go for it. But whether he's in or out doesn't really affect this next stage. What we have in our hands right now is what we're going to have, and we have to squeeze it dry."

"Okay," said Gadek. "Here's what we'll do. Those pieces of plywood in the hall are to put over the desks and make big tables. Then we're going to bring all the stuff up here and spread it out. Then we're going to specialize in different categories of stuff and work through it bit by bit."

* * *

We cleared the desks and brought in the plywood. Then we all went down to the basement, loaded the swag into stolen shopping carts, and maneuvered it all upstairs.

Papers were a large category, and we devoted one table to paper. There were two more for clothes, male and female. There was a table for miscellaneous items, some bedding, a few pieces of jewelry, a slide projector, a camera, a tape recorder, and a star attraction, a pistol found under the seat of Leonora's car.

Spreading it all out on four large tables was very efficient, but it made the rest of the office's functions more complicated. The phones had to go on the floor, along with all the other things that usually live on the surfaces of desks. When the phone rang the office resembled a prairie dog city in crisis, with its members suddenly disappearing below the surface. The aisles were only wide enough for one. Still, it gave you a clear view of what was there.

"It's a pile of shit," said Footer. You couldn't disagree, on the face of it. But Reyes remained hopeful.

"What we're looking for is firm connections between Henry Dorn and individual crimes, provable to a jury beyond a reasonable doubt. All we have at the moment is Julia Frome's identification, which, as you know, is problematic. One unarguable connection could be enough; several would be better. The more there are the better, because you can show a pattern even if each element wouldn't convince by itself."

Gadek said, "Guys, I won't kid you. I was hoping for a bombshell when we walked into Dorn's apartment. We looked for the stuff we could prove had been stolen from victims. We didn't find it. What we've got is a lot of stuff—"

"A lot of shit," put in Footer, and guffawed.

"No, Charlie," said Gadek firmly. "No. You don't know what we've got. You don't know whether it's good or not. That's my point. All the evidence we need may be right here—stuff the victims didn't miss, or didn't think was worth mentioning. We don't know. So this isn't the time to get discouraged, or to relax. It'd be too bad to miss good stuff just because we got lazy.

"We're going to sort carefully through all this, we're going to stay alert, and we're going to find what's there."

"Let's see," said Gadek. "Parkman, you and Dwornenscheck do clothes. Fry and Footer, paper. Blondie, miscellaneous. Let's do it."

Patty and I moved over to the clothing table. Gadek joined us.

"Go over the garments one by one," he said. "Obviously, you're looking for name tags or laundry marks that could be traced. Look for alterations, especially hand-sewing, because there's a high probability that a victim would remember it. Then look for stains: if we can analyze 'em we may be able to connect 'em to a victim. Look for hair, or fiber that doesn't come from that material. There may be things caught in seams. The stuff's all been jumbled up, of course, so hair and that sort of thing might start on one garment and be jiggled to another. Still, it's something. And when we're done looking at everything bit by bit we'll try to get some of the victims in to look it all over and see if they can identify anything as theirs. The more connections the merrier."

"Look for handwriting," Reyes was saying at the paper table. "Here's a sample of Dorn's. Look for others. Look for lists."

"I've never looked carefully at clothing," I said after examining several pieces. "It's really quite wonderfully made. Look how that little seam is fitted together." Patty looked. "It's so smooth."

"Bras could be your thing, Parkman," she said. "You're sure an attentive pupil. Now, what do you make of that?" She was holding a blouse with a whitish spot.

"Looks like a bleach stain to me," I said. "I'm not an expert on the subject."

"Well, it's distinctive," she said. "I think I'd remember having a blouse with that stain on it." She tagged the item and made a note in the catalog which lay on the table between us.

"But why on earth would he have stolen something like that?" I asked. "The underwear I get. But what's souvenirish about that blouse?"

"I dunno," said Patty. "But then I'm not a sadistic, psychopathic lunatic. Maybe folks like that see things differently."

"Now look at this," I said. I had a short nightgown. Near the hem was a dark stain almost an inch in diameter. "That's blood, or my name's not Detective Parkman." I tagged it and entered my observations in the catalog.

Bit by bit we moved through the pile. Gadek and Reyes circulated, coming frequently to us. They reviewed our discoveries, listened to our ideas, and gave us theirs. As we finished with each piece we tagged it and laid it neatly on the other side of the table. Some of it was promising: there were stains, some analyzable and therefore, perhaps, traceable to a specific victim; and some, like the bleach stain, simply distinguishing, so that the garment's former owner might reasonably identify the item as her own. Either way, a connection might be made.

"Of course," I said, "these items may come from some other, noncriminal source. Leonora said he bought them, and it might be true. Or even if they were stolen from victims and represent a provable link to a hit, it may well be an unreported hit, in which case we have nothing and no one to connect it to."

"Jeeze, Parkman. Brighten my day, why doncha? Now tell me what you make of this."

From time to time we all stretched our legs and wandered around the room to see how the others were doing. Nobody else was having as much luck as we were. There was a lot of paper, some of it highly suggestive, but nothing actually incriminating. There were lists of women, and many sheets, slips, and scraps of paper with names and addresses, almost invariably those of women. Footer and Fry were compiling a list of every name mentioned so that we could run through the case documents again and look for matches, but it wasn't much to hope for: victims' names we could hope to spot right away.

There was a lot of miscellaneous junk, but again, nothing good. Gadek had seized a camera from Dorn's apartment and Blondie was hopeful that we might find souvenir snapshots of victims, but his work seemed to be all "art" of a sort, and nothing to our purpose.

When we were done with the pile of clothes we had three possibly analyzable (all apparently blood), and three possibly identifiable: the bleach-stained blouse, a pair of jeans with alternations to the legs and a hand-sewn patch on the knee, and a bra with a hand-sewn repair to a torn strap.

Gadek and Reyes continued to circulate, conferring and examining. Reyes's face grew longer and longer as the hour grew late. By midnight, when Gadek sent us home, the bulk of the material had been inspected and cataloged. There were possibilities, and some follow-up remained, of course, but by this time none of us thought that there was going to be a breakthrough.

As I left, I heard Gadek whisper to Reyes: "We may be looking at it."

"Yes, we may, goddam it," said Reyes. "We may not make it. We may not have enough."

The next morning we reassembled at 10:00. Gadek gave us all chores. Leonora Hart was probably as ignorant as she was helpless, but she would have to be interviewed. The stained clothing had to be sent off to the lab, but first it had to be photographed. There were still reports and follow-ups from several of the more recent hits that were unfinished or undigested in one degree or another, and which might still produce something firm. He gave Blondie and me the job of recontacting as many victims as possible and persuading them to come in to the office over the next day or two to try to identify the clothing laid out on the tables.

That afternoon Reyes held a press conference, the first formal media event since the arrest. He announced definitely that the police had arrested Henry Dorn as the responsible in the rape series. Dorn was being held in lieu of bail. The case was being prepared for the district attorney, and he expected well over fifty counts to be charged.

Reyes stated his belief that many, if not a majority, of the rapist's attacks had never been reported. Now was the time, he said, for all those victims to come forward so that the police would have all possible evidence, justice could be done, and potential future victims protected. He gave the task force number.

It was an admission of weakness, a thinly disguised plea for something new that would hold our guy.

The media gave this conference very good play, but there had been a lot of media attention before. The persuadable victims had been persuaded already. There was no response. We had everything we were going to get.

Mike had lasagna ready when Walt came home on his dinner break. The apartment was clean as it had never been before.

"Place looks great," said Walt as they sat down. He said, "Great lasagna. Great. Excellent."

Mike grinned shyly. He still didn't make much eye contact, but every day it was better.

It's a great improvement, thought Walt. A vast improvement.

They weren't out of the woods yet. They had emptied the liquor cabinet and agreed to keep a dry establishment. Walt screened the papers and cut out news about the series. Mike had agreed not to watch the news when Walt was not home, and when they watched it together Walt kept the zapper at hand. He and Mike didn't talk about it. Mike had a shrink, now—the two of *them* could talk about it.

Herodotus was read, and Thucydides, and Mike was putting together a paper which had been assigned before he left school on the several Greek dramatists whose works were neatly piled on the floor by his rolled-up sleeping bag. Still, it was a grossly constricted existence. Mike could scarcely leave the apartment: he had lived most of his life in that town. If he ran into people who knew him, word was sure to get back to Melanie that he was around; and if he went out he was sure to run into people he knew. A little time and therapy had worked wonders, but he needed human contact. He needed home. The carriage house was out of the picture now, but he had a mother and a sister.

And of course, there were selfish considerations. Before Mike had moved in, Walt and Melanie had been using his apartment for purposes of vice. He was running out of excuses for going to motels instead, to say nothing of the expense. Walt was also footing the bill for the twice-a-week shrink, and Mike's appetite was returning along with his morale: the groceries were ruinous.

Perhaps it was not too soon. Walt swallowed a bite of garlic bread and said, "Y'know, maybe it's time to write your mother another note. Tell her you're on your way and you're gonna be home in a few days. I've got a friend who lives a couple of days' drive from here. He can mail it for us. What d'ya think?"

Mike was pushing a piece of tomato around his plate with his fork. He didn't raise his eyes, but he looked pleased.

"Yeah, Walt," he said. "Yeah. I'd like that."

Fourteen victims came in to look over the clothing we had seized from Dorn. For some, it was clearly futile: we knew beforehand what they were aware of having missed, and what they told us we knew was not in our possession.

They came through in ones and twos, usually with a friend for support. They paced slowly through the tables, running their eyes over each piece. I got the impression that there was a fascination in seeing close up the detritus of other crimes, other lives. Our guy had not been a visitation upon them alone.

But only one garment was claimed: a plain black sweater without distinguishing marks of any kind, one of thousands of identical pieces sold by a large retailer. Whether hers or not, an utterly useless identification.

We called the victims who had not come. Some refused, some promised. Eventually, four more came in, but they couldn't pick anything out.

The bottom line was that we did not have one single object positively establishing a connection between Dorn and a victim.

"That's it," said Gadek. "That's the lot."

Everything was boxed and stored away, and the plywood removed, when we assembled around the table on the fifth day after the arrest.

"Reyes goes to the D.A. this morning," said Gadek. "They have a regular review process. In a case like this, the deputy D.A. in charge of the case lays out what we've got and the D.A. and his staff decide whether or not to charge. I don't know just when this is going to happen. They have a lot of cases they run through, and Reyes didn't know when Dorn would come up.

"It's not a great case, you know that. I'm confident that Dorn is our guy, and Reyes is, too, but you have to convince a jury. Even if the case isn't terrific, they could do a plea-bargain that would put him away for a long time. Not long enough, but better than nothing.

"So we'll just have to wait and see.

"If you guys are anything like me, you're feeling kinda spacey and deflated. If you want to take a day or two of vacation time, go ahead. If you want to keep busy, we've still got odds and ends to take care of here. Let me know what you want to do.

"Most of you will be going back to your regular assignments soon. This is pretty much it. You've worked very hard and very well. We've done the best we could. Let's hope it all works out."

Nobody had much to say when Gadek was finished. Fry picked up some report he had been working on and plowed forward with it; Footer had a file of narratives that he was skimming for the umpteenth time, looking for something that might have escaped him before. Blondie drifted down to Sex Crimes to see what they had going—she would be back with them in a day or two. Patty and Marcia began taking down all the exhibits on the wall and filing them away. I wandered down to Patrol, where I schmoozed and read whatever was on the pillar.

But I hadn't been doing this for long before Sergeant

Bridey poked his head out of the office and said, "Parkman, Leo just called down. He wants everyone upstairs. Reyes just came in."

It was Reyes, looking unhappy, Gadek, looking pale, and Lieutenant Bloom, looking grim.

"My God," whispered Blondie. "They're not going to charge."

30

However he may have planned to break the news to us, Reyes must have seen from our faces that there was no point in beating about the bush.

They weren't going to charge.

The district attorney did not consider that the case that Reyes presented was strong enough to convince a jury beyond a reasonable doubt that Henry Dorn was responsible for any crime. It wasn't a hasty decision; Reyes had been giving him regular briefings on the development of the case. He declined to press inadequate charges in the hope of a plea-bargain, a practice he considered oppressive on its face.

It was a principled decision, Reyes felt. It wasn't reckless, or political, or corrupt; it was a judgment call. The issues were substantial. He disagreed, but there it was.

He spoke for about two minutes. There was nothing more for him to say.

Gadek was stunned. I'd never seen him at a loss before. He didn't speak a word. He just sat there, shaking his head.

It wasn't really a surprise. The case wasn't terrific; we all knew it. This possibility had been out there. But the actuality was almost incomprehensible.

Nobody shouted, nobody swore. We looked at each other,

we looked at Reyes and Gadek, we looked at the floor. All those nights, all those chases. Waiting, watching, straining. The victims, those poor women, what about them? Jesus H. Christ, it just fizzles?

And Dorn walks. He'll be back on the street. He'll be out this afternoon.

It's just hard to take these things in.

Lieutenant Bloom got up and made some avuncular remarks about . . . well, I don't know what he said, because I wasn't listening. I was thinking about what might have happened if he hadn't seen me. . . .

In the end Bloom sent us all home.

But how can you go home? What do you do at home? Dust? Do the dishes? Jesus H. Christ. We all wound up at Patty's apartment, sitting, pacing, drinking whatever she had on hand, trying to talk it through. It was all over so quickly. Had we got all the leads in? Had we looked at everything? The D.A. could reopen the case if we got something new, we reminded each other. He could reopen. We proposed things excitedly, new openings, and shot them down. We ordered pizza, we went out to get more beer. We were there till late in the afternoon. We struggled to get our minds around it. Nobody blamed me, but the thought was there.

When I got home I told Sara. I'd talked about the case being thin, but somehow I had given the impression—I suppose I was thinking—that all it meant was that we would have to work harder to make sure the ends met. When I told her what had actually happened she just looked at me. She didn't say "What?" or "How is that possible?" or "You're kidding." There was coffee made; she poured two cups. We went outside and sat wordlessly together, staring morosely at the garden.

I dreamt that night that I was lying in the pit in the woods where Sara and the kids had been hiding. Our guy was standing close to the edge of the pit, trying to make out who it was at the bottom. He had that guarded, alert expression. He leaned lower and lower, trying to see. I could smell him strongly now. He put out his hand, almost a tender gesture, to touch me. I leapt up and bit him hard across the face, shaking and chewing, grinding my teeth deeper and deeper. He made no sound, but he struggled and broke free, staggering backward. He recovered his balance and lurched heavily away across the broken ground, the blood streaming down his face and spattering thickly on the golden fallen leaves. It poured out of him, his face turning gray, his legs wobbling, until at last he stumbled and fell heavily. I crept out of the pit and began to circle in on him. He thrashed desperately, but his strength was gone. His eyes rolled, and soundlessly his mouth gaped upward, the lips bright with blood.

The next morning I described my dream to Sara.
"Don't you wish," she said. "Don't *I* wish."

I called in to the office. Suzanne, the DD receptionist, answered. She told me that the whole task force had been given the rest of the week off, and I should report back to my Patrol platoon on Monday. She said that Gadek was in and out of the office, picking things up and putting them down, starting to read things and then stopping, putting paper into his typewriter and then taking it out again. He'd spent a lot of time with Captain Claypool. She thought he was trying to convince the brass to lobby the D.A. to reopen. Everybody in the building was talking about that: would he or wouldn't he. Suzanne didn't think he would.

My left eyelid had developed a twitch over the past days. I kept wanting to do push-ups. I did them, but it didn't help.

Walt came over on his day off. We sat in the garden and drank beer. He told me that Melanie had gotten a letter from Mike saying that he was on his way home. Walt had thought she'd have a fit about Mike's dropping out of school, but these days she was so grateful simply for the sunrise that she wasn't terribly upset about it.

"I think it's a good idea," Walt said. He sounded very decisive about it, very firm. "I think he got jammed into school before he was ready for it. He can do something else for a year. Toughen up a bit. Hell, he's still just a kid."

Walt seemed very involved with Mike, very protective. I told Sara, and she said that Melanie had told her the same thing. Melanie thought that perhaps Walt was inclined to spoil Mike, but on the whole she thought he was a positive influence. Melanie worried about Mike, Sara said, and Walt's decisiveness reassured her.

"I'm sure they'll be getting married," Sara said. "He'd have moved in before now, but Melanie doesn't think she ought to live in sin as long as Heather is in the house."

I thought it was charming to have concerns on that scale.

I dug in the garden. I painted a chest of drawers.

It seemed very odd to be back in uniform, as if someone had said, you didn't really graduate, you're a sophomore again, and you found yourself back in the lecture hall. I listened to the roll call announcements, more or less, got my radio and car, and meandered by side streets to my beat. I pulled over a car full of kids for rolling through a stop sign. They had two six-packs in the car, but they hadn't started drinking yet. I made them open every can and pour it out into the gutter, took all their names so that I could call their parents later, and cited the driver for the stop sign. It was that sort of evening.

The radio was silent for a long time.

I towed a van parked by a fireplug.

All those victims, I thought. What happens to them? They don't go away. They'll still be there, somewhere, with their anger and shame. How he loved to hurt them. How good he was at it.

The security officer at the marina called to report a group of drunks on the embankment just outside his perimeter fence. He thought they might be thinking about climbing the fence and stealing one of the boats. My own assumption was that if they climbed the fence they would more likely be intent on using the rest rooms, but whatever their criminal designs might be, the Desk dispatched Tim Becker and me to thwart them, Becker to handle and me to cover.

I had some distance to come, and Becker was there before me. His car was on the road that runs along the top of the embankment to the marina gate, slanting across the shoulder, pointing toward the water. The driver's door was standing open, suggesting that he had exited in haste, but Becker is a hotdog: he does everything in a big way. He was lit by the headlights, herding a group of five people up the embankment. He was staying beside the group so they wouldn't be above him on the slope, and when I got there they were spreading out away from him. I left my car beside his and stepped down a few steps onto the embankment, which cut them off. He ordered them to stop just below the roadway, and called to me, "I haven't searched them." His tone was redolent with implications of menace. They all moved closer to each other.

There were two men, two women, and a girl of about fourteen. They all looked drunk or stoned, staring vaguely around them, reacting slowly. They were poorly dressed, mostly in jeans and fatigue jackets, the women in prairie dresses with sweaters and fatigues over them, except for the girl, who wore the tightest possible designer jeans and a ski jacket, all of it very expensive and none of it very clean. Her hair was dirty, but it was a stylish cut.

The wind whipped off the bay and swept the embankment, and they were frankly huddled together, shivering.

It was really quite cold. The girl was beginning to cry, but the women seemed not to notice her.

Becker had called for two more cars. There were four cops now to handle our five bodies.

"They're all going in," Becker yelled. "None of 'em's been searched. They're probably all packing knives. Hippies are always packing knives," he added to himself.

I searched the nearer woman, patting down her arms and waist, and tugging her clothes tight against her body to reveal at least large-sized objects concealed in the usual places. She had a caseknife and three joints of pot. I threw the knife into the water, scuffed the joints into the gravel, handcuffed her, and put her in the front seat of my car.

"I'm going in," I called to Becker. "I'll see you there." And then I thought to ask, "Who does the girl go with?" The woman said, "She's none of ours, Officer. She's a runaway. We've been feedin' her."

I got back out into the wind. "You, young lady," I said. "What's your name?"

She was shaking with cold, huddling by one of the cars.

She didn't answer. Well, of course not, if she's a runaway and she doesn't want to be sent home. We were twenty feet apart, and it's hard to be ingratiating at that distance, but the car door gave me some cover from the wind and I didn't want to leave it.

"Well, tell me your first name."

She thought for a minute, and then said, "Beth."

"We can't leave you here, Beth," I said. "Come on. It's warm in here." She came over. I put her in the back seat behind the woman.

"Have you searched her?" yelled Becker. No, and I didn't cuff her, either. I was sick of mistrusting everyone. I was sick of watching everyone's hands and looking for bulges in everyone's clothes and always keeping my back to walls. I wanted to have reasonable expectations. I wanted to relax. I rolled up the window and turned the heater to high. I called Control and announced for the tape that I was transporting two females and my starting mileage. The dispatcher gave a time check, 8:17 P.M., to show when the transport started. We had been less than twenty minutes on the embankment.

The wind had cleared the clouds away and the sky was thick with stars. So far away, and you can only see the nearest ones.

At the Hall of Justice I radioed our arrival and my closing mileage, and the dispatcher gave another time check. This is so that if someone were to accuse me of hanky-panky they would have to prove that it can take place in the amount of time indicated on the tape, minus the time it takes to drive in from the marina. I took my passengers to the squad room and told them to empty their pockets onto the little trays outside one of the holding rooms. The woman produced a wallet, a key chain, a packet of sewing needles, some change, and a comb. Beth produced a comb, a locket with the picture of a cocker spaniel inside, a film canister containing an ounce or so of hashish, and a straight razor.

Feel like an ass? And sitting behind me the whole way back. What was I doing? What was I thinking of?

I confiscated the razor and put the woman in a holding room. Then I took Beth to a bathroom and stood in the doorway while she flushed the hashish. That way I wouldn't have to charge her with possession, which wouldn't do her any good at that stage in her life, and she would know that I hadn't taken it home to smoke myself. I put her into the holding room with the woman. The other transporting officers were going through the same routine with their charges.

What was I doing there, riding herd on drunk hippies? Dorn. Christ, I'd had him at the end of the chase. He was in my sights. If I'd shot him then, before the chase arrived, I could have made up some explanation. We weren't ten feet apart. One shot square in the face. No more victims.

From the middle of the squad room you could see them all through their windows. They could not see each other. They were all sitting on the benches, staring out into whatever parts of the squad room they could see. They waited with dwindling interest for whatever might happen next.

I felt tired. I sat down for a moment at the squad room table. The Bulletin clipboard lay there.

"0450, Ofc Grimes reports family disturbance/battery in the street. Arrested: Nadine Baker, age 26, battery on vic: daughter Angeline Baker, age 13, for becoming pregnant."

I was having trouble fixing my mind.

All those offense reports I've taken, all those interviews. If you added up all the time I've spent waiting for the victims to overcome a new fit of weeping so that the questions could continue, how many hours would it be?

D'Honnencourt stood by the pillar talking to the Patrol lieutenant. Becker was typing smoothly away; the Beckers of the world have all the mechanical accomplishments.

The expressions on their faces when I finished and left: for some of them, relief that it was over; for others, the realization that the uniform and gun were leaving them, and that for the first moment since the police had arrived, they would be alone. For many of them the investigation was at least a structure for their thoughts, as awful as it was. They would discover, when they were by themselves, that their own thoughts were worse. And for the rest of their lives it will be with them. Never a day to pass without remembering and in some degree reliving.

Protect the weak. Nail jerks. Jesus, Jesus, Jesus.

The chair didn't seem to be holding me. I wished I could lie down.

I wondered what they thought when they heard he was going to walk? Jean Hayes and Claudia Murray and all the rest of them. I wondered what their faces looked like. I wondered what they said to themselves. I wondered what they thought of us.

D'Honnencourt's voice had fallen silent. I didn't notice.

What else could we have done? How else could we have handled it? What mistakes did we make? What did we omit? Bits of it flickered past me, snippets of reports, glimpses of the street in shadow and under streetlight, Dorn's expression as the headlights passed over us and he saw me sitting right behind him. Was *that* it? Was *that* where it all fell apart? Was it my error that lost the whole thing? What else could I have done? It was bad luck, simply bad luck. I couldn't have seen anything on the floor. I had to be where I was.

The blood had risen to my face. I was rocking back and forth in the chair, hands knotted in my lap, eyes fixed on some far place.

D'Honnencourt was behind me. He put a big hand on my shoulder and said, "Come with me, Parkman."

Everyone in the squad room was staring.

The lieutenant coughed sharply, and the faces turned guiltily away. D'Honnencourt led me out of the squad room and downstairs to the locker room. He waited for me to change. He walked me to my car. When we reached it he said, "You're going to take two weeks' leave. I'll arrange it. Call me in ten days and tell me if you need more, or if you're ready to come back.

"I'm not going to take your badge and gun. Please don't give me cause to regret it. You have nothing to reproach yourself with so far. But you're not on top of things, and you have to restrict yourself. I want you to know that I admire what you've done. Leo speaks highly of you, and he doesn't speak highly of most people."

I hadn't spoken a word.

He said, "Do you think you can get home all right?"

"Yes," I said. "Yes, I'm okay. It catches up with me."

"Yes. It catches up with everyone. Leo is showing it, and he's had this kind of thing happen before. Everyone feels it. It's one more thing you have to learn to deal with."

"Right. Thanks, Sergeant."

"Give my best to Sara and the kids."

So I was home by 9:00.

31

By 9:15 I was half a block down from Dorn's apartment. The blue two-door was junked, of course, but the brown sedan was in the favored corner parking place.

It was impossible to be anyplace else. Here, at least, there was some chance that something would develop. He might— well, who knows? He might see me and come over to pick a fight. He might pull a weapon. If he would do it in front of witnesses—hell, there are lots of people on the street at this hour. Someone would see, would tell the TV cameras how Dorn had started the whole thing. I'm on a public street, I've got nothing to apologize for. Self-defense. End of problem.

I'd drawn my pistol, holding it in my lap.

I'd pulled the trigger halfway back.

I was sitting there in my car on a public street with my gun in full view, about to blow my pecker off.

That'll be great revenge. That'll make him feel bad.

So I was home again by 9:45.

I was back in position by 10:45. At 10:50 a car pulled up alongside mine, blocking me in. Gadek got out.

"Sara called me," he said. "She's invited us both over to

your place for a drink. I'll meet you there." He got back in his car and waited while I pulled out. He followed me home.

"Hey, guys," said Sara when we came in. "How nice of you to come by. I was feeling lonely, and worried about my husband."

"Tell you what," said Gadek. "Let's give our guns to Sara. That way we won't get into a shootout if we get drunk and quarrel." He laid his automatic on the kitchen table.

"Okay," I said. I put my snub-nose beside it.

"Drop guns," said Sara. Gadek looked startled, but he produced a .22 magnum from his jacket. I pulled mine from my hip pocket. "Thanks," she said, scooping them all up and leaving the room.

"Thanks for coming out to get me," I said. "I don't think I'm doing this very well."

"It's hard to do. It's real hard. There's no getting around it. I haven't been sleeping much lately, and especially not since the night Dorn walked. I put a lot into that case."

Sara returned.

"I was promised champagne," said Gadek.

She produced some very fancy ice cream, a box of elegant chocolate cookies, and a bottle of champagne.

"Open that," she said, and went to get three glasses. I poured while she dished up the ice cream and stuck a cookie into each dish. "We should have had mint leaves for color," she said. "Well, we'll have to rough it. I—" She stopped. She looked as if she was about to cry. "I'm sorry," she said after a minute. "I just can't believe it."

There was nothing to say.

I was afraid that if I went around the table to comfort her I would start to cry, too, so I stayed where I was.

But the cloud passed. We ate ice cream and cookies, and drank champagne. Gadek told about going to take a report, back when he was in Patrol. The guy he was supposed to talk to was a music teacher—he coached opera singers—and when Gadek arrived he had a student there. He said, look, her lesson isn't over for ten minutes—can you wait? And Gadek says, sure. So the teacher leads him into the living room where the piano is. The singer is there, this very attractive young woman. The teacher takes a big high-backed armchair, plants it right in the middle of the room, about ten feet from the piano, and sits Gadek down in it. Then he sits down at the piano, and the singer stands by it right square in front of Gadek, and sings "O mio babbino caro" from *Gianni Schicchi.*

"D'you know that piece?" asked Gadek.

"Yes," said Sara.

"No," I said.

"It's very sentimental," he said.

Anyway, this girl has a beautiful voice; the teacher plays very well. And she's right there, ten feet away, looking him in the eye and singing this marvelous aria.

When it was over, the teacher came around and stood by the singer. He asked Gadek his opinion. Asked really sincerely. They both stood there and waited to hear what he would say.

Well, he said the singing was beyond his praise. But that he had noticed that the singer had an odd way of leaning forward when she sang, sometimes so far that he was afraid she was going to fall over, and that distracted him.

They both laughed delightedly and clapped their hands. They said that that was *exactly* what Somebody-or-other, the famous singing teacher, had told her, and she was trying to correct it. They congratulated him on his observation.

That was the end of the lesson. The singer left, and Gadek took the report.

He treasured the memory of that quarter hour. It seemed to him a precious moment in life.

Sara laughed. She laughed easily, the last few days, unless Dorn was mentioned. But right now she wasn't thinking about Dorn. She said that when she was in law school her whole class went on a retreat to ponder the moral aspects of the law. It's this place out in the woods, it's very rustic, log cabins, the whole nine yards. And the last night they're there they have this big dinner in the dining hall—rough-hewn beam ceiling, knotty pine walls, deer heads, naive paintings of pioneers fighting grizzly bears—and the focus of the event is a speech by this famous lawyer-minister on "The Law and the Polis," very grand and noble. He's sitting at the head table on the dais all through dinner, and he really stands out because all the faculty are dressed like lumberjacks, and he's wearing a black leather suit and a cream-colored silk clerical shirt and collar with a big cross made by an Amazon Indian out of monkey bones. So he does this speech, which is full of the common touch, and how he's really young at heart just like you young people, blah blah blah, and it's very well received.

There's a wineskin passing around the room. For a joke, somebody passes it up to the head table. The first guy it's passed to is this very cool young professor, and instead of just laughing and passing it back he stands up, raises the wineskin, starts the stream and gradually extends his arm until it's straight, then brings it back in and cuts the stream with a twist of his wrist. The room bursts into applause— the kids eat it up. Well, the next person at the table is this middle-aged professor of Constitutional law, and she's not going to be outdone; she stands up, takes the wineskin, and does the same thing. She hasn't drunk from a wineskin before, but she's game. She dribbles a little on her plaid shirt when she cuts off the stream, but she laughs, and everyone's delighted. She sits amidst great applause, and passes the wineskin on to the next person, who's the dean, this white-haired old gentleman. He takes the wineskin, stands up, starts the stream, extends his arm till it's straight, and just holds it there, the wine arcing through the air, until he must have swallowed half a pint; then brings it in and cuts it off. *Thunderous* acclamation. The place goes wild. Everyone's delighted.

Next is the lawyer-minister. The dean passes him the wineskin. He holds it like it's a cow paddy. He does this little grin and glances around the hall. Every eye is fixed on him. There is a hush. He leans forward to the microphone and says, red wine will really stain this shirt. He passed the wineskin on. You could hear people catch their breath. Someone snickered. The lawyer-minister departed shortly after that. Everyone saw him go. The door had no sooner closed behind him than the whole place burst out with a great whoop of laughter. He must have heard it, but he didn't come back to find out what had caused it. No doubt he knew.

We had another bottle of champagne in the refrigerator, and while Sara was finishing her story I was easing the cork. It popped lightly, and while I poured I told about an ambulance run I responded to once. It was a heart attack, and I was quite close when the call went out. I went red light and siren and got there just half a block before the ambulance. I left my car double-parked and ran up to the house. There were two or three people standing in the front door, and they pointed into a bedroom. There was a woman lying on her back on the floor in the narrow space between the bed and the dresser. You know when you get your CPR training they give you this healthy-looking, squeaky-clean mannequin to practice on, and the instructor is always wiping the lips off with alcohol. But this woman was old. Her skin was mealy and pale gray. Her eyes were yellow slits. Her lips were yellow and flecked with a gray crust. I took one look and thought, Jesus, I hope she's good and dead. I sure don't want to do CPR on *that*.

She was stone cold when I touched her. The first paramedic came into the room right behind me. He knelt down and took her wrist. He let it go immediately. He didn't even open up his kit. He whispered, "She's been dead for hours." He got up and went out to tell her family.

I went back out to my car. I thought, I've got a hell of an attitude: maybe somebody needs me and I think, gee, I sure hope she's dead. That's great. If I want to save the world I'm going to have to learn not to be so prissy. I thought about it a lot, and the next time something repellent came along I did much better.

We'd each drunk a glass while I told this. I distributed what was left in the bottle. We drank it and chatted. Gadek said it was time for him to go, but we said why didn't he spend the night where he was. We got out a pillow and blankets and made him up a bed on the living room sofa.

"Don't you love the streets at night, Walt?" said Melanie as they ambled along. "Don't you, Mike?" They had started out after dinner three abreast, but the sidewalks were too narrow, and the bushes too encroaching, to accommodate them, so that they proceeded in various combinations as opportunity permitted, or in single file.

"I love to see the streetlights shining through the branches. I love all the shadows, and how some of the windows are lit and others are dark. All the different sorts of curtains and blinds."

Walt and Mike looked, and indeed it was just as she described.

"And I suppose it's a selfish feeling," said Melanie, gently guiding Mike ahead of her as they came to a narrow place, "but it's very nice not to have to worry about getting mugged. Not everyone can be so well protected."

She was being very good, Walt thought. Mike had arrived home that afternoon. Walt had found occasion to suggest to Melanie that her son would be in a fragile state, leaving school and all, and he would need gentle support. Melanie's instinct ran more toward a good hard shaking. But she was learning to respect Walt's judgment, and she forbore.

Then, following her train of thought, she said, "This man Toby caught, what's his name? Dern?"

"Ah, Dorn," said Walt. "Ah, y'know—"

"It's so terrible, just letting him go."

From behind, Walt could see Mike's shoulders fall in a little, his arms get tight. He said, "Yeah, it's a bummer. Look at that bit of trim on that Victorian, up around the attic window."

"Not Victorian, really," said Melanie. "Queen Anne. And I still don't understand why he got away with it. You said there was a great pile of evidence."

My God, thought Walt, for good or ill you cannot turn this broad. Straight and simple seemed to be the quickest way to dispose of the subject.

"It's because there was a lot of evidence but none of it connected him to any individual, provable crime. There was never an actual connection. We never caught him in the act. If anyone has the goods on him they never came forward. And nobody could actually identify him: none of the victims ever saw his face."

Walt saw Mike stop dead on the sidewalk, six feet ahead. He began to turn, his face in the streetlight an awful yellow, the whites of his eyes enormous in the sharp shadow cast by the brows. He began to form a word as Walt and Melanie came abreast of him. He put a hand out toward Walt.

Walt thought that Melaine had not seen. He stepped between them, grabbed Mike by the upper arms and spun him behind them as they passed. He said pretty loud, "Hey, pioneer, stub your toe? Better let us lead the way." And to Melanie, "I thought Queen Annes *were* Victorians."

While she discoursed he glanced back once or twice. Mike was stumbling along behind them, his arms dangling as if they were broken, his eyes focused on some altogether different scene.

Jesus! Walt thought. It's what I get for being so goddam sensitive. I never even asked him.

"It's not a satisfactory end," I said. "I keep saying that. I guess I'm hoping that if I say it often enough, it'll come out different." I had turned out all the lights except for the small lamp at the end of the sofa. We were casting monstrous dark shadows across the walls and ceiling.

"No," said Gadek. "Not satisfactory."

"Maybe . . ."

"Maybe. Don't hold your breath. But the champagne was good."

"Thanks." I didn't want to hear about the champagne. I wanted some hope.

"He's lying low," Gadek said, perhaps relenting a little. "I've been going by every day. He hasn't seen me, so far as I know, but he must know we're not letting go. I'm not making predictions. I don't know what pieces are out there. But we only need one break. There are lots of possibilities. We only have to have one of them break our way."

He yawned. "But I don't suppose anything's going to happen tonight." He sank down on the sofa. "I haven't been sleeping at all well lately." He began tugging at his shoes. He chuckled. "But then I don't usually drink most of a bottle of champagne before bedtime. I wonder if it'll make any difference."

I left him and went upstairs. I had just got one sock off when the phone rang.

It was Walt.

I sat on the edge of the bed listening to what he said. I had one sock on my foot and one in my hand. Sara was just coming out of the bathroom, and she saw more or less what it was. She sat beside me, almost touching. I could feel the thickness of my body, the density of it, the tautness of my skin, as if my face and limbs were slowly expanding with the volume of my blood. We sat side by side, perfectly still, while Walt explained.

When he was finished I said, "Hold on a minute. Leo's here. I'll go get him." Putting down the receiver on the covers I met Sara's eye and whispered.

"Bingo."

When I got downstairs, Gadek was fast asleep. He was propped up on pillows at one end of the couch under the small lamp, the blanket pulled up to his armpits, a magazine lying open across his chest. I brought the phone on its long cord, put it on the coffee table, and shook him gently. I told him briefly what Walt had to say, and put the phone in his hand.

"Gadek," he said, as if he were in the office.

I could hear the distant buzz of Walt's voice at the other end. Gadek listened so impassively that watching him I wondered if he were quite awake. Walt was laying it out very logically, and Gadek didn't need to ask questions. His eyes were fixed on the phone, and he was silent except for an occasional "Mmm" or an "Uh huh."

Finally he said, "How is he? Can you bring him in now?" There was a pause for consultation at the other end and then Gadek said, "Good. Half an hour." He handed me the phone, threw off the blanket, and swung his feet onto the floor.

He was pulling his shoes on when Sara came down the stairs in her bathrobe.

"We've got him," said Gadek, glancing up at her. "Do you remember where you put my firearms? Toby, why don't you go to bed. Walt said his victim would prefer not to have you there. Come in first thing in the morning. There'll be plenty to do before we go get him. Of course, you're on leave, officially. I assume you want to be in on this."

"You bet," I said. "I'm fine."

"Good," he said. He paused in tying his second shoe, and looked up at me. "By the way, Toby, this business with Walt's surprise witness—did you know about this?"

"No," I said. "It's a complete surprise."

"Good," he said, returning to his shoe. "It's not kosher. But Walt's a fast talker. I expect he'll have some convincing tale."

The following afternoon, his foot jittering at a great rate, Charlie Footer watched Dorn enter his apartment at 2:15. Ten minutes later, Leonora followed him in. He didn't see them come out again.

The raiding party had been standing by since early afternoon, waiting for current news of Dorn's location. By 2:45 it was briefed. We were reminded that a pistol had been found in the brown car when it was searched, and we should consider him armed. A few minutes after 3:00 we drove out of the parking lot, the task force people in two cars and the Patrol officers in three more. Patty, who had been spotting on Leonora's apartment, moved to hook up with Footer. In order not to arrive in dribs and drabs, we all paused two blocks back from Dorn's building. When Gadek had confirmed that everyone was in attendance we started in at a moderate pace, without racing engines or squealing tires to attract attention.

Each group paused at different places around the block and advised Gadek by radio that they were ready. The object was for the whole party to arrive simultaneously and snap the cordon tight before any warning could be given. Thirty seconds would give him time to move into any gap that might be open. If he got loose from his apartment into the building, our work would be complicated greatly; if he got out into the block, we had a major problem; if he could cross a street—or, worse, if he could escape direct observation so that we didn't know whether he had crossed a street or not, and had to cordon off two or more blocks—he might get clean away.

On the word, the Patrol officers swept in from all sides toward the building. They darted into the passageway behind the building, the parking area below, the second-story breezeway above Dorn's unit, and into the street in front. As they sprinted in they hustled neighbors and bystanders indoors or out of the way. They were still settling into position when the task force hurried in from the street and up the stairs to the first level, all of us running absurdly on tiptoe, for silence. Patty raced past the door to cover the farther windows that looked onto the breezeway, Footer held at the top of the stairs, while Gadek, Blondie, Fry (carrying a battering ram), and I stopped on opposite sides of the door. Except for Footer and Patty, who were in plainclothes for spotting, we were all in uniform. There is some moral ascendency to be gained from visibly overwhelming force in these situations, and no advantage in concealment. Uniforms also help to clarify the situation for bystanders.

Gadek glanced around to make sure that everyone was in position, drew his automatic, and punched his left hand forward. Delicately, briefly, he touched the bell.

For a moment, nothing happened.

Then in the window nearest the door the curtain parted slightly and instantly snapped back.

"Police!" yelled Gadek. *"Open up!"*

Perhaps five seconds passed.

"Okay, go," he said. Fry and I stepped up smartly with the ram, a heavy piece of pipe with handles to heave it between us. The door was lightly constructed, and with the first impact the ram struck out the entire lock and a large piece of the surrounding paneling, hurling the gaping remnant around on its hinges to crash noisily against the wall inside. Gadek and Blondie bounded through the gap while Fry and I dropped the ram, drew our pistols, and followed. Leonora stood frozen in the middle of the room.

"He's not here!" she screamed. "He's not here!"

"Get outside," said Blondie, throwing an arm around her shoulders and sweeping her out onto the breezeway and up toward Patty. "Where is he? He was here an hour ago."

"I don't know!" she cried. "I don't know!" She grabbed the rail and clung to it. Blondie pushed her down into a crouch. "You stay right where you are," she said, and plunged back into the apartment.

Fry had stopped just inside the door while I jumped straight across the room and stood at one end of the couch.

The living room was empty except for the large couch, a much-scarred coffee table, two chairs, and a television. The kitchen beyond the dinette to the left had cupboards large enough to hold a man. The short hallway to the bathroom and bedroom were straight ahead.

It wasn't going to be a straightforward surrender. He was holed up here someplace, playing it out to the end.

Nobody spoke. There was no point in giving him a clearer idea of our movements than we could help. Gadek pointed to Fry, then to the hallway, and made a flat gesture with his hand. Fry was to hold where he was and watch the passage. Then he pointed to Blondie and to the dinette. She moved quietly forward so that she was holding her pistol over the counter that divided the dinette from the kitchen. He pointed to me and then to the end of the counter. From there I could shoot into any cupboard in the kitchen.

When I was in position, Gadek moved into the kitchen and flattened himself against the counter with his free hand on the door of the broom closet, the only enclosure in the kitchen large enough to hold a man standing erect. Gadek would yank the door open, I would cover him, and while we were focused on that one place, Blondie would keep an eye loose in case he popped out behind us.

I leveled my pistol on the closet door. People hiding will often try to hold a door shut, and you don't want to get into a pulling match. Gadek caught my eye, yanked suddenly and jumped back. The door flew open, bounced off the wall and clapped shut again. But in that moment I'd seen to the back; there was no one there. Gadek, who couldn't see in from where he was, glanced at me, and I shook my head. Gingerly, he opened the door again and peered inside, the muzzle of his automatic forward, just to make sure.

We were 0 for 1.

The rest of the kitchen was less promising. It was physically possible for him to be in any of several other kitchen cabinets, but not likely. It would take a while to squeeze in, after all, and we'd come in awful fast. He was probably someplace else. You don't like to leave unsearched hiding places behind you, but Fry could watch the kitchen as well as the hall while Gadek and Blondie and I moved on to the bedroom and bathroom.

We searched them very carefully, and with great caution. We went through all the closets and cupboards. We looked under the bed and prodded the mattress. We picked the whole bed up a few inches, to test it for weight. There were several cardboard boxes piled up in a closet, and we unpiled them to make sure they didn't form a hiding place. We took the drawers right out of the bureau so we could see to the back. He wasn't there.

"Okay," whispered Gadek. "If he isn't anyplace else, he must be in the kitchen." We went back. Fry was still spotting on the hall, and we took the first couple of steps out of the bedroom sedately, so as not to try his nerves.

We started with the larger cupboards under the counter. He might have removed some of the dividers and opened out a little hideaway in there—you never know. We worked from the larger cupboards to the smaller. Some were only twelve inches deep, but we went through them one by one. We looked in the refrigerator. We looked in the oven on general principles, the door making a loud squawking noise; wherever he was, he'd surely hear that and know what it meant. He'd be getting quite a chuckle out of it, if he were a chuckling sort of guy. But in any case, he wasn't there.

Okay, he wasn't in the kitchen, after all. We stood for a moment scratching our heads.

He was seen going in. He wasn't seen coming out. There's no rear exit. Of course, he could have jumped out one of the rear windows and gotten away between the time Footer saw him arrive and our arrival, but since he didn't know he was about to be busted he had no reason to put himself to that trouble.

We'd searched each room.

The building was concrete slab construction, so there were no crawl spaces between floors above or below for him to squeeze into. There were no big drains or ducts.

Where was he?

Blondie looked around and said, "The couch?" I glanced over my shoulder into the living room.

The pillows erupted and for half a second I had a picture of Dorn rising out of a space below them. He was onto his feet as we turned toward him. He leapt clear of the couch toward the door. Blondie was closest and she dove at him, but he was heavy and already moving fast. He shook her off, darted through the doorway inches ahead of Fry and me, sailed over the breezeway rail, and disappeared from sight. The parking area was ten feet below.

We reached the rail just behind him. He landed awkwardly on the roof of a pickup parked beneath, twisting one ankle sideways and scraping his face and scalp harshly across the rough steel cargo rack behind. He rocked back, stunned, the quick blood pouring down. Drunkenly he lurched upright, but his ankle failed him and he toppled heavily over into the narrow space between the cars. The uniforms stationed below were on him in an instant, hemming him into the slot formed by the cars and the wall. We broke away from the rail and bounded down the stairs two at a time. When we got to him he was still struggling to get up, but his bad leg would support no weight and the slick concrete floor was oily. He heaved and floundered, dragging futilely with his big gummy palms at the towering fenders and the coarse block wall as if he would crush out handholds with his fingertips. His mouth gaped and closed. He tossed his head this way and that, trying to clear his eyes, almost sightless under the mask of blood.

32

Walt found Adam and me at the kitchen door, replacing the lock. Apparently it had been malfunctioning, undetected, for some time.

"Hey, Tobe," he said. "Hey, tiger."

"Hey," I said. "I was thinking about you today. How'd it go?"

"Oh, it was the usual review board. The captain made a hanging speech about how I'd done a naughty thing, blah blah blah, and the lieutenant agreed, and the city manager's rep agreed. Y'know D'Honnencourt agreed to be *my* rep, surprisingly enough. He talked about how cops have hearts, too, and if he had a hundred more like me, even if they weren't any better groomed—I thought he was going to lose his train of thought there for a second, but he didn't—the world would be a better place, and so on."

"Frankly, I'm astonished," I said. "Still, good for him."

"I'm with you," said Walt, "believe me. Anyway, that turned the stampede. They're going to recommend something to the chief. They'll let me know."

You don't jinx these things by saying so out loud, but Walt had won. If a board can't work up a feeding frenzy, it just writes a pompous finding to protect its dignity and everyone forgets about it.

"So how's the house hunting?" I said, gracefully turning the conversation.

"Grim," he said, sinking down on the top step. "It's grim. Well, you know Melanie. She's got standards. And Heather's like her mom—polite up to the gills, but she's got standards, too. Makes it hard to find a place."

"And you?" I said.

"Nah. Fortunately for all concerned, I've got no standards at all. Anything they can live with is fine with me."

We had the new lock spread out on a tray, together with its incomprehensible instructions. Adam sat cross-legged, somewhat encumbered by Robert Peel, in deep contemplation of the mechanism. They had been there for some time. I was coming to the conclusion that the door had to be hung upside down.

Walt eyed the tray without enthusiasm. "I don't think of you as being handy, somehow," he said.

"Handy or not," I said, "the beauty of home ownership is that you're never forced to have an idle moment, if you don't want one."

"Ah," said Walt. "Middle-class diligence. How wonderful it is. I wonder what it's like."

I was just opening my mouth to say that anyone intending to marry Melanie was about to get a crash course, but instead I said, "How's Mike?"

"He's okay," said Walt. "He's . . . well, he'll be okay."

"He calls?"

"He writes. Needs a little distance."

"It must be hard on Melanie," I said.

"Yeah. Well, these things are hard on people. Anyway, I think he's glad to be back in school. He wants to be busy. But he needs a little distance."

"He blames her?"

"No, no." He glanced at Adam, who was still absorbed in the lock. He dropped his voice a little. "It's that I've talked about the series with Melanie, and she knows pretty much what was done to 'im. Technically, and all. And it makes him feel, well, walked in on, if you know what I mean."

"Christ."

"Yeah, Christ, at least," he said. "And y'know the funny thing—I mean funny *striking,* not funny *ha ha*—the funny thing is, Mike's right on the money: she thinks about it. It's kinda eerie, how alike they are, how their minds run along the same lines.

"Anyway, she keeps busy, too. There's a reason the house hunting is so assiduous. But he's working it out, and she will when he does."

"Ah-*ha!*" said Adam abruptly. He picked up the lock, slipped a part out, reversed it, and slipped it back. This was clearly the solution.

"Hey," I said.

"Out*standing*," said Walt.

"Shucks," said Adam.

"Well, I guess you can drill the holes," I said, "if you can figure *that* out. But let's go over it together before you start."

"Okay," he said, and turned happily again to the diagram.

"So now you're getting married," I said.

"Well, why not, at this stage?" he said. "I'm kinda intrigued. I want to see how things work out."

"Well, that's good," I said.

"Yeah," he said. "It's good." And then, "Have you ever had Melanie's rutabaga fritters?"

"No," I said. "I'm pretty sure I haven't. I think I'd remember rutabaga fritters."

"No, no, really, they're great," he said. "She does—well, I don't know what she does. Takes hours. They're *so* delicate. Really great."

"Melanie's a super cook."

"We have to do something special when we've got our new place. Housewarming. Maybe I can talk her into making those fritters."

"Feel free," I said. "We'd love it."

"We can have some music. Y'know, Bach. It's pretty good stuff."

"It *is* pretty good."
"It's sort of consoling," he said.
"Yes. We'd like that."
"Great," he said. "That'd be great."
"Good," I said. "Good."
"Good."